THE DEATH

HUNTING

Book One
By Emma Steinbrecher

ISBN: 978-0-578-36733-0
Editor: Kenna Karlson
Interior Graphics: Erin Esther (Instagram @erin.esther)
Map Artist: sekcer
Cover Artist: Mousam Banerjee

For those who see the shadows in others and still call them beautiful

Trigger Warnings

Dear reader,

It is my desire to ensure that everyone who picks up this book feels comfortable in doing so. Because of this, I have provided a list of trigger warnings below.

Trauma
Explicit Sexual Scenes
Death
Violence
Kidnapping
Torture
Car Accident
Violent Shooting

The Wasteland

Vulcan

Ohriid

Adhara

The Court of Shadow

Ascella

Zora

Namid

The Court of Light

Tiranna

Nashira

Debnar

Velas

N

The Fae Realm

Death

The man was sleeping—eyes fluttering along with the rhythmic breathing of his chest. His portly figure lay sprawled across the bed, blankets tangled around his meaty limbs.

Death lurked in the shadows of the one-bedroom apartment, waiting to set events into motion. The studio apartment was littered with empty beer bottles and crumpled-up food wrappers. Death wrinkled his nose at the smell of desperate failure and disgusting hopelessness. He scrutinized the man responsible for the mess while taking in every detail. In the nightstand drawer lay a weapon, one that would prove just as useful as the balding man who was now snoring—thick mucus sounding at the back of his throat.

Death pulled the cigarette from his lips with his finger and thumb, flicking it out the sliding glass doors behind him. The embers extinguished as the butt hit the damp stone balcony outside. He didn't care about leaving this trace of himself there. It could have easily fallen from a balcony above this third-floor shithole.

Death took in the peeling green paint on the walls and the stove by the kitchen coated in blackened grime. He winced, the smell of beer still lingering in his nostrils and assaulting his senses as it replaced the comforting scent of tobacco. Maybe he shouldn't have tossed the cigarette.

He strode forward, boots silenced and padding across the wooden floor. Careful steps ensured the man remained unconscious. Death ran his hand over the case, feeling the darkness pull from his skin. He sighed, allowing pleasure to seep into his bones before unclasping and opening the container to reveal what he was looking for.

The man shifted in the bed, and Death's gaze snapped in his direction, hand stilling over the container. He could exit this place as quickly as he needed to if the man woke, but then it would delay his job for another day, and he hated being late.

The stranger flopped onto his stomach, his snoring continuing in blissful ignorance of the predator mere feet away from him. Death looked away and returned his gaze to the weapon that sat before him. The semi-automatic gleamed in the city lights streaming in from the balcony, sleek and concealable—utterly perfect—utterly human.

Death hovered his hand over the weapon, allowing shadows to twist and curl in his palm, pushing them over the metal. When the man would wake in the morning, this darkness would call to him, and he wouldn't be able to deny what it wanted. The weapon would demand use by manipulating his mind, and it wouldn't rest until the bloodlust was fulfilled.

Death ran a tattooed hand through his dark hair, shaking off the shadows he just used. The magic was heady, and it needed to be controlled. He had spent centuries controlling it, but the lingering pleasure that coasted through his veins whenever he called the shadows forward always threatened to drag him under.

He strode out onto the balcony, sliding the glass doors closed behind him before jumping down onto the gleaming street below. The remnants from the warm rain splashed up as he landed, the shadows keeping him concealed in the darkness.

Death had one more place to visit before the night was up. This time, he wasn't instilling the desire for blood into anyone. He merely had to check on the intriguing blonde for the last time. He had been watching the woman for weeks, feeling the familiarity of power surrounding her. It fascinated him, and he needed to know who she was— what she was. There was a subtle threat in the power he sensed coursing through her veins, something that drew him in, gripping his interest like a vice.

This time, the draw of the shadows wouldn't fail him. The man he had picked would surely complete the job, and when he did, the blonde would meet Death once and for all.

One

Morana pulled the keys from the ignition, opening the door as she exited her beat-up car. The black paint was peeling, rust seeping through the cracks to reveal a deteriorating body beneath. It wasn't pretty, but it got her from point A to point B. Besides, she liked that it had character. Even if that character was screaming metal death trap.

The air was thick with humidity, pressing in on her chest as she slammed the door behind her. It was only seven in the morning, and it was already sweltering. The sticky August heat would be the death of her.

She tied her flannel around her waist, tugged at her dark cut-off shorts, and peeled the oversized band tee from her sweaty frame. Moisture was already running over every curve of her body, plastering the material to her slim waist and accentuating her chest, something she didn't need as she moved to the massive steel building ahead of her.

The Ashford Gun Club sign was crooked again, and she huffed before pushing the door open. It was unlocked, which meant Morton and Axton would already be here. She needed to get those assholes to fix the sign.

The shooting range wouldn't open until eight, so she had some time before she had to be back in the shop. Morana grabbed everything she needed, poking around the doorframe into Morton's office before heading out to the range.

"I'm going to go shoot for a bit." She pushed a blonde strand of hair behind her ear. "Where's Axton?" she asked.

Morton turned around in his chair, arms folded across his chest. He was in his late seventies with slight wrinkles around his mouth that peeked out from under his thick mustache and indicated years of frowning—the same way he continued to frown every time Morana showed up for work. Morton was heavier set and bald beneath his Ashford hat. Despite his unfriendly demeanor, Morana enjoyed working for him. He had started this place from nothing and preferred to hide his kindness from the world, holding it captive for only those who earned it.

"Shit, if I know," he grunted. "That boy's an adult. I raised his mother, I raised him, I'm done keeping tabs on people."

"You're the very image of compassion and kindness, Morton. I'll see you in an hour." Morana twisted away from the doorframe, holding the gun case in her hand.

"Make that thirty minutes. I need you to help open up shop," Morton yelled from his office. She chuckled while using her boot to kick open the door, bells rattling as it slammed shut.

She walked out to the range; heart pounding as sweat slid down her spine. It was still ungodly hot out here. Rain would help to cool things down, but this morning, the sky was cloudless.

She set the case down on the wooden table, pushing earplugs in before gripping the cool metal of the handgun. This was her favorite part about working for the shooting range. She could play with every weapon that Morton stocked his shelves with, and she had the space outside to do it. She liked the feeling of power that came with each shot, knowing that she could handle something so deadly made her heart pound and adrenaline run through her veins.

Each shot sent a ringing over the grounds. She pinned the target and placed her finger over the trigger, pulling until the familiar jerk sent fire through her limbs. She had been shooting since moving here and securing this job. The thrill was becoming a part of her. She felt a familiar sensation coat her arms as she aimed for her last shot of the morning. Darkness swirled in her vision for a moment. She blinked it away before readying herself to pull the trigger.

"Morton's looking for you," Axton's smooth voice slithered across the gravel. She flinched, lowering the gun, and turning on the safety. She scowled when she met his hazel eyes.

"Shit, Axton. You can't do that." Morana pulled the earplugs from her ear, giving up on her last shot. The heady feeling that had accompanied her moments ago had disappeared. She sauntered past Axton, pushing her shoulder into his as she made her way to the case opened on the table. Checking the time, she cursed under her breath. Her private shooting time was over. It was the one moment where nobody demanded anything of her—the promised solace of a moment alone and the sensation of complete control brought a certain freedom. It was the one time she didn't need to worry about being needed, and the one time the guilt of leaving her struggling father alone to his own devices didn't infiltrate her swirling thoughts.

The thoughts were now back, consuming and demanding. She wanted to hide them from herself, return to the life she had built away from the smell of beer and sadness—the desperate hopelessness she felt obligated to fix. Running was comforting and pretending long enough could make the monsters disappear. She was still running, but at least she had the assurance of Axton's careless banter and occasional asshole attitude. She bit her lip, fighting off the smile that threatened to lighten her face. For an asshole, he could surely charm anyone into a dog willingly rolling for its master.

"Actually, I can," Axton flashed a crooked smile at her, the dimple on his cheek painting a picture of innocence. "My grandfather owns the place. I can sneak up on shooters if I want to."

Morana's brows shot up. "Yes." She locked the case and leaned into the carefree feeling that came from unattached and harmless flirting. Her voice dripped sarcasm all over the cocky bastard in front of her. "You are welcome to sneak up on shooters and get yourself killed on accident. It would save me the pain of dealing with you at every turn."

"You love me." Axton smiled, leaning his elbows on the wooden table as he looked up at her through his wire-framed glasses. There was no doubting he noticed the smile she pretended to fight off. "Admit it, Ana."

She leaned forward with her hands on the birch surface, trailing her gaze over his full lips, and admiring the sharp cut of his jaw. Her blood heated as her gaze smoldered, begging him to respond to her. His lips parted, and the smile fell from his face. She watched as he took an unsteady breath, eyes dropping to her lips. *Got him.*

"Is that what you tell yourself to get you through the night?" A knowing smile broke across her face. "You have always been, and will always be, a royal pain in my ass." She slid the case off the table and turned to walk down the gravel path to the shop.

"So, I'm royalty in your eyes?" Axton lingered behind her, and she could hear him jog away, but she didn't bother to look back. He eventually caught up behind her, and she stole a glance. A strand of brown hair fell across his forehead as he shoved something into his pocket. His scent wrapped around her, eating away at the thoughts she had now successfully kept at bay. The sweet aroma of tobacco and the familiar heat of his tall figure made her cheeks burn. She swallowed, building back the charming mask she presented to those surrounding her.

"You're a peasant, Axton." Morana turned back, eyes narrowing as she looked up and made her last point. "A peasant through and through."

She ignored him as he trailed her to the door. Before she pulled it open, she gestured to the sign overhead.

"It's crooked again." She yanked the door open and stepped aside, holding it with her black boot. "After you, your highness." She bowed her head and lowered into a taunting curtsey as she encouraged Axton to move inside.

He walked past her, a dark chuckle rumbling in his chest. She didn't like what that noise did to her, so she shoved the feeling away and followed inside after him. A little attraction was fine—just enough to distract and entertain, but too much, and she felt far too vulnerable—easily manipulated. She had kept a careful distance between herself and anyone in this city. They knew little about her past, little about her family, and she intended to keep it that way. The less she thought about her father, the less he existed.

Morton was standing behind the counter, glasses pulled down to the tip of his nose, analyzing some small piece of metal—likely fixing another gun. The old man liked to stay active in tinkering with the weapons he sold. He was convinced it kept him young.

"You miss any?" he asked, looking over the large spectacles perched on his bulbous nose, his gray mustache moving as he spoke.

"Every single one." She spun as she moved behind the counter, returning the case to its proper location. Axton pointed at her, that stupid dimple appearing on his cheek again.

"That right there is a liar, Granddad." He leaned over the counter, pulling out a folded paper from the pocket of his jeans and laying it flat on the counter. "She made every shot. Here's the proof."

"How did you get that?" Morana opened the mini-fridge, brushing off the invasive way Axton had complimented her before grabbing a cold water and leaning against the wooden wall behind the counter. Her gaze settled on the faint stubble Axton was scratching around his strong jaw, causing her cheeks to flush. She snorted, chiding herself for letting his effortlessly attractive features affect her so easily.

"That's what you get for running away from me and calling me a peasant." He pushed his glasses up on his nose, his smile wide. Her stomach curled and flipped, but she took another sip of cool liquid and turned away.

"You've got an eye, girl." Morton glanced at the paper and then gestured to the door. "Go ahead and flip that sign to open for me. It's about that time," he grunted.

She strode forward, flipping over the rectangular piece of plastic, and walking back behind the counter. She retied the flannel around her waist and pulled the crystal necklace from under her tee. Her fingers played with the chain as she waited. People usually started showing up quickly after opening. They liked to get an early start, shooting before the heat of summer took over the grounds.

"Axton," Morton's gravelly voice stopped her coworker in his tracks. Axton's shoulders tensed. "I need you to help me with some licensing information in the office. The damn font is so small. I need to figure out how to make it bigger on that computer in there." Morton turned to walk to his office.

Axton shot a pleading glance to Morana, and she chuckled. "I think I deserve double the salary for being the IT department as well as a normal employee," he chuckled.

"You're salaried?" Morana gasped in mocking surprise. "Maybe you're right, Axton Lee Keres. You absolutely are royalty." She pressed her hand gently to her chest. "I don't know what a peasant like myself would do with such riches."

Axton winked at her. "I won't forget you, Morana Rowley. Even as I rise to the very pinnacle of high society." He blew her a kiss before prowling after Morton, leaving Morana to run the shop on her own.

It wasn't long before the bells on the door rang, and she looked up at the portly man walking through the entryway. His eyes flicked wildly about the room, glancing at the displays before landing on Morana. A shiver ran up her spine as he walked to the counter, hands jittering at his sides. The man appeared distressed, sweat beading and dripping down his temples.

"Can I help you?" She fought through the heavy pounding in her chest and the strange feeling that overtook her body. There was something untrustworthy about this man. The smell of alcohol and bitterness wrapped around her senses as he moved closer. Forcing a friendly smile, she buried the discomfort beneath a careful mask.

"I'm here to buy a gun," the man grunted.

"Great, I'll just need to see your gun owner's license, and I can help you out. What were you looking for today?" She turned to the computer, pulling up the system they used to see what they had in stock.

"License?" the man asked, eyes narrowing on her and his jaw clenching in frustration. "I didn't need one for my other purchases. Just an ID."

"New law sir." Her voice was level despite her rising anxiety. "It's happened a lot recently. You know, customers coming in and being surprised by the big changes in gun ownership." Morana rested a hand on the cool glass of the counter to ground herself, remind her of where she was. "It's easy to get approved. There's a basic questionnaire you have to pass, takes about thirty minutes online. If you'd like, there's a kiosk over there in the corner. We can get you approved today."

"I don't need fucking approved," the man growled, his irritation making Morana shift uncomfortably.

A stabbing fear gripped her gut as the man shifted his hand behind him. The rest seemed to happen in slow motion as the man pulled a gun from his back. She stared into the barrel in disbelief as he pointed it directly at her. Morana could feel the adrenaline pick up as she glanced to the button beneath the counter. She just needed to get to the other side.

"Hey!" Morton limped as he came out of the office with Axton following behind. A shot rang out through the air, and Morana dropped to the floor behind the counter, slamming her back against the wall and covering her ears. Her mouth was dry as she desperately fought to keep her mind clear.

She could hear Morton's body hit the ground and watched the intruder's feet as he shifted toward Axton. Her mind was reeling as she heard more shouting, but she couldn't make out what was happening or what was being said. Beneath the counter there was a small gap at the floor where she saw Morton's body still and lying in a pool of blood, glasses missing. The world froze, suspended in the current moment where fear was still engulfing her very being, like flames in a forest. She couldn't breathe as she fought the churning in her stomach. Another shot rang out, and she felt the sharp sting of a bullet pierce the flesh of her stomach. In her shocked state, she hadn't even seen the man point the gun at her.

She screamed, closing her eyes and breathing through the pain. Darkness flooded her vision, and she could feel the blood leak through her fingers.

Everything went silent for a moment, a black void consuming her before she opened her eyes again. She was in a glass castle, consumed by the yellow glow of sunlight streaming through the windows. A woman turned, pale skin and white hair. She cocked her head, observing Morana's still figure sitting on the floor. The last thing she saw were rose-colored eyes flashing with fury before she woke up to the same nightmare surrounding her.

Morana's brows furrowed in confusion as the pain dulled from her wound. Figuring it was the shock, she gathered the courage to stand, but there was no blood coating her fingertips, something she swore had been there moments ago.

Axton was standing with a gun pointed at the dead body on the ground. His eyes hardened, the wildness disappearing when he spotted Morton still lay in a pool of crimson. The rogue customer slouched against the wall in the corner, a bullet wound in his chest.

Axton was panting as his hazel eyes met hers. She looked down. There were no marks on her, no blood to indicate she had been injured. Her ears were ringing as she tried to piece together what had happened. She was sure she had been shot—positive.

"Call the cops," Axton commanded, but she didn't move. "Now!" His tone was sharp, and she jolted before pulling the cell phone from her back pocket. She quickly dialed the number with trembling fingers, awaiting the voice on the other line.

Two

The street was damp again. An overcast sky looming above the city and making midday seem akin to dusk. Morana's white tennis shoes hit mud on the sidewalk, and she cursed. The ends of her leggings were damp, but she was thankful that the rain had taken away the heat from the week prior. She wished it would have taken the scars from the event still lingered.

Her pulse quickened with every passing figure as she made her way to the local coffeehouse. The familiar brick building appeared on her right, and she carefully ducked through the door, making her way into line. The sound of the bells smacking the glass sent adrenaline racing through her bones. She stiffened as all the noise disappeared, carefully turning to the door. Nothing was amiss.

Morana shook off the feeling and walked up to the register. It was slow today, but Wednesdays at ten typically were. Most people were at work already. She ran a hand over her oversized sage button-down, pressing it firmly to her stomach. It was almost as if she could still feel the bullet there. How had she not been shot?

"I said, can I help you?" The brunette's voice cut through her thoughts. She glanced over the girl's nose piercing, round-framed glasses, and sleeve of tattoos peeking from beneath the cuffed sleeves of her black t-shirt.

"Oh." Morana cleared her throat, pulling her hand away from her stomach. "Just a chai tea latte, please."

"Got it." The barista gave her a strange look before turning to the monitor.

"Actually—" She crossed her arms. "Could you just add 4 shots to that?" Morana tucked a strand of blonde hair behind her ear. "And cinnamon powder on top, too."

The girl nodded but failed to hide her irritation at the minor inconvenience. She huffed as she gestured to the card machine, and Morana placed her debit card in the slot.

A week ago, she would have probably made some snide comment, calling the girl out on her shitty mood, but this week was different. She wanted to cave into herself, to disappear entirely. She shivered as she touched her stomach again, the clinging memory refusing to leave.

With Ashford being closed, she had little to distract her. The café was airy and open, with hanging plants and cozy fireplaces. She slid into one of the vintage wooden chairs. Even with the open space, being inside still made her throat tighten. She felt trapped, unable to get a grip on her emotions. Morana had spent so much time fighting for control, fighting for any sort of freedom to choose her own fate, and it slowly felt like it was being ripped from her fingertips. She could still hear the shots sounding, see the crimson blood. Taking a steadying breath, she shoved the feeling down. She just hoped Axton arrived here quickly.

Being out in public now was difficult, but when Axton had texted her to meet here, she couldn't turn down the challenge. She wouldn't let death taint her experience of the world, and she surely wouldn't let hardship keep her from doing the things she wanted—keep her from living.

She pulled the coffee to her lips. Her eyes roamed the room, searching for anything that would trigger a warning. She could hardly taste the liquid, her body refusing to register anything over the pounding in her head.

The fireplace on the other side of the room flickered. The flames weren't real, serving to light the coffee shop for the aesthetic alone. The rain had cooled the sticky heat of summer, but not enough to speak of fall and justify fire. She glanced at the dark-haired man sitting in the chair near the fire. He was leaning back, a tattooed hand wound around his cup as he pinned her with his gaze. His eyes were dark and searching, causing a chill to run up her spine, the hairs straightening at her neck. She couldn't look away from his captivating gaze.

His legs were stretched out as he casually rested his elbow on the arm of the chair. She started taking note of his white shirt, his leather jacket, and the black boots, memorizing his features—just in case. She fought the fear that rose in her throat, the stench of beer and frustration that reminded her of the man who held a gun pointed at her. Her hand tightened around her cup. The panic was suffocating and consuming.

"Morana."

She broke eye contact, shifting to Axton, who was now standing over the table, a coffee in hand. His brown hair was mussed, and stubble lined his jaw. Axton was usually put together. Nothing phased him, but in the wake of what had happened, he was clearly shaken and hiding it. A sentiment Morana heavily related to. A sentiment that built a small semblance of trust in her gut as he took off his brown jacket. The white long-sleeved shirt underneath had some obscure symbol on it in black.

"Hey," she whispered.

Axton sat down across from her, adjusting his glasses before throwing her a strained smile. The dimple on his cheek didn't appear, and she knew the expression was forced.

"How are you?" he asked. His knee was bouncing impatiently beneath the table. Axton was nervous, too, eyes wild as he glanced at the door.

She didn't respond for a while, trailing her eyes over to the fireplace again. The man had disappeared, and she took a deep breath, sagging into her chair, fingers tightening around her cup. The café somehow felt less suffocating now that he was gone. Had he been watching her before? She hadn't noticed.

"I'm—" Her brows furrowed as she held her cup, staring at the writing on the cardboard sleeve. Vines twisted around the café's logo, constricting it almost, and she let out a shaky laugh. She felt like there were vines wrapped around her throat, keeping the words from coming out. Emotions were hard for her. She had kept everyone out for so long. Maybe she regretted this decision. Maybe this was a bad idea to trust Axton, but the way he was looking at her, the way he was glancing around the room, desperately trying to memorize every detail—

"You don't have to answer that, Ana." Axton reached forward, brushing her fingers with his own. His touch was warm. She let go of her cup, allowing him to take her hand into his own and allowing the walls to crack ever so slightly. Her eyes met his, and she fought the tear that threatened to escape. Would she regret letting him in? There was a part of her that desperately wanted to.

"Have you been to the club?" she asked.

"No." Axton's jaw ticked, and he released her hand, the warmth it lent her disappearing with it. He leaned back in the metal chair as he brought his coffee to his mouth. "I haven't."

She hated feeling like they were drowning. The waves had crashed over them, and they couldn't do anything to find their way to the surface. In a way, it made her trust him.

"You know," she smirked, "you really don't look like you belong at a gun club, anyway." She glanced up to gauge his reaction to her half-hearted attempt to anchor them both with humor like she always did. "You're too—" She trailed her gaze over him, waiting for the telltale signs her actions made him feel something for her. "Dark academia," she finished.

Axton huffed a laugh, his hand still clinging to the coffee on the table. "It's the glasses," he offered. "They make me look smart."

"Well, they certainly try to." She rolled her eyes playfully. "It's not an easy task, and I have to say I can see through all of their attempts at dragging you up from your very low placement in society," she taunted.

"I like it when you say such nice things, you know." Axton placed his elbows on the table, leaning forward as his eyes flicked to her mouth. She noted how they seemed less distracted and lighted with amusement and longing. "It gets me all kinds of worked up."

Her heart skipped a beat, a sharp inhale giving away her true feelings. She cursed inwardly as the mask she presented to the world slipped. Using humor to hide again still left a hollowness in her chest. She certainly didn't want a relationship with him—not romantically. At least she hadn't thought of it before, but something about the way he was looking at her now brought a sense of comfort—of understanding. Morana desperately longed to be understood.

The dimple appeared on his cheek, and she watched as he rolled his tongue along the inside. Her brows knit together, as she glanced out the large window to the damp street. Her grip tightened on the cup before she changed the subject.

"Something happened a week ago, Axton." Her voice was barely a whisper. He looked at her with intrigue. "I was shot," she confessed.

"You were shot?" he asked, tilting his head and scratching at the stubble that peppered his jaw.

"I thought I was. I—"

A towering man with a toned and demanding stature stood over their table. His short black hair had a strand falling just across his forehead. His dark gaze pinned Morana before he interrupted their conversation. It was the man who had been sitting by the fire.

"Your car's been hit." He gestured out the window. "You parked in the lot about a block down, right? Black car?" His voice was deep, coated with an unearthly rasp. "I saw you get out. We arrived around the same time, and I parked nearby. I was just trying to leave." He licked his lips. "I'm the one that hit it."

"Shit." She glanced to Axton, who was already rising from his seat.

"Do you want me to come with you, Ana?" His hazel eyes searched hers as if he was looking for more than the answer to his question, peering through to what she wouldn't let him see. The events at Ashford may have made her feel weak, but she could fight that feeling, keeping her trembling hands in check, stilling her thoughts.

"No, that's fine." She abandoned her coffee cup on the table as she stood. "This shouldn't take long. I'll be right back." She threw Axton a reassuring smile. "Promise."

Axton's eyes followed her as she exited out onto the damp sidewalk with the stranger who hit her car, but he didn't move. She could feel the man's presence at her back. He kept a comfortable distance, and that brought her a sense of peace as she swiftly made her way to the parking lot.

The fresh air cleared more of her nerves, letting frustration build in her chest as she silently cursed her luck. She couldn't afford repairs right now, and she had very basic insurance for her car. With Ashford closed down, she wasn't receiving a paycheck for a while. The timing couldn't have been worse. She spotted her car up ahead and jogged forward to look at the damage. There was none.

"I needed to get you alone." The raspy voice near her ear had her skin prickling as she whirled around. He was so close that she could smell the sickly sweetness of his breath. His jaw tightened; lips pressed into a firm line. Morana glanced at the rip in the knee of his black jeans. He didn't look like a murderer. He looked edgy and attractive, his tall form dwarfing her in the parking lot. Edgy and attractive is probably what would make him so good at taking a life.

He inched closer, wetting his lips as the scent of mint invaded her senses. His eyes were dark, lighted with curiosity and amusement—and danger. She had one second to choose, and she chose flight. There was no way she would be in another situation like this. She had hardly wrapped her head around what had happened a week ago. Morana spun around, pumping her arms as she ran full force for the warehouse on the other side of the parking lot. Her heart rate picked up when she heard the heavy boots hit the pavement close behind her.

Her hands hit the stone windowsill, and she climbed through the punched-out glass, cutting her shoulder and slicing open her shirt as she went.

She could hear him grunt in frustration as he threw himself through the window after her. She had almost died a week ago at the range, but it seemed death was not done with her yet. The son of a bitch couldn't have her.

Morana moved faster, sprinting through the dimly lit halls of the abandoned building. Her lungs burned from the damp air and dust. The building grew darker with the windows disappearing, and she could hardly see where she was going. Glancing back, she found that the man was relentless in his pursuit. This asshole really wasn't giving up.

A door opened to her right, and she ducked inside the room, twisting and pressing her back against some old metal shelves. Her leg stretched out in front of her, kicking metal across the concrete floor. She noticed the gun, fingers trembling as she reached forward to pick up the weapon that had been conveniently sitting in this abandoned place. It was loaded. She briefly wondered if this was his plan, to chase her here and use the gun for her own end, stowing it away in this abandoned room.

The man burst through the doors, his leather jacket removed, and she could barely make out the tattoos over his arms in the shadows of the warehouse. She had the gun pointed directly at his chest, steady and waiting to release her final defense.

"Don't," he growled.

"Don't what?" she spat back, surprised at the power behind her words. They resembled a calm she didn't feel. Her voice was steady, but the vivid images of her imminent death crossed her mind. She wouldn't be the one to die. Would she have to live with the consequences of her actions? What would she become after she killed a man? Morana was pulled from her spinning thoughts by a sudden tingling in her limbs. Inky shadows spilled across her arms, caressing her skin. She blinked, and they were gone.

"If you shift realms again, you may end up where you don't belong."

She shook her head to ground herself, noticing that the man was stalking towards her, and she gripped the gun tighter. "What the hell are you talking about?" The trigger was touching her fingertip. The feel of it was burning and shooting fire into her blood, demanding her to take this life in front of her, but something stopped her.

"You avoided me a week ago." He took a step forward, eyes still trained on her. He didn't flinch despite the gun pointed in his direction, as if he had no reason to fear her. That would be his mistake, a choice that would end him. She had been someone to fear, capable of abandoning all she cared about in the middle of the night.

"Who are you?" she asked. It felt like the floor had fallen from beneath her when registering what he had said. A week ago? This man definitely wasn't the insane customer that had shot up the club last week. "Who are you?" she repeated. Her voice reverberated in the empty space.

"Before I tell you, promise me you won't tell the boy about what happened to you." He raised his hands up in defense as if he were trying to tame a wild animal. Morana's knuckles screamed in protest as she squeezed the butt of the gun even tighter. He was about to find out how wild she could be.

"That gun can't kill me," he spoke. "And apparently, it can't kill you either. You were shot last week, weren't you?"

"How did you--?"

"Promise me," he growled.

"Okay." She was shaking now, mind reeling and bound by what he claimed he knew. Did he read the news article or something? She hadn't had the strength to look herself, but she was sure he could have gotten some of the information from there. That's probably how he knew about the incident, but the part about her thinking she had been shot?

"I fucking promise." She was panting now. "Who are you?"

He lowered his hands, a cocky grin appearing on his face as he squatted in front of her with the gun now pointed at his skull. "You can call me Death."

Three

Morana lowered the weapon slowly, biting her cheek in concentration. He didn't even flinch. This guy was insane.

He reached out and grabbed her arm, the touch bruising as he dragged her back out into the hallway. She struggled against his grip, trying to tilt the gun toward him before he used his knee to knock it out of her hand, leaving the weapon on the dirty floor.

Her chest still stung from the damp air inside the warehouse, and sweat was sliding down her temples, plastering small strands of blonde hair to the sides of her face. For a moment, she felt the vulnerability of her disheveled appearance in the face of a stranger, the uncertainty of the situation surrounding her. She had always been good at fear, burying it six feet deep so that no storm could unearth her true emotions. This situation was no different. Morana packed the soil harder, keeping Death away from the fear she refused to touch.

"That's not an answer, asshole," she grunted. "Death isn't a name." She was still fighting his grip, but he continued dragging her through the empty warehouse.

His jaw flinched in the faint light, but beyond that, he didn't react. "It's not." A smirk finally formed on his lips as he looked at her, keeping his hand tight around her bicep. His eyes were dark, a swirling mix of ebony and brown, dancing like deep secrets unknown. In the depths of his gaze, something shone, as if there was some light buried within—something she was missing. For a moment, she almost believed he wasn't crazy, but filled with the wisdom of an uncomfortably long life. "It's a title," he finished.

She let out a harsh breath, reality crashing back into her like a flood. Could he hear her heart pounding in her chest as he pulled her through hallways lined with metal vents and forgotten dust? He headed toward the hall with the windows. Hope rose, chasing the adrenaline pumping in her veins. Morana didn't respond to him, and she could tell it was irritating him. He wanted a reaction.

"I'm a god," he informed.

She laughed loudly; the sound echoing over the metal vents and running along the ceiling. "Yeah," she started. "Me too."

"Maybe," he speculated.

She grimaced and tried to fight out of his grip. If he wanted to threaten and test her with his cocky arrogance, she would throw the same conceited attitude around, pulling him from whatever high horse he sat upon. Fighting against his hold and twisting away from him, her back slammed against the concrete wall. He had let her go, and she didn't want to find out if it was on purpose. There was no time for games. She froze there with the concrete steadying her emotions. She took comfort in it. Death wouldn't unearth a damn thing about her.

"Where are you taking me?" she asked, jutting her chin out and squaring her shoulders.

He didn't offer her a response. He merely pinned her with that dark gaze. It was almost captivating—almost.

She moved forward, pushing her hands into his chest to send him backward. It was useless, but she pushed him again. Again.

Rock steady and unyielding. Those eyes bore into her soul, creating a feeling of discomfort as his gaze stripped her bare. "You're coming to my home," he spoke calmly. "One of them."

"You're insane," she spat, backing up against the wall again. Deep pleasure pulsed along her skin, a familiar sensation took over, and she longed to close her eyes and get lost in the abyss as darkness coated her vision momentarily.

Death glanced down at her arms, but his features didn't betray his emotion. Could he see something there?

"You must be too, then," he countered. "Because I use the same power you do to travel between worlds." He took a step forward. She needed to run again, but the roots of fear dug into the floor, holding her captive. "To shift realms," he finished. "Don't blink."

He grabbed her arm again, and the world faded away. She was descending into a canyon and staring into nothing but an empty void. Shadows twisted in her vision, and though she fought them, she soon succumbed to their darkness.

With a stumbling step, Morana felt the firm grip on her shoulder before snarling at the man called Death.

"Get your hands off me," she hissed, yanking against him. Morana pulled out of his grip before realizing her surroundings had changed. She froze.

She was standing in the middle of a massive foyer. Balconies rose around the perimeter of the large room, carved with intricate details. The deep brown wood could almost be considered a work of art and reminded her of the balconies lining an old theater. The large ceiling stretched up three stories, a glass roof overhead that illuminated the blue-green walls. There was an antiquated feeling to the space, as if it had been around for centuries.

Her throat bobbed as the first dig of a shovel pushed into her carefully curated mask. A trickle of shock spread across her face before she could wish it away. Her eyes were wide as she looked back at the man in the white t-shirt, now dirty and soaked with sweat. His leather jacket was draped over his arm, and his tanned skin was glistening with sweat, making his tattoos stand out in the misty sunlight.

He gestured to a room off the main entryway, and Morana dug her heels in, refusing to follow. Curiosity won the battle, and she pushed on after him, noticing the crows inked into his toned forearm.

They walked up a short set of three steps carpeted in deep red before emerging in a dining room. The man sat at the head of the wooden table and nodded to the high-backed chair at the other end. Statues and carvings decorated the dining room. Candles sat at the center of the table.

Morana shifted uncomfortably where she stood, slowly running her finger along the rich, brown-colored furniture. She finally sat, fists tight, while her nails bit into her palms. Her gray eyes locked on her shoulder. A bloodied cut remained where the glass had ripped her shirt, but it was all dried now. A mere stain of what this stranger had put her through. Her blood was boiling. Anger was easy, and she allowed it to fester when her pale gray eyes met his onyx gaze across the room.

"Hungry?" he asked casually, leaning an elbow on the table. Place settings sat on the rich oak slab the table was constructed from—as if he had expected her to be dining with him. Even cutlery that smelled of money lay before her, tucked into silken table napkins. Pushing repulsion down, she held onto the rage of her situation.

She had been kidnapped, hunted like a helpless fawn, and pulled into the safety of whatever this place was.

"No." Her gaze shot shards of ice in his direction. "Why the *fuck* am I here?" she asked, hands clenched at her sides beneath the wooden surface of the table. There was no one else in the room.

"How long have you had these abilities?" he probed, running his pointer finger over his bottom lip.

"Answer my question first." She lifted her chin, her lips peeling back. She didn't bother with his strange interrogation, not understanding whatever ability he spoke of. What she wanted to know was what he planned on doing with her, and how she had ended up in what looked like a castle. "*Why* am I here?"

He raised an eyebrow at her and picked up the silver cup that sat on his side of the table. The furniture fit the lofty appearance of this palace, the long table stretching miles away, keeping him distanced from her. It allowed her to breathe for the briefest moment. He took a drink of whatever was in there, delaying his answer. Something about his presence held her under his power, despite her furious attempts at keeping her emotions in check.

"You're here," he began, "because you avoided me a week ago." He leaned forward against the table. "You're here because I've seen something familiar in you, and you walked into another realm with a blink of your eye." His dark gaze pinned her as he waited to finish. Morana assumed the pause was for effect, but his empty and useless words did not impress her. He was clearly insane. "You're here because only a god can do that."

Morana let out an exasperated laugh. She folded her arms across her chest after tucking a strand of now frizzy blonde hair behind her ear. "And you're a god," she stated in disbelief.

"More or less." His jaw ticked again, holding back a smile that dug up another layer of frustration in Morana. "Yes, I'm a god." His answer was definitive. She observed his features, looking for a crack in the confidence he was showing. Her stomach churned at the realization that this man really believed what he was saying. There was no crack to be seen, no sign that he was even lying about what he spoke of. She didn't look away from his dark eyes, challenging him to give in and admit it wasn't true, but the longer she stared at him, the more she believed it, too.

When he looked at her, it felt like her mind was wrapped in a veil—like her own decisions were just out of reach, and he could see beneath the layers of her thoughts. Something took root in her chest, making her shift uncomfortably again.

Morana sealed the lid on her emotions. "And you're Death, I suppose." Her eyes narrowed.

"Yes."

"Do you have another name?" She cocked an eyebrow, returning the challenge. Whatever he saw in her, he didn't have permission. Not even Axton was allowed into the deepest truth of who she was, what she felt. And he was the closest thing she had come to having as a friend since leaving her old home, leaving her father behind.

"Yes," he answered. His lip twitched, holding back a smirk once more. She watched the amusement dancing in his eyes, her stomach dipping.

"I assume I'm now Death's prisoner." Her nose scrunched in disgust.

"You're not a prisoner," he said calmly. "You're free to go." A knowing look appeared on his face. "But I've gathered that your abilities are new to you. You probably can't control them since it appears that you hardly knew they were there. So—" His finger tapped impatiently on the oak surface. "Without my help in teaching you, you can go where you will, but my guess is it won't be home."

Her face fell as her throat clogged with something like hopelessness, her heart squeezing in her chest— another layer uncovered. Who was this man? She looked around the room, longing for an exit. She needed to run, but she had to be smart.

Morana cleared her throat. "You want to teach me to use my powers, then?" she asked, shoving the nerves away from the surface. Adrenaline was racing under her skin.

She thought back to the darkness she felt when she was shooting, the way she had been shot and lived without a wound to prove it. Her mind traced over the seconds she had seen a strange woman in what she assumed to be a dream during the attack on Ashford. Maybe he could explain to her what she saw.

He didn't answer. Death merely stared at her, moving his gaze down her body. Heat washed over her under his scrutinization. What was he looking for? What did he see?

"What do you want in return?" she asked. Her cheeks heating as his eyes continued to track up her body. Her gut churned at the thought of what he was doing, why he had kidnapped her.

"Fuck." She slammed her fist on the table, snapping the tension. He didn't flinch. Morana laughed then, loud and manic. If he wanted to be mad, she could play the game. She would meet his madness with her own.

"I am not here to be mocked." His deep voice rumbled with power across the stone floor. He stood up abruptly, the scrape of the chair sending shivers up her spine. He strode towards her, and she fought her reaction but failed as she reeled back away from his towering figure. "There's room for you here if you wish." He pushed off the table, turning to exit the room. She watched as the muscles in his back shifted. When he got to the door, he turned back, his dark hair falling in his face. "You can call me Matthias." He didn't even make it to the door before he vanished. She blinked, willing the image to correct itself, but it was no use. Death was gone.

Morana sat in silence, peering into the cup in front of her. She wrapped her hand around the cool metal and brought it to her nose to smell its contents. It looked like water, but she didn't trust it. She pushed up out of her chair, making her way to the entrance where they had come in.

"Miss Morana?" A silvery voice halted her in her tracks. She turned back to see the petite figure of a woman standing across the room. Her black wavey hair hung loosely at her back. She was wearing a simple brown dress and boots that laced up her ankles. "I've been sent to escort you to your rooms."

Morana looked her up and down before meeting her large blue eyes which were wide with curiosity.

A servant.

How many did he have? She shook her head. It didn't matter, and she wouldn't dwell on the way this madman lived his life, the way he thrusted her into—she didn't even know what. Her stomach felt hollow, the anger slowly fading, draining out of her and leaving a forgotten emptiness. She didn't want to stay here any longer. Something about the connection she felt to this man, the way his words twisted in her mind, begging to be believed, made her uncomfortable. It touched on an experience that was just out of reach. Something she couldn't explain and a reminder of the event she still couldn't fully escape from. But she refused to be trapped.

"You can escort me out," she said curtly.

The girl bowed. "Of course," she answered. Moving swiftly and removing her apron, she led Morana back out through the foyer and through the large black doors that exited to the world beyond.

Four

Morana didn't look back at the girl that had led her outside, hellbent on getting out of this nightmare. She burst through the doors, realizing her mistake.

Outside of what she now knew to be a castle, the misty forest wrapped around her. The grounds were completely isolated from the city she left, and it dawned on her. He was right. She wouldn't be able to find her way out of here. She didn't even know where she was.

Panic swelled in her chest as she took to the gravel path at her feet. The air was cooler here, and she folded her arms across her chest. The wound on her shoulder throbbed as her shirt separated from the dried blood, leaving the cut open to the air.

Her mind was spinning, but she refused to lose focus. Where would she go? She stopped by a tree, resting her arm against the bark and closing her eyes. She needed to think. Where had he taken her?

The world went silent, and her mind descended into the void. She glimpsed a flash of a familiar woman. Rose-colored eyes appeared more shocked than the first time. Her mind was playing tricks on her, hardly able to wrap around the words *Matthias* had spoken. Maybe she was dreaming, something her anxiety-riddled mind conjured in the wake of the Ashford shooting.

When she opened her eyes, she realized her arm was leaning on a lamppost in the parking lot next to her car. She spun around, frantically looking at the abandoned warehouse. Morning had quickly turned into dusk, the golden light filtering through the city as streetlamps slowly turned on.

Morana pulled the keys from the pocket on her leggings and jumped into the rusty car, pleading with whatever gods—save for the insane one she had just met—would listen. The engine clicked but refused to start. She slammed her hand against the steering wheel once before resting her head there.

"Shit," she breathed. The weight of the last few hours crashed over her like a raging storm. As far as she knew, she was alone. It wouldn't hurt to unearth some fears she had. It wouldn't hurt to accept the stinging behind her eyes that begged her to release the dam of emotions she had pushed aside to act. As she got out of the car, touching a finger to the fresh blood on her shoulder, she realized her hands were shaking. Her gaze shot to the warehouse. The gun.

Morana sprinted ahead, summer wind whipping at her hair before she crawled into the broken window, her hips squeezing through the dilapidated opening. She paused in the abandoned space, trying to remember where she had run, where she had dropped the weapon. She moved through the hallway, down deeper into the dark. With the sun setting, the warehouse was eerie, and her heart pounded with the fear that he might have come back here. She couldn't shake the feeling that the man called Death wouldn't keep to his word. He had told her she was free to go, but she hardly believed him. Too easy, and if life taught her anything, nothing was that easy. She liked to pretend that walking out on a drunken, depressed man as she had with her father, was easy, but it wasn't. Protecting yourself always came at a cost.

Something glinted in the retreating sunlight pouring into the dusty hallway. *There.* Morana reached down to pick up the discarded handgun, tucking it into the waistband of her leggings before moving back through the hall to exit into the parking lot. She would need to walk back to her apartment. She'd deal with the car later.

Morana moved through the city streets with the lights flickering on overhead. She had eight blocks before she would make it to her small apartment, eight blocks before this nightmare would be over. Eight blocks until she could allow the well to spill over. Tears stung at the corners of her eyes. When she was alone, when no one was looking, she would let this all out.

She ran a hand over her face, wiping the damp moisture of salt and sweat. It was still humid from all the rain, and she wished the sky would open up if only to hide the tears dangerously close from spilling. But she wasn't that lucky. Hell, these past two weeks showed her she wasn't lucky at all. She wrapped her arms around herself tightly—trudging forward—always pressing forward.

Cars passed, many of them blaring loud music. A couple of teenagers across the street were stopping at a food truck. She tucked her hair behind her ear, looking down as she moved faster. Seven more blocks.

A dark figure stopped her in her tracks. She halted, looking up into the magnetic green eyes of a man now standing in the way. She scoffed, her nose twisting in frustration.

"Sorry, dude," she muttered. Morana cocked her head, noticing that he was wearing a cloak. His hood was pulled up, his dark skin illuminated in the streetlights. She made to step around him, but he moved, blocking her again. Scowling, she clenched her fists at her sides.

"What's your problem?" Morana tried to move again, but he followed the motion, lowering his hood to reveal ears pointed at the top on either side. She backed up a step while he continued analyzing her. She didn't speak before she took off, sprinting down the alleyway to her left. His footsteps followed, keeping pace with the pounding of her heart.

Her lungs were burning, body protesting from the exertion earlier in the night, but she continued moving through alleyways and streets, refusing to stop for cars. After a few blocks, she stopped to hide in the shadows of a dumpster with a metal ladder hanging above her head. She looked back to find he had disappeared. She caught her breath and carefully walked deeper into the shadows. Her confidence in having shaken him wavered when she heard a rock skid across the asphalt.

When she turned, he was there again. His hood was pulled back up over his head, and his black boots echoed off the walls of the alley as he moved toward her. A brick wall boxed her in with her would-be assailant. She reached behind her, pulling the gun from her waistband and pointing it at the second stranger to chase her down today.

"Don't move," her voice was shaking. "I know how to shoot."

Before she knew it, the man had lunged, grabbing her wrist and freeing the gun from her grip. The weapon went flying across the ground. He slammed her back against the brick wall, holding her chest with his forearm while moving a dagger to her throat. The man snarled, blowing hot breath in her face.

Morana could do nothing but press into the solid structure at her back and beg any god to listen.

"A dagger? Doesn't that seem a little archaic? What do you want?" Her voice was strained, barely containing the underlying terror. There was no hiding her fear. It was out in the open, despite her best efforts to conceal it.

As if this were a game, his eyes lit with cruel excitement. One she had no patience for or desire to play. She turned her head away from him, nails digging into the skin at her palms. When she braced herself against the tip of his knife, a shot rang through the empty alley. The man grunted, releasing her, and stepping backward, gripping his side. Morana turned to where the shot had come from. Relief flooded her when she saw Axton was standing there, hair mussed and eyes wild as he held her gun out in front of him. Her mind flashed to a week ago, but she shoved it away.

She watched as the cloaked stranger ran his hand over his side, golden light moving and covering the place where he had been shot before he turned and ran off.

Axton moved forward, grabbing her arm and hauling her toward the metal ladder.

"Did you see that? What just happened?" Axton wasn't reacting to the strange light the man released. He wasn't really reacting at all. Her brow furrowed as she tried to understand how he had gotten here. Something settled low in her stomach, but she chalked it up to being chased by two crazy people and too much cardio with nothing but caffeine to fuel her. Axton turned and walked back up the alley. "Where are we going?" she gasped, following him blindly in the dark, not wanting to be alone should one of the men be waiting in the shadows for her.

"My apartment." His eyes flicked down to hers before he gently shoved her toward the ladder, coaxing her to climb. "You're the one in the alley next to it."

A crease formed on her forehead before she stepped up, climbing her way to the fourth balcony before halting. Axton opened the window, and they both crawled into his loft.

Her heart was threatening to burst through her chest in the same way the tears now flowed freely down her face. The well had broken, and the weight settled. Sweat lined her neck as she backed up away from Axton. She reached for something to steady her, and he ran to the kitchen to grab a first aid kit from beneath the sink.

"What the fuck was that?" she whispered. Her hands were shaking again. She couldn't get enough air into her lungs, damp fear running down her cheeks.

Axton didn't answer as he rummaged through the kit, pulling out bandages and alcohol wipes. "Let me see your arm, Ana." Axton held a tube of antiseptic ointment between his teeth.

She quickly unbuttoned her shirt, leaving her standing in a black sports bra and leggings as he examined the cut on her shoulder. He worked quickly. "Breathe," he grunted before pressing the alcohol wipe to her arm. She cried out as he quickly worked to place the bandage over the cut. Her entire body was shuddering as the adrenaline raced out of her system.

"You shot him," she stated, her mind tracing over the details of what had happened, trying to remember everything. "You shot him, and he walked away."

Axton didn't look up. He moved his glasses up on his nose, pressing his other hand to the bandage now covering the cut from earlier. When he was done, he gently grasped either side of her face. "Where were you?" he demanded. His voice a strained rasp.

She couldn't answer. Not because she didn't want to, but because she still didn't know. The adrenaline washed out of her, leaving her with the overwhelming pain of what had happened. The new trauma settled in with the remanents of what happened at the gun club. A tear escaped her as Axton traced her features. His hazel eyes were pleading, but she still couldn't give him an answer. She didn't want to talk about it, anyway.

She leaned forward, wrapping her arms around his waist and burying her face in his solid chest. His warmth engulfed her, and she loosened the reins on it all. He smelled like leather and spice. He pulled her closer as her body shook vigorously, new tears dampening his shirt.

"You can stay here," he whispered, moving a hand to her hair and stroking gently.

She nodded, pulling away from him and wiping her hand across her face. Her clothes were damp with sweat, muscles aching.

"Go take a shower. You can use some of my clothes. There's a guest bedroom at the end of the hall past the bathroom." Axton moved a hand to rest on her cheek. He looked as if he were about to say something before blowing out a breath and walking away.

Morana strode down to the bathroom, opening the door. A fresh towel was hanging on the rack, and she hurried to turn on the water.

She washed the grime away from her skin, scrubbing at every part of her that had been touched by strangers today. The steam filled her aching lungs, and she closed her eyes, running her fingers through her matted hair. It had been three years in this godforsaken city. Three years of isolation, and now she was here, welcomed into Axton's apartment. She was desperate for connection—desperate for someone to see her after all that was happening around her. At work, there was a careful distance, one she placed to protect herself and maintain the freedom she had established. Here, however, there was the budding knowledge that he had been there. In the gun club, he was there. In the street, he was there. Axton had always been there, and now he was opening up his home to her.

When she finally padded out of the bathroom in her towel, the hall was empty. She quickly made her way to the guest bedroom to find a clean pair of sweatpants and a t-shirt waiting for her. Without thinking, she crawled into the bed after putting them on. She knew Axton was across the hall, and she was thankful for his presence, but she was more thankful that she could descend into sleep. The darkness provided an escape from the worries and constant action required to push forward—to keep moving, regardless of how she felt.

Morana sat up abruptly, her head pounding as she pressed her fingers against her temples and glanced toward the glowing numbers on the nightstand in Axton's apartment. The clock read 2:04 am. She had hardly slept.

She fingered the bandage on her shoulder and shuddered. It was the one sign it had all been real. She pressed her finger to it, feeling the dull pain move under her skin. She winced.

A shadow moved in the corner, and before she knew it, she was held by the obsidian gaze of the man standing in her room. She recognized the sleeve of tattoos. Crows gathered in ink on his skin, and she immediately scooted back, slamming her back into the headboard.

He didn't speak, and she doubted that what she was seeing was real before he started prowling toward the bed.

"I'll scream," she warned him.

Matthias grabbed her arm, pulling up the sleeve of the oversized tee to reveal the bandage on her shoulder. He ripped it off, the biting sting hitting her skin. A fog settled over her mind, and she remembered the green eyes of the man that had attacked her.

"They found you," Matthias breathed, glancing at the minor cut where the dagger had been on her neck. She tried to pull away from his grip. "Shit."

"You're not taking me out of here." She fought him off to no avail before he finally let go of her.

He was pacing now. "They're going to kill you," he warned, his strong jaw clenching.

"And you're not?" She glared in suspicion. "Almighty god of *Death*?" she mocked. "Isn't killing your job?"

He huffed, folding his arms across his broad chest. Her ears were ringing, a reminder of the gunshot, the vulnerability, the strange sensations that saved her. Panicked, her eyes flicked across the room. She didn't hear anything outside of the door, but panic was becoming a close friend. Would someone barge in, ready to take her away? Or was that person standing in the room with her already?

"Who tried to kill me?" she pleaded; voice softer than before. Maybe if she softened her delivery, if she showed an emotion other than anger, he would give her some actual answers.

Death simply snarled, his lip peeling back in disgust, anger a vivid presence beneath his tattooed skin. The moth was shifting on his hand, moving as his fists clenched tighter.

"Who?" she demanded.

"You know where I am." He stepped back, facing her as she sat on the bed. "Come by the warehouse when you want to learn how to use those abilities of yours. Maybe it won't leave you so vulnerable."

Without an explanation, Matthias disappeared.

She pulled the blankets up to her chest, tears gathering at the corners of her eyes as they flicked wildly around the room. She wanted to fear the dark gaze of the first stranger to attack her today most, but all she could see was green, and it sent her into a panic.

The door opened, and she jumped. Axton was standing there in gray sweatpants and no shirt. His toned chest was cleanly shaven, skin taught around muscles she hadn't realized he possessed. He ran a hand through his brown hair, concern evident on his bare face. She couldn't recall a time she saw him without his glasses.

"I'm sorry," he stuttered. "I was just checking on you."

She straightened where she was sitting, hardening her gaze and placing the mask over her face so he wouldn't suspect anything was amiss.

"Go back to sleep, Axton."

He nodded, pulling the door closed until she was alone in the dimly lit room.

Morana tried to settle into the bed. Her mind wouldn't shut off, and she had the strongest feeling that this wasn't over. Death would come for her again.

Five

Morning light hadn't appeared when she looked over at the clock. Sweat made her borrowed shirt stick to her, and Morana peeled it from her chest as she moved from underneath the comforter in Axton's apartment. Her throat was dry, and her mind was still hazy from everything that had occurred yesterday. She swallowed down what felt like sand and got up to get a glass of water.

She slowly opened the door, stepping into the hall and carefully walking out to the kitchen. It was still dark outside, the high-rise buildings blocking the early traces of morning light from creeping through the blinds. Morana opened the cabinet, grabbing a glass and filling it with water from the refrigerator. She leaned against the cool granite counter to breathe and take in her surroundings.

She hadn't been to Axton's apartment before. She had known him since applying at Ashford, never daring to get closer than a friendship. Relationships weren't something she could tolerate, not with the guilt she carried with her. Morana had run from everything, walking out on her father as soon as she turned eighteen. That guilt held firm, keeping her from connection and drawing on a deeply rooted fear that she would be trapped and useless—unable to change or fix all that crumbled. Maybe that's why she clung to senseless flirtations and nothing more. Roots were binding.

Her mind ran back over the way it had felt to have his body pressed to hers, hands comforting her while she came undone. He had seen her raw emotion, and he hadn't run. That had to say something. Either that or she was more desperate than she thought.

A loud shot rang in the night, causing her to flinch as the glass slipped from her hand, shattering on the tiled floor.

Fear made a dramatic reappearance, carried into the night by a loud noise that left her ears ringing. Everything moved in slow motion briefly as she turned.

"Idiots setting off fireworks." Axton walked out from the darkened hall—voice smooth. She turned towards him. He was wearing the gray sweatpants still, his chestnut locks gently tousled, making warmth pool in her stomach. His chest was bare, revealing the toned muscle beneath his usual clothing. As her heart slowed back to a normal pace, she tried to hide the trembling in her fingers.

Her gaze flicked back up from his broad chest. She hadn't looked long, but the way the corner of his mouth pulled up and the dimple appeared on his cheek. He noticed. The heat from her stomach shot up to her face, coloring her cheeks and scalding the turmoil leftover from the fireworks.

"Yeah," her voice was still unsteady, lined with an unsure rasp. The sound had startled her. That was all. She looked down at the shattered glass on the floor.

"Oh my god," her brows knit together with concern. "I'm so sorry. Let me clean that up." She shifted forward, but Axton was already there with a dustpan and broom. His warm hand wound around her wrist, tugging gently to draw her attention to him.

"It's okay," he spoke gently as if he were afraid of frightening her. "It's been happening to me, too." His eyes softened. It was a fleeting comfort She still didn't like the pity she found in his gaze. Her gut twisted with unease, and he winced. Axton let go, kneeling to clean up the mess.

She watched as he scooped up the shards. She couldn't help but stare as the muscles in his back shifted with each movement. The dim light of morning cast shadows over his skin, and she longed to be taken by such darkness. Her skin was still heated where his touch had been around her wrist. She shoved the feeling away, taking a step back and chuckling.

Fear was palpable, and she longed for an escape, but she was determined to keep those feelings at bay, masking them with careless amusement. Could Axton see through it?

"Maybe we could warm each other's beds to chase the nightmares away." Her voice was filled with casual taunting, begging him to fall for the mask she presented, the one that said she was in control of herself. With all that had happened in the past weeks, she wasn't so sure her resolve would hold. She longed to be lost in someone, laid bare but too afraid to admit it.

Axton poured the broken glass into the trash can, leaning the broom and dustpan against it, and moved to stand in front of her. His hazel eyes pierced the mask.

"Don't do that," he whispered, voice taut.

Her stomach dipped as his breath fanned over her face. The pity in his eyes had mocked her, and she longed to wipe the memory of it away.

"Do what?" she asked. It was a challenge.

"Don't bait me and then throw the walls back up." His gaze was intense and unyielding. It was so different from the lighthearted man she worked with, the one that tolerated the teasing and distance.

"I'm not," she defended. He was standing closer now. Her heart was pounding in her chest, desire pooling in her core.

"You are." His brows furrowed. "You've done it forever. At some point, I'm going to need a straight answer." He was so close that her back arched over the countertop. "I can see right through it all, Ana."

Her eyes widened in surprise, the smell of sweet tobacco invading her senses. Her lips parted as she took him in, and hungry eyes dropped to watch the movement.

"A straight answer to what, Axton?" she finally asked. She wanted him to say it. The feeling of comfort from last night returned. He had saved her—defended her.

"A straight answer to how you feel about me." He leaned forward, looking down at her short frame.

Her thoughts emptied, leaving nothing but pure desire.

"Do I make your heart race, Ana?" he asked, trailing a finger down her neck towards her chest, the traitorous thing pounding to meet his touch. He held her wrist again with his other hand, and she looked down, relishing in the feeling of his skin on hers. "Do I steal the breath from your lungs?" Her breath caught as he continued to trail his fingers even lower. "Does my touch place fire beneath your skin?" He dropped the hand, causing liquid fire to flood her while tightening his grip ever so slightly on her wrist. His bare chest was now brushing against hers, separated only by the shirt she wore—his shirt.

"Why should I have an answer to that?" Morana's voice wobbled. She couldn't think straight with him this close, and she was seconds away from giving in to him.

"Because you do all of those things to me," he admitted. "Every second of every day." He leaned in so his lips almost brushed her ear. "I can't get my head on straight."

"I've liked my freedom," she confessed, lifting her chin. For all the time she spent running, she also wanted to be chased. Though it wasn't entirely true. It was also an excuse—a last-ditch effort to avoid where this was going, but she wasn't sure she wanted to run from whatever this was anymore. He could see her desire, and she could feel him pressing into her hip.

"I'm not here to steal your freedom, Ana." He pulled back, and pain flashed across his features as he searched for an answer.

A part of her feared everything that Axton was, feared what it would mean if she accepted him, the intensity of it. If she were being honest with herself, he already owned part of her. She wasn't sure when it happened, but she was tired. She was tired of fighting it, and it couldn't hurt to lose herself for a night. Maybe it was time to open up to someone. After everything that happened, she deserved something steady.

"Okay," she finally breathed.

Axton moved, lifting her onto the counter, his hands on either side of her as his lips crashed into hers. Every thought in her mind emptied as she gave in to the feeling of his skin. He pressed forward, his hard length pushing into her center, and she ran her hands up his bare back to tangle into his soft hair. Morana tugged gently to deepen the kiss. He groaned, releasing every ounce of need he had bottled up for the past three years.

Her skin was on fire as she fought to regain control of her breathing. The small part of her whispering that this was a mistake reappeared, circling—hunting. She cast it aside for the headiness of it all. She liked the feeling of losing control to chaos for once.

Axton placed a hand to the side of her face as he continued moving his lips, gently adding pressure. His fingers tangled in the hair at the back of her head before he pulled his mouth from hers. Morana slid down from the counter, allowing his forehead to rest against her own. She could feel his breath ghost over her skin, and she shivered.

"You have no idea," he breathed, voice like gravel. "You have no idea how long I've wanted this."

She chuckled and pushed her fingers into the waistband of his sweatpants, pulling him closer. "Oh, I've known," she said.

"I suppose I knew that." He smiled against her lips. He reached a hand around her and opened the drawer to her left. She could hear the wrapper before he slammed it shut. She tilted her head in question.

"Junk drawer," he answered.

"Condoms in the kitchen?" she pressed.

He smiled again, revealing the dimple on his cheek. It only confirmed her decision. She wanted to lick him there.

"I prefer junk drawer." His hazel eyes lighted as a car passed in the streets below, shifting the light over his face. "I sound insane the way you phrase it."

"Or you just sound like a poor peasant that lives with limited storage."

He laughed, the rich sound rolling over her skin, making her body hum with fire and need. She clenched her thighs together to relieve the pressure. Her stomach wound into knots as her walls came crashing down.

"Or that," he whispered before returning his mouth to hers. One hand threaded through her hair, and the other reached down to grip the back of her thigh. She hopped up, wrapping her legs around his waist and holding his face in her hands. She brushed her thumb over the dimple there as he moved them down the hallway to the open door leading into the guest room.

He placed her on the bed, and she smiled before pulling his shirt from her torso. She revealed herself completely and leaned back on her elbows, daring him to look longer.

"Fuck, Ana." Axton ran his hand down his face, hazel eyes burning her skin with every glance.

"Keep staring, and you'll give me enough time to change my mind." The longer he stood there watching her, the more she couldn't keep the thoughts at bay. She longed for this vulnerability, the escape he was offering, but there was still a part of her that questioned if she was making the right decision. Death's presence still lurked in the corners of her mind, muddling her emotions. If she was going to do this, she needed to do it quickly. She didn't have enough excuses to keep him away from her.

Axton growled, moving forward to rip the sweatpants off her body, throwing them on the floor. He kneeled on the bed, pressing a hand to her knee and spreading her apart. He ran his fingers up her torso as he drank in the sight of her sprawled out before him.

Her heart was pounding in her chest, limbs trembling as she looked up. Light finally reached the apartment windows and was filtering into the room. Golden rays splashed across his tanned skin, highlighting the toned muscle of his arms and chest—flexing with each fevered motion. Desire returned tenfold, and she squeezed her legs together at the intensity of it. Axton smiled wickedly as he hooked her knee with his forearm to open her legs and drag her closer to his face.

He leaned down and kissed her hip, eyes looking up at her, full lips brushing over her skin and sending chills everywhere. Keeping one hand on her stomach, and one on her thigh, he held her open to him, daring her to close her legs again. He trailed his kisses lower, the hand on her thigh slowly moving upwards. She closed her eyes, letting the heat of his skin melt into her own, burning the fire in her veins brighter.

"You haven't changed your mind?" he asked against her skin, and she almost laughed. How could she change her mind when every movement felt so damn good?

"No," she breathed. His finger traced outside of her entrance, tempting and toying.

"You know this doesn't take your freedom, right?" he spoke. The rasp in his voice coated her skin. "No strings attached."

"I don't know if I'd object if it did at this point." Her breathing was ragged as he kissed the inside of her thigh. The dark sound of his laugh had her arching into his touch, begging him to continue.

"I won't ask for your freedom, Ana." His finger moved up her slick center, and she moaned, hardly focusing on his words. "Not yet anyway."

His mouth moved on her at the same time his finger entered her, curling upward as he moved his tongue across that spot that sent her mind spinning. She moved her fingers to his hair, tangling them in the brown silk.

She couldn't help moving against him, begging him to take faster, harder. She would shatter beneath him. His tongue had her gripping his hair tighter. Death was a mere figment of her imagination. There were only three years of released tension.

He pushed into her again, licking his way across her flesh, and sending her spiraling out of control. She panted, feeling the pressure build when cool air kissed her flesh. She opened her eyes to see he was standing now, pulling the pants away from his body and frantically grabbing the condom.

"Hurry up," she barked. The dimple appeared on his cheek, making him look innocent. Axton was far from innocent. He was quickly holding his weight above her.

He pressed a kiss to her neck, moving down to her breast, and taking her nipple between his teeth. Her breath caught as she arched into the sensation, his hand moving to run his thumb across her other breast, causing it to pebble in need.

"Good god," she breathed.

"If that god had anything to do with you." His breath fanned over her collarbones. "I can guarantee he wasn't any good, and I will never stop thanking him for it."

Axton placed a kiss on her lips, and Morana ran her hands over his back, fingernails digging into the skin. He kissed her once more before thrusting himself inside her, filling every part of her.

"Don't you dare stop," she breathed as he continued moving. She needed this, needed the demons hunted down and shattered.

"I wouldn't dream of it."

He hooked her leg over his shoulder to angle himself deeper. His eyelids fluttered, and his movements turned erratic. Both of their breathing turned ragged as he pushed into her, tearing down every wall she had ever placed in front of him. She could feel herself ready to fall, and she would be damned if she didn't take him down with her. She let out another noise as she pulled his lip between her teeth, biting gently.

His muscles tensed where her hands touched, and she knew they would go over the edge together.

"Axton," she breathed. The plea was his undoing. She followed him into the darkness, refusing to think about the consequences. Refusing to think about the walls now laying in ruin around the heart she so carefully protected.

The unfamiliar scent of clean linen and fleeting comfort woke her up. She rose a hand to block the steady stream of sunlight that met her sleepy gaze through the window.

Morana shifted onto her back, staring up at the white ceiling above. For a moment, her heart rushed into a fierce beat as she flicked her gaze to the corner of Axton's guest bedroom. She expected to see Death standing there, but as she was met with empty wall space, she realized the thought was ridiculous. Death lurked in the shadows, and it was clearly mid-morning.

Shifting upright in the bed, Morana took in the empty space next to her. She could feel Axton's lingering touch on her skin, sending shivers down her spine. She brought her finger up to meet her tender lips, gently tracing the sensations away. When she got out of bed, she quickly grabbed his oversized t-shirt and draped it over her naked body. The shirt wasn't huge on her, hugging her breasts and falling to her thigh, but it covered enough.

Morana pulled the door open and walked into the hallway. She could hear faint noises in the kitchen where Axton took the first battering ram to her defenses. Smiling, she followed the sounds of coffee brewing and the quiet "shit" Axton muttered under his breath.

When she rounded the corner, he froze—mug and coffeepot in hand. It was like he was holding his breath, waiting for her to bolt or disappear. She wrapped her arms in front of her chest and offered a small smile before breaking eye contact.

"Hi," she broke the silence.

"Hi." Axton jolted, breaking from his trance, and moved to pour the coffee into a mug, muscles flexing beneath his white t-shirt. "How are you feeling?" he asked, passing the coffee over the counter. She grabbed it and inhaled deeply before taking a sip.

"Fine."

Axton swallowed, his throat working. She finally met his gaze and smiled as the tension rolled off his shoulders.

"No regrets?" he asked.

"No regrets," she assured him, and his body visibly relaxed.

It was the truth. She didn't regret spending the night with him. It had kept the demons away, and she had too many demons to count. One of them had paid her a visit in the middle of the night. It was still unsettling, but she wouldn't linger on the thought.

"I wanted to ask you something." Axton leaned over the counter that stretched out and divided the kitchen from the living room, a mug in his hands as he watched her expression. "I just don't want to spook you."

She huffed a laugh and set her mug down on the counter. Leaning forward, she placed her elbows on the granite and gazed up at him. His brown hair was mussed, stubble lining his jaw. Her mind went to how her hands tangled in his chestnut locks, and the way she had grazed his jaw with her teeth. Clearly remembering as well, his mouth parted, and she could feel his breath fan over her face.

"Axton," she smiled. "You're not going to spook me." She placed her hand over his coffee cup, coaxing him to lower it as well. She watched the way the veins in his hands flexed, remembering the heat of him. When he set it down, she looked back up, tugging her bottom lip between her teeth before speaking again. "You fucked me. I don't regret it. Stop acting weird."

He chuckled, dark and sweet, like the faint smell of tobacco that clouded her senses. Leaning forward, Axton kissed her. He straightened and ran a hand through his hair, a smile playing on his lips.

"I was thinking we should stop by the gun club today."

Morana froze. A familiar rush racked her body. She hadn't been back since the shooting. Axton's apartment started to feel as if it were closing in on her, but she couldn't break now. She tried to school her features, ensuring that Axton knew she meant what she had said. He wouldn't spook her. Maybe going to the gun club was exactly what she needed to get over this fear—an opportunity to open up to him.

"If you don't want to—"

"I do." She picked up her mug, sipping on the black coffee. She winced at the bitter taste. "I think it'll be good for me."

"I need to wrap up some things for Granddad." Axton swallowed hard. He looked away and picked up his own mug. "I think it'll be easier with you there."

"Yeah." Morana could see the sorrow there, but she didn't want to touch it, or she didn't know how to. "I don't have any clothes."

Axton's eyes tracked her movements, roving down her body, taking in the shirt she wore and nothing else. "You can borrow something."

She winced. Axton probably had clothes here from the other girls he had been with. Her stomach twisted in knots. She didn't like the idea of him sleeping with another woman, and she really didn't like the idea that she cared. Maybe last night had been more than comfort. There may have been more meaning lurking beneath the surface. The deep desire to be wanted and to connect had won. There was no longer a war within herself, no longer a desire to keep the distance she had previously built between them. It was frightening.

"You can borrow something of mine. It might be a bit big, but I'm sure it'll work."

She released a breath, the smile reappearing. "Oh." She set her mug down and turned to walk down the hallway. "Are you going to serve me peasant, or will I have to work for said clothing by searching myself?"

Axton scrambled around the counter and wrapped an arm around her shoulder before whispering into her ear. "If I were going to make you work for it, I would choose something much more fun than digging in my drawers." He released her and headed down to his bedroom, leaving the door open.

Her blood heated at his words, stomach in knots as what he said sank in. She desperately wanted to learn what kind of work he was referring to.

"I didn't peg you as a concert kind of guy." Morana watched as he pulled the concert t-shirt from a drawer.

"I'm not." He tossed the tee at her, along with faded ripped jeans.

She pulled the jeans on, rolling them once to make them fit better. The t-shirt was larger, so she tucked it into the front, hoping to look halfway decent. Her blonde hair hung around her shoulders, wavey and untamed.

He looked her over with a grin that showed off the damned dimple. It brought back feelings from last night, reminding her of the touch of his skin on hers, the way it burned in the most desirable way.

"We should go," she stated.

Six

Ten minutes and the city sounds had disappeared. There was nothing but gently curving roads and partly cloudy skies. The silence stretched on between them, but Morana didn't mind.

Axton's hand rested on her thigh, eyes forward as they traveled to the gun club. She tried not to think of how it would affect her—being in the club where she died—or almost died, rather. Instead, she focused on the warmth of his hand through her borrowed jeans. It seemed to burn through any unease, leaving her with a different sensation in her stomach.

She traced a finger along the black interior of the car, gazing out of the passenger window. The rain had brought a tolerably hot day, and a gentle breeze was kissing the leaves of dense forest appearing to either side. They would be there soon. Axton cleared his throat, interrupting her thoughts.

"I don't want to bring up anything you don't want to share." His voice was gentle as he glanced over at her. Brows furrowed and mouth a straight line, Axton finally brought up what she had been avoiding. "What happened at the coffee shop, Ana? Where did you go?"

She leaned her head back against the seat, breathing deeply. The scent of wilderness and trauma danced together to form the perfect dreaded thought. She was good at dealing with trauma, picking up and moving on with little emotion to cloud her thoughts. Careful detachment was her specialty, but Death had been hunting her, and she feared she would see him again.

"That guy in the coffee shop," she began.

"The one who hit your car?"

"Yeah." She blinked hard at the memory, staring at her hands in her lap. "He was—" the memory of the lavish castle, and the strange woman that escorted her out cut her off. The glass roof that stretched overhead, and the intricately carved wooden balconies. "Insane." She finished, but the word tasted strange in her mouth.

On paper, Matthias was insane, but she had experienced so much since then. She briefly questioned that thought. The strange man in the alley had chased her down, and there was genuine concern on Death's face when he visited Axton's room.

Maybe she was the crazy one.

"Was he the one I shot?" Axton grunted, gripping the wheel tighter.

"No, that was someone else." She was looking at Axton, running her eyes over his features. The dimple was gone—no good humor then. "I don't know what's happening to me," she whispered.

His grip tightened on her thigh and then relaxed again. He cast a glance toward her before pinning his eyes to the road once more. Time passed as they drove on.

Morana couldn't help the memories crashing through her skull. This time, it was more than just her recent trauma. It was the way her father looked when she had left him—a ghost of who he used to be—consumed by his own demons. He had become a slave to the desperation and hopelessness of his circumstances, and in turn, made her a slave to the same. There was nothing there for her, and she had to lock the guilt of abandoning him—of running.

"You know, my mother left me when I was five." Morana broke the silence. She needed to unearth some of her past—to dig up the things no one knew. Even if the hole she dug became her grave.

"You never talked about your family," Axton replied cautiously, his hand tightening on the steering wheel.

"I had reasons for that." She smiled while glancing at the hand still resting on her thigh. He was warm and safe, someone to be trusted. "She left, and my dad fell into a deep hole of depression." She paused, choosing her words carefully. "I experienced a lot of neglect."

Axton hummed, a sign that he was listening while leaving the space for her to open up.

"I had to take care of myself. There was no space for what I wanted or felt, but recently I've been afraid. I'm afraid of what my choice to leave did to him. I haven't been able to get close to anyone since then."

"Do you still talk to him?"

"No," she admitted, leaning her elbow on the car door and resting her head in her hand. "I walked out when I turned eighteen. In three years, I haven't looked back."

"And he hasn't reached out to you?" His voice was hesitant, brows pinched together.

"That's the part that scares me most. I left him, just like my mom. I'm more runner than fighter—bound to avoid anything remotely uncomfortable. If I don't think about it, I don't have to be guilty." She winced. "I don't know why I'm sharing this." She cleared her throat. "I'm not trying to scare you away." Morana wrung her hands in her lap. "I just needed to tell someone. You seemed safe."

He squeezed her thigh gently before placing both hands on the wheel. "I'm glad you did."

There wasn't much more she wanted to talk about, and he seemed to read that well. It felt good to unlock some things she kept hidden, to allow someone to see the truth. She liked to put on a brave face, but behind it all, she was afraid. Afraid of disappointing others, and now afraid of a madman that called himself a god, afraid of what Axton would think if she told him the truth of what had happened. Especially when the shadows had looked so real.

Morana looked back at the forests lining the road, limbs of leafy green moving quickly around them. They would be at the club soon. As much as that event scared her, the words Death had spoken scared her more.

"You're not a prisoner," he said calmly. "You're free to go." A knowing look appeared on his face. "But I've gathered that your abilities are new to you. You probably can't control them, so without my help teaching you, you can go where you wish, but my guess is it won't be home."

As if she conjured him, a familiar figure stood on the side of the road; arms folded across his broad chest. Tattoos trailed up his arms, and dark hair hung in his face. He wore a black tee, the chain around his neck glinting against the stark background of it. A lit cigarette hung loosely between the fingers of his tattooed hand.

Morana sat forward, heart racing. She gripped the door, eyes looking back to where he stood. It looked like shadows were swirling around his boots, consuming any light that dare fall their way.

"Shit," she whispered.

Axton was leaning forward, one hand on the wheel as he desperately tried to see what was happening. "What is it?" he asked.

When she turned to face forward, Death was standing in the road. It was quickly replaced by the lights of an oncoming car.

"Axton, watch out!" The scream was cut off by a jerk of the wheel, and then time slowed. Her body pressed against the glass, pain pulsing through her skull.

They were airborne, the car catching and flipping into the other lane. Adrenaline gave one last heaving push before she lost her grip on reality.

She blinked, the image of deflated airbags becoming clear. As she became more aware, she heard Axton's steady breath next to her, the gentle inhale and exhale of a man unconscious. Morana opened her eyes and looked over to see Axton breathing rhythmically, right side up. Her passenger door was crushed inward. Trying the handle was useless. She jerked and pulled, but it wouldn't budge.

"Axton." Morana laid a gentle hand on his shoulder. He was unconscious, blood running down his temple and streaked across the spot where his dimple should be. "Axton." Her voice was a mere whisper.

Morana removed the seatbelt, and slowly squeezed her way across Axton's body. His door opened, creaking as she slithered out of the car on her hands and knees across broken glass.

"I'm so sorry. I'm so fucking sorry," she spoke to the wreckage. There was no one out here, no car in the other lane, nothing that showed they had crashed. No evidence but the crumpled car and the unconscious man inside. Morana touched her shoulder where she had been injured while climbing through the window of the warehouse. It was bleeding again. She ran a finger down her jaw, feeling the dampness of blood on her fingers.

"I could heal that."

She whirled around to find the source of the voice laced with shadows and gravel. Death was standing there casually, his thumb and finger resting on his chin as he looked at her shoulder. Morana could make out the moth tattoo on his hand. Atop the moth looked like the image of a skull. She took a step back.

Death pointed at her shoulder. "It could get infected if I don't. You cut it on a surface in the warehouse."

She didn't respond.

"I could heal him too," he added, glancing to Axton, still passed out in the driver's seat.

"No." She didn't know what he was talking about, but she wouldn't let him touch Axton. Axton wouldn't meet Death. She would ensure he never did.

"You'd let him stay like that?" Death cocked an eyebrow, a quizzical look crossing his face. His muscles flexed as he moved forward, just a few steps. Morana was pinned in place by his menacing presence and hulking size. The power emanated from him, calling to something deep within her.

"I don't trust you," she hissed.

He kept moving until he was close enough to brush his hand over her shoulder. Faint shadows danced over her flesh. She could feel a gentle pull in her chest, drawing her to whatever magic pushed into her skin, stitching the wound back together. She could feel the firm tug of her flesh, the magic sparking something within that gave her a strange sense of peace. The skin itched, and she fought the urge to touch it.

She took a deep breath. When her eyes opened once more, she looked down to see no injury there. It was gone.

"I can heal him, too." His voice was rough, entwined with something dangerous and enticing. She blinked. He could heal. She didn't know how, but this man called Death healed her. If she didn't let him heal Axton, if she left him like that, she would never forgive herself.

"Fine."

Death moved to the car, squatting in front of the open door and running the same golden light over Axton's unconscious form. She watched as Axton shifted, body moving to get more comfortable. His breathing was relaxed, and he almost looked peaceful now that the blood on his temple was gone.

"Why are you here?" she asked, snapping her head towards the man—god—she didn't know. She wouldn't be afraid of Death; she would face it head-on— embrace whatever shadows he wielded. Beneath the surface, she was afraid. Afraid of all that she could do and afraid of the strange cord that pulled from her chest, the familiar power she could feel stored there—the one that wanted to rise to meet him—challenge him.

"Testing your powers." His tone was mocking. "You're being hunted, you know?" He was standing on the asphalt, face a mask of indifference.

"By you," she hissed. It was clearly him. She hadn't been able to get away from the supposed god that kept appearing before her eyes, bringing chaos with those damned shadows of his.

"Come with me." He raked his gaze over her body, taking in the oversized ripped jeans and band shirt. His head tilted to the side. "Come with me and you can find out who's after you. It isn't me anymore." Morana noticed a gentle tick in his jaw, as if he were holding back a smirk.

Her gaze moved to Axton. She couldn't leave him here. She needed to find her phone, get help—move. Tears threatened to escape as the guilt that crept up her throat held her in place, her gray eyes firmly locked on his sleeping figure. When she had left her father, she had left him alone and in need. Even so, she wanted to leave—to run.

"He'll be well taken care of." Death's voice gently caressed her skin. "I'll have someone take him back to his apartment." It felt sincere, but she still wasn't sure. She got out of the castle the last time. She could do it again. He wouldn't keep her there, and she just watched him heal wounds. Her heart tugged as she looked back to the sleeping form of the man who ripped down her walls. But then there was the matter of the strange powers he kept mentioning. Could Death remove the final walls so she could truly be free and understand the thing waking up in her? So she could know what had happened at the gun club.

"You swear he will be taken care of?" she questioned through gritted teeth, daring him to lie to her. There weren't a lot of choices here. Morana was caught between the cord that kept tugging, the depth of *something* she hadn't begun to explore, and the recurring nightmare that was her tendency to long for escape. They were out in the middle of nowhere, surrounded by trees and the remains of metal scraps and broken glass strewn across the asphalt.

"Swear it," he answered.

She couldn't say no.

"Okay." Her voice sounded with little thought of anything else. Morana stepped forward, making to stride past this strange creature of a man. He reached out, latching onto her hand before whispering.

"Don't hold your breath." His voice was low as they descended into a thick darkness, vanishing from all that was familiar.

Seven

She couldn't move. Shadows still ran across her skin as she stood in the familiar palace, intricate woodwork and large spaces greeting her upon arrival. The heavy mist coated her skin, sending a shiver of pleasure down her spine. Something about them felt right—felt like home. She was waking up to the idea that the dark power he used was what caused their movement to this place, and maybe it wasn't something so new after all.

Death stood in front of her with his back turned. Behind her was a fireplace, raging along and twisting in the dim sitting room. A small wooden coffee table sat amidst the seating arrangement, littered with pens and books. A twinge of regret made its way along her skin, the books reminding her of the comment she had made to Axton about his appearance. *Dark academia.* She had left him—left him to a stranger. There was no hiding that she was running again, and the guilt was restricting her throat. It was something she didn't want to feel—a reminder that beneath what she presented to the world; she was afraid.

She didn't want to be afraid, and she sure as hell didn't want to feel trapped by the asshole standing in front of her.

A fire iron caught her eye. Desperation took root in her blood. What was she doing?

"Come along." Death's dark voice rumbled along the red-carpeted floor. He walked to exit the room.

Morana strode forward, quickly grabbing the iron as soundlessly as possible. She moved, a deep, heady need calling out to her. When Death stopped at the door, turning his head to glance over his shoulder, she lunged.

Pushing him backward into the wall, and shoving the fire iron up to his neck, bracing the makeshift weapon against his skin. There was a whisper of a tattoo appearing just above the neckline of his shirt.

"No," she whispered. She was testing him. Her eyes widened and burned with the challenge. How firm were the walls he now built around her? How much choice did she actually have in coming here?

Death didn't fight her. He stood stock still with the metal pressed to his skin. His jaw flinched as if he were holding back before he gave in and allowed the ever so frequent smirk to overtake his features. Morana's stomach roiled. No man deserved to have this much power over her decisions, not even a man that called himself a god.

"You're going to answer my questions," she hissed.

"Fair enough." He licked his lips, eyes alight with amusement.

"Who is hunting me?"

"The Court of Light." Death's eyes glanced at the object against his flesh. His smile was gone, but there was no urgency in his expression. Morana pushed the tip a little harder. Blood welled up where it gently cut through flesh, and she begged the crimson leaking down his flawless skin to give her some sort of control.

"What the fuck is the Court of Light?" she snarled.

There was a pause. The fire crackled in the distance, but all she could hear was the blood rushing in her ears. She breathed deeply, longing to shove the iron into his neck to see if that would make him take her seriously, but she needed information. Shadows danced over her skin; the fear floated away with the mist—anger rising in its place.

"Take this fire iron off my throat and maybe I will tell you." He was cocky, arrogant, and unaffected. He hadn't flinched at the blood pooling at the base of his throat. Shadows seemed to spark across his features, rising to meet whatever darkness lurked on her own skin. Her lip peeled back in disgust as she pulled the iron away. Taking a step back, she gripped the weapon close. Death turned to look at her, his dark eyes boring into her own, that infuriating glimmer that told her he thought this was comical returned. "Or drive it through my throat." He stepped closer. "I'd love for you to see what happens."

She lunged forward, swinging the weapon through the air, penetrating the shadows that surrounded the god. Death vanished on a black mist, appearing behind her. He grabbed her, causing her to drop the iron. He caught her in his firm grasp, immobilizing her. Morana was trapped and panting with frustration. She could feel his chest rising and falling behind her, and her shoulders went rigid. His hot breath caressed the shell of her ear, causing her hairs to stand on end. The sensation made way for a new feeling, a sudden desire to feel and know the power that coursed through his veins.

"This is my house, Morana." The amusement was gone, replaced with something that tasted like rage.

"This is my life," she seethed in return, jerking against his grasp. "And I don't know what is happening with it."

"As I said before, that is fair enough, but I won't be threatened here." His hand tightened on her bicep; her arms still pinned at her sides. Morana bit her lip, the anger and panic rising in her throat.

"Let go of me."

He leaned in closer, his lips brushing against her skin. It sent electricity through her veins, sparking a rage so deep she couldn't control it. Whatever desire she had to know him was gone now. She felt bound in the way that death, actual death, lurked in the darkness, ready to bind anyone it pleased.

"No," he taunted. She jerked against him again, trying to wriggle free, but it was no use. He was pressed flush against her, his powerful muscles keeping her locked into her stance. "I rather like this position."

Her stomach bottomed out. Before she could react, the darkness took them. They appeared in the dining room, the long table stretching across the space set for two at each end. Back where they started. She was no longer being held, but she didn't dare make another move against him.

"Sit." He gestured to one of the chairs—the same table setting as before—as if he had expected her. Morana reluctantly sat down, a loud thump echoing by the way she threw herself in the chair. Death found his place across from her.

Silence emanated through the room, and Morana became acutely aware of the ticking of a clock somewhere in the distance. How long had it been since she left Axton on that road? She didn't know why she agreed to come here. Maybe it was desperation, or maybe there was a small part of her that believed in some of what he was saying. The power he had spoken of was unmistakable. She'd watched him vanish, heal, and swim in the darkness that surrounded him. She watched herself survive a bullet wound and couldn't get the rose-colored eyes to disappear from her memory.

"This is the land of the gods," he began, shifting in his chair and picking up the glass in front of him. He took a sip, his full lips ghosting over the glass, his neck moving as he swallowed. "This is my home, but I have another. The land of the gods houses many realms." He twirled the glass in his hand, ice cubes clinking on the crystal sides. "We are currently in mine."

Morana kept her lips tight together as she refused to respond. He had already bested her, shown her that there was no escaping. If she didn't speak, maybe her defiance would irritate him enough to bring her some satisfaction—something to say he hadn't won—not fully. Her eyes were dead as she stared at him, waiting for him to reveal some important piece of information—waiting for him to address the power he claimed she had.

"There are two courts in the fae realm. That's separate from here."

She blinked once—twice.

"The what?" she asked, brows knitting together. "Fae?" She huffed a laugh. "As in faeries?"

"Yes," he continued. "In the fae realm, I rule the Court of Shadows. Inara is the goddess of light and rules the Court of Light." He leaned back in his chair, running a tattooed hand through his dark hair. His eyes never broke contact. "She's hunting you."

"I thought you were hunting me?" Morana arched a brow, condescension dripping from her lips.

"Death is always hunting." A smile pulled at his lips, dripping with sweet promises. "You're intriguing. Able to avoid me with those powers you claim to know nothing about." His eyes focus in as if searching for something. "It is why I have been watching you. You can travel through realms. Only a god can do that."

"A god like you?"

"A god like me." He tipped his glass in her direction, approving of how she was starting to put it together.

"I'm no god, so why am I here?" she asked, and he shrugged.

"I want to help you." She scoffed, leaning back in her chair. "Despite what you may believe, and even as you held a fire iron to my throat, I want to help you figure out this power of yours." His tongue rolled over his cheek. "I also need to figure out what Inara wants with you."

"Figure it out?" She glanced at the cup on her side of the table. Thirst tightened its grip on her, and she gave in, drawing the cup to her lips. The water was satisfying after the crash and after being plunged through shadows into this strange place. Death tracked the movement.

"I want to train you," he corrected. "I want to train you and see what you can do." He looked back down to her lips. A spike of fear and something more flashed through her chest. "Here in the land of the gods, you won't be bothered. There are others here who could help you. I can bring a lord from my court to help. You can stay and be taken care of. Inara needn't find you until we can get you controlling whatever gifts you have. It would give you an opportunity to defend yourself."

Morana shifted in her seat. She looked at the plate sitting before her, void of food. Remembering the woman who had escorted her out previously, she realized who he was referring to, who would take care of her.

"You wish for me to just leave my life, and come to this strange place to be taken care of by servants? You're the god of Death. Did they start out as your trainees too?" Her lip peeled back in disgust. He had let her go once, but maybe this was merely a trap. If he ruled a fae realm, odds are he operated in bargains and promises. Odds are he would take advantage of a human like her. She'd read enough mythology to know better.

"My *servants* work here by their own choice." Her back straightened, chin held high in a refusal to admit the assumptions she had just made about him. "I pay them and some live outside my castle." His eyes roved her features. It was as if he were reading every stray thought she had had. "Most of them reside in the Court of Shadows."

"And if I say no?" Morana leaned forward, challenging him to keep her here, begging him to prove what he had just stated about his servants—their freedom. Something dark swirled in her chest in response to the eyes that refused to break contact from across the table.

"If you say no, she will kill you, and your guns will do nothing to stop her." He traced a hand along the table, casually touching the surface. "Human weapons only kill humans." He continued trailing his hand over the dark wooden surface. "You may stay here and refer to me as Matthias. Make yourself at home and be ready to train when summoned."

"Summoned," she scoffed. "Like a dog." Her mind lingered on a buried memory, trudging up old wounds.

"You need to work. We don't have money for the rent payment." Her father's eyes were hollow and sagging, burdened with the days of worry and too much alcohol.

"And what if I say no?" she asked, scowling as he sat at their wooden table, setting his beer down to cover the chipped surface. She lifted her chin in challenge.

"You live here, you can't say no." He stood up, his tired frame swaying as he moved forward, his height dwarfing her despite the way he slouched.

"And what have you been doing to make the rent payment?" Her voice was a harsh whisper, barely containing the fury boiling within. He had stolen everything from her, but he would continue to take. This man would continue to make demands despite how he spent his time.

The slap burned when it landed, leaving a red mark across her cheek. Her father was slurring when he spoke again. His breath reeked.

"You earn your right to exist," he hissed. "Your existence demands sacrifice." His eyes were drooping now, body swaying again. Any strength he had shown when he slapped her was gone. She held her jaw, tears burning the corners of her eyes. "She left." He moved to sit back at their table. "You won't be leaving either." He cleared his throat, his body lowering into the chair. "I need you, Ana."

The confession was more painful than the red mark decorating her flesh.

"Don't mock the gift of my council." Matthias was looking at her now, his brows lowered. Something about the way his eyes burned into her caused her to shift in her seat, the only sign he would get of her true feelings. She refused to break and refused to be told what to do. Death couldn't guilt her.

"I'll do what I like." She leaned in more, elbows resting on the table. The wood creaked beneath the weight. "I will agree. I've seen enough to know there is truth to your words, but I'm telling you, *Matthias*, I will do exactly as I please."

Matthias grunted as darkness encircled him. He disappeared. Moments later, he was leaning over her, hands on the table before him.

"Fine." The statement surprised her. Her lips parted as the anger drained out of her. It left her with the towering presence of the god of Death—the man that she had yet to figure out. Her eyes trailed over his neck, corded muscles straining with whatever emotion he was holding onto. He was hard to read.

Matthias pushed away from the table.

And with that, he was gone.

Eight

"Miss Morana?"

It was the woman again, the servant that had escorted her out the first time she had found herself in this palace. The woman walked in carrying a tray of food, her pale blue eyes wide. Morana carefully observed her. You could tell a lot about a man by the company he kept. Maybe she could learn something.

"Matthias asked me to bring you something to eat, Miss." She approached carefully, as if she were trying not to frighten the strange creature in front of her. The scent of marinated chicken and rice flowed off the tray. With her mouthwatering, Morana shifted in her chair, now staring at the table.

"Is he kind to you?" she whispered, never moving her gaze.

"I'm sorry?" The girl's voice was soft and rich. Her blue eyes were bright and wise. She set the tray down on the table, standing with her delicate hands clasped in front of her tall figure.

"Has Death been kind to you?" Morana finally looked up into the woman's pale face. There was a wisdom there in her eyes, the look of someone older than she first appeared.

"*Death* has not been kind to me." She sat down in the chair to Morana's left, leaning forward. Her mouth was in a firm line. "Matthias has." She paused for a moment; sincerity trapped within her gaze. "He's been kind."

Morana tilted her head. If he was who he claimed to be, if he was Death, then wouldn't he have been the entity that caused this woman suffering? How could he both cause pain, and not cause pain?

The woman gave a knowing smile, carefully observing Morana's expression. Sinking back into the plush cushion on the wooden chair, she played with a small charm from a bracelet encircling her wrist. Morana couldn't make out the shape of the metal piece in her hands.

"Matthias is the god of Death, but he is not death itself. Death occurs on its own, without his intervention."

"Have you experienced death?" Morana's gaze and tone were flat—unfeeling as she fought to hide anything she could in this ridiculous realm. Something about Matthias and this place chipped away at her walls, making it impossible to ignore the turmoil within.

"Everyone I cared for has died. If that is, in fact, what you're asking." She pushed away from the table, shoving the tray forward. "Now eat." Her tone was sharp. Morana's brows stitched together. Something had changed in the woman's presence. Where she was soft and meek before, she was now all sharp edges and harsh lines. It was fitting with her facial features. They were not as soft as Morana first thought. She must have hit a nerve.

"If you want to know more about who Matthias really is, what it means to be the god of Death, you can find out tomorrow when you train with him." She turned on her heel to move from the room, clearly done with the conversation.

"Thank you," Morana spoke gently. She admired the woman's strength, the way she didn't balk at the intrusion of questions.

The strange woman turned her head to glance over her shoulder, stopping just before exiting the dining area. "You're welcome." She cleared her throat. "I will be in soon to take you to your rooms. I figured you would want to eat alone. Take some time to think. There are more who work here, many more in the Court of Shadows, but we've been instructed to go easy on you."

The bedroom was spacious. A plush, light gray comforter lay neatly sprawled across the four-poster bed's surface. It was complete with airy beige curtains and lights strung around. A small bench was at the foot of the bed with a vase of baby's breath flowers. It was a stark contrast to the dark wood decorating the rest of the palace.

Morana turned, locking eyes with the woman she now knew as Willow. She had her raven waves pulled back in a neat knot that revealed pointed ears. She was fae.

"There are clothes in the wardrobe," Willow stated. "Though I will warn you, they are clothes fit for the Court of Shadows."

Morana glanced at the large wooden wardrobe and the adjacent vanity. There was a fireplace and cushioned seating arranged in the room. Matthias clearly preferred luxury and had prepared this place prior to bringing her here. Her throat burned, the air turning fiery and suffocating. Had this woman known what the god of Death planned? Her eyes went back to Willow's.

"Why are there clothes here for me?" Morana questioned. Confusion swirled in her chest. The possibility that this room belonged to another crossed her mind, especially if the clothing was fit for the fae.

"Well," Willow began, her tone firm. For all the meekness she had portrayed previously, the woman was certainly capable of being assertive. She didn't balk at Morana's temper. "He sent things up for you." She took a step forward, gesturing to a wooden door off the bedroom. "There's a bathroom attached to your quarters as well."

"When did he do all this? Whose room was this?" Morana touched the flowers at the foot of her bed, a crease on her forehead. Confusion. That's what she felt.

Matthias had chased her through a warehouse, followed her, and allowed himself into her bedroom at Axton's. He had taunted her—goaded her. The delicate flowers, the way Willow had spoken of him—nothing made sense. It only increased her curiosity and muddy the feelings stirring in her mind.

"He had this prepared for you the last time you were here. This is a guest room." Willow tucked a stray strand of black hair that had escaped its binding behind her ear. Morana tilted her head, assessing the fae before her. The name was fitting. Her limbs were thin and long, but there was a grace to her. She waited there as if she had more to do.

"You can leave," Morana stated. She needed space to breathe—to figure out what she could expect from this place.

"Are you sure? I was asked to make sure you were comfortable—"

"It won't be necessary," Morana's tone was harsh. She tried to soften it. This woman had done nothing to deserve such treatment. "Please." Her voice echoed gently across the stone floors.

"Of course." Bowing her head, Willow turned to exit the room. The wooden door clicked as she left. The room filled with the crackling of the fire, and the silence of one accompanied by only their raging thoughts.

Morana was alone.

Without hesitation, she moved to the wardrobe, quickly finding several delicate dresses. They were lavish and well made. Dark colors of rich purple and royal blue, black and gold. Morana cringed, desperate for something comforting—something that didn't feel so foreign. There were some leggings and a few shirts. She looked down at Axton's dirty band tee that she still wore. She couldn't take it off, not after all she had been through. It served as a reminder of the guilt resting at the back of her mind. Did she have no loyalty?

Pulling on the leggings, she moved to the bed, turning off the string lights, and falling into soft blankets and pillows. There was a balcony off her room, curtains gently pulled back to reveal the stars casting sleepy light over the forested landscape of the land of the gods. The stars were gentle and seeking—at odds with what she knew of the god of Death. It was cooler here. Not hot like the summer she left behind.

Morana pulled the blanket up over her shoulders and turned, facing the stars. Glancing at the twinkling lights hung in a sea of black, she realized the moon wasn't out.

The weight of emotion was heavy—the emotions she had refused to acknowledge or show. Her mind spun with images of the portly man entering Ashford Gun Club, Axton's panicked look when she had come out of whatever darkness consumed her the moment she felt the bullet. She thought of the coffee shop, the dimple that appeared on Axton's cheek when he smiled. The memory of his skin on hers followed her as she closed her eyes, allowing the tears to come.

Part of her had trusted Death in healing and taking care of Axton, but if he hadn't, if Axton had been left to the wreckage, it would eat at her soul for the rest of her existence.

Morana brought a palm to her face, smearing the dampness across her cheek.

"Fuck," she whispered into the lonely room.

A shadow moved out of the corner of her tearful eye, but she didn't have the energy to look or to care. Too much had happened too fast, and she was slowly losing herself. If Death had let himself into her room once more, if he was here to taunt her about courts and hunting and magic, she wouldn't listen.

Morana closed her eyes and lost herself to the deep nothingness of peaceful sleep.

She was falling.

And then she wasn't.

Morana sat up abruptly; the comforter twisted around her legs. The world came into view around her, early morning light trickling in from the balcony of the strange room.

The fire was low, barely crackling behind the grate. She rubbed her eyes before registering the other presence in the room.

"You're awake." A honey-smooth voice sounded from the seating area by the fire. Morana's eyes snapped in that direction to find a stunning woman draped across a chair. Her brown skin was dewy, burnt umber eyes, and strange silver webbing tattooed across her forehead and arms. The webbing shimmered like that of the silver dress she wore.

Morana's heart came into her throat. She didn't know this woman, and she definitely didn't know how she got into her room.

"A note from Matthias." The woman smirked subtly before vines tumbled from her hands, moving a piece of paper until it landed in Morana's lap on the bed.

She grabbed it and stood up, backing away from the strange creature and opening the note.

We start in the library.
-M

"Do you work here?" Morana asked, steeling her spine. Irritation stirred as bile rose in her throat. *We start in the library.* As she said before, she was being summoned—like a dog.

The woman chuckled, a rich sound that tasted like earth and soil. "Absolutely not." She stood up. She was tall, the slits in her dress revealing toned legs beneath. "This is, after all, the land of the gods."

"You're a god then?" Morana's brows furrowed.

"More or less." Without another word, the strange woman exited the room.

Morana's heart was still fluttering rapidly in her chest. She gripped the note tighter. She didn't know how she would find the library, but she hurried and looked through the clothing provided.

There weren't many options that she would have chosen for herself. Lavish and expensive weren't part of her vocabulary—they never had been. She walked into the bathroom and stripped down to take a shower, the grime from the day before still coating her skin. Thankfully, herbal soaps and lotions were lining the ornately carved wooden shelf beyond the large metal tub. Morana climbed in when the water was hot, wincing as her skin burned against the liquid. She fumbled with whatever items Death had to offer, choosing something that smelled of jasmine and coconut milk to wash her body.

The steam cleared her senses, helping her prepare to meet Matthias. There was a deep curiosity mixed with acute dread. He was unpredictable, but according to Willow, Matthias was kind. Maybe she would see this other side of him.

The castle was eerily quiet, and she remembered Willow stating that few were here now. Most of his staff worked in the Court of Shadows—wherever that may be.

When she was done, she turned off the water. Stepping out of the shower, she grabbed a towel and dried off. Morana walked to the wardrobe again, struggling with the clothing placed there for her. She settled on putting

Axton's clothes back on. They were dirty, but she couldn't help it. Something about the scent of him on the shirt comforted her. She fought the tears that dared to threaten their presence.

"Miss Morana?" Willow was standing at the door. When she turned, the woman winced while looking Morana over. Her hair was damp and slowly becoming wavey.

"Why are you staring at me?" Morana moved to pass her, striding toward the door. "Also, you can just call me Ana." A pang struck her chest at the memory of Axton's nickname for her, and she thought better of it, not ready for the feelings that tried to surface with it. "Morana," she corrected. "*Just* Morana."

"Of course." Willow's nose wrinkled. Was it her clothes that offended the fae? Morana took a whiff of the shirt. It wasn't terrible, but it didn't smell like the fancy lotions in the bathroom either. "I'm here to escort you to the library."

They walked down long castle halls. The desire to explore the various alcoves passed through her mind. So many details existed in this castle that contradicted what she knew of Death. She didn't know what to believe. Still, something about the shadows had felt familiar—calling to the deepest parts of her. The best way to learn about someone would be to stand in their presence. They walked down a set of stairs that opened to a balcony overlooking the main foyer where she had originally arrived. They glided down, and she ran her fingers along the cherry railings.

When they made it to the foyer, they crossed to the large entrance doors.

"Matthias is waiting for you." Blue eyes glanced down over her jeans again. "Did you find the clothes?" she asked, a note of concern in her voice.

"Yes." Morana didn't want to provide anything more as an answer. Her thoughts still circled back to the man she had left, the stress of the hunt. She smiled. "Thank you again, Willow." Morana turned, opening the heavy doors into the large space ahead.

She was met with vaulted ceilings and rows and rows of shelves stacked with leather-bound books. The scent of parchment and ink permeated the air.

When the door closed behind her, Morana flinched at the sound. There were still some reactions she couldn't suppress. Maybe the time to think alone without Willow's presence wasn't good for her. It allowed vulnerability to creep into her thoughts and made the mask more difficult to keep in place as she prepared to meet Death.

Shadows flickered in between stacks and out walked a tall, tattooed Matthias with a cigarette between his lips. The habit sent pain through her chest as it reminded her of the tobacco scent of Axton. Matthias's clothes were different. He was wearing a black button-up with the sleeves rolled revealing the veins in his forearms. The first few buttons were left undone, revealing a tattooed chest.

Morana fought to keep her stomach from curling and heat from rising to her cheeks. His attractiveness aside, this was a death god. He was objectively insane.

"You're late."

"You didn't give a time," she tossed back. "Should you be smoking in here?" She waved a hand around. "A lot of flammable items."

He pulled the cigarette from his lips, flicking it onto the floor near a shelf of books. Morana's pulse picked up, but before the cigarette hit the ground, the object vanished in a wisp of darkness.

"Point taken," she grunted, folding her arms across her chest. She glanced over to a desk on her left. An older woman sat hunched over the desk and hardly noticed their presence or the intimidating god standing amidst fae that were organizing the books. Not a single soul looked their direction. Maybe nobody questioned Matthias's actions. She assumed that would be despite their better judgment.

"You didn't find the clothes?" When she turned to him, his dark eyes were tracing over her body, taking in every scrap of dirt and blood that painted the worn outfit.

"I didn't like them." She tilted her chin in defiance.

"Oh." He strode forward, circling her. His eyes never moved from her figure. Dark boots scuffed across the stone floors of the library. When he had rounded her once, he stopped in front of her, close enough for her to smell the alluring darkness and mint laced in his breath. "I didn't realize providing you with a wardrobe would be so difficult." His dark eyes glittered, but the stoic mask remained over the rest of his features. "Tell me, did your mortal man go to such lengths to appease your specific tastes?"

Anger pierced her gut. "Fuck you." Morana narrowed her eyes, straightening her stance. "I didn't want the dresses."

"That's fine." His eyes flicked to her lips briefly. She licked her lips instinctively, and something flared there in the dark pools before he steeled his expression. "You'll need some for the Court of Shadows, but I will try to find something more appealing to send to your room." He turned on his heel, striding through the stacks. "Follow me."

Morana scrambled to keep up, trying to listen as he spewed facts about her new reality. Fae servants scuttled away, avoiding them as they walked through the maze of the massive palace library.

"You need to learn about what is out there." Matthias began. "We are in the land of the gods, but the land of the gods contains many realms." His hands were in his pockets as he floated through the stacks. "I want you to learn about those other realms today." He turned, crowding her space. His face was inches from hers as she halted abruptly. Her eyes briefly caught on his full lips and pulled back to the onyx gaze. "Then, and only then, will we talk about using your gifts to move. I'll take care of any travel today."

"Sounds like I'm a prisoner," she scoffed.

"You're free to leave, but if I'm training you, we play by my rules." He smiled then. "Knowledge first."

"I've said it before. I will do as I please."

"Then the Court of Light can take you." He tilted his head, a dark strand of hair falling across his forehead. His eyes dropped to her lips, and she felt his gaze everywhere. Her cheeks flushed at the interaction. There was no denying how attractive he was. No hiding that under different circumstances, she may have enjoyed the heated way he stared at her. He smirked again before turning down the stacks again. "Choose a book, Morana." The way he said her name sounded as if he were still smiling knowingly. Irritation skated along her flesh, sending her huffing as she looked around.

She glanced at the leather-bound books lining the shelves. Her finger landed on one with intricate silver vine designs skating up the spine. They vaguely reminded her of the woman that had appeared in her room. Morana placed her hand around it to feel the gentle thrum of life racing through her fingertips. It reminded her of flowers blooming and vines wrapping around trees.

"Perfect." Matthias was behind her in an instant. He placed a hand on her shoulder. The shadows wrapped around them and then they were gone.

Nine

When the darkness lifted, Morana glanced around the mossy wood blooming with life in a thousand different directions. Intricate vines snaked up the mysterious trees looming above them in a suspended mist. Vibrant mushrooms grew on a dark log covered in moss and magic. It was like looking through a kaleidoscope, and her eyes strained from taking it all in.

"Oh yes," Matthias interrupted her thoughts, his low voice coating the limbs in power. He seemed different here, too—more vibrant. It was as if the entire forest brought everything to life as the damp earth and sounds of trickling water begged the plants to grow—to create. "I will give you a moment to adjust."

"Where are we?" Morana asked, eyes snapping to his. Matthias leaned against one of the strange trees, his powerful form relaxed as he watched her with that stupid glint in his eyes. He was clearly enjoying himself.

"A different realm. You know, you could have taken us here." He leaned against a tree casually, shadows skating across his skin. Picking a flower from the vine, he eyed the almost fluorescent petals. "You can shift realms, Morana. You need to learn what is out there, so you don't end up somewhere you shouldn't." His eyes looked through the stray strand of hair that had fallen across his forehead again. "Lucky for you, you chose a relatively safe place through the book you picked up." He smirked, alluring and devious.

"You mean the book I chose—"

"Detailed where we went. It tells you everything about this realm. Why read when we can visit?" He cocked an eyebrow in question and flicked the flower to the muddied ground below his boots.

"Now that we are here, I assume you're going to teach me how to get back." She took a step forward, glancing at the flower that now lay in the mud. The mist surrounded her, coating her skin in what felt like life itself. She didn't mind it here, but if different realms existed, she assumed different creatures did as well. And Matthias did say *relatively*.

Matthias straightened and pushed off the tree, adjusting the rolled sleeves of his black buttoned shirt. Morana watched the flexing of muscles, the corded veins, and the detailed ink across his skin. Her lips parted, and she looked up to find his eyes dancing with knowledge of her body's traitorous reaction. A half-smile tugged at the corner of his mouth. She tried to hide the reality of how he affected her. The fear she felt around him took a back seat to the way her curiosity drew her in. He unearthed something within her—a longing and a call felt amidst the chaos. Heat pooled in her core under his watchful gaze as her loyalty to Axton withered in stark contrast to the budding life around her.

I'm not here to steal your freedom, Ana.

A dangerous thought.

"I could teach you to get back." He strode forward, boots sinking in the cool mud below his feet. "Or--" He paused inches from her face. She refused to move back. His scent was intoxicating, invading her lungs like a drug. Despite his habits, she didn't smell tobacco like she did with Axton. This was something darker, headier. "Or I could leave you here and see what you can do on your own." His voice was a mere whisper.

Morana narrowed her eyes, blood boiling in her veins at the suggestion. He couldn't possibly leave her in a strange realm. He couldn't possibly be that callous.

"You wouldn't," she dared, but she shuddered as she realized she knew very little about him beyond what she had seen, and what Willow had told her. What she had seen wasn't promising.

Matthias reached a hand up, brushing a strand of hair behind her ear. His touch lingered there, warm fingers trailing down to trace over her lips. She couldn't fight the way her breath quickened, or the way her heart pounded in response to his touch. To be caressed by Death was to be consumed entirely.

For a moment, she saw Axton's hazel eyes flash just behind the veil that now existed in her mind, that useless fog that took hold of her in Matthias's presence. She stepped away, leaving a careful distance between them.

"You know nothing about me," he chuckled. "I'm the god of death, Morana." His face fell as the mirth disappeared from his features. He narrowed his eyes at her. "There's nothing I wouldn't do."

He was gone. She frantically looked around the misty forest, waiting for him to appear somewhere between the vibrant trees, but there was nothing but a faint trickle of water in the distance. Her stomach bottomed out. The emotions she kept carefully buried unearthed like a grave robbed in the night. Panic gave way to a raging storm that roared like the blood in her ears.

Lucky for you, you chose a relatively safe place through the book you picked up.

At least she hadn't chosen whatever option wasn't *relatively safe.* Morana tried to focus, tried to feel what she had felt when he had first taken her to his castle. Every time the shadows had appeared, the pleasure pulsing over her flesh; she had been experiencing intense emotion. She had gotten back somehow, made her way to Axton's with ease. What had she felt then? Fear? She was already afraid, though she'd never admit it aloud. There was no time to think.

With each passing second, something dark rooted in her blood, coaxing its way to the surface. She could feel it pulling her under, heady and consuming. She paused, glancing at her hands. Shadows were moving across her skin, skating the way they did around Matthias. Had he really left? Pulling on the thread of darkness, she unlocked something. The shadows moved, consuming more of her skin until magic covered her arms. It was a familiar sensation, one that took root when she was shooting at Ashford. It was the same pleasure she had felt ghost over her skin as she held the fire iron to his throat. She closed her eyes to hold on to it.

"Thank the gods he's gone."

Morana twisted to find the woman who had entered her room this morning standing near a tree. The shadows disappeared the moment she dropped the thread from within. She looked at the stranger. The webbing tattooed across her forehead was more vibrant in the muted light of the woods.

"What the fuck? Why are *you* here?" Morana's shoulders tensed, but she didn't feel danger, not yet at least.

The woman smiled, bright teeth flashing white. "I was curious," she answered.

"About what?" Morana asked. Her voice came out quickly with a harshness she couldn't suppress. There was a reason this woman was in her room this morning.

"You." She was wearing the same silver dress. It almost glittered here in this place. "You," she began, "and

Death's strange interest in a human girl. It's not often he brings women into his home. Usually, he's just out killing them."

Bile rose in her throat. She thought back to what Willow had said about death happening on its own. This directly contradicted what she had been told. Was Matthias more dangerous than she had originally thought?

Morana wrapped her arms around her stomach, turning away from the bizarre creature. She hardly had time to think about the way Matthias had left her stranded here. The way he had said there was nothing he wouldn't do—even to her.

"Oh, don't behave like that." She sat down on a fallen log; her dress spread out like a blanket of stars. "He's the god of Death. It's to be expected." She casually inspected her fingers painted black and red before cupping her hand out in front of her face. "He doesn't actually kill anyone." She smiled wide. "Not usually." A small plant formed in her palm, rising from nothing much like the vines that trailed from her back in the land of the gods. "I make things grow."

"The god of growth," Morana guessed.

"Flora." Her umber eyes found Morana's. "But growth sounds delightful, too." She tilted her head, her full lips falling into a questioning frown. "So, what does he want with you?" she asked. "He doesn't seem keen on actually killing you. I also want to know why he's taking you to different realms."

Morana scowled, refusing to answer. The goddess would certainly change her opinion about the killing if she knew Matthias abandoned her here.

"I told you I was curious," she smiled again. "It's not like I don't have free passage to enter his home in the land of the gods. We get along—me and Matthias. Flowers wither and die too."

Morana scoffed. "You act as if you are friends, but yet, he hasn't told you what he wants with me." She cocked an eyebrow at the goddess in challenge.

The Flora god's eyes glittered. "Privacy is important to Matthias. He—"

"Sarnai," the familiar gruff voice broke through the mist. Death was behind Morana in an instant, gripping her shoulder possessively. She shook him off, not entirely trusting him or his motives. Besides, no one owned her.

"Of course." The woman, Sarnai, rolled her eyes, the plant in her hand withering and fluttering to the ground before she stood up and turned to walk away. "You owe me an explanation, Matthias." She glanced back over her shoulder. "Especially if you're bringing strangers into my kingdom. Remember all the places I travel." She disappeared through the trees.

Morana glanced up at the dark expression on his face. He looked fierce, his jaw ticking in frustration, gaze never leaving the goddess.

"You left me," Morana whispered. The noise sounded too vulnerable, too soft. It left bile in her throat at the thought of showing him weakness—especially after what he had just done.

"Hardly," he clipped. He was still staring at where Sarnai had disappeared, as if she would appear again.

"You know her?" Morana asked. He was still standing close, and something about his presence sent heat down her spine. "She claimed you were friends." They certainly didn't look like it now.

"I know her. She frequently visits my home." His expression was now blank, revealing nothing. The phrasing of his comment revealed enough. They *were* close, but not just as friends.

"You're—" She cleared the tightness from her throat. "You're involved with her?"

He finally looked at her, gazing down with one eyebrow raised. His eyes traced down her face, her neck, and back. "Also hardly," he answered. "Though I'm curious why you'd ask." He tilted his head to the side.

She scowled, releasing a harsh breath in disgust. Morana folded her arms and looked away. The seed of doubt had been planted, and she desperately needed to learn more about what Matthias had done with Axton. She was here to learn about her powers, not be distracted by a death god. One thought ran unbidden through her mind.

I'm not here to steal your freedom, Ana.

If she could ignore the guilt of abandoning Axton, if she could harden her heart the way she had when she left her father, then she didn't have to feel more shame at the feelings she was now having.

"Close your eyes," he whispered.

She did as she was told, keeping her arms firmly in place. She felt him move behind her, hands on both of her shoulders, lips close to her neck. Her pulse pounded; any thoughts of the human realm wiped from her mind.

"What is this for?" she asked a bit breathlessly.

"I'm going to help you shift. You're going to take us back to the land of the gods, Morana." His voice carried a subtle rasp, though it was gentle. She relaxed her shoulders, moving her arms to her sides. This was what she was here for. She was aware of his touch on her shoulders, the way her skin burned there. Her gut twisted with guilt once more.

She should be with Axton. What was she doing here toying with Death? What would he think if he saw the way Matthias had his hands on her now, knew the way she was responding?

"I need you to stop thinking," Matthias's voice rumbled. If she didn't know any better, she would think it affected him in some way, too. He was still so close, and she hoped he couldn't see the flush creeping up her neck.

"How do you know what I'm thinking?"

"The shadows know no secrets." She felt his lips brush her ear, and she shuddered. Guilt pressed heavily on her chest once more. His touch was intimate, a slap in the face for all she had experienced with Axton before abandoning him. She left him on the side of the road. She abandoned him the way she had walked out on her father, and she had asked no questions. It had only been a day since she left Axton—abandoned him in the same way her mother had abandoned her father.

"You'll be back, right?" Her father's slurred words indicated exactly what state he was in.

"I'm working." Morana's tone was tight and filled with resentment toward the man. "Of course, I'll be back." She was picking up trash that littered the kitchen table where her father sat. Her keys rattled in her hand. "We have to make the rent payment, right?" She wouldn't meet his eyes.

She flinched as a firm hand gripped her wrist and prevented her from moving toward the door.

"She left us." Her father's eyes were glassy and begging for pity. She had no more pity to give—not when she sacrificed day after day while he drank himself into oblivion.

Something softened in his features, causing her to pause. "You look so much like her, Mor."

The tears threatened to break free as she desperately fought the rising sorrow. It was as if the entire world revolved around him and his loss. There wasn't a soul to recognize what she had lost, too. She had lost a childhood—a mother.

She ripped her wrist from his grasp, her voice coming out in a hoarse rasp. "I'll be back, but I have to go."

He coughed, and when she turned, the vomit spewed to the floor. It was foul.

"Shit, dad." Morana dropped the keys, running to the small closet in the hall, next to the hole decorating the plaster. She was used to cleaning up his messes. Always there. Always loyal. The realization stung like bitter alcohol coating her throat.

There was pain here in this memory. It was the moment she decided she would eventually leave. His mess wasn't enough to keep her. Maybe she lacked compassion, and maybe she was just as bad as her mother. There was no loyalty she could hold—not now.

"Stop thinking, Morana. I told you I'd heal him, and I did. I had someone deliver him back to his apartment. He's safe." Her head snapped as she twisted her body around to glare at him, now facing him. She hadn't been thinking about Axton anymore, but maybe she should have been.

"What did you say?" she asked.

"He's safe. You're thinking of him." He tilted his head, curiosity dancing in his gaze. "Or someone."

Panic stirred where the guilt once wrapped around her. It felt violating. He was so close to her deepest fears and regrets. Death touched on the things she wished to keep locked away. As Matthias stared at her, she questioned his abilities and the strange shadows that she felt tugging in her gut, begging to be released. His expression gave away nothing.

"Close your eyes again."

"Answer me this time." Tired of his ridiculous games, she refused to relent until he gave her a straight answer. "Can you read my thoughts?"

"I can sometimes. To be the god of death has a lot to do with the mind. Now, let me help you use your powers." A small fragment of frustration broke through his mask, betraying the emotion he tried to keep concealed.

"And if I refuse?" She was goading him, and she knew it.

"If you refuse—" He took a step forward, crowding her space. "If you refuse, you will remain in the dark about your abilities, making it easier for the Court of Light to hunt and kill you." He moved to stand behind her again, hands pressed to her shoulders. "This is what I brought you here for. Now, close your eyes."

"This feels an awful lot like I'm your prisoner," she spat. "Blackmailing me to stay is no better."

"I never claimed to be good."

She closed her eyes, waiting for instruction. If she were honest, she knew she needed to understand what lay within her. The shadows that had moved across her skin, the strange shifts that seemed to happen when she needed them most.

"I want you to think about the castle." He spoke gently, like the night slowly overtaking the dusk. "Think about it and pull the image into your mind. Will yourself there."

"What does that mean?"

His hand traced slowly down her arm, sending fire sparking across her skin. She tried to picture the castle, the balconies and intricate carvings, the stacks in the library. Her mind kept circling back to the way his fingers trailed across her skin. The feeling returned. Her mind kept emptying at the way he was making her feel—making her forget.

"You're distracting me," she admitted, voice thick with desire.

His hand stilled. "You're distracting yourself. You can think of the castle. I'm trying to help find your power." He shifted closer, his chest against her back before whispering in her ear, molten heat tracking across her flesh. "When I distract you, I promise you will think of nothing else. *This* is not a distraction."

The castle appeared in her vision as she felt his shadows caress her skin. The darkness took over, and her power met his own. Before she knew it, she was back in the stacks of the library, standing before the shelf where she had taken the book.

A redheaded boy looked to them, scuttling away in a hurry to the back of the library, so they were alone.

Morana glanced at Matthias, his comment still ringing in her ears. Her eyes were wide, mouth hanging open. She closed it firmly. "That's enough for today." Spinning on her heel, she plowed her way through the aisles, past the library entrance, and out to the castle foyer. She could barely remember where she was going, but her mind was racing, hating the way his touch sent shivers over her skin, the way her breath responded to him.

Glaring at her feet, she took the first stairs she saw and began climbing. Inky mist trailed across her skin as the thoughts were shoved deeper and deeper into the abyss. She didn't know when it happened, but their presence was almost comforting now, and she needed comfort. This castle was a prison, and she wasn't learning fast enough to get out of there.

She stopped at the landing just before the first floor above the entrance, closing her eyes and inhaling deeply, willing herself to calm. She thought of the dimple that appeared on Axton's cheek when he was truly amused, the way he cared for her after being attacked, the way *his* skin felt on hers. Morana pulled the memories out as she stood on the step with her eyes shut. She would picture *him* to cover up this wretched place.

When her eyes opened, she found herself standing in Axton's kitchen, pressed against the counter where she had given in to temptation just days ago. She couldn't focus, her eyes flicking wildly around the space. Was he here?

"Axton?" Her voice rang in the silence, bouncing off the white walls and tidy furniture. Her heart picked up as she stood there. Matthias had said he was here.

The door was closed, but the balcony door was open, the curtains billowing in the heated wind. Her pulse picked up and panic crept up her throat. Either Axton had left, or Death was a sweet and manipulative liar.

Morana pushed off the counter and moved down the hallway to the guest bedroom. There she found the bed still unmade; her dirty clothes thrown over the dresser as if someone had been in here. She glanced across the hall into Axton's bedroom to see everything overturned.

Bitter rage took root in her stomach, branching out in catastrophic limbs that climbed to her chest. Morana slammed the door behind her, a frustrated scream bursting from her lips as she stood in the hallway. Back to the wall, she slid down, holding her knees close.

Matthias lied to her. He lied about it all. She should have known he wouldn't bring him back here. What was Death but whispers of sweet promises to be broken?

"I'm leaving."

"Let me know when you'll be back." Her father was sprawled across the couch, a half-empty beer bottle set on the wooden coffee table. Morana pulled the backpack tightly over her shoulder. There was nothing here for her anymore, and she desperately wanted out.

The night was thick outside their small, shitty apartment. The apartment she had helped to pay for. There was no doubt that her father loved her, but after all that she had done, all that she had given up and sacrificed, she figured he would do something. He never did even, though he promised.

"Right." Her voice was nearly a whisper. She swallowed, turning the handle on the door, then closing it

behind her forever.

"Fuck." Her head landed against the wall, tears streaming down her face. What good was she if she could only ever run? Only ever think of herself. At least that's what he had told her—that she was selfish. She liked to believe that it was the right choice to leave, but it would have only been the right choice for her, and the world doesn't honor people making choices for themselves. People will lie about it, but in reality, they value self-sacrifice. And she was sacrificing herself. Every day in that hole, she felt as if she was dying just a little more with every passing second.

"He's safe," an unfamiliar voice broke into her sorrowful haze. Morana looked up to see a cloaked figure standing at the end of the hallway. The dark skin and green eyes pulled at some forbidden memory.

"Do I know you?" she asked, using her hands to push herself up. She was now standing, backing slowly to the end of the hallway towards a linen closet.

"You do not." The man didn't move.

"Why are you here?" she asked.

"Matthias had him delivered here, but we let ourselves in. He's safe," the man repeated, pulling down his cloak to reveal two pointed ears. A sinister smile broke across his face. "But you're not." Lunging forward, the man pulled a knife from inside his cloak.

Morana frantically ducked into the bedroom, closing the door and looking around for a weapon. Who was this guy? The loud banging on the wood made her jolt. Sweat trickled down her temple as panic made pain shoot through her lungs. Axton had to have a gun in here somewhere.

She dug through the sea of band shirts in his dresser, frantically looking for where he would keep a weapon. Axton had to have something. He worked at a shooting range damnit.

The banging continued. When Morana looked up, light shone from under the door. Her eyes were wide, fear paralyzing her. She closed her eyes to picture somewhere, anywhere but here. It was no use. Where would she go? A faint memory appeared, placing the man on the other side of the door in a dark alleyway. She remembered him from the night Axton shot him.

There was no denying now that people were hunting her. She couldn't go back to the castle, and she couldn't get her mind to cooperate. As much as she hated to admit it, she needed Matthias. She had to go back to the castle. What had the man said? Matthias had him delivered here. He had kept his word.

"Shit."

"I wasn't going to charge for the training, but now you definitely owe me," Matthias grunted as he materialized in the corner of the room.

The banging on the door continued as the gold light leaked from the crack by the floor. The sight of Matthias startled her. His hair was disheveled as if he had been running his hands through it incessantly.

"I owe you nothing," she spat. She wouldn't bow to him, even if she needed him. Matthias was there in an instant, dark and menacing.

"Mark my words," he warned. "You owe me, Morana. I take lives. It is rare that I spare them." He kneeled in front of her, keeping his body close. The sheer power of him pinned her against the nightstand. She couldn't move as he reached under the bed, looking up at her through thick lashes. He pulled a familiar black case out, flicked it open, and pulled the gun out before slowly standing once more.

"He won't die from this. It's a human weapon." She could have sworn he smirked as he said it. "But he will be slowed. I wouldn't dare take you with me without a little fun first." He turned to the door that was now trembling from the force of whatever power the monster possessed. Matthias glanced over his shoulder. "I am the god of death, after all."

When the door lit up in flames, disintegrating before her eyes, Matthias lifted the gun and shot at the intruder. The ringing sent something deeply wrong swirling in her gut, reminding her of the portly man entering Ashford. Morana shut her eyes, squeezing them tight before feeling a familiar hand grip her arm. When she opened them, they were in the bathroom of her suite. She was trembling.

Matthias's face was soft as he looked at her shaking hands. "It's only a gunshot." He was oddly gentle as his hand rested on her shoulder. She could have sworn she saw concern there.

"I know it was only a gunshot," she hissed. "Now, get out." She needed the space to breathe, time to heal from the events she hadn't yet dealt with. The echoes of Ashford rumbled through her veins, reminding her that pain wasn't easily avoided, and reactions couldn't always be controlled. Her mind was a confused mess. He hadn't lied to her. He had delivered Axton there, but then again, who could she believe?

"I'll let it slide this once," his hand slid away. "Get cleaned up." Matthias looked down at her, his eyes scalding her flesh with their intensity. "That man was an assassin, and he will be back, but not here." Anger pulsed from his shoulders. "They can track the shadows in the human realm—use them to find you. The same can be done in The Court of Light." His expression darkened. "I just need to figure out what they did with that fucking boy."

"Get out!" she yelled, the pain of Axton's disappearance ripping her to shreds.

"You still owe me." Matthias didn't waste time disappearing. Morana collapsed on the tile, wishing she could disappear too.

Ten

Morana had sat long enough in the extravagant tub that her skin wrinkled, and the bathwater was no longer hot. She didn't care. She was numb to it like she was now numb to everything that happened. Shadows danced over her flesh, sending pleasure rippling through her veins. She liked this new ability and the feeling of comfort it provided. Death was powerful, and she liked the idea that she held some of the same power, some of the same protections afforded to the god. It was calming. Or maybe it was the jasmine-scented soap left on the table near the tub. Her mind was as blank as the inky black mist floating between her fingers, ghosting over every inch of her hand.

She had cried on the floor until her soul was dry and withered—covered in wrinkles like the skin at her fingertips. There was no point in allowing the trauma that plagued her to continue to haunt her. She had lived with guilt weighing heavily on her shoulders for so long that she desperately wanted to let go. The black mist continued to snake between her fingertips in mesmerizing patterns. The tears had stopped flowing, and her head had cleared. She would fight to understand her power and the mysterious court that continued to prowl even in the light to hunt after its prey. She would fight even if she didn't know who she was fighting against.

Soft candlelight flickered over the tub's surface, trailing along the water. The light was consumed by whatever magic dripped from her hands. As she toyed with it, she found she could move the shadows away from her skin, breaking their soft caress to cover the light in front of her, cloaking it in shadows.

"When were you going to tell me about that?" Death's voice came suddenly, intruding on the peace she had found these past few hours. "I've seen them on you. I know you can shift realms, but I didn't know you had that much control."

Morana pulled her knees to her chest as the water splashed up around her, her heart stuttering as her limbs desperately fought to conceal her naked body. Matthias was in her head, and now he was in her bathroom. As if the way her emotions opened up in his presence wasn't enough. Now he was here to see her stripped bare. The fear of that vulnerability coated her flesh and twisted into a bitter rage. He had no right.

The shadows disappeared as she fought to conceal something—anything. Morana stared at him, eyes swimming with a cool rage. He was standing in the corner in the same way he had before, eyeing her. She didn't make a noise. She just clutched her legs closer, allowing her thick blonde hair, damp and heavy, to stick to her slick shoulders. Her stomach churned before a hollow sensation took over there. It was icy as she fought to conceal her opinions about his intrusion. The privacy of her rage wouldn't last long in his presence, and she supposed nothing ever did. He was the god of Death, after all.

"I can't help you if—"

She didn't let him finish as her face twisted in disgust. "You're an ass." The words tasted bitter on her tongue. "No consideration for how I've been thrown into all of this. You treated that man that attacked me like this all was a game. You treated it like *death* is a game." Morana was tired of the taunting remarks, the cold carelessness he continued to show. When did it all end? "You were treating my death as a game, Matthias." Her tone hardened as her voice lowered. "He said you had Axton delivered there. Is that true?"

"It is." Matthias ran a hand through his dark hair. "I had Hames take him there."

Her brows knit together in confusion. "Hames?"

"One of the lords in the Court of Shadows." He licked his lips. "He's trusted. Inara must have gotten there. That was her assassin going after you."

After going back to the human realm, after being attacked in Axton's apartment and then being attacked, she knew she couldn't return there, not until she mastered all the power humming in her blood. She needed the strength that came with the shadows. The calming presence they had brought as they twisted and danced between her slick fingers. She still needed Matthias to understand the power she held, but she hated that she needed him all the same. Resentment ran deep—no amount of attraction could cover that. He had left her in the Flora realm. When they had returned here, he was so cold to her, as if his involvement in her life were a favor. The part that she hated the most was that she supposed it was.

Matthias took her in, assessing her in a way that showed she was a puzzle to solve. His intense gaze sent shivers down her spine. "I'm not here to coddle you," he grunted.

"Why are you here, then?" she snarled.

"I came to check on you."

"Oh, how convenient," she started. "Coming to check on me while I'm butt ass naked in a bathtub. How noble." Rage was swarming and creating a perfect storm behind her gray eyes. She was mad at Matthias, mad at herself, and mad at the fucking assassin that broke into Axton's apartment. She didn't know what to do with all the anger burning beneath her skin.

"One, I never claimed to be noble," Matthias began, "and two, don't flatter yourself." His eyes narrowed; arms folded across his broad chest. He was wearing the same clothes from earlier, sleeves rolled up. The crows on his forearm, a symbol of what he ruled over.

"I will flatter myself if I please, and you know what?" She stood up, naked but unwilling to be bullied by even a god. She wouldn't tolerate it. "You claim you want to help me." She stepped out of the tub, water dripping from her hair down her chest. She supposed she could throw her anger at him. He claimed he wasn't noble, and she wanted to fuel that fire by challenging the truth of his words. "But I can't figure out your reasoning. Your tactics for training are shit." She lifted her chin, advancing toward him as the cool rage melted and ignited into a flaming entity. Morana was propelled by the burning fire within. Fanning it with the memories of being stranded in the forest. His eyes roved over her naked form to betray what he had said, but she didn't care. "You're barging in where you don't belong." Each claim allowed the bitterness to sink deeper into her soul. "And you've taught me nothing." It was a lie. "I don't care what kind of *god* you are. You are an ass, a liar, and an absolute waste of space." She could have sworn he flinched at that.

Matthias picked up the clothes off the counter and threw them at her. They were a pair she had picked for herself—something he had sent up to her wardrobe. She noticed the new clothes when she had finished crying.

"Put those on." His deep voice portrayed no emotion. Any traces of the power of her words disappeared as his onyx eyes immobilized her, refusing to balk at all she had thrown his way.

"Why?" She was holding the clothes close to her dripping body.

He stepped forward and grabbed her arm, yanking her closer. His eyes didn't slip down again. He simply stared into her face—menacing power and anger radiating off him. "You want me to help?" His lips peeled back. "Then I'm going to help." His grip was rough before he released her. Shoving her away. She pulled on the forest green jogger pants and black crop top before following him out the door.

He walked quickly, refusing to wait for her as he descended stairs and moved through endless halls. Morana knew she had pissed him off, but she had almost been killed multiple times now. The only thing he could do now would be to put her out of her misery.

"Call the shadows," he finally commanded when they reached a new room in the castle. A mahogany desk sat in front of several large bookcases. Maps hung on the walls detailing places she had never visited, and she assumed they were the places she could have gone if she had chosen another book from the library.

"I—"

"Do it," he growled.

Morana let the inky black spill over her arms, willing it to the surface. The power invaded her head, her lungs, and filled the well of fear she carried with her. The more she touched that hidden power, the easier it became to call on. It was as if the darkness had a mind of its own. It was filled with the secrets of power and pleasure, sending shivers down her spine.

"You can hide with the shadows," he informed. "In fact, there are lots of things you can do with dark magic, Morana." Matthias disappeared. In an instant he was behind her, face close, taking her back to the way he had touched her in Sarnai's kingdom. "You can move with them." His voice dipped to a whisper. "Call people to their death."

"Is that what you do?" she asked, magic still coating her arms.

"That's not what I'd do with you." His voice was darker—richer. She felt a gentle caress run up her leg, sending heated bliss across her skin. A subtle gasp left her lips. That pleasure was short-lived when she realized what was happening. His power was meeting her own, caressing her body, running along her skin, making her own darkness seem even darker.

Her breath quickened; lips parted. She took an unsteady breath as Matthias trailed his magic along her sensitized flesh, the temptation extinguishing her rage in the most delicious way.

"Everyone has to die sometime, Morana." His voice made her shudder, sending chills down her spine as if he were making a vow that would bring her to her knees. The black mist floated along her neck, her shoulders, her hips. She should still be angry, but he was touching her everywhere and nowhere at once, and she may hate herself later, but she enjoyed it.

"Practice using them, and tell me what you find."

"I thought you were helping me?" her voice was breathless.

"I am." His power floated down her neck, her back, and back up. She leaned into the touch of the shadows. "I told you what you can do. Now I want to see if you can do it. You already have a lot of control."

"You want me to touch you with dark magic?" she rasped.

He chuckled, low and bold. "No. I want you to hide. I want you to disappear." The gentle caress of Death left her. "However tempting your offer may be, I already told you." His voice was smooth, coated in promises she never knew she wanted. "You owe me."

His magic intensified, and Morana drew in a breath at the meeting of shadows. He wanted her to disappear, and she supposed all it took was covering herself in her own darkness. She called more to the surface, drawn up to meet every ounce of Death's power until she was consumed.

"Good girl," his voice rumbled, and Morana opened her eyes. She could see him standing in front of her, but aside from that, the room was void of any light.

"Did it work?" she asked breathlessly. A tendril of power ran down her throat and a small noise escaped her. She could see Matthias's lips pull into a deadly smirk.

"It worked." He stepped forward; his eyes filled with wicked delight. "It doesn't seem like you needed as much help as you let on."

"Can I touch things with the shadows?" She winced at her own question and the way her desire was so apparent. There was no hiding with him—no running. She didn't care to admit how much she liked it. "I mean, can I move objects or something?"

The smile remained on his face. Eyes glittering with wicked satisfaction. "I'm not actually touching you," he admitted. "The shadows control the mind. They can make people believe things that aren't real." She felt a featherlight touch on her shoulder. "I can make you believe I'm touching you, without ever laying a finger on you." Suddenly the touch changed, feeling less like the shadows and more like Death's warm grasp. "I can make people believe all sorts of things."

"Is that how you kill them?" She swallowed, remembering what he had confessed before he shot the assassin. "You torture them by manipulating their minds."

"I don't actually kill beyond my duty as king in the Court of Shadows." He dropped his own magic, the ghost of his touch disappearing along with it. "Death happens on its own. Sometimes it claims people abruptly, sometimes it's slow." His expression hardened. "I can bring peace to someone before they die. Manipulate their mind—their desires." His finger ghosted over her temple, sending sparks across her skin. "I usually choose to take the pain away before they disappear."

"Have you been manipulating me?" she asked. "Have you been manipulating my desires?"

He smiled. "I can honestly say that your desires are your own." His eyes flicked hungrily down to the bare skin at her stomach before dragging them back up to meet her incredulous gaze.

She stared at him then, allowing her own magic to fall away. The room came into view—utterly still. The silence was deafening, the air stagnant as if the entire space were holding its breath.

He used his ability to bring peace to people before they died. Matthias eased pain; he didn't cause it. Why was that so easy to believe despite everything?

"Don't look at me like that." His voice was soft, face almost pained as he watched the warmth flare in her gaze.

"Like what?" she whispered. For as bare as her emotions became around him, maybe she could strip his as well. There was something here—something lurking beneath the hard planes of his chest. Compassion? Could a god even feel that in a world so cruel?

Matthias grunted and moved to the door, dispelling the tension that hung in the air between them. His back flexed beneath his shirt. "I'm going to figure out what happened to Axton." She swallowed at the mention of his name, hating that she hadn't thought of him with Death so close to her. "Later, I'll teach you how to guard your own mind. It'll be useful." He reached for the handle. "Then you can really be sure that I'm not manipulating you."

Morana just stared at him. Maybe there was more to the god than she originally thought. Willow's words were true. Death was supposed to be evil, but deep down, she didn't think he was.

"Please don't leave," he whispered, glancing back from the doorway. "I want you safe. You have to be able to protect yourself, and whether you like it or not, you need my help to do that right now. I don't understand what the Court of Light is planning." He didn't look back again as he closed the door behind him.

Eleven

The light spilled softly through the open window of a dusty cabin. A gentle buzzing wrapped around her mind, and Morana stepped slowly toward the noise. White and yellow flowers were carefully arranged on a table to her left. A cup of steaming tea with a golden spoon set on the saucer caught her attention.

She didn't know where she was, only that she was dreaming.

Morana ran a finger along the white cup painted with delicate purple flowers. She could smell its enticing aroma. Drawn by the scent and the desire to drink, she pulled the cup to her lips before the buzzing caught her attention again. She set the cup down with a soft clink.

Wooden floors creaked beneath her bare feet until she made it to the window and the source of the sound. A honeybee flew in the air. She tracked each movement, mesmerized and dazed from the sweet fog of sleep.

The bee landed on the wooden sill in a puddle of honey that slowly dripped to the floor. A clock ticked in the distance, and Morana felt a presence in the room. She turned, met with the green eyes of a familiar figure. Dark skin and cloak draped over his broad shoulders. She couldn't quite place him.

He pulled his hood down to reveal two delicately pointed ears beneath.

"We've been looking for you," his voice was smooth and sweet like the honey that coated the sill. "I thought I had found you."

Morana glanced at the tea again, drawn in by the floral scent. She walked to the cup and picked it up, stirring with the golden spoon.

"Have you?" she asked, taking a sip of the warm liquid. She glanced sideways at the stranger.

He smiled—something sinister shadowing his features. "Queen of Darkness." His voice contained a sharp edge that had Morana whipping her head around, spilling hot tea on the floor below. She stared at him, unafraid of this stranger invading her mind. In the end, it was only a dream.

"What did you call me?"

He stepped forward. "You," he began, "are the Queen of Darkness. Are you not?" Something like fear wrapped its tendrils around Morana's spine. "The Court of Light is looking for you. We don't enjoy dusk in our court."

The cup slipped from her hands, shattering on the ground. A strong and low voice entered her mind. It was laced with unforgiving malice—ripping power from wherever it existed—claiming it as its own.

"You have no right to be here." Matthias wasn't anywhere in this dream, but his voice was clear. Darkness pooled around the corners of her vision, drowning out the soft golden light coming in from the window. A look of fear overtook the man before her, and she was suddenly falling away from the confines of her own mind.

She sat up abruptly, still in Death's palace. Matthias was standing at the foot of her bed, face curiously hardened.

"What was that?" she asked, still dazed from the dreamland she had entered.

"That," he began, "was the reason I was going to teach you to guard your mind." He moved around the bed, the mattress dipping beneath his weight as he sat next to her. "It seems that lesson needs to be moved up."

"I don't understand what happened." Her brows furrowed.

"They're finding you." He leaned forward, pressing a finger to her forehead. "Here." He moved his hand away. "He entered your dream. They are trying to hunt you, and most likely know where you are now. They won't be able to get here, though. I went to my court." He pinched the bridge of his nose in frustration. "I have duties there, things I'm responsible for, and now I'm worried about them entering your dreams." His eyes were glowing with a new intensity. "I asked around. Axton is somewhere in the Court of Light."

"He's a prisoner?" she asked, the fear skating up her spine. "We have to get him out." Her words were frantic.

"We will." He assured her. "But we need to get you guarding your mind before I take you to the fae realm. They're already looking for you."

"You were in my dream too," she stated, staring up at him.

"I told you." His face was serious. "The shadows manipulate the mind. I want you to learn how to keep me out of your head." He cleared his throat. "As well as others."

"I didn't know you could get in my head."

She flinched as dark vines of magic wrapped around her, giving her over to Death's grasp. She closed her eyes, breathing in the scent of power. Then he was there.

"You're here." Morana was staring at Matthias as he stood in this new dream. Aside from his presence, the space was stagnant and empty—a void between thought and reality.

"I am." He stepped forward, prowling toward her with predatory focus. "I want you to kick me out."

"Kick you out of my head?" she asked.

"Yes." He circled her, eyeing her carefully. She could feel the heat radiating off his body. It was difficult not to get sucked under.

A warm hand gripped her shoulder, sending a shiver down her spine. It felt so real in the way the pressure from his hand pushed into her flesh. The heat of his body ignited a desire within her.

"Force me out." Matthias was standing behind her again, lips close to her ear. Closing her eyes, Morana tried to think of a way to get him out of her dream. His presence and his touch were intoxicating. He felt like the shadows, the way they wrapped around her flesh. When she had felt the power previously, it had guided her and begged her to take more—use more. She felt she was only touching the very top of that well of power that lived within her. In the same way, Matthias exuded that same power and demanded that same use—teasing the depths left to explore—the things she still didn't know about the god standing so close.

"I can't," she admitted. Her voice dropped to almost a whisper. "I am not hiding my abilities from you. The shadows have been acting on their own, but this level of control—" Did she have any control? Matthias seemed to think she did.

"Build a fortress around your thoughts. You'll need to keep me away from you. That's your first task since I'm already touching you."

"But you're not," she scoffed. "This is only a dream." She was thinking of the way he had stood there before, using his magic to ghost over her skin.

This wasn't real. It was only a dream.

"Is it?" He moved his hand along her arm, brushing his chest against her back. Her breathing halted. Desire stirred her senses to life as she heard the subtle shift in his voice. His tone was deeper and coaxing—drawing her into whatever it was he wanted her to know or do. "This feels pretty real to me." Matthias leaned down, placing his lips on the sensitive flesh of her neck. She didn't pull away as he tested what she would allow.

"Are you going to force me to leave like I asked?" he questioned. His voice was low—tempting. His hand ran along her arm, sending sparks across her skin. "You're beautiful." Voice nearly a whisper, Matthias placed another kiss on her skin, lower this time. "Did you know that?" Another kiss. She was lost, floating weightless in this space, ready to forget the outside world existed. She didn't have time to be embarrassed by her panting. If this wasn't real, if it was only a dream—

She leaned back into his touch, grinding herself against him, a soft breath exiting her lips. If he was going to break down all of her walls, she might as well give herself this one moment to give in—a moment where she didn't have to fight her body's reactions. She wanted him, and in this space, she didn't have to sit with the guilt of how quickly Axton had fled from her mind.

Matthias groaned, and she felt the noise vibrate through her bones. She reached up, threading her fingers through his dark hair and pulling his head down toward her, begging him to continue. A hiss left his mouth, and she couldn't help but think of the way his full lips looked when he spoke, and how they would feel on her own lips.

"You're supposed to be pushing me away from you." His voice was raspy. "You're not supposed to be pulling me closer." She ground into him again, abandoning all dignity. "Or doing that," he hissed. The noise sent a thrill through her and heat pooled at her core. He pressed closer; desire evident by the firm length she felt at the arch of her back. It seems she wasn't the only one affected.

"You started it."

"What would Axton think if he knew you were standing here, allowing me to touch you?" His finger traced her lower lip, her legs nearly buckling from the sensation. "What would he do if he saw us?"

Her mind registered that last question, the words acting as a bucket of icy water extinguishing the burning desire to touch him and force his walls to crumble in the way hers did in his presence. The floor dropped from beneath her as she realized how close he was to her thoughts. He was in her mind—the vulnerability of that ignited a familiar rage, lifting the fog that had overtaken her mind with his close proximity and lightning touch. If he knew how to play her like this, how much control did she really have over her own fate? She would have no freedom here—not with a god that shared the same power she held. Matthias couldn't be safe, not if he was willing to play this game and use her emotions to toy with her.

*"No." Her voice was strong as she took a step
forward. "No." Morana spun, staring at Matthias, his eyes
glittering. Rage twisted its way around her chest, creating
an unbearable pressure. It needed to be released.*

*A wall shot up between them, forcing Matthias
stumbling back. She felt power working through her,
begging for more release. She strengthened the wall,
adding every ounce of energy she had into its construction,
blocking him out, creating distance.*

*Morana heard nothing—felt nothing. Until her eyes
blinked open, and she was once again sitting on the bed in
the palace.*

"Good." Matthias stood up from where he was
sitting. She couldn't read his expression. Was he
impressed by her power? "I don't want to have to touch
you again." He disappeared, and an emptiness took over
her emotions. He was the closest person to her true
feelings, could burn right through the barriers constructed
by her pride and anxiousness, but he wouldn't let her in.
More than that, he was still playing a game. What was the
life of a mortal to a god?

A crease formed between her brows; eyes glued to
the spot where Matthias had been only moments before.
There was no trace of his magic, just silence. She wrapped
her arms around her stomach, nails gently digging into her
sides. Had he meant that? Was touching her so terrible?
Embarrassment washed over her, and she felt the flush
work over the skin he had trailed his lips over. She

remembered the way his voice sounded when she pressed back into him, his arousal. How could he fake something like that? She couldn't. Even now, her body betrayed her thinking of it. She was completely undone around him.

Twelve

"What did you do to him?"

Morana sat up abruptly, pushing the white comforter off her tired frame as she registered the goddess in the room. She wrestled the stray strands of champagne blonde hair back into a loose bun atop her head. The nightclothes she found in her room, leggings and a large sweatshirt, paled in comparison to what the graceful creature was wearing.

"Sarnai?" she questioned. The woman was sitting in a chair by the crackling fire. The webbing across her forehead glowed in contrast with the delicate black dress hanging across her lean body. Sarnai's hand rested on her chin, her fingertips painted with black earth and scarlet.

"What did you do to him?" Her sideways glance revealed a brightness to her eyes—one that said she found the entire situation entertaining. "Matthias has been in a mood all morning." Her lip quirked up at the thought. Sarnai leaned back further, making herself comfortable in Morana's room.

"I'm not sure what you're talking about," Morana answered, pulling the covers aside and getting up off the mattress. "Also, why are you here again? It didn't seem like he wanted you around?"

"You speak your mind." The goddess's eyes glistened with appreciation. "I like that." Sarnai got up, moving gracefully. Everything about her spoke of earth and life, the way that forest had been filled with it. "You should come down for breakfast with us."

Willow appeared at the door; her black hair tied back gently in its usual knot. She glanced at Sarnai, unsurprised and almost pleased by the woman's presence. It gave Morana some sense of peace that it wasn't abnormal for the flora goddess to be slinking around the castle. "You beat me to it," Willow stated, a soft smile on the woman's lips.

"Of course." Sarnai chuckled, moving to the door to pass the servant. "She's not in the mood to answer questions, though," Sarnai pouted. "And I already told her we would wait for her to come down for breakfast, so I wouldn't waste your time." She opened the door with a subtle creak. "Besides, Matthias is already pissed, which is a common theme since our guest here showed up."

Willow chuckled as Sarnai disappeared from sight. It was the first bit of joy Morana had seen in the servant. Willow moved forward, straightening the bed and pulling at the comforter. "Go enjoy your breakfast," she said, unfazed by Sarnai's comments, presence, or the situation at hand. In fact, Morana thought the woman to be amused.

"You're friends with the goddess?" Morana questioned.

"We get along," Willow responded, tucking the sheets under the mattress. "She is here a lot. Active in the fae realm as well. If you were to see the palace in the Court of Light, you'd know that she has a lot of responsibilities there."

"Does she favor them?"

"She hates Inara," Willow stood up, adjusting the apron around her waist. "She's trustworthy, though." There was a pause. "If that's what you're asking, I mean." Willow's big eyes were lighted. "Though she is a bit strange." A smile pulled at her lips as she moved to the other side of the bed.

Morana thought for a moment, glancing at the flowers that still sat on the chest at the foot of her bed. Daisies this time. When had they been replaced? Her brows pinched together. "Should I be worried about his mood?" She thought about the way his solid form had felt against her, and the way he had responded afterward. She wanted to hate herself for wanting him so badly, for the way she had embarrassed herself.

I don't want to have to touch you again.

"Forget it," Morana answered her own question as she snatched the faded dark jeans and white t-shirt from the wardrobe, chiding herself for how one statement stung. She had wanted him to touch her. Heat washed over her at the thought—first from desire, then embarrassment. She snorted. "He's always moody." And despite her better judgment, his actions made her moody as well. She peeled the sweatshirt off her body and shoved it to the bottom of the basket next to the wardrobe.

Willow chuckled again, tucking a stray strand of hair behind her ear. "That is very true. And you've only been here for a few days, Miss Morana."

Morana cringed. "Please don't call me that."

She finished changing and donned a pair of brown combat boots. She left Willow and made her way through the endless halls, observing the décor of Death's palace. Everything was beautifully made—old and expensive. Tapestries hung on the walls, and the lavish carpets ran through the hallway. She needed to find time to explore this place, to learn what really lurked behind the endless rooms in the hallway. A man she assumed was fae by his pointed ears walked past her, nodding as he made his way up a set of stairs.

When she came to the foyer, she saw a woman dusting one of the carved statues sitting next to a skull encased in glass.

The red carpet looked freshly swept. Morana cleared her throat, heading up the short set of stairs into the dining room, where Matthias and Sarnai were seated at either end of the table. The place was set for her next to Matthias, and she winced.

I don't want to have to touch you again.

Morana forced the shame trying to color her cheeks down, and walked forward, her eyes meeting his as she strode confidently through the room. There was no way she would sit next to him. She grabbed the high back of the wooden chair and dragged the piece of furniture noisily away on two legs down the length table, putting distance between herself and Matthias. She didn't look away as she moved to grab the dishes, making her way to her new spot. Matthias just looked amused at her display, and Morana's fingers twitched around the silver fork she grabbed. He wouldn't be amused if she shoved it in that damn tattooed hand of his. Then he really couldn't touch her, touch anyone.

Sarnai let out a muffled laugh. She glanced over her cup, a knowing smile on the goddess's lips. Setting the cup down, Sarnai raised her brows in question, knowing something had happened between the two. Her question was ignored.

Morana sat on the chair, and food was quickly brought out to her. She noticed Willow wasn't among the servants bustling about the room, appearing and disappearing with various food items.

She chose scrambled eggs with potatoes and peppers, as well as toast with blueberry jam, not hesitating to satisfy her hunger, unable to remember the last time she had eaten. The food tasted better than she expected. It was a fine distraction from the tension swirling in the air.

"How did you sleep?" Matthias's voice broke the silence. He was staring at her, his black button-up hugging his chest. She glanced at the moth tattoo on his hand as he picked up his cup and took a drink. Her gaze lingered on those full lips. The ghost of a sensation on her skin, the feeling of those lips on her, the way they had been last night. She steeled her spine, straightening in her seat to hide the thoughts away from him.

"It was unpleasant," she finally said, meeting his gaze with shards of ice. "The first half anyway." It was bitter and petty, but she pushed on, allowing the train to derail entirely. She could cut with words too, and she hoped the cut would run deep.

Matthias grunted, returning to his food. She hated to admit it, but his lack of reaction stung. For someone so invested in how she slept, he seemed unable to muster enough energy to continue the conversation. It added coal to the firebox on the train of rejection.

"I had a wonderful dream the second half of the night." Morana looked away, picking up her fork to take a bite of potato. She knew it was ridiculous the second the words left her mouth. She swallowed, hardly looking at the gods in the room, but she wasn't backing down now. "You know my friend, Axton?" she asked. "Such a way with his hands. With his—"

He had slammed a fist on the table, rattling the cutlery and Morana, causing her to halt her words.

Matthias got up, pushing his own chair back loudly. It didn't take long before he was standing across from her on the other side of the table, the wood creaking beneath the weight of his arms. She looked up at him. His eyes were dark, swirling with some sort of promise she couldn't quite name.

A tendril of fear crawled across her skin. Power was radiating off him in waves as if the room couldn't contain everything that he was. Morana risked a glance at Sarnai, who seemed to enjoy this little interaction.

"Problem?" Morana asked, barely containing the smile breaking through. If his lack of interest offended her before, she surely wasn't showing him now. One eyebrow raised in challenge.

"A way with his hands?" He asked, disgust dripping from his tone. He leaned forward, dark hair falling just over his eyes as the scent of bergamot and mint invaded her senses. The corded muscles in his forearms flexed with his movement, and she glanced away, refusing to react. This was a challenge, and she would rise. She squared her shoulders and met his gaze once again.

"Not just his hands." Her brows flicked up as she pushed her tongue into her cheek. Matthias leaned forward, the wood creaking again beneath his strong grip. His chest was rising and falling rapidly as his jaw clenched. She liked this reaction. Something about it wiped away the rejection from earlier. Never mind that the rejection train had completely tumbled into the raging river below. She was fully taunting him. There was a certain thrill in goading a god. It spiked her adrenaline—made her feel powerful. Despite everything he had said, despite stating that he didn't want to touch her, this reaction proved something else entirely.

Morana licked her lips, her eyes looking up at him with wicked challenge—begging him to say something.

"You're a petty child," he spat.

Sarnai coughed, and Matthias moved, the table shifting as he pushed off its surface. He stomped out of the dining room, tension moving through his shoulders. Morana watched as the muscles in his back flexed beneath his shirt. She took a drink of water, allowing the small smirk to form on her lips as her heart raced in her chest.

"I think I understand." Sarnai leaned back in her chair, propping her feet on the dark wood of the table. The delicate black fabric of her dress parted to reveal lean legs. "He's moody because he's sexually frustrated."

Morana's head snapped to the goddess. "He doesn't want to touch me," she hissed, cursing herself for allowing the mask to crumble away, revealing that it irritated her, hurt her.

"Do you want to touch him?" Sarnai asked without hesitation, a knowing smile playing on her lips. She was clearly enjoying this breakfast.

"No." It was a lie that tasted bitter on her tongue. Matthias consumed her thoughts, and it was hard not to think back on every time he had touched her or pretended to touch her. It was all smoke and mirrors with Death.

In an instant, Morana was thrown into her own mind, greeted by the image of Sarnai standing in the void. She tensed as her eyes turned wild. Nobody had a right to invade her space like this—not again. The goddess was trying to read her thoughts. This is what Matthias had tried to warn her about. He had tried to protect her from this. *No.* He had taught her to protect herself.

The fortress went up, resurrected in the way she had done the night before. It thrusted her mind back to the present—back to reality. Her eyes focused and when she looked at her hands, dark shadows inked the skin there before fading away.

"Impressive," Sarnai mused. "I'm starting to understand why you may be here. That's not typical of a mortal." She pulled her feet off the table. "I guess I'll have to get to know you the old-fashioned way." The goddess took another drink. "Tell me, Morana, would you like to leave the land of the gods?"

"And go where exactly?" she asked.

"The Court of Shadows." Sarnai chuckled. "The place where Matthias is king."

"Matthias is a god that rules the court," Morana corrected, thinking back to what he had told her.

"And sometimes they are one and the same." Sarnai gave her a curious look, trying to solve the puzzle of the mortal in front of her.

"What's it like?" Morana asked. "Matthias mentioned the courts. What are they like?"

Sarnai didn't look surprised. "There are two courts in the fae realm: light and dark---life and death. Matthias is a god, and gods dabble in all the realms. For example, I'm here." She gave a devious smile. "However, Matthias and Inara are different. They are gods, but they also rule in the fae courts."

"Matthias said the Court of Light is hunting me," Morana admitted. "Why would he keep me from them? What does Inara want from me?"

"Tensions are high between the courts. They call for peace around the Autumn Equinox that takes place in a couple of weeks. Mabon." Sarnai rested her elbows on the table, leaning over her plate. "The courts will be together to celebrate." Her face fell, the webbing on her forehead moving as her brows furrowed. "I'm not sure why they want you if you're only a mortal. Though I assume Matthias is planning to bring you to the Mabon celebration." She swirled the liquid in her cup, observing it pensively. "I didn't realize the Court of Light was hunting you. I tend to the gardens in the palace, but I avoid the place. The Flora realm gets boring and so I prefer to hang around fae—specifically ones that enjoy the darkness."

"Why?" Morana asked.

"Sometimes the darkest evils lurk out of the shadows and in the brightest of light." Her eyes were serious, burning with intensity and churning with some story Morana didn't have the time to ask about.

"Morana?" Willow appeared through the doorway from the kitchen. It was beginning to feel like she was specifically assigned to Death's new guest. "Matthias would like you to change."

Morana glanced at the pale woman, blue eyes glittering despite the dim light of the dining room. "Seem's rather presumptuous that he believes he could tell me what to wear."

"I assure you; he merely wants you to be comfortable where you are going," Willow added. "The fae realm is different."

"Should I put my nightclothes on again?" Morana asked. "For comfort."

"You'll want a dress."

Not comfortable then.

She looked back at Sarnai, taking in what she had learned about the courts from the goddess. "Where exactly is he taking me?" she asked.

"Hell, if I know," Sarnai responded. "Though I would wear the dress, and possibly a cloak."

Morana huffed before standing up. "That asshat," she muttered.

Sarnai chuckled at her reaction. "Looks like someone wants to flaunt his kingdom." She leaned back in her chair, a smile playing on her lips. "Whatever you see, it's important to note that Death does not compensate."

Heat rushed to Morana's cheeks; a cocktail of embarrassment, anger, and need. She moved swiftly across the room, leaving the flora goddess behind.

Crossing through the foyer and heading up the stairs, she tried to blend in so the servants wouldn't see the pink tint to her cheeks.

Morana bounded up the stairs, keeping her gaze on the floor. She trailed her fingers across her lips, the way Matthias had when he was in her mind. It had felt so real—so raw. Her stomach curled as she remembered the sensation, how it had overtaken her entirely.

Her walls were crumbling. There was no judgment from the god, even as he saw the rawness of her emotion. He had been in her mind—an act so intimate and profound that she could hardly make sense of it. The scariest part was that she had *wanted* him there. Morana wanted the shadows and his presence—and wanted to see how far he would go to unlock everything she had kept hidden for so long. The stubble on his jaw, the way his breath had fanned over her skin, all of it had ignited a deep desire to make him feel the same wild recklessness she felt with him. Maybe that's why she had delighted in goading him earlier.

"Shit," she muttered to herself.

"What are you thinking about?" Matthias was standing at the top of the stairs, leaning against the wall with his arms folded across his broad chest, as if her thoughts summoned him. Morana halted a few steps lower, dread seeping to fill every pore.

"I thought you were pissed," her voice was low, her eyebrow cocked in suspicion. He was standing casually, with a delighted charm about him.

"Whatever do you mean?" he asked, dark secrets hidden in his voice as he pushed off the wall.

Morana stared at him as he extended a hand toward her, anxiously waiting to escort her up the last four steps to the hall. She kept her gaze on that outstretched hand, the moth tattoo inked over veins and bone. He had nice hands.

"What are you playing at?" She didn't trust this shift in his mood. Not when he had dragged her from the bath, pulling her away to taunt her with shadows, forcing her to cloak herself in darkness and disappear from the world. Death had a firm grip, a moody disposition, and an exhausting attitude.

He smiled brightly, still holding his hand out. Morana took it, waiting for an answer.

"You do realize I'm not just a god?" He hauled her closer to him, the dark black and flecks of brown in his eyes glittering in the dim light. "Allow me to show you something different." She just stared at him. "I am also a king that lives in a beautiful city. Let me convince you."

"I'll believe it when I see it." She strode past him, her footsteps heavy as she made her way to her room.

"Perfect," he called out from behind her. "Wear one of the dresses. You'll be treated by the king."

She muttered a curse under her breath, rushing to get away from him.

Thirteen

Morana could hardly remember her life before it existed between the planes of different realms and gods. It had only been a few days, but it had felt like a lifetime. The ancient city around them flourished with well-kept streets and quiet corners—all pointing to the presence of a good king. His demeanor was different here, too. While he was almost always confident, there was an easiness here.

Matthias glanced sideways at the midnight blue dress twisting beneath a black cloak. Morana sighed, her heels clicking on the stones. She was walking the streets of a fae realm with the god of Death, the king of shadow.

He promised an impressive city too, and on that, he didn't disappoint.

"I'll admit that it's beautiful," she spoke as they walked down the narrow, cobbled street that spiraled through stone homes coated in vines and delicate flowers. She pulled the black cloak he had given her tighter around her body, glancing at the road ahead. There was still tension from breakfast, and she hated herself for allowing the sting of rejection to hurt her this long. Though goading him was enjoyable, his new attitude felt like a game.

The air was cool, and Matthias looked somewhat out of place with his dark tattoos peeking out from the rolled sleeves of his black button-up. He looked every bit a king and a god with power radiating from his tall, athletic frame.

"The city also seems old," Morana mused, attempting to break the silence again. She had gotten ready. Matthias met her just outside of her rooms, hardly speaking before he used the shadows to shift to this place. Morana expected to see fae walking the streets, dressed in intricate and elaborate dresses and cloaks. The quaint streets were void of fae but blooming with life from the intricate gardens spreading out and decorating the short iron fences in front of some homes. She could admit she was nervous to see what was out there. A week ago, she had known nothing about different realms and their existence.

"It is." He glanced at her, but his expression was difficult to read. She didn't know what he was thinking after the things she had said, the way he had acted before they left. It was as if nothing had happened for him while it wouldn't stop replaying in her mind.

"Well," she began, "you know I'm human. I know very little about this." He smirked at her ignorance, still not responding with conversation. "So," she tried again, her voice cracking on the word. She cleared her throat.

"What do I need to know about the fae realm, *your highness?*"

Matthias grunted, his eyes rolling at her remark. He was utterly unamused at her jibe. "So, now you're willing to be respectful."

She scoffed, increasing her pace and crossing her arms over her chest. There was a fog in the air, a mist that made this place seem even more magical. The clouds muted the sunlight overhead, and she saw a fae woman, dressed in a simple tunic and brown pants, working a garden outside of her small house. Her face fell at the sight.

"You said I had to wear the dress." Her brows furrowed—tone tight as she stood motionless in the street. As if being thrust into a different realm wasn't enough, she was now being told what to do. Summoned like a dog and trained for his amusement.

"I suggested it." He paused his stride, fixing his amused gaze on Morana as he chewed on his cheek.

She swatted at him; her fist colliding with his broad chest. "You arrogant, self-centered, callous, belligerent, domineering—"

"Are you done?" he interrupted, but she continued.

"Obstinate, tactless, and sullen son of a bitch!" She pushed at his chest, rage swarming as he stumbled back a step. Every part of her felt ignited—fire burning. She felt as if he were trying to control her, instructing her on what to wear. Maybe it was because she had goaded him. This was a power move. "Is this payback for breakfast?" she asked.

"So, you admit you were being petty." His hands were in his pockets now, the fae woman behind him now staring with her jaw dropping. Did she know who he was?

"Don't call me names." Morana's gaze flicked back to his dark eyes. He saw the hypocrisy of her statement, the way her careful control slipped in his presence. He didn't balk at it, as if he could take whatever she threw at him—even if it didn't make sense.

He chuckled, running a hand down his face. "Right." He glanced back at the fae woman, smiling. It was a strange thing to see. Matthias appeared more relaxed here, more welcoming. The woman bowed low, muttering something to herself about the king outside of her home. "You're walking around with me; you should wear a dress and be willing to learn." Matthias turned back to Morana as the fae woman disappeared into her house, leaving them alone on the cobbled street.

"I *am* willing to learn." She stiffened, realizing that she had just insulted him in front of his subject, pounded at his chest in frustration.

His hands flexed at his sides, and she saw a flash of the temperament she had come to know cross his face. Nerves wracked her body as she remembered all the times he had been firm with her. The way he had left her in the flora kingdom. The harsh way he had dragged her for a lesson after she had bathed.

The last part of her statement came out as a whisper. "I want to learn," she admitted. "And then maybe I want to go home."

"You can go home." He stepped forward, still facing her on the quiet street, gaze hardened. "I want you to understand, Morana. I *am* trying to help you. You can shift realms." He gestured to her. "You can enter minds as easily as I can once you learn to wield that power." For a moment, she thought she saw compassion cross his face. "I don't trust Inara. What began as curiosity has changed for me." A serious expression shadowed his features. "She wants something from you, and I'm not sure what it is. She's taken Axton to get to you. You have to be able to protect yourself."

Her heart stuttered at the mention of Axton. "You almost sound like a noble king, eager to protect your people." Morana narrowed her eyes. "Does the fae realm have some incredible power that changes you from an asshole to a caring teacher, longing to help me figure out what's going on in my blood?"

He laughed then, a sound that tasted sweet on her tongue. She was surprised at how much she enjoyed it. "Are you hungry?" he deflected. "We need to eat before we go to the palace. It's nearly noon."

"I am hungry." Her stomach growled in agreeance. Matthias arched a brow but said nothing as he continued down the cobbled streets.

She followed him until they met a larger road paved with the same delicate masonry at the bottom of the hill. The buildings were taller here and fae men, women, and children walked through the streets, buying and selling goods from stalls. She paused, taking in the sights and smells. The street was glistening with the remnants of rain. Morana hardly noticed when fae stopped to look at Matthias, glancing at the woman standing with them.

Matthias quickly ducked into an alleyway, avoiding being seen. She followed swiftly as magic coated her skin, swirling around him like a dark mist in the night.

"What are you doing?" she asked.

"Making us disappear. They recognize their king."

Matthias pushed forward, and they crossed another street, bustling with cloaked figures. This time, she could feel the shadows pressing in, masking her appearance. They ducked into what appeared to be a restaurant, accessing it from the side door.

"I don't want to be recognized." Matthias smirked as a lanky boy with sandy blonde hair and an apron moved around to greet them. His blue eyes flicked away from Morana, and he bowed while wiping his hands on a white towel.

"Your highness," he spoke. He couldn't be older than eighteen. He was shaking, clearly nervous in Matthias's presence. "Your private room, I'm assuming?"

Matthias nodded.

"I'll let father know you've arrived." His eyes moved back to Morana. "I will inform him of your guest. We will prepare for two today." The boy's eyes tracked over her ears, and Morana pulled her hand up to touch the rounded ends out of insecurity. She wasn't usually like this, but something about being thrown into this alternate universe made her feel uncomfortable.

The boy hurried away. Matthias gestured to the stairs just to their left, leading up to a room unknown. She moved forward; the wood creaking beneath her shoes.

When they reached the top, a private table set for lunch came into view. It was encased in glass, with plants hanging and decorating every inch of the space. She could see the vibrant sky where clouds were breaking, allowing a soft blue to overtake its vastness, lighting the glowing streets below. They could see everything from up here. So much for not being recognized. The city was beautiful—nothing like the dirty streets outside her apartment.

"I don't remember seeing this from the street," she spoke, looking through the sunroom at the city beyond. "But everyone will see us."

"A glamour," Matthias answered. "There's a lot to take in. We should eat first."

They moved to sit at the table, and food was brought out. Morana draped the cloak over the back of her chair, glancing at the dish served by the boy who had greeted them in the kitchen.

They ate in silence while Morana lost herself in thought. She saw herself over the past three years, the way she had refused to grow close to anyone, the loneliness that accompanied her. She supposed it made her stronger, being on her own, but desperation came in the end, begging her to open up to Axton. Even that was short-lived. She was known for running, known for making selfish choices at the expense of others, and something about the change in Matthias's demeanor set her on edge. Every fiber of her being was gearing to run because the god of Death was showing he was capable of kindness. And what was this kindness, anyway? He was treating her to lunch in a beautiful city seated in the kingdom he ruled. It contrasted everything she had learned about him.

She didn't look at him, but her mind started pulling her vision away from the ancient buildings that surrounded them. Whether he was requesting access or testing her, it didn't matter. She sank into the inky veil to meet him.

Morana saw him then, standing in her mind. She was tempted to build that fortress again, but she let him in. She wanted to be seen.

Matthias walked up to her, mist swirling and twisting over his skin. He was standing directly in front of her now, dark eyes pinned to hers.

"You are supposed to kick me out," he whispered.

"Have you come to read my thoughts?" she asked him. "Since we've been eating in silence." Her blonde hair loosened from where it was pulled back at the base of her neck. She brushed the stray strand aside, tucking it behind her ear.

"Possibly," he responded.

"Then maybe I don't want to kick you out." Tears stung at her eyes. He was here, eroding something in her

she had kept carefully covered, the truth of who she was. She wanted to know if he meant what he said. She's said many things since being here, most of them not reflecting what she really felt. "Maybe someone needs to know what's going on in my head for once," she admitted. "Axton isn't here. I had opened up to him, but I ran from even that."

His face communicated nothing. Morana saw no emotion there, but she took comfort in it. He hadn't judged her for the way she acted, and she didn't believe he would judge her for this. She was falling apart, all the emotion she had kept hidden the past few weeks slowly coming to the surface now. She was about to break.

"You want me to look through your thoughts?" His voice was soft, and it was the first time she could hear something in it other than his usual bravado. If Morana wasn't looking at him so intently, begging him to see her, she would have missed the longing in those dark pools of his. Her limbs felt heavy, and the swirling of the mist around them seemed to still. She wanted to run, but the heaviness in her chest kept her rooted in place before him.

Morana nodded, and then he reached out, resting a warm hand on her cheek. She closed her eyes as the shadows took over, forcing her to relive the one thing she regretted; the moment she walked out of her father's apartment.

Opening her eyes, Morana realized they were still in the restaurant. Her cheeks were damp, and Matthias was leaned back in his chair, running his fingers over his chin. He was staring at her, eyebrows furrowed and a look she couldn't quite read. She felt like she had to say something. She had told Axton about what had happened, but having someone see it, live through it with her, felt more intimate.

"It was my father," she whispered. "I walked out when I was eighteen, moved to the city, worked at the gun club, and never looked back." She swallowed, the untold story weighing less as she released it to him. Whether he deserved to hear it was a thought she didn't want to spend time on. "He was depressed. My mother left when I was seven, and everything I did from that point on was out of obligation." Her throat bobbed at the memory of his hand smacking across her flesh. "The jobs to keep us afloat, the caring for him. All of it. I got fed up, so I turned eighteen, looked at him half-drunk on the couch, and walked out without saying hardly a thing." The tears had dried, and she pushed forward. "I left Axton and came here," she admitted. "I don't even know what I'm doing, but no wonder I'm being hunted." She thought of how she had felt seeing Matthias standing there after the accident. His presence had pulled her in, or maybe it was his power. "I'm being hunted because I'm a damn good runner." Tears were falling freely down her raw cheeks, and for once she didn't try to damn them back up behind her mask. "And I'm selfish," she whispered.

Matthias didn't break his mask. All the warmth he had shown on their way here disappeared. Her stomach sunk and she looked away. The physical rejection was one thing, but this?

"You can't judge me," she added. "You're a god of Death. Maybe that's why I thought I could tell you." She shook her head, picking up the cup of water on the table and thinking about the memories she had laid bare while he was in her mind. "Show you," she corrected. "You said there was nothing you wouldn't do."

"I meant that." His deep voice rumbled through the air as he sat casually across from her. Their plates empty.

"Well," she said, calling on the callous temperament, the fiery attitude she held so closely to keep herself safe. "I'm realizing that I'm capable of all manner of things."

There was a moment's pause before he leaned forward and answered. "Being capable of selfishness once in a while is hardly a damning quality." Something genuine flashed in his dark eyes. "I don't believe people are selfish enough."

"Not surprising coming from you," she laughed.

"I've watched many people die from the selfishness of their decisions." The admittance sent guilt shooting through her chest. "But I've also watched people lead miserable lives, giving up every piece of themselves for others because the world tells them it's the right thing to do." He eyed her carefully. "They die unfulfilled and sick because they allow the desire to be good to run them ragged. Life is about balance." He ran a finger along the table, tracing the wooden surface. "You spent eleven years of your life caring for your father, sacrificing yourself. He didn't care for you or himself. You now shame yourself for walking away, but maybe he has been using that time to do the work to heal. He had to stop relying on you." His voice dropped lower. "You isolated yourself for three years and lived with this shame because you think you ran. Don't you think eleven years of service was enough?" he asked. "When do you get to stop and decide for you? When is it enough?"

Morana stared at him, gray eyes wide in the afternoon light. Those were questions she had asked herself once, and she had felt guilty for the answer. The answer was the reason she left, the reason she walked away. She couldn't bear to see the look on her father's face or hear his condemning voice as he slurred every comparison that left his lips. He saw her mother in her, and he begged her to stay. He had needed her, but she could never be enough for him. Let him call her selfish in the way he had labeled her mother. Even so, the guilt crept back in like a creature in the night, joining her in the grave that she had dug for her emotions.

That feeling never left and was unearthed again in the past few weeks. Because of *him*. The intensity of it scared her. This was nothing like what it had been with Axton. With Axton, she was desperate for anyone to listen, but with Matthias, she was desperate for the one who could understand.

"A god," she mused. "A god trying to enlighten me." She huffed a laugh.

"I don't think my name has ever been associated with enlightenment." His jaw ticked as if he were about to smile. "At least not in the way you're saying. I'm always the thing people are avoiding." He got up, pushing his chair away from the table and extending a hand. "Just not here. Here, I am king, and I want you to learn how to fight like fae—like a god."

She stood up, a weight leaving her as her hand touched his. Something new blossomed in her chest at his words. Not only had he seen the deepest regrets she housed internally, but he was offering her a way to defend herself and claim her own power. There was no condemnation here—no comparisons—just the gentle cracking of the walls she wrestled with. It felt good to be known—seen. She was beginning to realize that Matthias wasn't who she had believed him to be, and a part of her believed he spoke truth when he said she wasn't a prisoner.

Fourteen

The quaint cobbled streets of the district they were in faded away as the late afternoon sun shone overhead. Matthias walked swiftly through crowds, avoiding recognition with the shadows encasing them both. She glanced at his eyes, then his lips, before tracing the stubble lining his jaw with her gaze. The softness remained on his features; shoulders relaxed as if he could carry the weight of all she had told him—the weight that didn't feel as heavy now that she wasn't the only one carrying it.

They made their way to an uncovered shop, located down a side street where few fae were wandering. An iron sign hung off a wooden post speaking of the owner's craftsmanship.

Morana read the sign. *Ore Else Blacksmiths.*

They were meeting with a blacksmith?

A confused expression covered her features, and Matthias halted before an iron gate, blocking off the space where heat was radiating in waves from inside the building.

"You can't kill fae without a fae weapon," he informed. "I want to have something made for you." He was standing close, looking down at her with those dark eyes. "You'll need to learn to fight, too."

"Could a fae weapon kill you?" she asked, brows raised.

Matthias laughed, resting his hand on the iron gate. "No, it couldn't."

"Well," Morana began, "I won't need training on how to use a gun." She folded her arms in front of her chest, confidence emanating from her.

"No guns." Matthias smiled. "You're not in the human realm any longer."

He pushed through the gate, leaving her to follow.

A small, framed woman stood over a workbench with a fire blazing behind her. Sparks shot through the air where her hammer struck true on a piece of metal. She looked up, moving the face covering to the top of her head. Her green eyes went wide at the sight of Matthias, and she dropped the hammer to the table, flinching at the sound.

"Y—your highness," she stuttered. Her voice was smooth and rich, like the sap from a tree. She wiped her face with her sleeve, smudging black soot over some of the smattering of freckles decorating her tanned skin. "I'll get my brother."

"Unnecessary," Matthias spoke. "We were looking for you, Reese."

She bowed low, moving around the table and whipping the face covering off her head, setting it on the stone workbench.

"I'm not sure why," she smiled, tucking a strand of long brown hair behind one pointed ear. There were burns etched into the skin on her hand, a sign of the work she did.

"I need a few weapons made. A dagger and a sword."

"Oh." Reese cleared her throat and tugged at the pointed tip of her ear. Morana understood the overwhelm the poor fae was exuding. It was something Matthias caused naturally anytime he was in close proximity. "Don't you usually send someone for orders like that?"

"These aren't for me," he revealed, casually leaning on one of the worktables. "They're for my guest." He gestured to Morana.

Reese looked confused for a moment before observing Morana carefully, her long hair wavey and draped over one shoulder, reaching her waist.

"I can have some things made." She glanced at Matthias. "It will take about a week."

"That's fine. In the meantime, do you have a sword and a dagger that she could borrow? Something she could train with. There's also the discussion of magic I would like embedded in her blades."

The conversation faded as Morana turned to a map hanging at the end of the workshop. The tables surrounding were cluttered with pieces of metal and half-formed weapons. She stepped away and up to the map, looking at the layout of the city she had spent her afternoon in. Ascella was printed at the top of the crinkled map, and the paper was fading with the age.

This place was real.

The entire day had felt like a dream, weaving in and out of the pain she felt surrounding her old life, and the way Matthias had taken her to the roof of a restaurant just to treat her to his court.

"Morana?" She turned to see Matthias holding two weapons in his hands. Reese was nowhere to be found. "We should head to the palace." His brows furrowed.

"Ascella," she said. "That's the city we are in, isn't it?"

"It's the capital. There's more than just this city in the Court of Shadows. This is where the palace is. Four other cities are spread across the court, ruled by the lords."

"Lords?" She glanced back to the map, trying to imagine what the rest of the cities looked like. "Does it look like your home in the land of the gods?" she asked.

"Similar enough," he answered. "We really need to go. I want you to train with these as soon as possible."

Nodding, Morana turned and took a step forward, standing just in front of Matthias. He leaned toward her, minty breath mingling with her own, before a gentle hand gripped her shoulder. In a blink, she was whisked out of the shop, thrust into the throne room of a different palace, one similar to the isolated one that had provided her refuge.

The obsidian floors glistened in the light of the grandiose chandeliers hanging above them. The sides of the throne room were lined with gold embellished columns. Atop the columns sat various carvings, all symbols of death. She looked at the crows, skulls, and moths that matched the tattoos inked across Matthias's skin.

Morana turned from staring at the throne atop a dark dais. She glanced at the tattoos peeking from beneath Matthias's rolled sleeves. Her gaze met his and her hand tightened on the weapons they had retrieved from Reese.

"Good to see you," a gravelly voice came from behind them. A man wearing a cloak over leathers entered the throne room. The lights from above illuminated his dark skin and cropped hair. Pointed ears gave him away as fae, and his piercing amber eyes hinted to the lethalness contained in his built frame. That and the many weapons strapped to his body.

"Garian," Matthias spoke, turning to greet the man that had entered the throne room.

Those amber eyes turned to Morana, taking in the woman standing in the throne room with Death. Morana shifted uncomfortably before lifting her chin, feigning confidence in the presence of a stranger. His hulking presence sent unease racing through her veins.

"The girl?" he asked, jaw tight. Garian's gaze lingered, observing her features with indifference.

"The girl," Matthias confirmed. "Where is Hames?" Matthias asked.

"Gone. He returned to Vulcan after he escorted the boy from the wreckage. You know how his city is, littered with mountain creatures," he spat in disgust. "He can never leave for too long."

Garian turned to Morana, acknowledging her presence once more, though he didn't speak.

"You knew about me?" she asked, suspicion woven into her tone.

Garian nodded at the sword and dagger Matthias still held at his side. "I'm the one that will need to train you with those," Garian confirmed. "Though I wonder why Matthias has insisted on me teaching defense to someone he ripped out of the human realm." Garian turned to her, challenge in his gaze.

Her mouth hung open; voice caught in her throat. She wasn't sure what to say, what to reveal to the man standing before her.

"He knows you can wield the shadows," Matthias answered. "Garian is the lord over Nashira, a city to the south of Ascella."

"Have you told the other lords about her?" Garian asked, eyes assessing Morana before returning to the god in the room.

"No," Matthias answered. His shoulder brushed hers, flexing beneath his shirt. She could see the tension through his shoulders at Garian's remark. Something about it comforted her—it felt protective. They began walking away from the throne to the two large doors stationed at the other end of the room.

"I will warn you then," Garian started, but laughter cut him off, trailing in from the doors that opened ahead.

A younger man walked in, sandy blonde curls atop his head, blue eyes glittering with amusement. He walked casually through the room, confident and easy. Something about his presence was more welcoming.

"Ronan," Garian finished.

Ronan stopped, gaze catching Morana's before he stepped forward to greet Matthias. "So, he returns." The man stated, smiling widely.

"Ronan," Matthias spoke. "It's good to see you, though I wonder why you're still here."

"Just visiting," he responded. "Things were doing well in the city. I wanted to visit my mother."

"Ah," Matthias nodded. "And how is she?"

"The same," Ronan chuckled. "Old, crotchety, and still whipping me with a towel every time I show up at home without a wife." Ronan winked at Morana; his arms folded across his chest. He was tan, with crystal blue eyes and bright white teeth, adding to his allure. Morana blushed.

Matthias glanced in her direction, a crease forming on his brow. "A nice *fae* wife to help you lord over

Adhara. I can't say I disagree with that." Matthias shifted uncomfortably.

Garian stood stoically next to them, though Morana swore she saw an irritated expression flash over his features.

"Garian is going to train this one," Matthias informed.

"Ah, a mystery woman." Ronan stepped forward and gently grabbed Morana's hand. Bowing low, he placed a gentle kiss on her skin. She cleared her throat, noticing the subtle shadows swirling around Matthias. His fists clenched. "Tell me," Ronan began, "what is your name, darling?"

"Morana," she responded. "And you're Ronan, I've gathered. Another lord?" she asked.

"A lord indeed," he answered, bright smile and genuine joy radiating from him. "Though I would never flaunt my status around a beautiful woman." He winked again.

"That's a lie." Garian's gruff voice broke the silence as Morana's head swung in his direction. He was taller than Ronan—broader and more intimidating.

"Garian and I are old friends," Ronan confessed, patting the man that appeared more of a warrior than a lord on the back.

"Also a lie," Garian grunted.

"I would never tell a lie." A dimple appeared on his cheek, adding to the innocence of his expression. "How would a liar honor his mother and find a wife?"

"He wouldn't," Garian chimed in again. "He would continue lying and sleep with every woman in Ascella."

Ronan grunted, stepping back from the warrior.

"Nothing wrong with sleeping around," Morana smiled, trying to ease the tension between the two lords— the tension that was beginning to feel one-sided. "Just make sure you get yourself checked." She glanced just below his belt before returning to Ronan's gaze. "Right?" she asked.

Matthias laughed under his breath, encouraging her to walk ahead of him out the doors as he handed her sword to Garian. He leaned in, his breath sending shivers down her spine as he wrapped his arm around her shoulder, whispering as they walked through the doors. "Welcome to court," he breathed.

The palace differed from the one in the land of the gods. The obsidian floors were consistent throughout, lights glittering like stars above in the hallways. There were more people here too, fae walking through halls in elaborate clothes that made her realize why Matthias had suggested she wear a dress.

"Should you have your arm around me?" she asked, voice quiet.

"And leave you to him," he flicked his gaze back to Ronan, who was trailing them with Garian in tow. "Absolutely not."

"He's charming," Morana admitted, and Matthias's grip tightened around her shoulders. It was the truth.

There was a kindness about him, though his flirtations may have been a bit too much.

"That boy has charmed his way into the beds of many women." Matthias chuckled. "You, however, are taken."

She paused, glancing at him. Her heart was in her throat as her mind traced back to their conversation at lunch. She had opened up fully to him and he hadn't balked. Matthias's arm dropped away as they faced each other in the dim light of the hallway. What had he just said?

"Axton." He stared at her and licked his lips. "We are going to figure out what the Court of Light wants with him."

Her heart slowed as she realized her mistake. She didn't know why she had reacted so suddenly to the statement. Maybe it was the way she had let him in, lowering her walls willingly. The protectiveness and kindness made her want him more despite his claims that he didn't want to touch her again. Of course, she wasn't here to be with Matthias, and he had done nothing but listen and understand. The change in his demeanor was messing with her mind.

"I needed to speak with Hames," Matthias spoke, breaking her thoughts. "He was the lord that took Axton back to his apartment. He, however, is not here, and I should get you back." Matthias turned to Garian. "Send for Hames, would you? When he returns, I'd like to speak with him about the boy."

Garian nodded, a hand on the hilt of the sword he held—her sword.

"We will be back tomorrow." Matthias handed her the dagger, placing it firmly in her palm. "We will see you in the morning, in the training room. Bring the sword."

Matthias turned to her, touching her arm gently and readying her to leave the Court of Shadows. Without another word, they disappeared in a cloud of mist.

Fifteen

Morana's black cloak dragged across the stone floor of the castle hallway. A few servants moved past her, casting welcoming glances in her direction despite the weapon she now carried. She supposed she could have tucked the dagger under her cloak, but felt comforted by the weight in her palm.

Matthias had brought her back, encouraging her to take the weapon to her room, stating she should keep it close. She ran a thoughtful finger over the intricate hilt. He trusted her. Yet, a part of her wondered if he trusted her with the weapon because he knew they couldn't kill him.

It was strange how hospitable the staff had become in the land of the gods. They were there, a constant presence throughout the home, but after her first interactions with Willow, and the requests to be left alone, they hardly bothered her now. The only individual insistent enough to annoy her wasn't employed by Matthias at all.

Morana tugged on the metal handle, the wooden door creaking as warm light greeted her from her room.

Sarnai was sprawled across her bed, reading a book and making herself at home.

Speaking of the goddess.

Sarnai's brown eyes glittered in the light from the fireplace, catching on the dagger that Morana held in her hand. Sarnai closed the book, her painted fingers lingering over the leather. Morana gripped the weapons tighter. The metal became heavy, and she involuntarily tucked it beneath the cloak that still wrapped around her shoulders.

"I see he's treating you to fae weapons and finery," Sarnai remarked, closing the book in her hands.

"He wants me to be able to defend myself."

Sarnai stood up, golden dress twisting around her body as she strode forward. "Hmm," she mused, umber eyes narrowing as she circled Morana. "What is it about you that makes you worth defending?" she asked. She licked her lips as she assessed Morana, attempting to determine if she saw what Matthias saw. There was no malice to her tone, simply a testing curiosity—one that begged for an answer.

Morana tensed, grip tightening around the hilt in her hand. Shadows coated her skin like honey poured over a spoon. The heady sensation eased the anger slightly.

Sarnai stopped circling and sat down in the chair, waiting for a response. Morana let the image of what she wanted to unfold in her mind. If Sarnai couldn't already see what made her worth defending, she would give her something to look at. Matthias had taught her enough for this trick. Morana smirked before being thrust to the other side of the room, her power coursing through her blood. Standing casually, she leaned against the wall near the fireplace, refusing to glance at the seated goddess in the chair.

"Not entirely sure," she answered finally, amusement woven in her voice.

"You're certainly not mortal." Sarnai's face fell, her brown skin glowing in the firelight. Her eyes were now trained on Morana standing by the hearth, one eyebrow raised. "And he's been training you well."

"I am mortal." Morana finally looked at her, straightening her stance.

There was no response. Sarnai got up from the chair and glided toward the door. It wasn't until her hand met the knob that she cast a glance over her shoulder. A knowing smile played on her lips. "Enjoy your night." She smiled. "I look forward to breakfast."

And then the goddess was gone.

Morana shook her head, dropping the dagger on the cushioned chair where Sarnai had been sitting. The delicate embroidery shone a brighter gold, as if Sarnai's presence brought new life to the thread.

Stripping off her cloak and dress, Morana pulled on comfortable leggings and a sweatshirt that was on the floor from earlier. She fell into the comfort of the bed, and allowed herself a moment to rest, dreaming of the Fae and the sunroom atop the restaurant where she truly bared her soul for the first time in her life.

The palace was made of glass. There were no intricately carved designs on dark wood, no strange dining rooms where Morana was forced to engage in cryptic conversations about the powers she possessed. There were only beautiful flowers decorating the gilded space, while golden light shone from every window in the room.

"It's beautiful, isn't it?" a honeyed voice drifted across the glass. There was a musical quality to the tone.

Morana turned, meeting rose-colored eyes belonging to the stunning figure of a woman seated on a white sofa.

"Where am I?" she asked, her mind foggy in the haze of light. It was always like this in her dreams.

"Does it matter?" The woman stood up from her seat. Her white hair was flowing freely to her waist, sharp features contrasting with the softly flowing dress she adorned herself with. Her head snapped to someone standing on the other side of the room. Morana's eyes locked with a familiar green gaze. The man with dark skin stood waiting for instructions with his back rigid. His presence pulled on some forgotten memory. He was difficult to place in this state, but she could remember a dark alleyway, a dumpster, and a gun. "Fetch us some tea," the woman commanded, moving a cushioned chair across from the small table before the white couch. *"Please, sit down."*

Mind still veiled, Morana sat, trying to place the man she had just witnessed. The woman returned to the couch as delicate teacups were placed in front of them. They were white, purple flowers painted on the surface. It pulled at some memory just out of reach.

"Sugar?" she asked, smiling at Morana.

"Sure."

"How is Death treating you?" the woman questioned. Morana's heart picked up in pace, but there was less fear to be felt here. It was as if the strange palace of golden light and winding plant life dampened all her senses.

"He has been kind," she answered honestly, thinking back to the words spoken over her atop the restaurant. How long had it been since she had been in the fae realm?

The woman hummed, raising the cup of steaming tea to her soft pink lips. *"Strange, since just a number of weeks ago, Matthias was trying to kill you."*

Morana shifted uncomfortably in her seat. *"What do you mean?"* She recalled a time when she had been running through a warehouse, desperately trying to flee the madman that had lured her from the coffee shop, but Matthias hadn't actually been trying to kill her.

"Ashford, of course." Rose-colored eyes pinned Morana, scaling her features to measure the emotions that still were not coming easily.

"The gun club?" she inquired, a shiver working its way through the haze. Her palms were sweating at the memory, the fear slowly breaking through to greet her. "How do you know about what happened there?"

"Don't be a fool," the woman scolded. "You know the shadows can manipulate the mind. Who do you think placed the idea in that man's head to shoot you?" There was a bitter bite to her words, something that had teeth. They struck the flesh and held on, digging in until blood trailed from the wound.

Morana's brows furrowed as she fought to process what had been said. Matthias had tried to kill her? Her heart clenched in her chest. She trusted Matthias—didn't she?

The green-eyed man with fae ears stood stoic in the corner, avoiding her gaze. Light fluttered around him, trembling in the hazy air. It was trembling like a door Morana could almost see—almost.

"Matthias is using you, you stupid girl." All sweetness disappeared from her tone to reveal the bitterness of hatred that coated her careful words. "A queen of darkness is a threat to his power—his precious court."

Something about that phrase, the Queen of Darkness, split some of the haze that had settled over her. Morana's mind began to clear, remembering a phrase spoken in a room much like the one she sat in now. She glanced at the teacup and then at the golden light coming in from the window.

"I've heard that before," Morana whispered. "I've been called the Queen of Darkness before. Where have I heard that?"

The woman blinked.

Morana's eyes snapped to the man. He had been the one to call her that. He had been the one to invade her dreams. It started coming back. She should block this woman out—but curiosity broke through the fear.

"Who are you?" Morana asked through clenched teeth.

A wicked smile pulled at the woman's lips. "Dear child, I am the Queen of Light—the goddess of life."

Morana tensed. The woman before her was Inara, the one who had sent the assassin. She was right in front of her, making claims about Death and his involvement in what had happened. This woman. She was in Morana's mind.

"Get out."

Inara flinched at the authority in Morana's tone. It was brief, but it was there. She hadn't expected to be challenged. "Ask him to take you to the hall of relics." Her voice was casual. "Use the Basar to see what Death was up to the night before you were almost shot."

Morana started constructing the fortress, slowly blocking the woman from her mind. The ground trembled below her feet as she worked quickly.

Right before she shut Inara out completely, she heard her speak. "I look forward to seeing you at Mabon, Queen of Darkness."

"Miss Morana!" Willow shouted as Morana sat up in bed. Sweat was trailing down her temples, deep scratches running up her arms that were exposed where the sleeves of her sweatshirt were rolled. They stung.

Willow's blue eyes were wild as she let her grip drop away from Morana's arm. The woman was frantic. "Are you alright?" she asked.

"I'm fine," Morana answered. "I'm—" She glanced away, folding her arms over her chest. Inara had been in her dreams with the assassin.

Queen of Darkness

"Willow," Morana began. "Has Matthias ever spoken of taking a queen or of a queen threatening his power?"

Willow's eyes widened. She stood up, smoothing down the front of her dress.

"I don't even know if the gods do that," Morana added.

"Well, it's nothing I've heard about," Willow answered. Her hands were still pressing into her dress as if she were avoiding something. "Though I believe there was a time when Inara had almost taken a king." Willow gave a quizzical look. "Did something happen with Matthias?" she asked. It was a loaded question, one that Morana ignored.

"What happened to the man?" Morana asked. Her brows stitched together, deep curiosity burning her chest. "The one that Inara almost took as king."

"She never did," Willow answered. "The man died before they were wed. He was said to be a powerful fae. Not equal to a god, of course." Willow cleared her throat. "You can read the story in the libraries. Matthias has detailed histories there."

Morana nodded, thinking back to the library she had visited that first day. There had been a woman at the desk, and other fae working throughout. She supposed they could help her find what she was looking for.

Willow made her way to the door, indecision weighing heavily on her delicate features. Morana could tell that the fae was struggling with leaving her alone. "Goodnight, Morana," she whispered, before exiting to the hallway beyond.

Shadows danced in the corner of the room as Morana pulled the blankets tightly over her body. She could have sworn she saw dark eyes peering from the darkness. She shook off the feeling of being watched, fully believing that if Matthias were here, he would have been the one to wake her up. Not Willow.

She traced over what Inara had spoken, the way she had accused Matthias of trying to kill her. It wasn't impossible, but he had weapons forged for her, taken her to dine above the city of Ascella. She didn't fear Death. But then again, something about what Inara said struck a chord.

Morana closed her eyes, shifting as she held a wall in her mind, keeping the demons at bay, and when the darkness found her, sweet relief found her as well.

Sixteen

There were firm, black mats on the floor of the palace training room. The shiny surface glared under the harsh lighting of the room, intimidating Morana, who stood in the flexible black pants and cream tunic. Matthias had brought the items for her to wear earlier this morning, demanding she hurry.

She barely had the tunic over her head before he materialized her here in the palace in Ascella, leaving her with the fae warrior that now stood on the mat. A grim expression etched into his brow.

She swallowed.

"So," she started, gripping the hilt of the sword firmly. "Do we just start swinging?" It was uncomfortable, especially after such a brief introduction to the fae. They hardly knew each other, but Matthias had planned on Garian training her for a while. He had known when she had shown up at the palace for the first time. Even so, he hadn't said a word since Matthias walked out. How long had it been? Five minutes?

It felt like an eternity.

Garian sighed. He was wearing fighting leathers, his own sword sheathed at his side. He looked every bit a fae warrior from the way his huge frame moved to the muscles flexing with each motion.

"Do *not* just start swinging," he ground out, full lips cast downward in a permanent frown.

"Well," Morana began, irritation making a dramatic appearance. "You *are* supposed to train me." She raised a brow, swinging the sword up, so the blade sat directly in front of her face. It was heavier than she expected, and she nearly lost control of the weapon.

She could have sworn he almost smirked. "You look ridiculous," Garian sighed. "I suppose we will start with how you are standing."

"What's wrong with how I'm standing?" Morana allowed the blade to turn, placing the tip on the floor, and leaning on it casually with her legs crossed. Her weight pushed the sword into the mat, a ripping sound causing her to flinch, losing the confident air she had tried to portray.

Garian's frown deepened—something she could have sworn was impossible.

"Fine," she huffed in defeat. "How should I stand?"

Garian walked over to her, grabbing the sword from her hand and tossing it away. It landed on the mat with a loud smack.

"Eyes here," he barked. She looked up at him, his frown still sinking lower. She cringed.

"Your left foot is the leading foot, so it is the front foot." He gestured to her leg, and she moved it forward, planting herself firmly on the ground. Garian revealed nothing about her performance. "Right, your hips should face your opponent, your right foot toward the back."

She attempted to move her hips, straightening them towards the fae man. He moved, and she shifted slightly as he stood beside her, her body now twisted at an unnatural angle.

"What are you doing?" he scowled.

"You're my opponent." She had her hands on her hips. "I'm trying to make my hips face you, but you're moving."

His glare made the silence seem worse. She winced, knowing this wasn't going well.

"Forward," he grunted. "Face your hips forward." He grabbed her waist firmly, moving the way she was standing until her weight was evenly distributed. He let go, glancing at his hands as if she had burned him. Great. Another man who didn't want to touch her.

Walking over to pick up the sword, Garian muttered something under his breath.

"I can hear you; you know!" She focused on keeping her feet in the same place, not moving from the way he positioned her. She didn't want to fuck this up, didn't want it to take longer than it had to.

Garian handed her the hilt of the sword, directing her to hold it at shoulder level. The weight was awkward, but she did her best to follow his council.

He stood back, observing her carefully before speaking. "Now, bring the sword forward. This will help you with any kind of counterattack." She did as he said, and he nodded his agreement. It was at least something. "Make sure you step a bit to the right, out of the line of your opponent, bringing the sword down straight."

She acted it out to the best of her ability. After she completed the movement, she stared at Garian.

His finger and thumb were resting on his chin, a crease cut across his forehead. What was he thinking?

"Good," he spoke finally. "Again."

Morana whimpered. It was going to be a long day.

Cool water washed down the burning in her throat, replacing what she had lost because of the sweat skating down her back, down her neck—everywhere. She was sore, the weight of the sword growing heavier with each drill Garian put her through. There were no gentle encouragements from the fae man, only harsh commands. Morana didn't mind. The physical exertion eased some of her worries and Garian didn't require conversation. She relished in his silence—the way he only spoke when necessary.

He was standing off to the side, organizing a rack of weapons, when the doors opened. Morana didn't move from the table she was sitting on.

Ronan walked in, running his hands through his hair, a wide smile on his face. Morana was surprised when the second figure entered the room with him. Sarnai was dressed in orange today, dark brown hair pulled away from her face. She thought back to what Matthias and Garian said about Ronan and women, wondering if there was history there too.

Morana shifted on the table, the muscles in her back stiff from training. Ronan's eyes met hers after hearing the creaking noise of her movement. His shoulders were relaxed, a broad smile stretching across his face.

"I see you've been working hard." He was standing in front of her now. Sarnai moved to sit on the table as well, adjusting the flowing skirts of her dress.

"You're here?" Morana questioned, looking at Sarnai.

"Tending to the palace gardens," she answered.

"How is she doing, Garian?" Ronan shot over his shoulder.

The fae lord ran a hand down his face. His leathers were gone, leaving him in a t-shirt and pants. Morana flushed, already expecting his response. "She knows nothing about swords."

"Well then," Ronan began as he pulled his shirt over his head, lean muscle on display. He clearly wanted her to enjoy the view, but her mind continued to wander to the dark-haired god that had brought her here to begin with. She could smell the mint and shadows, imagine running her hands along the tattoos that decorated his arms, trailing her touch higher until she revealed what lie beneath the buttoned shirt he always wore. Her cheeks heated at the thought while Ronan's cocky smile remained as he walked to the rack, grabbing two wooden swords, and tossing one to Garian. "Go on then, if she has a lot to learn, let's give her something to learn." He turned, winking at Morana. She ignored it, barely refraining from rolling her eyes as she took another gulp of water. The curling in her stomach had nothing to do with the cocky lord, though she supposed it could have if she weren't so distracted.

"Lose the shirt," Ronan commanded, pointing to Garian with the wooden sword. "We want her to pay attention, don't we?"

"Gross," Morana muttered, staring at the cup in her hand, willing her thoughts to cooperate before Ronan was asking for her hand in marriage to appease his own mother as he thought her reddened cheeks were for him.

"Speak for yourself," Sarnai chimed in. "I love a good show." Leaning back, she stretched her arms behind her as she glanced at the now shirtless lords positioning themselves on the mat.

"Fine," Garian stated, twirling the wooden sword in hand. "But I hope you're ready to have your ass handed to you."

Ronan pulled the curly mop of hair into a bun atop his head. Morana could see sweat already gathering on his back as he circled his opponent. He struck first, eager to get started. Garian met him with a counterattack, prepared for whatever Ronan tried to throw his way.

Morana listened and watched as they sparred. Her eyes fixed on the lords of the Court of Shadows, seeking any movement she had learned today. Garian and Ronan were moving too quickly, their skill level clearly bounds ahead of where Morana was. She ran a hand down her face, wiping the sweat away.

"God, I love this court," Sarnai mused. "Matthias's lords don't really visit all that often. They're usually busy in their own cities doing whatever it is they do." Her hooded eyes tracked the men, admiring every flex of toned muscle and flash of bare skin.

"How often do they come here?" Morana asked. She had opened up to Matthias and was seeking pieces of his world. How close was he with the lords of his court?

"Only when something has to be discussed." She ran her tongue along her teeth. "Your arrival, for example." She tapped a finger on the wooden surface of the table. "Your," she paused, thinking of the right word, "male friend's abduction into the Court of Light." Her umber eyes met Morana's. "Ronan was filling me in."

Morana's stomach flipped at the mention of Axton, her jaw tensing as she kept from saying anything else. What would Sarnai think of her if she knew? She had abandoned Axton, and here she was thinking about Matthias, living in his home. She *should* feel guilty; be more concerned, but how well did Axton really know her to begin with? Morana could still taste the bitter coffee he had handed her the morning after she had slept with him. She hated black coffee.

Garian swept a leg out, ducking under the swipe of Ronan's sword. His foot met the blonde lord's leg, knocking him onto his back. Garian quickly placed his foot atop his chest and pointed his sword at the man's throat.

"I thought you were training *her*." Matthias's familiar voice rose from the corner of the room where he stood, tattoos on display from the rolled-up sleeves of his signature, pressed button-up.

"I am." Garian looked up, a flash of panic crossing his features as Ronan caught him with his guard down. The lord shot up, sword in hand, swinging at the man in front of him. The surprise served him well as he struck Garian in the ribs, eliciting a grunt from Morana's trainer.

"I'm learning by example," she threw out, smiling in Matthias's direction. She hated herself for it, but part of her was happy to see him. It had been a long day, and as her shoulders relaxed, she realized the way his powerful presence brought a sense of comfort. Just like the shadows, she was beginning to trust him. Matthias was teaching her to defend herself with magic and asking a lord to teach her to defend herself with weapons.

"You wouldn't be watching Ronan's sorry ass if you were learning by example." Matthias chuckled, striding closer to the table. His steps were measured, his hands in his pockets. "He's hardly seen battle."

"You've been around for a while," Morana started, hopping to the ground. She ignored the way her muscles tensed as her feet hit the floor. "You've probably seen a battle or two, so why don't you show me what you've got?" She cocked an eyebrow in challenge, loving the way his eyes glittered in the dim light of the training arena.

Garian laughed, his tone deep and the volume loud. It was the first time he had shown any emotion other than solid indifference or utter irritation in the hours they had been here. "You're hardly ready for that," he scoffed.

Morana shrugged. "You were hardly ready for Matthias to walk in the room. How do you think Ronan bested you?" She smirked before tilting her head in challenge. "You thought I wasn't paying attention."

Ronan pointed at her as he looked to Garian. "See, losing the shirt, man. What did I tell you?"

"Well, if the men are done," Sarnai interrupted, "I have places to be." The goddess disappeared; a cloud of gold mist left in her wake. Morana made a note to ask Matthias about what kind of power the other gods possessed. She had seen the way Sarnai could grow things, but the gold mist was new.

"I don't care," Morana looked back at Matthias. "Garian's shown me a few things, and I'll just wing the rest."

"You'll wing it?" Matthias was smiling, the stubble on his face shadowing his sharp jaw.

"I don't care how much I've shown you," Garian chimed in. "You're not using a real sword. You're clumsy, uncoordinated, and a real weapon in your hand would be dangerous." He walked forward, pressing the wooden sword into her palm. "Not in a good way."

Ronan chuckled, bringing his practice weapon to Matthias. "Good luck with that one," he chuckled.

Matthias started unbuttoning his shirt. "Fine," he sighed.

Morana's heart picked up as he revealed the tattoos across his chest. More crows were inked there, flying over a large moon over his pectoral. There was a dead tree tattooed on his rib cage, extending down beneath the waistline of his pants. "Must you really strip for this?" she asked, swallowing hard.

"I'm hardly dressed for sparing." Matthias's eyes glittered as he looked up through a stray strand of dark hair, undoing the last button on his shirt and shrugging it off. "Are you afraid you'll like it too much, Morana?" She looked up to meet his gaze, realizing she had been caught staring at his movements. One side of his mouth quirked up. It infuriated her, reminding her of all the things he had said to her, the ways he had rejected her.

"Don't flatter yourself," she ground out, repeating what he had once said while viewing her naked in a bathing room. She didn't care to admit she had been picturing the solid planes of his chest earlier.

Morana caught a familiar glint in his eye as he held the sword, adjusting his stance. She matched him, move for move, preparing to spar with a god. Her heart pounded fiercely in her chest, her mind tracing over all the moves she had learned. There was no way she was going to let him knock her on her ass. He would never let her live it down. She rolled her shoulders, begging the soreness to hold off, hoping that she would be able to at least hold her own.

Morana swung first, stepping forward and moving to the right, placing her weight on her right foot. Her hips were facing Matthias, straight forward, as Garian had taught her. The wood of her practice sword met his as he blocked her from bringing the sword down on his shoulder.

Matthias chuckled, dark humor weaving with the sound. Her blood was boiling, angry at the way he was making fun of her, mocking her. When he started swinging, Morana focused on blocking every blow, keeping him at bay. She was clearly overpowered, barely keeping up with every change in direction from his sword. Still, she persisted, slashing in any way that felt natural since all her training had gone out the window as she felt it out.

Matthias nicked her arm, but she ignored it, pushing forward, trying to catch him by surprise. He was ready for every move she had. If she were going to win, she couldn't fight fair. The shadows twisted over her skin, begging to be wielded. The power guided her; dark secrets whispered in the confines of her mind. An idea surfaced— conjured by the darkness. She knew how to succeed.

Channeling her power, Morana disappeared from sight and reappeared behind Matthias in the same way he had done to her so many times before. Forgetting the sword, she swung her leg out in the same way she had watched Garian when he was sparring with Ronan. Matthias fell back, caught by surprise.

He was on his back when she reappeared in front of him, using the shadows to her advantage. She could have sworn she saw a touch of his power snaking from his skin, begging to meet her own. Unrelenting, she stepped over him, straddling his torso while she pressed the tip of the wooden sword to his neck.

Matthias was smiling, but his face fell as he took in the shadows, flicking across her flesh. Dark shadows appeared along his arms, rising with the rapid movement of his chest. His head whipped in the direction of two lords standing in the room, watching the exchange. Discomfort replaced his previously delighted expression Matthias had worn a moment earlier.

Morana looked at the lords. Ronan's eyes were wide, his mouth hanging open in surprise. She had almost forgotten what Matthias had told Garian before. They didn't know why she was there, or what power she possessed.

"The human wields shadows." Ronan's voice broke the painful silence. His brows were knit together. "She wields shadows, and she's not from our court."

"You were supposed to fight fair," Matthias spoke in a low voice. A rumble of anger came from his chest, but there was no going back. They had seen her. It didn't matter.

"If I were in any real danger, do you think fighting fair would help me survive?" She knew she had a point as she glared at the death god laying beneath her. He didn't answer right away.

"I didn't use the shadows," he gritted out.

"And I thank you for that." Morana tossed the sword across the mats, extending a hand to help Matthias to his feet, though she knew he didn't need it.

Something hissed through the air, cutting along her cheek. The sharp sting and feel of blood struck her but quickly vanished when adrenaline pumped its way through her veins. Her heart stuttered as she turned to see a woman dressed in black charging at her, dagger in hand.

Morana brought her hand up to her face, pulling it away to see crimson liquid staining her fingers. The cut across her cheek sent her mind racing. She could see Inara seated across from her, hear the bitterness that had replaced her sweet tone. Matthias had said something about the Court of Light being able to track her magic when she wasn't in the land of the gods. The color drained from her face, blood now dripping down her cheek, staining her shirt. No wonder Matthias had been so upset. Her magic had led them right to her.

Matthias was on his feet in an instant, covering distance quickly by shadowing to retrieve a sword and standing between Morana and the strange woman. The assassin's features were twisted in determination. The hood of her cloak had fallen to reveal pointed fae ears and black hair that hung low around her waist, tied in a ponytail at her back.

Garian's blade came down, only to be met by a solid glittering golden thread that appeared in the air. The room smelled like magic as the woman battled with an artificial sword, meeting Garian stroke for stroke.

Her eyes flicked to Morana, and Morana realized what was happening. This was another assassination attempt, and where the Court of Shadows wielded the same darkness she carried within her, the Court of Light held a different power, one this woman was using to battle the lords surrounding.

Panting, Morana ran to the table, grabbing the dagger she had borrowed from Reese. They had focused on the sword today, but there was no way she stood an actual chance against the assassin. Morana held the knife blade out in front of her, squaring her hips in anticipation.

The light whipped out from the assassin's figure as Matthias fought to meet the attacks. She was holding off both men while Ronan snuck up behind her. She struck him in the arm with whatever magic she possessed, unfazed by the man's movement.

Ronan hissed as he fell to the ground, clutching his arm where a dark burn seared his flesh. Morana cringed at the sight.

The light grew in size, becoming more powerful with every passing second. Her black boots struck the floor as she made one last push of power, knocking

Matthias and Garian out of the way just enough to charge at the human in the room.

Morana braced herself as the woman lunged. She counted in her head from three, waiting until the woman was close. When she was so close Morana could feel the heat of the women's power, Morana shadowed. She appeared behind her and recklessly drove the dagger through her back.

The assassin clutched the front of her stomach where the tip of Morana's knife had punctured through. Blood spurted from the wound, and Morana fought the urge to vomit all over the mats that were now under her feet.

The woman fell forward, and Morana yanked at the knife, driving it out of her body. The woman crumpled to bleed out on the training room floor.

She hardened her gaze, turning back to see Garian panting, a sword in hand. Morana was breathing hard, too—the muscles in her back burning like fire ignited and exploding across a night sky.

"Well," Garian began. He swallowed deeply. "That's one way to learn," he finished.

Morana dropped the dagger to the floor, keeping her emotions at bay. This wasn't an act rooted in skill. She had been panicked and relying on the shadows to do most of the work. Her stomach roiled at the thought of how close she had come to dying. "I suppose so," she answered, just before curling over and allowing the contents of her stomach to spill across the floor.

Seventeen

Morana sat on the table of the training room as a woman entered from the large doors. Her brown hair was curly and short, cut just below her jawline. Morana glanced at the woman wearing the simple dress, carrying a case with bandages.

"Sit," Matthias growled. He stood in front of her, hands resting on either side of her, boxing her in. She didn't know why he was being so bossy. She was the one with the injury. Not to mention the one who saved the day.

The woman dropped the case as Matthias stepped aside, a deep scowl on his face. The woman's icy hands cupped Morana's chin as she tilted it to the side, observing the dried blood across her cheek, just over the bone.

"Well, it wasn't poisoned," she observed, releasing Morana's chin in a rough movement. Morana brought her hand up to the wound that now stung. While everything was happening, she had hardly noticed it, but now that Ronan and Garian were off, sending for the other lords, the wound had a bite to it.

Morana glanced at her fingers, stained pink. A cold pad hit her cheek, wiping away the blood and bacteria. The sharpness had Morana tensing as the woman disinfected the wound.

"Can't you just heal it?" She looked at Matthias, who was standing and observing her with intense focus.

"She needed to check for poison first. That woman was from the Court of Light, and I still can't figure out what the fuck Inara wants with you." He crossed his arms. "If it isn't cleaned, it would risk healing the wound over any poison, allowing it to fester."

Morana glared at him. "And you took that risk with my shoulder?" she spat.

Matthias shrugged one shoulder, a faint smirk appearing on his lips.

The woman's cold finger met her flesh, slowly working as the pain dulled.

"Wait," Morana grabbed the woman's wrist. A frustrated scowl crossed the woman's face as she halted her healing. "Don't heal it all the way."

The woman looked at Matthias. He didn't react.

"I want to remember," Morana spoke, eyes bright with fire. There was something to be said about being left with the scar of what had happened. She wanted to remember why she was here. She wanted to see it when she woke up in the morning, remind herself of the demons chasing her. Most of all, as she thought about the attack, she wanted to remember that despite the shaking that wouldn't work its way out of her hands, despite the fear that challenged her bravery, she wanted to remember that she could kill—if she needed to.

The woman nodded—brown eyes bright. She worked to heal the wound, stopping just before the pain fully subsided. She wiped her hands on a damp cloth and packed up the case she had brought with her.

Morana hopped off the table, touching the raised flesh on her cheek and looking to Matthias. He had said nothing about her request, but his dark gaze fixed on the scar now decorating her flesh.

"Still beautiful," he whispered. It was so low that she almost didn't hear it. A crease formed on her brow before he grabbed her hand.

There was a shout from the hall outside of the training room. She didn't recognize the voice, but they were demanding Matthias's presence, his hand still wrapped around her own. He gave it a gentle squeeze.

The comforting presence of his magic wrapped around her before they were swept away, reappearing in the empty throne room of the palace.

"Why are we here?" Morana asked.

"Privacy."

"Isn't the throne room the first place they'd look?" She smirked.

"I only use it for official business. Mostly when I'm trying to intimidate." There was a wicked delight in the way he said it.

Morana huffed a laugh, striding over to the throne. Her pants were still coated in blood, but she didn't care as she threw her ass on his chair atop the dais. She threw her legs over the arm of the intricately decorated chair, and Matthias followed each of her movements with a dark intent.

"Not all that comfortable," she goaded, her gray eyes meeting his.

"Did the healer get everything?" he asked, voice thick with something that made her body warm as he surveyed her. Heat washed over her. That same feeling returned, the one that she had been fighting.

I'm not here to take your freedom, Ana.

She turned, sitting forward on his throne. "I'm fine," she choked out, hardly able to breathe.

Matthias stepped forward, boots softly clicking on the surface of the steps leading up to the throne. He moved until he was directly in front of her before kneeling at her feet. His closeness sent shivers up her spine.

"Morana," he placed his hands on her knees. His touch burned her with a desire she could hardly contain. "You just took a life. Some wounds run deeper than the flesh." Something softened in his features. "Now tell me, what other scars have you earned?" He moved his hand up, placing it on the left side of her chest. "The ones that reside here."

She took a shuddering breath, unable to wrap her mind around what he was saying. She knew it was something important—profound, but all she could focus on were his full lips and the way he was staring at her. The way he looked like he wanted to consume her.

He licked his lips, looking at her neck where her pulse fluttered. Her chest was rising and falling with the force of a wild storm, and she knew he could feel it beneath where his hand still rested, just over her heart.

Matthias was kneeling between her knees, kneeling before her as she sat on the throne of *his* kingdom. It felt powerful, heady.

"Tell me," he asked, moving his hands to rest on her thighs. He slid them up slowly, stopping midway. Her eyes fluttered. "Do you like sitting on that throne while I kneel at your feet?" One hand moved upward, sending sparks across her skin, igniting despite the barrier that separated them. He squeezed gently, and she let out a soft whimper.

"What would Axton think?" He was slowly circling his thumb on the inside of her thigh, distracting her from thinking about anything but the god in front of her.

"He probably already thinks the worst." She admitted. "He's gone." She would hate herself later, but for now, she would break the tension. "If I don't think about it, then it isn't real."

"That's no way to live," Matthias whispered, bringing a thumb to her face to trace her lips. She fought the moan that threatened to break free. He smiled—eyes still dark with desire.

"It's the way I'm living now." She leaned forward. Pausing just before her lips met his. Morana looked down, waiting for him to draw back, but he didn't. He looked into her eyes, waiting for confirmation, and she nodded, remembering the way he had defended her and the way she had let him see the things that haunted her and the guilt that she carried. He had still chosen to protect her despite the way she had abandoned her father.

His lips met hers, tasting of rain and secrets. She gave in to the sensation, allowing him to pull her under. Matthias rose, bringing his hands to tangle in her hair. He kissed her like a starved man, groaning as she shifted forward on the throne.

A harsh breath left her when he bit her lip, and she brought her hands up, moving them beneath his shirt to feel the planes of his chest. She traced her shaking fingers over where she memorized the tattoos decorating his flesh.

Morana moved to stand, but he pushed her back down. "No," he breathed. "I actually like you sitting there."

She moaned again, pressing her mouth to his before a thought entered her mind. Intruding and insistent, it caused her to draw back.

Queen of Darkness

Matthias noticed her pause, pulling back and gazing into her eyes, his hand still twinned in her hair

Matthias is using you, you stupid girl.

Her breathing was still rapid, lust and desire replaced with subtle panic as she took in the death god. He looked confused, almost like he didn't understand her pause.

Use the Basar to see what Death was up to the night before you were almost shot.

"Tell me, Matthias," she whispered, face still close. She pushed the panic down, burying it in the familiar grave that housed her innermost thoughts. She had started to trust him, but what were his motives in all this? He was training her, bringing her to court, protecting her from assassins. What game was the god of death actually playing? "Were you the one trying to kill me at Ashford?" She drew back, trying to gauge his reaction. Trying to decide if this was a mistake.

A sharp cold replaced the fire that had sparked between them. It was dead as winter, icy and full of truth. Anger and betrayal wrapped around her heart, choking out everything she knew.

"I knew you wouldn't die," he finally spoke, eyes hardened.

Not knowing how to react, the storm built behind her eyes. There was some truth to what Inara stated—the truth in the words she had spoken. There was no denying that the assassin held the power of the Court of Light. It was familiar, the same power she witnessed in Axton's apartment.

Even so, Matthias had tried to kill her. He told her the shadows manipulated the mind. Morton died because of him.

She shoved him off, putting the fullness of her strength into the push. He stumbled back, surprised by her movement.

Her room in the land of the gods appeared clear in her mind, sailing on the shadows that sat dormant in her blood.

In an instant, she was gone, slamming the door. There was nowhere else to go, nowhere else she could escape to.

"Wait." Matthias was in the corner, and she flinched, backing up until her back met the wooden door to the bathroom.

"Of course," she hissed, her body shaking with fear and fury.

"Let me show you," he spoke, stepping forward. "Go into my mind."

"Now isn't time for one of your ridiculous lessons, Matthias. What do you want with me?"

"Let me show you." His tone was sharp, commanding, slicing the air with the dominance of a god. She flinched again, pressing her back into the door. "Please."

Her eyes met his, wanting to believe him, wanting to know the truth.

"How?" she asked. She hadn't done this yet, hadn't attempted to use the shadows to thrust herself into someone's mind. But she wanted to see, to find some lie in the truth that was shaking her to her core. She had trusted him.

"Focus on me," his voice was low as he took another step forward.

"That's close enough." Her spine rigid as she held a hand to ward him off. Shadows twisted between her fingers to provide the comfort of her power. She wasn't helpless in the face of Death.

"Focus on me, allow the shadows to carry you."

She closed her eyes, reaching her power toward him, begging it to work. In an instant, she was standing in the void of what was now open to her, staring into the innermost thoughts of Death.

She was standing in the woods, watching the range at Ashford, watching herself through the eyes of Death, feeling his emotions, hearing his thoughts.

He observed her carefully, keeping to the shadows. Morana stood, a gun in hand, her cut-off shorts hanging loose from her body. This had to have been a few weeks before the incident at Ashford.

Morana had her fingers on the trigger, aiming at a target yards away from where she stood. The morning air was crisp, and she shifted uncomfortably—no—Matthias shifted uncomfortably as he trailed his gaze across her body. She could feel the heat there, knew what he was thinking about her.

That was when she saw it, the shadows twisting and the familiar call of power. It darkened over her flesh, coating her skin with something she hadn't realized she had.

Matthias watched. This wasn't the first time he had seen this, observed the power that she held.

His gaze flicked to the gravel pathway. Axton was standing there, brows furrowed, and arms folded across his chest. He didn't move, didn't make a noise. She hadn't realized he was there when she thought back to her own memory of this moment.

Light flickered in the distance, just next to where Axton stood. Death tensed, nerves coursing through his veins. Axton turned and left—undetected—just before Morana turned to put the gun away.

She was thrust once more into a different memory.

Jumping from a balcony that sat over a glistened street. In that moment, she became Matthias—Death.

Death had one more place to visit before the night was up. This time, he wasn't instilling the desire for blood into anyone. He merely had to check on the blonde for the last time. This time, the draw of the shadows wouldn't fail him.

He had been watching the woman for weeks, feeling the familiarity of power surrounding her. It intrigued him, and he needed to know who she was—what she was. The man he had picked would surely complete the job, and when he did, the blonde would meet Death once and for all.

Then he would know. The fear would send her spiraling. The shadows would work on their own, calling her somewhere else, healing her wound, and proving what he had feared all along. She was more like fae than human.

She blinked, staring at Matthias in front of her. "You think I'm fae?" she asked. "My ears—"

"I don't know what you are." Matthias strode forward, standing close. He touched her chin gently, lifting it so she could look into those onyx eyes, marbled with dark shades of brown. "I know that I wouldn't kill you. I thought that was clear at this point."

She wanted to trust him, wanted to believe the words he spoke, the way he had kissed her in the throne room, and she supposed a part of her did. However, the seed of doubt remained. That trust would have to be repaired—the truth uncovered about Inara.

"This doesn't change things," she breathed, steeling her spine.

"That's fine." His tone was flat as he gently swept his thumb across her jaw. The movement sent a familiar heat throughout her body, one that she longed to fight. "I will continue to protect you, regardless."

She inhaled, a sharp breath moving between her parted lips. His eyes darkened, not with desire, but with something more sinister. She was suddenly reminded that Matthias was not only a king but also a god, a powerful one.

"What made you believe I was out to kill you?" he asked.

"Nothing," she replied. She wasn't willing to give up this secret, wasn't willing to tell him about Inara. The woman had planted doubt in her, and did she really have reason to doubt him? He had put her in a dangerous situation and sent a man to kill her, knowing she wouldn't die—assuming she wouldn't die.

Matthias also abandoned her in the flora realm, leaving her to her own devices—but not really. This wasn't new, and she realized she should have known that a god of death could never truly be safe.

She needed answers about what Inara had said, what the goddess had called her

The Queen of Darkness

Her only hope was the Mabon festival where the courts came together. If Matthias brought her there, she could meet with the goddess, figure out what she wanted.

She felt the scar that was now permanently etched into her skin. Would she be able to defend herself from the goddess? Garian hardly had time to train her, giving her one day with a sword.

"I'll leave you to your thoughts," Matthias whispered, his expression pained. "Just know, Morana, I don't regret a thing."

Whether he was talking about the kiss or the savage way he continued to test her powers, she didn't know. Matthias was gone, but she could feel herself building and reconstructing the walls that he had demolished. The pain of betrayal pounded in her head as she brought her fingers to the bridge of her nose, hoping to pinch away the unbearable headache.

There were so many contradictions in Death. Death was protective and gentle. It coaxed secrets from its prey. Was that what she was? *Prey.* He was still willing to teach her, to give her space. Did a monster train its prey to defend itself from the hunter? She had startled Matthias in the training room when she had wielded the shadows. The same ones that were now coating her arms. They had revealed the path to victory, but there were more secrets she needed to uncover—lies she needed to expose.

Eighteen

It had been a week. A week of practicing with the sword. Matthias brought Garian to the land of the gods, something she didn't realize was a possibility. In the end, he was trying to hold up his promise. Keeping her in the land of the gods was protecting her, but at what cost?

She had more time to focus, to sit with her emotions. More time to trust Matthias, but also time to run over every word Inara had spoken in that dream. It was driving her mad.

Matthias had heard nothing about Axton's whereabouts. Hames had left him at the apartment and returned to the Court of Shadows promptly after. She would have prayed to the gods that Axton was still alive but knowing the gods she was praying to made her realize one of them could be the reason he wasn't.

The only light in the darkness, the one thing that could give her the answers she needed was attending the Mabon festival and learning about Inara to the best of her ability while she was here. Being kept tightly packed away in the land of the gods didn't help the first option, so she made her way to the library. She didn't know what she was looking for, but something told her it was here among the many stacks and buzzing fae.

A fae woman was sitting behind the desk. She had glimpsed her before. She didn't look up from her book as Morana approached. The woman's golden eyes remained pinned to the story that consumed her.

"Excuse me," Morana began, fidgeting with her hands. "I was looking for a book."

"Most people are," the woman responded. There was no emotion in her tone. "You are, in fact, standing in a library."

Morana frowned, now tapping the desk in front of her. "Yes, in fact, you do seem to work here." The woman didn't bother to respond. "I want a book about Inara, the goddess of life. One that details her histories."

That got the woman's attention. She looked up, pulling her glasses up on the top of her head, brushing back strands of white hair. "Interesting," she mused. "First floor, the one below us, toward the back. There's a shelf with the *Histories of the Seelie*. That should give you what you're looking for, but I will admit, that tome is a bit temperamental."

Morana rubbed her temple. "I didn't realize there was another floor."

"Stairs to the right." She looked back down and returned to reading.

Morana rolled her eyes, turning to the right to look for the steps.

"My right." Annoyance coloring the fae's tone. Morana cursed under her breath, changing direction, and pulling her hair back as she found the stairs to the first floor.

The lower level of the library was different, older. She passed books with strange symbols and unfamiliar languages. Dust settled over the quiet space as she walked through crowded shelves and moved toward the back. When she got to the last shelf, Morana started scanning the spines, looking for the title.

Running her hands along the books, she froze when she spotted it. *Histories of the Seelie*—perfect.

She brought the large tome to the table, dropping the worn leather book on the wooden surface before sitting in the chair. She stretched her legs, stiff muscles aching when she moved.

Tracing the edges of the book, she moved to open it but was confused when it wouldn't budge. There were no locks or mechanisms keeping the book shut, and she figured something had made the pages stick together. If she just pulled hard enough, she could pry it open.

Every muscle in her body was sore, but she fought with the book, huffing as she tossed it back on the table.

"The book has to trust you." A young boy stood in the corner of the dark library, watching her intently.

"Books are not sentient beings." Morana tapped a finger on the cherry table. She leaned back in her chair, glancing at the boy. "Can I help you?"

"You took my spot," he smiled. "No worries, though. You're free to sit there." A curly strand of red hair fell in his face as he tilted his head—clearly intent on watching her struggle.

"That book wants to know what you will do with the knowledge you find." The boy smiled again, highlighting the freckles smattered across his face. "Maybe whisper the answer. See if you can convince it to change its mind."

Morana scoffed as the boy walked away. She spent the next twenty minutes trying to pry the book open, using the shadows to twist and creep between the pages, begging it to provide information about the goddess.

"I only want to know answers," she whispered, feeling somewhat insane for talking to a book. "To understand the things I've heard. I want to know why Inara sent assassins to kill me." She sighed, resting her head on her arm and giving in to the ridiculous charade at last. "I want to know who the fuck to trust."

The book snapped open, sending dust up her nose and into her eyes. She sputtered, hoping she wouldn't die from millennia-old dust inhalation. The boy was right. Not only was the book sentient, but it also had an attitude. A clock sounded in the distance, and Morana swung her towards the sound. It was late, too late, but she didn't mind. She needed to know, needed to understand the woman she was going to approach, the woman who had Axton in her clutches.

She skimmed the pages, finding a section about Inara. There was a faded sketch there, showing the goddess and her familiar rose-colored eyes glaring at a man she stood over, sword in hand, ready to attack.

The man looked fearful, dressed in full armor and cowering away from the goddess. Morana rubbed her eyes, trying to keep sleep at bay.

The text told the story of Lux, the god of light that existed prior to Inara's reign. Lux had been seated on the throne of the Court of Light for hundreds of years, during a time when it was known as the Seelie court. Morana ran a finger over the page as she took in the story of Inara rising to power. She was a woman living in the fae court with unlimited amounts of magic, something unheard of except for the gods.

As she grew, she became power-hungry, seducing Lux and eventually turning on him in a battle against the Unseelie court. She killed him with a sword, one designed to take down any enemy, even a god. There were no details on the origin of the sword, where it had come from, just that she had retrieved it, and used it in a ruthless act to seize power.

Morana closed the book.

"Did you find what you were looking for?" Morana jumped as Sarnai appeared from in between the shelves, looking at Morana with bright eyes. "*Histories of the Seelie*," she remarked. "That's a tricky book."

Sarnai sat at the table, a black dress clinging to her form, making her look every bit at one with Death's court.

"I was just reading." Morana slid the book away from the goddess and leaned back in her chair, arms folded. "Trying to learn about the court."

"I can see that." The webbing across Sarnai's forehead grew brighter. "The question is, why are you reading about the other court?"

"Just curious." Morana leaned forward, elbows on the table. "Tell me, Sarnai. You spend time in the Court of Light. It's my understanding that Matthias and Inara don't get along. How do you go back and forth between the two?" There was a bite to the words. After the truth came out with Matthias, Morana wondered if she was wrong to be relaxed in front of the goddess before her.

Sarnai laughed, low and heady. "I have my preferences, but my gifts lie with the things that grow from the soil." A vine wrapped around the surface of the table, the plant snaked down the leg of the table and over the floor until it reached the shelves behind them. "Inara is not to be messed with," Sarnai warned. "Matthias *will* protect you, Morana." Her eyes were intense.

"How do you know that? Matthias tried to kill me."

"Try as he might, you're still not dead." She smiled, a calculating expression forming on her features. "There's something within you, something that Inara may want. You learned for yourself how she craves power." Sarnai tapped a long fingernail on the wooden surface of the table. "We still know little about your powers, but you keep up with Matthias. That is enough for her to fear you." Sarnai traced the pad of her painted finger along the table. "She knows something of your power. Especially if she's tracking you."

"Do you think she is trying to kill me for that power?" Morana asked, her back tense. "Like Lux?"

"I don't know," the goddess admitted. Her features softened. "Matthias has me looking for Axton."

Morana's heart sped up, her mind instantly attentive to what the flora goddess had to say. "Have you seen him?"

"I haven't, but I've heard he's in the palace." Sarnai gave her a pitying look, taking her hand into her own. Morana let her, feeling the warmth seep through her skin. "You need to learn to trust him fully—trust someone, at least."

Morana didn't react, her mask having returned. She knew she had been a runner. Knew that Matthias's admittance of his attempt to kill her, regardless of what he thought would happen, was a perfect excuse to draw distance. She had confessed her innermost thoughts, allowing him to go deeper than she had let Axton by letting him fish through the memory of her walking out on her father. She had given into him in the throne room, and the passion of it scared her.

The realization that she had given up on Axton entirely hit her in the chest and robbed her of breath. Panic bloomed from the impact while guilt collided with it to give it teeth. How could she after he had attempted to save her from the first assassin Inara sent while she was still in the human realm?

Morana drew her hand back, running it through her unruly blonde hair. She would deal with this later, in private and away from the knowing umber eyes looking at her with pity. Preferably after a bath. She hadn't changed after training, and it was getting late.

"If he's at the palace, do you think he'd be at Mabon?" Morana asked.

"Possibly."

"I just don't understand what they want from him," Morana whispered. "If they're using him to get close to me, that hardly makes sense. We were together for all but a day."

"A day is something," Sarnai responded.

The guilt stung at the corners of her eyes. She looked at the goddess, gaze intense. "Is it?" she asked, thinking back to the way Matthias's lips felt on hers, how his presence washed the memory of anyone else from her skin.

She needed to go to the Court of Light. Needed to attend the festival. She supposed she could trust Matthias for now if it meant he would tell her yes.

Nineteen

"Your weapons arrived today." Matthias looked at her from over his cup, the moth tattoo shifting with the movement. The dining room was quiet, and the lingering exhaustion settled into her bones. It was nearly morning by the time Morana returned to her room after her late night in the library with Sarnai. Her head barely hit the pillow before it seemed like she was up, shoving her tired limbs into a new training outfit. She wasn't ready to wake, but training didn't wait, especially not now.

"Can you repeat that?" she asked, resting her head on her hand.

"Your weapons arrived today," he spoke, voice deep and gravely. "Reese is waiting in the grand hall to explain how they work." He set his cup down. "When we are done—"

Morana stood up abruptly, the tired fog leaving her mind at the mention of the new weapons. The new sword and dagger held more power than the ones currently sitting in her room, the ones Garian had been working with her to understand—to wield. Matthias had explained that the ones Reese brought were designed for someone who would wield the shadows—someone like her.

"Then why are we still here?" she asked, before bounding for the exit.

Matthias appeared next to her, carried on the inky mist that they used to shift realms, a smile on his face as he gripped her arm gently. He chuckled before moving them out of the dining room and into the grand hall toward the back of the palace, heading for the grand foyer where she had taken to training.

Reese was standing across the room, shifting nervously from one foot to the other. Her brown hair pulled back and braided over her shoulder to reveal her pointed ears. She held two weapons in her hands—Morana's weapons.

"Does she wield the shadows too?" Morana asked, glancing at Matthias.

He chuckled again, leaning in to whisper. His breath was a ghost against her skin, reminding her of the sensations she had felt in the throne room. She quickly worked to shove the feelings down, store them away as she had for the past week, allowing it to ease the guilt. "All the fae in the Court of Shadows hold that power. The strength, however, varies. My lords, whom you met, hold more power, but they too can run out. I, on the other hand, have yet to find an end."

A shiver worked up her spine at his nearness. He had stopped touching her while they worked together. This moment was the most contact they had had. She still wouldn't let herself get close, not with the threats looming overhead. She still didn't know who or what to believe, and though she had chosen to trust Matthias, believing that he wouldn't kill her, not yet, she still had a sliver of doubt on the matter. Doubt that remained because of his history in hunting her down just to abandon her in foreign realms.

"Cocky as always," she responded. "I assume *that* is what makes you a god."

"More or less," he smiled. "I'm still a king, too."

"I think I prefer the king," she admitted. "You were much nicer to me in the Court of Shadows."

He paused, onyx eyes meeting her own. "I was?" he asked, a small smirk forming on his lips. "I seem to remember that as well." His voice was laced with dark undertones as he referred to a part of their history she didn't want to be brought up.

They approached Reese, her green eyes glittering in the light of the space, a smile crossing her sharp features.

"I hope you approve," she began, looking between Matthias and Morana. "I'm familiar with your abilities. Matthias has had me forge his weapons in the past."

"Reese's weapons that channel your magic, enhancing your strength." Matthias gestured to the weapons, and Reese stretched them out, encouraging Morana to take them. "This should help since you have had little practice with a sword, Though Garian said you've been learning quickly."

Morana glared at him.

They were heavier than the sword and dagger she kept hidden away upstairs. Morana grabbed the sword first, pulling it out of its sheath. The hilt was silver, shapes like the shadows that roamed over her skin delicately crafted where her hand would hold it. The dagger matched the intricate workmanship.

"They're beautiful," she breathed. She had been used to guns, but those weapons couldn't kill the fae. These weapons could. Something about that sparked fire in her blood. The knowledge of that power filled her with excitement, eased her worries about assassins showing up in this palace.

"We should start working with them." Matthias was standing just behind her, dark eyes observing her reaction. There was something about the way he was looking at her that made her heart stutter.

She nodded.

"Reese, you're welcome to stick around. Someone can escort you through the castle. Potentially lead you to the armory, where you can check on your previous works. I may commission you for more."

"Of course," she bowed before moving out of the room, leaving Morana alone with Death.

Inara's words echoed through her mind, forcing her to tense in his presence.

Matthias was trying to kill you.

She couldn't fully shake what Inara said to her, what Matthias admitted. It made her nervous, forcing her to push that wall up between them, never getting too close.

"We can start with the dagger." Matthias reached out, brushing her hand before taking the sword and moving it to the table in the corner. When he turned, there was a glint in his eye, something that told Morana he was about to enjoy this training session. Fine. If he was going to act like this, she was more than happy to knock him on his ass again.

He faced her, arms flexing beneath his black shirt. "Try to catch me," he taunted before disappearing. He wasn't fighting fair then. She wouldn't either.

Morana's senses were in overdrive, in tune with every faint sound, or shift in light across the room. She desperately tried to find him, wondering if he had exited this realm entirely. Her confidence waned, and her heart rate picked up with every passing second. Seeds of distrust took root in her core, spreading out over her organs, and gripping them tightly.

Genuine fear struck as Matthias materialized behind her, gently brushing her shoulder. Whipping around with her dagger in hand, she slashed at the fading mist where Death once was.

Sweat beaded at her temples. The wild strands escaping her low bun from her frantic movements stuck to her face. She would never catch him like this. When she had sparred with him before, she had the upper hand. She had been the one shifting through shadows to attack. She didn't know how to find someone who was doing the same.

Her legs carried her across the room, brown boots hitting the stone floors until she halted with Matthias's tall form in front of her. She lunged forward, dagger in hand, but he was gone again. This strategy wasn't working.

Something tugged at her power within, dark secrets whispered into her mind in the way they had before. The dagger was calling the shadows to life, connecting her in a way that transcended what she already knew about the darkness. In those depths, the whispers were stronger, and she could feel Death, his amusement radiating off a figure she could not see. She reached out with the inky mist, feeling for the parts of his mind she had seen in other sessions. When she met his thoughts, there was a wall keeping her out, but she could see more than just his mind. He appeared a few more times in the room, but Morana wasn't looking. She closed her eyes, sensing his presence, allowing the shadows to take her.

"Having fun?" she heard him whisper. A smile crossed her lips. She could see it right before it happened. He was getting ready to appear in front of her. Her hand tightened on the hilt of her dagger.

In a split second, she reached out, grabbing his wrist as he materialized. She wrapped the shadows there, pushing them into his mind, making him fear her. He couldn't move as she infiltrated the crack in his fortress. Pushing him back to the ground, she climbed on top of him, straddling his hips with the dagger pressed to his throat.

The bloodlust hit, and she pressed in. A trickle of red blood leaks from his neck, the cut stitching back together before she had a second to process. Her brows furrowed, watching him heal himself beneath her. If Inara was right and he wanted to kill her, there would be no way for her to win. He hadn't killed her yet.

"Am I going to Mabon?" She hated that she was panting while he sat so coolly beneath her. She could already feel where the soreness would settle into her body from their fight, and she doubted he even broke a sweat. "Or were you planning on hiding me away in this castle forever, fearful of what would happen?" She spat to the side, trying to rid her mouth of the coppery taste of blood. "I've protected myself before in your court."

The amusement left his eyes. "You can go if you wish." His expression was thoughtful. "You'll need to wear a dress again. If you don't like the ones you have, select a color, and I'll have one made."

Her eyes narrowed, that tiny sliver of distrust working to the surface.

"I saw Sarnai in the library last night," she stated. Her thoughts were racing a mile a minute, and she had trouble nailing down the questions she wanted to ask, what she wanted to uncover. "She informed me that Axton is alive somewhere in the Court of Light."

"She told me the same this morning." Matthias was calm, even with the dagger still touching the skin at his neck. He didn't move her off him, either. Suddenly, her body was on fire, heat washing over her in waves. "Sarnai has her own things to do, but she will be at Mabon as well. She's faithful and will help look for him." He shifted a bit. "If that is what you're asking."

"Will I meet Inara?" she questioned.

"You will."

"If she's hunting me, then aren't you just delivering me into her hands? How are you planning on protecting me then, Matthias?"

"She's bound by the Fae rules as much as I am at a celebration like Mabon. It's a time of peace. The Fae and the gods that lead them won't be able to touch because of a more powerful ancient magic." His eyes hardened in the light of the hall. "There won't be a repeat of what happened last time." His voice was practically a growl. "No one will touch you."

"So, I will come face to face with Inara. She wants me, and she can do nothing about it?" No matter what his answer was, she had to be sure. "I'm being dangled in front of someone who can't have me."

"Seems like a common situation for you to be in." Matthias's gaze trailed over her body briefly. "Do you really no longer trust me?"

She froze. That was exactly the problem. She wanted to, and she had become comfortable in his presence, but she knew the truth. She couldn't trust him— not after what he confessed.

"What was it in the throne room that changed it for you?" He asked, moving a hand to rest on her thigh. "Was it the kiss?" Her heart picked up at his touch. She had forgotten how much she enjoyed it, the way it sparked fire in her blood. "Or is it Axton?" A crease formed on his brow. "Or," he continued, "is it that I sought to send that man after you at Ashford?"

"Both," she whispered. "I mean all. All three."

"I highly doubt all of those things are bothering you." Matthias smiled. One eyebrow raised. "Especially considering that you're still straddling me." He looked down at where she was still pinning him before meeting her gaze again. "Do you just prefer it this way? You never answered my question about kneeling before you."

Her stomach twisted, damp heat working its way to where she didn't want it. She was trying to fight the effect he had on her. Morana got up, the dagger in hand. She stared at Matthias.

"Maybe check with someone you trust about Mabon and the safety surrounding it." He sat up, resting his weight on his elbows. "Then maybe you'll trust me again. Understand that I would never intentionally hurt you."

She wanted to believe it. She wanted to believe him with everything she had. He disappeared and Morana stood alone, questioning everything.

Twenty

She was still sweating when she entered the library, her mind spinning. Morana thought back to the sunroom in the Fae realm. The way Matthias had seen the memories that haunted her, the things that kept her running. She had trusted him then, allowing him to see the deepest, most guarded parts of her. When she had trained in the Court of Shadows, she had trusted him then, too. He had shown her his world, the places he went when he wasn't with her.

Then maybe you'll trust me again. Understand that I would never intentionally hurt you.

If she was going to attend Mabon, she had to be sure. There was only one person who hadn't led her astray, hadn't lied to her at some point or another.

"Where is the fae boy? The one with the red hair and freckles. He's young." Morana asked the woman sitting at the desk, glasses sitting low on her nose. "I mean, I think he's young." The woman looked up this time, taking in Morana's sweaty form. This was the second time she had interacted with her, never bothering to learn her name.

"He works at the back downstairs. Technically, he's a scribe. I wouldn't interrupt his work." The woman's golden eyes were fierce, burning with a fire that Morana didn't expect, almost making her uncomfortable.

"Thank you," she answered before pushing away from the desk and walking back to where she was the night before. No wonder he had said she had taken his spot. Lights flickered overhead, and the woodwork looked ominous in the inconsistent light and dusty haze of the lower level of the library.

Morana ran her hand over the books stacked on the shelves, feeling the leather binding and remembering the first time she had come here. Matthias had left her in the Flora realm, disappearing without a thought. It had bothered her, but she couldn't help noticing that he never really left. Recognizing the gentle way he had spoken to her when she received the scar that now decorated her face, a reminder of what she was up against, of who she could become.

At the back, she saw the boy, hunched over parchment, and focused on copying something from the book in his lap. He had been here too when Matthias had brought her to the library to learn about different realms. She remembered him then, the way he had walked away from them.

"Can the Fae hurt me at Mabon?" she interrupted as she studied him. He had helped her open the book. Maybe he could help her with this. Ease her fears, though, despite the fear, she was certain she could shove it down regardless and do what needed to be done.

He looked up; wavy red hair mussed at the top of his head. He couldn't have been more than sixteen, but with him being fae, who knew. She hadn't asked Matthias about how the fae aged, nor how old Matthias was. Part of her was afraid to know the answer.

"The fae are bound by certain rules at the four festivals. It's a forced peace." He cracked a smile. His teeth were a little crooked, but it was charming. "I saw you got the book to open." He tapped his fingers on the wooden surface, the pen held between his pointer and thumb. "So, you know the courts don't typically get along. That shouldn't concern you, though."

Morana wasn't content with that answer.

"And the gods?" she asked. "Are they bound as well?"

He sat back casually in his chair, setting the pen down. "You have nothing to worry about if you're concerned about Mabon. Your precious Death god will be bound just as much as Inara." He eyed her curiously. "You are worried about him, aren't you? You don't want to be, but I can see it in your eyes, the part of you that is unsure."

"*Should* Death worry me?" she asked, refusing to break his gaze. She hated how vulnerable she was being, allowing this boy to hear the way her voice trembled at the thought. He spoke as if he were older, as if he knew things she could only dream of, as if he knew more about her presence than he originally let on. Did anyone else in the castle know why she was here? It seemed Matthias was trying to help her—get her to understand her powers—but what did he have to gain from that? What did Inara have to gain from her powers as well?

"Only if you wish to be worried about him." The boy winked at her. Morana tensed. Maybe she shouldn't have asked. She should have just found a book about the fae festivals and read the information instead. The last book wasn't so simple, taking her way longer than it should have. With all the secrets in this library, this route of asking a scribe made more sense.

"He isn't someone to fear," the boy added, sensing her concern. "Do you think you're worried about Matthias for the obvious reasons? Or is something else bothering you, something keeping you from trusting him fully? Something you have even been keeping from yourself."

She didn't answer.

He sighed before continuing. "People fear the darkness, but it's in the light that corruption can be masked best." His face fell, the previous amusement vanishing from his features as his jaw tensed. "That answers your question about Inara. The other one, though, the one where you're avoiding your own darkness, that's another answer entirely."

Her brows furrowed. She didn't understand what he was talking about. "Are you from the Court of Shadows?" Morana glanced at the delicately pointed ears. None of the gods she had met so far had them, and if he was only a scribe. He was just fae—maybe.

"I am," he answered. "But I wasn't."

She didn't know what he meant. "What kind of answer is that supposed to be?"

"It means Inara is not to be trusted." A shadow crossed his face. Morana remembered the distrust she felt in her dream, the way the goddess hardened when she realized she wasn't getting to her prey. Matthias had been helping her and helping her grow in her power. Someone who was seeking to kill her surely wouldn't help her become stronger.

"What is your name?" she finally questioned. If he was going to help her, she might as well get to know him.

"Cain."

Her brows furrowed, and she looked away briefly. "*Cain*," she mused. "That name doesn't fit you well."

"The name doesn't have to fit me." He looked down at his work and picked up the pen. "It's only a name."

And Death was only a name as well.

Morana turned, stalking through the library to return to her room. Her mind traced back over the fae's words. He had been so sure of what he said about her avoiding her own darkness. The shadows twisted in her palms, reminding her of their comforting presence. She knew she masked her emotions from others, but maybe she had masked them from herself as well. Her emotions had become a stranger to her, an unfamiliar presence that she struggled to understand to the point of distrust. She didn't trust her previous judgment of Matthias, but maybe she should.

When she finished cleaning up, she intended to explore the castle—unlock some of the answers she sought. Maybe there was something hidden in the walls that would clue her in to Matthias's intentions. After all, he told her she was free to go. She figured free to go also meant free to go lurking around the place she had stayed in for nearly two weeks. A smile pulled at her lips.

The dark halls had become comforting, and she admired the delicate woodwork and ornate red and gold carpets and furnishings. There was a peace in being here, something she hadn't had in a long time. At the top of the stairs, she turned to walk toward her room, struck by the things the boy had said. Her actions were all over the place. She wasn't sure what she truly felt about Axton being alive. She hadn't touched that part of her, nor did she want to. Her emotions were becoming unfamiliar—she was running from herself.

Pausing at a random door in the hall, Morana let herself trail her fingers over the carvings. Ancient writing, and an image that resembled a fish, were etched into the cherry surface.

"Were you looking for something?" She jumped as Matthias's voice appeared behind her. There was no telling how long he had been following her around.

"Nothing in particular." She turned to face him, noticing the way he glanced at her recent scar. He was freshly shaven and had changed out of his outfit from earlier, reminding her current disheveled state. He wore a white button-up that contrasted with his tan skin and the ink on his arms.

"Going exploring?" he asked. "I could show you more around the castle. If you're curious."

"You were in my head?" she snapped. "I didn't even notice. Is this some new trick? Some training exercise where I can't sense you? I—"

He chuckled, the smile breaking across his face. "Don't show all your cards at once." His dark eyes met hers. "I'm not in your head. I just figured you'd want to see more of this place." His smile fell, replaced by what she would call sincerity. "I also want you to trust me, understand that I *want* to help you."

She didn't know how to feel about that, but maybe he could show her something more than what she could find on her own, and she was curious about what he had in mind. "Okay," she answered.

He stepped forward, caging her between his body and the door to her back, the one with the fish. Her breath caught, and her gaze glanced off his chest and back to his eyes. He hadn't dared come this close, hadn't dared reignite what had been between them in the throne room.

The other one, though, the one where you're avoiding your own darkness, that's another answer entirely.

She had done more than run from Axton. She had abandoned him. It only took her a few days to do it. Had she been concerned about him all this time?

Matthias was smiling down at her, dark hair still damp from his shower. "Excuse me," he whispered before turning the handle on the door behind them. He stepped around her and entered the room.

When she stepped through, a room filled with curious objects greeted her. There were swords, daggers, instruments, rings, and trinkets lining the shelves. In the center sat a large fountain pressed up against the back wall. She could hear the gurgling from the water that gently cascaded down rock and pictures carved over the surface. A light blue glow came off the water, dappling the surrounding room.

"What is this?" she asked.

"The hall of relics." Matthias trailed his fingers over a golden chalice on the top shelf. "It's where we keep the important objects—the magical ones." He eyed her, gauging her reaction.

Something caught her attention in what he had said. Inara had mentioned the *Hall of Relics*, mentioned something about—she couldn't remember. There was something she was supposed to see.

Morana stepped further in, closing the door behind her. Words of strangers wound around her thoughts. The things Inara said, the amount of trust Cain had in Matthias.

"What is the fountain?" Morana walked over, looking in at the small silvery fish that swam beneath the surface. Their skin had a bluish tint, causing the glow that decorated the walls of the room. The stones at the back had pictures, images of people, and objects etched with incredible detail. The glowing water intrigued her, drawing her in with a gentle pull. Morana reached to trail her finger across the surface before being stopped by Matthias's warm but firm grip around her wrist.

"I wouldn't do that." His tone was serious. "The fish might suck you under."

She looked at him, his fingers still wound around her wrist. "You're serious," she observed before taking a step back. He let go slowly, his touch lingering on her skin.

"The Basar fish can show you images from the past. If you're not careful, they will try to keep you pulled under the water and take you as payment for the gift of sight."

Basar. That's what Inara had said.

"Fantastic," she winced. "So, you keep a fountain of fish that will eat you."

"They will if you're not strong enough to pull out of the vision. It just takes a little awareness."

She stood there a few feet away from the fountain. Her mind swirling with ideas. For a moment, she touched the part of herself, of her emotions that she had covered and left for dead. It was the part of her that ran out on Axton. The part of her that had ignored the depth of what she felt for him, running instead toward a stranger with the promise of something new. She touched on her fears and the realization that she was being selfish. She had abandoned him, barely considered where he was. Not only did she feel guilt, but a well of truth sprung up within her. Worry and panic and the things she didn't long to experience raced through her blood, making the tears form at the corners of her eyes. "Do you think they could show me Axton?"

Matthias didn't show emotion, but he observed her carefully, seeing the change. He cleared his throat before looking at the fountain. "They could," he answered. "You would be able to see him, but only in the past, not as he is now. You could see why he was taken."

Her brows furrowed, the well threatening to drown her. "He was probably looking for me," she whispered.

"Don't flatter yourself."

Her gaze snapped up. Deep anger bloomed in her chest, crashing and burning into the sadness and guilt. it ignited her emotions, searing and turning them to ash. She took comfort in the storm. "You asshole!" she shrieked, lunging at him. Catching him off guard, she pushed at his chest, and he stumbled back dangerously close to the Basar.

Without missing a beat, she stomped out of the room. Fury and confusion pulsed through her veins, making it hard to think. It was almost overwhelming. Morana ran a hand down her face as she prowled through the halls of the castle. She wished Axton was here. She needed someone familiar, something she didn't have to figure out. He was easy to read, easy to understand, and steady. She wiped the tears away at the flashes of memories that came. Long nights at Ashford working in comfortable silence. The flirtations, all of it. It was predictable and easy, but there was still a mask, something that kept her from letting go fully. The memories lacked the same wild passion that erupted the moment she set foot in this court. Was she so terrible that she would throw him away? He was the closest thing to a friend she had had in three years.

Was this what Cain was referring to? It was easier to run from it.

Matthias appeared in front of her, halting her in her tracks. She drew on the shadows, planning to disappear.

"I know you're mad." He grabbed her wrist again, the same way he had when he was protecting her from those stupid fish. "I kept my promise, Morana. I did what I said I would."

The tears burned. "You could have gone looking for him. We know where he is—where he was."

His features softened. "He could have been looking for you when The Court of Light came, but you were still being hunted. You still are. Who knows what promises they told him, what bargains he could have entered?" He rested a hand on her cheek, gentle and comforting. "I think you should wear black to Mabon."

She tensed. "Why?" A tear trailed down over the raised flesh on her skin. He wiped it away with his thumb, looking carefully at the reminder that what he said was true. She was being hunted.

"It would align you with me. I know you're angry, you don't fully trust me, and I don't expect you to accept what I'm offering. The gods and the fae will be bound by a deeper magic. We won't be able to hurt you, but afterward—" He trailed off.

"Someone could come after me," she realized, looking up into his dark eyes. "What would wearing black do?"

"Send a statement," he answered. "A statement that I'm protecting you." He shifted uncomfortably. "A statement that is very much true." His hand fell away. "Should you choose to believe it."

She held his gaze, mulling over the words he had just spoken. There was a truth to it she couldn't deny. Matthias *was* protecting her. He had given her weapons, shown her the fae realm, introduced her to his court. Maybe she should have trusted him more to begin with.

"I'll wear black." Morana folded her arms across her chest, gathering the courage to admit what she wanted to tell him. Extending an ounce of trust to the god. "Inara was in my dream."

Matthias stiffened, a dark expression taking over his face. "You blocked her out?" he asked.

"Not before she spoke to me." She met the intensity there when she looked at him, reading the anger radiating off his features. "She said you tried to kill me first," she whispered. "You were hunting me to begin with." Her voice was small. "She mentioned these fish."

His brows were knit together as he thought about what she confessed. She didn't know if he would answer honestly, but she needed to hear what he had to say. She needed to know if Inara was lying.

"She wanted you to doubt me." He wouldn't meet her gaze. "I wouldn't hurt you, Morana."

"But you did." Her voice was still a whisper. "In the past, you tried to."

"I did."

At least he was honest.

Morana stepped around him, emotions stirring in her chest. She didn't know what to feel. She should be angry that he had sent the man to Ashford, left her in a strange realm, risked her life, or at least had something to do with it, but she was more preoccupied with the reality that he had told her the truth.

"I'll wear black," she answered over her shoulder. "But I don't need protection."

And with that, she left him standing alone in the hall.

Twenty-One

Willow brought the dress in the morning of Mabon, and just as she requested, they made it black. It was stunning. Skillful hands didn't miss a single detail from the off-the-shoulder straps that draped on her toned shoulders to the sweetheart neckline accentuated by the hairstyle Willow helped her with. Soft waves fell loose from her pinned hair, framing her face. Morana stood in front of the mirror in her room, barely recognizing herself and anxious to get out of this godforsaken castle for once.

She ran her hands over the silk fabric. Her hand moved lower to feel for the dagger sheathed safely at her thigh. The slit in the dress hit just under where she had placed it, concealing it well. Even with the promise of peace, there was no telling what she may or may not need to do, and she was human, bound by nothing.

It had been difficult to realize how much the events of the past rattled her. The assassin attacking her in the alley and in Axton's apartment had left her shaken. Stabbing and killing a strange fae woman responsible for the new pink feature on her face, and the constant battling within her thoughts, the ones that told her she was worthless for what she had done, had chosen. The ones that told her she should have found Axton, gone after him, brought him home.

It wasn't until recently that she realized *this* was the reason she stayed in the castle. It was the reason she refused to go back to the human realm despite her abilities and despite her concern. The reason she refused to acknowledge that Axton was somewhere in the Court of Light, and she had done nothing to go in and retrieve him.

She was still running.

A knock sounded on the wooden door just before Matthias walked in, clad in a black suit. She glanced at him through the mirror and watched as shadows danced across his form, moving like wisps of clouds circling the eye of a fierce storm. It didn't escape her notice that it matched her dress or the way he was looking at her through the mirror.

Morana turned to face him. His dark eyes lingered over every inch of her exposed flesh. Heat took over, and she buried the guilt so deeply that it didn't matter. Let her run while she could. Soon, she would have to confront everything that plagued her. She cleared her throat, moving forward and smiling.

I'm not here to steal your freedom, Ana.

It had been so long since she heard that nickname—heard his voice. And here was the excuse she pulled out every time Matthias made her feel something, made her want him. Hiding away in this palace was easier than facing the way she had abandoned those she cared for. She couldn't bring herself to give in to these feelings fully with Matthias, not when she had already done so much damage.

"Black suits you." Matthias's voice was rich, mixed with something that sent her heart galloping in her chest.

"Being protected suits me, you mean." She raised an eyebrow in his direction. "I'm bringing my dagger."

"I expected nothing less." He chuckled, glancing at her thigh briefly. "Though this is a time of peace."

"Yes, a time of peace that binds the fae and the gods." She smiled, a knowing and wicked expression. "Good thing I'm mortal and not bound by those rules."

"You couldn't kill me with that dagger," he informed before striding forward. The air crackled with tension—untouchable.

"And how does one kill a god?" she asked. He was standing directly in front of her now, a small portion of a tattoo peeking from the collar of his shirt.

Matthias touched her chin, lifting it to get a better look at her. "I imagine with a dress like yours."

Her heart stuttered before she was thrust into the shadows, descending into the glass castle that haunted her dreams. Falling into the Court of Light.

Moonlight shone over the floors, streaming through the vast windows lining the entire palace. Morana stood in the entryway with Matthias, arm laced through his. He looked to her, searching her face as if to ask if she still wanted this. Fear may have twisted her stomach in knots, but so did determination. She gently squeezed his arm for reassurance, and they strode through the double doors leading to a massive hall where fae were mingling and dancing.

The music floated through the air, richer and purer somehow. People were dressed in vibrant colors, smiling as they carried cups filled with drink. Everywhere she looked, she saw pointed ears and elaborate clothes. The room smelled of power and magic. The shadows she held thrashed in her chest, begging to escape, begging to be revealed.

Matthias leaned down to whisper in her ear. "Be careful of the wine," he warned, his hot breath fanning over her neck. She shivered at the sensation.

"What's wrong with the wine? Is it drugged?"

"As a mortal, you can consider it drugged. It will be incredibly strong. I don't want you to be vulnerable."

She deadpanned, unlacing her arm with his and picking up a glass from a waiter making their way through the crowd. She held his gaze—strong and unwavering. "I can hold my liquor." She raised a brow and took a drink. The wine tasted faintly of orange and spice. "Mm, citrus." Morana turned to walk away, sauntering through the crowd.

Matthias materialized next to her. He took her arm once more. "Now I'm really glad you wore black," he joked. "No one will take advantage of you when you end up shitfaced on the stairs somewhere."

"I certainly will not end up shitfaced." Morana took another sip, the heat working its way to her cheeks already. She swirled the drink in the cup, looking at the liquid and smiling. She leaned in as they walked forward. "I may end up shitfaced," she whispered, giggling as she smelled the wine in the cup.

Matthias rolled his eyes and tightened his grip on her arm. Shadows continued to move around him. It was then that Morana noticed the eyes on them, the intense stares and faint whispers coming from fae in the crowd. They were stopping their conversations and turning to look at them, questioning expressions on their faces. They must have looked like a couple entering this place.

"Everyone's staring."

"As they should," he answered. "You look beautiful. Did you know that?"

She inhaled, remembering another time Matthias had spoken those words. The wine was going to her head faster than she could fight it. It was hot in the room, filled with bodies and drenched starlight shining through the windows. "You're flirting with me?" she questioned, her voice light. She took another drink, allowing the alcohol to burn her throat.

"I'm flirting with you," he admitted, his voice dropping as he leaned in again. "If you would allow me, I'd like to do more."

She tilted her head back and laughed, ignoring the way her stomach tightened and her heart picked up its pace. When she looked across the crowd, she saw a familiar face, blond curly hair, and a wicked charm floating through the fae and heading toward her. Perfect timing. She needed to escape Death and the desire that statement caused.

"I've come for a dance," Ronan smiled as he stopped in front of them, staring directly at Morana. She downed the rest of her glass, placing it on an empty tray that moved past her.

"I love to dance," she laughed, grabbing his hand. "Though I don't know any dances." Morana was pulling him to the dance floor, swaying gently with the way the room moved. That wine was strong.

Ronan trailed after her until they were in the center of the floor. He spun her around, resting his hand on her waist and winking. She couldn't stop smiling as she clung to the lord to keep her balance. The room was swaying, every sound and sight sending pleasure through her veins.

"It's been a while since I've seen you, Ronan." He pulled her closer to his chest. "How have you been?"

"I've been around." He started moving, leading her in an unfamiliar series of motions that kept time with the strings. She was lightheaded, content, and unworried. Every ounce of stress slipped away as she stayed present in the moment.

"You really are a wicked flirt," she scolded, trying to keep up with what he was doing. Her movements were sloppy, but she didn't mind.

"I'm harmless." Ronan was smiling down at her, enjoying the night, and giving his best attempts to impress her. His bright teeth flashed behind his soft pink lips, full and enticing. For all his strong features and casual charm, he didn't elicit a response beyond the warmth of blooming friendship.

"According to—" she paused. Mocking him with an expression that elicited a chuckle from the lord. "According to yourself?" she finished.

"According to women who are uninterested in me, and far more enamored with another." His eyes flicked across the room to where Matthias was talking with Garian, getting an update on her swordsmanship, no doubt. "Women like yourself." He spun her once, catching her and quickening his pace to meet the sounds of the band playing.

"And to the women who are interested?" she asked, her mind still floating from the wine.

"I'm an absolute nightmare." His smile turned wicked at the statement, but she didn't believe it for a second.

"I find that hard to believe," Morana remarked. "A harlot, maybe, but never a nightmare."

He paused for a moment, halting their movements with his hand on her waist. His smile was soft, his eyes light in the glittering moonlight. "I could still get you to fall for me yet, Lady Morana."

She put some distance between them, glancing at Matthias, who was now observing them with a careful gaze.

"I'm not a lady." Her smile had fallen, distracted by the intensity radiating off the god of death standing in the corner.

"No," Ronan whispered. "You are much, much more." He spun her then, finishing off the song with one final move, one that left her dizzy. She fought the haze to get another glimpse of death, but her mind couldn't keep up with the movement. The wine begged her to let go, release her thoughts for the pleasure of freedom.

Ronan bowed in exit as Matthias approached, putting his arm around her shoulder. He whispered in her ear, low and lurking. "Having fun?" he asked.

The wine was still thick in her body, making the entire room seem brighter.

"The most," she offered. When she looked back across the crowd, she was met with rose-colored eyes, wide and approaching rapidly.

The woman's white hair was pulled back, a rich amber-colored gown contrasting against her pale skin. She stood before them, looking at Morana with an expression that seemed like she was holding back disgust.

"Inara." Matthias's voice had changed now. It was harder, more intimidating.

"Would you introduce me to your guest?" Inara spoke, that fake sweetness appearing in her voice again. She looked over Morana slowly, her eyes catching on the place where the scar rose from Morana's cheek.

"You already know me," Morana revealed. She longed to grip Matthias closer to her but ignored the urge. She wanted to stand her ground, appear strong even with the wine. "We've met before."

Inara gauged Matthias's reaction. He didn't flinch, merely stood there, darkness radiating from his presence. "Yes," she finally answered. "I must have forgotten." Inara bowed slightly. She was taller, accompanied by an overwhelming grace and powerful presence that had to have been associated with her status as a goddess. Morana recognized the same air around Sarnai. "Enjoy the festival."

Inara turned and walked away.

"She was looking for a reaction from you," Morana observed. "She didn't expect I'd tell you about the dream."

"I don't think she was all that surprised," Matthias admitted. "I have some people I should talk to. Are you okay to enjoy yourself?"

"You think I need you to have a good time?" she scoffed. "Maybe I'll find Ronan again." She laughed, patting his arm in reassurance. "I'll be fine."

Matthias nodded and disappeared, leaving Morana to gaze around the room. She spotted more wine. Inara's presence had a sobering effect, and she longed for the heady bliss that came from the fae wine.

She approached a waiter, grabbing the citrusy liquid and downing it in three gulps. She placed the glass on the tray and let the wine ease her worries.

That was when she saw him—brown hair and hazel eyes meeting her own from across the room. Her heart stopped beating as she watched Axton stand through a crowd of fae. Everything stopped moving, frozen in place like the walls of glass that surrounded them. There was no air, no amount of alcohol that could have distracted her from this moment. She ran a hand over the dagger at her thigh.

He was here, and he was looking at her now with a hardened expression that made her heart clench. The dancing moonlight slowed, and the fae seemed to halt in their steps. Morana couldn't focus on anything but the raging sea of guilt churning in her stomach. She still hadn't breathed, hadn't been ready to face all that was before her, the emotions she kept carefully concealed.

Twenty-Two

It took Morana an eternity to register exactly what was happening, to formulate a plan. Yet, one never came. She stood suspended in her shock, stunned to see him here now, alive and unhurt by the looks of it. Something didn't sit right with her about it, but she didn't care. Axton was here.

Axton flicked his head, gesturing for her to follow him out and away from the party. She didn't question him, propelled by her guilt and surprise—the desperate desire to know if he was aware of what she had done.

"Excuse me," she whispered as she moved through the crowd. The room swayed as the wine she consumed settled in, and she followed the mirage out into a hallway.

Walking past the glittering glass stairs, Morana spun, looking for the man she had abandoned. Would he understand? Would he listen to what happened to her? Was he even really here?

She thought she was going crazy, that the wine was messing with her head until a familiar hand pulled her into an alcove beneath the stairwell. She was staring up into familiar eyes. A sense of relief washed over her at the image of the man looking at her as if she hadn't left him stranded in a car after giving herself to him so fully. He knew nothing of her senseless flirtations with Matthias, nothing of the weeks she had spent in the land of the gods. At least, that's what she assumed.

"You're here," she breathed, fighting the urge to reach up and touch him, to make sure he was real.

Without another word, he wrapped his arm around her waist, pulling her flush against his solid form. His lips were warm when they came down over hers, and her eyes stayed open before she gave in to what he was offering. He was hungry as he kissed her, and she fell into that hunger with him, accepting forgiveness in any form, even if he didn't know she needed forgiveness. His lips moved with hers, tongue requesting access to her. She obliged, groaning as he pressed her against the wall of the alcove. Panting breaths escaped her at the sensation of his hands on her body, roaming across her skin.

The act unwound her, allowing emotion to seep from her pores. She was crying now, barely keeping it together. Vulnerability was a stranger, but slowly becoming a friend in every moment she was surrounded by gods.

What would he say when he learned the truth? She had to tell him—tell him everything.

She pulled away; the confessions tumbling from her lips. "I ran," she admitted. "We got in that accident, and I ran, Axton. Strange things have been happening. I don't know what's going on." Her brows furrowed. "How are you here? Are you even real?" She ran her hands over the toned muscles of his arms, unable to stop speaking.

Axton smiled, the dimple appearing on his cheek. She touched it gently, soaking in that familiar dent, the one that ensured his emotions were true. The tears were still falling, coating her skin with desperation.

"Inara found me," he spoke, his voice low.

Morana tensed at his words. She frantically tried to understand what he was saying. "She—Inara?" Her brows lowered, nose wrinkling. "Axton," she began, "Inara can't be trusted."

His smile faded. "No, Ana." He gripped her shoulders firmly, forcing her to look into those soft hazel eyes flecked with concern. "You don't understand. That man," he sneered with a hatred that surprised her, "that god wants to kill you."

"What are you talking about?"

"Look at you." His eyes glanced to her dress and back to her face, dodging her question. "You look beautiful, but I could guess that the black wasn't your choice." Her heart plummeted. The room was spinning, making it hard to focus. "He's claiming you for himself, but he isn't safe."

"Inara isn't safe, Axton. I—"

"Ana, listen to me." He shook her gently. "I made a bargain with Inara. She's the goddess of *life*. Do you think she'd honestly be out seeking to murder you?"

"I don't know." She glanced away before wiping the dampness from her cheeks. Confusion and bitterness mingled in her blood. Everything she had seen from Matthias, his promises of protection. She couldn't have been wrong. She looked up into Axton's eyes. He was pleading. This was *Axton.* Matthias had taken a sledgehammer to the walls she crafted for her own safety. Axton had tried to do the same, and maybe it had been her own fault in failing to let him. She had known Axton for three years, and maybe this was a chance to right the mistake of failed loyalty from when she had abandoned him.

"He's trying to find a way to kill you. He doesn't know how yet. Not with your abilities." His tone was urgent, entwined with concern for her safety. "Inara doesn't know what your abilities are, but she's certain he's trying to piece together what you can do. She's convinced he wants to use you for something. Either kill you or strengthen himself with your power. Those assassins, the ones she sent, they weren't for you." He ran a finger over the scar on her face, pain taking over his expression.

She felt like a fool. Her mind was reeling, tracing over every interaction. How could she have been manipulated so easily? There was truth to this. There had to be.

"I made this bargain with her to get you out, Ana." A warm hand still rested on her cheek, gentle and forgiving. She leaned into the touch, closing her eyes. "Inara came to my apartment after the accident. I didn't blame you. I swear it. She explained what she knew, offered me a solution I couldn't resist." She opened her eyes, met with the forgiving familiarity of the one constant in her life since leaving her father. "I want us to go home."

Home.

The word struck her, causing more tears to well up. He wanted to take her *home*, and she wanted him to. She stood on her toes, a gentle kiss ghosting over Axton's lips. She could taste sweet tobacco and gunpowder that would anchor her in the mortal realm.

"Let's go home." She reached for the shadows, but Axton halted her with a firm grip on her wrist.

"No." His tone made her pause. "He has the shadows, too. He will sense you." Axton tucked a stray strand of hair behind her ear. "Did you use the Basar?" he asked.

"The fish?" Morana glanced at her wrist, where his grip still held tight. "No, but Matthias let me into his memories. I saw the truth there. Whatever Inara wanted me to see about him attempting to kill me. I saw it from his eyes."

Axton tensed. She could feel it beneath her touch on his shoulder. He said nothing else about the Basar, but that clearly wasn't the answer he was expecting. "There's a portal beneath the castle. We can go now, but we have to go before he finds you."

Morana nodded as Axton led her out of the alcove. They walked through glass halls, moonlight glistening over the silver floors. Axton turned left to descend stairs that were closed off from the sky above. The now stone walls were cold in contrast with the rest of the palace. They dripped with unfamiliar magic. Morana could feel it in her veins.

Her hand was still in his as he dragged her down deeper into the bowels of the castle. It was dark and her eyes struggled to adjust until she saw a shimmering light glisten at the bottom of the stairs. The golden veil rippled, lighting the gray concrete steps as they descended. A shiver ran down her spine at the damp chill of this place. It felt like death—not the gentle and seeking death she associated with Matthias—this was harsh and full of pain. It smelled of broken promises.

"That's the portal," he whispered. Axton was frantically looking around the stairwell, as if waiting for Matthias to jump out from within the walls. "Quick," he whispered, the sound harsh. He shoved her forward, pushing her toward the strange light.

"Wait." She halted before the portal, hardly able to wrap her mind around what was happening. A moment ago, she didn't even know portals existed. Everything was moving so fast. "Axton, do you know this portal will take us home? What if they are both lying?"

He ran a hand down his face in exasperation. "Do you trust me?" he asked.

She did—undoubtedly, but something dark came over his features, and she took a step back. She paused, her hand moving to the dagger strapped just beneath the black fabric of her dress. He watched the motion, and she panicked, grabbing the knife. Lifting the dagger she intended to drive through his heart, something stopped her. She couldn't thrust the knife forward, her hands bound in front of her until he shoved her through the shimmering light.

It wasn't the same as the shadows. Her head spun as she was spit out onto cold stone floors that reeked of piss and vomit. She sat up, the motion further disorienting her as she looked for Axton. Her dagger had been lost, thrown out of her hands, and disappeared somewhere beyond the portal that still stood.

When he appeared, his expression was different—harder. He stepped forward to where she was lying on the ground, bending down to get a better look at her.

Something was missing in her chest. She tried to call the shadows to no avail. This wasn't right.

That's when she noticed the iron bars around the dark room the portal had spit them into. It looked like a dungeon. Frantically, she dug for the darkness, the things she could call to keep her safe. She had no weapons, no way to leave and shift away from the nightmare standing in the form of her closest friend.

"I told you," he spat, squatting next to her. Morana put a hand to her head. The pain was getting worse. Axton pulled a white sleeve up over his forearm after unbuttoning the cuff. What she saw there, she didn't understand. There was a long scar across his forearm. Golden light shimmered just beneath the surface of his tainted skin. "I made a bargain." He pulled his sleeve down and stood, backing away from her on the floor. The light from the portal had disappeared, leaving her in what would now become her prison cell.

"Axton," she croaked.

His features softened with regret. "You can't get out of a bargain with the fae, Ana. He obviously hasn't taught you much."

Yes, a time of peace that binds the fae and the gods.

Realization sunk in, hardening her stomach while the sound of her heartbeat thrashed in her ears. Axton was neither. He was mortal—like her.

"The bargain is bound by magic. I have to do this." He stepped back, closing the cell doors with a harsh click.

The strength had left her as she looked up at the man she had known for three years. Her vision blurred as she tried to fight off her tears. The one that now felt like a stranger. Pain hit her chest all at once, raging like a vicious storm. Her hands trembled as she tried to stand, waiting for him to confess that it was a lie. Waiting for him to save her.

"You promised me my freedom," she spat, lunging and gripping the iron bars. The walls were closing in around her as they pulsed with an unfamiliar magic. The magic she had experienced in the previous weeks had brought her comfort. The shadows had made her feel powerful, and Matthias had made her feel *safe*. This didn't feel the same. It felt vicious and malevolent, magic stronger than anything she had ever felt. It burned— stinging the flesh on her palms. She hissed as she released her grip.

Inara walked in, a deceitful smile on her face as she strode up to Axton. She gripped his face with long fingers. Her touch looked bruising as she dragged him forward, kissing him without saying a word. Axton accepted it. He didn't flinch, as if she had done this before.

Morana's heart shattered. Sharp glass lying on the stone floor of a dungeon in some mysterious location, somewhere she didn't know. Would Matthias find her? Keep his promise to protect her? Would he even know she was missing?

Inara broke the kiss, patting Axton's chest before turning to look at her new prisoner. Axton was staring at Morana, his expression absent of feeling, void of the softness or taunting she had come to love.

He walked out without another word.

She was alone with the goddess of life, but Morana had never felt less alive.

Twenty-Three

"Have you heard the whispers?" The sweetness had disappeared from her voice.

Morana pressed her face against the cold iron bars, her grip punishing on the metal. The magic embedded in the substance stung her flesh, speaking of immeasurable power, but she was desperate. Axton was gone. He ran from her in the way she had run from him, but the god he had aligned with wasn't Matthias. That was clear.

"They call you the *Queen of Darkness,*" she continued. "The lords in my court have given you this title." Her lip peeled back in disgust. "It's a ridiculous sentiment."

Morana didn't respond. Sweat and dirt streaked her face from when she had entered through the portal. She watched the goddess pace from the other side of the bars. The room was dark except for a few torches outside of her cell, lighted with a strange orange fire.

"Where are we?" she asked, teeth clenched. Morana allowed the sting of betrayal to wipe the guilt from her conscious. Bargain be damned—everyone had a choice, and Axton had made his.

Inara's head snapped in her direction; her gaze cold. "Does it matter?" She moved forward, prowling with preternatural grace. Her anomalously colored eyes peering through the metal. "I want to know what you know about their whispering."

Sweat skated down her temples as Morana held the vicious woman's gaze. How she could have ever trusted anything she had to say, she didn't know. Matthias was not the threat. He showed her the truth, and she ignored it—tried to fight it. "I don't know anything." The latch clicked, and before she knew it, Inara was in the cell with her.

Morana's power still lay dormant. She couldn't feel the familiar caress of ink across her skin, the comfort she knew in training. Fear coursed under her flesh, causing her to step back, peering at the tall form of the goddess in the room.

"You lie," Inara seethed. She was standing there, her height forcing Morana to look up at her.

Panic increased, but Morana would leave it in the grave. A goddess of life had no reason to unearth what was already dead. She couldn't touch her. Morana wouldn't allow it. "I don't know anything," she repeated.

The slap stung, sending a sharp pain across the scar marring her face. It was a reminder of what she was up against, and she drew the strength she needed in this moment from it. Inara slammed her hand against flesh a second time, the smack echoing through the chamber. Morana's face turned on impact. Her hand rose to cup her sensitive skin as she moved her jaw. Inara snarled and reached forward, caressing the place she had just hit. A reminder of something her father had done a lifetime ago. This time, there was no way out.

"You're lucky the deep magic around Mabon is keeping me from doing more." She drew her hand away. "That security won't last." Her eyes hardened as she muttered a curse under her breath. "*Queen of Darkness. The implications of something like that,*" Inara began, piercing eyes pinned to her prisoner. "An imbalance of power," she scoffed, stepping forward and crowding Morana's space. "A desire to conquer."

Morana frowned, not understanding what the woman was talking about. She felt it then; the intruder demanding access into her mind but wouldn't allow it. She bore down, erecting the fortress she had been pushed to master. She built it with everything she had left, instantly shutting the goddess out of her innermost memories. No shadows to comfort her now, but she would remain strong.

Inara shrieked and struck her a third time. "Your magic is useless here," she informed, distaste and disgust coating her voice. "I'll see to it you rot in this cell." She stepped back, slamming the bars and turning the lock. "I expect answers eventually, Morana." Her lip peeled back in a snarl. "You can't hide forever."

With that, the woman was gone.

Morana collapsed against the bars, the strength she called upon leeching from her body now that she was alone. Her limbs were heavy, and they shook with the weakness she felt but didn't want to show the goddess of life. The beginning of betrayal tasted sweet, like honey crafted from a harmless bee. A bee that could then turn and sting with poison in reckless defiance, but Morana knew the truth. That honeybee could inject poison, but afterward, it would surely die.

Every kiss, every look, had been a lie meant to lead her astray. Axton's actions had kept her close in order to bring her here, to destroy her. She couldn't help but think about the bargain he had made, and what that entailed. How much of this bargain could he fight?

The kiss between him and Inara made her stomach roil. There was no way of telling what was real and what wasn't. The only thing she could cling to was the promise of Death finding her, carrying her away from the dungeon that now consumed her fragile figure.

The effects of the wine wore off. Morana curled up against the wall, the damp dripping of water on stone filling her mind. She pulled her knees to her chest, covering her head with her hands.

The image of the kiss she shared with Axton in the alcove burned her thoughts, just as the remnants of his touch scared her skin. She could feel his deceit everywhere all at once. The lies lurked beneath her skin, permanently taking residence in her bones.

"Some wounds run deeper than the flesh."
Something softened his features. *"Now tell me, what other scars have you earned?"*

"So many," she whispered in the empty cell, a tear breaking free, coating the stinging wound with damp desperation.

With no shadows to keep her company. Morana closed her eyes, waiting for her nightmare to end. Waiting to wake up from the awful dream that now consumed her.

Two days of deafening silence had left her exhausted. Morana's mind fought to cling to reality every second she remained in the cell.

After the first day, the smell of her own shit and piss made her vomit in the corner, worsening the stench that coated the cold and unforgiving walls. Since then, she had become immune to the aroma. Her dress was covered in dirt, and the harsh stone made sleeping difficult.

Morana had no more tears to cry. She had paced the length of the cell, desperately fighting to find the shadows in her blood, but they were gone. She was so hopelessly weak and alone, with nowhere to run. Morana grabbed the bars, an enraged sound escaping her lips as the magic stung her flesh. She screamed then before moving across the empty space, dirt scuttling across the barren floor.

Slamming her palm against the wall at the back of the cell, Morana shrieked. How could she have been so foolish? Her head fell to her arm while she leaned against the stone for support. It was so dark in this dungeon, just one torch flickering outside the cell, offering the faintest amount of light to see. She had expected the light to go out, but it remained bright.

Morana turned, sliding her back against the wall as she moved to sit on the hard ground. Her gray eyes pinned to the light, and she watched the way the flame danced in her vision. The image was her only thought, the only thing occupying her mind.

"It's faefire." Axton's boots clicked on the floor as he walked up to the iron bars of her chamber. The good humor she knew and loved was gone, nothing remaining of the man she had slept with. She didn't look away from the light—she couldn't.

Her stomach felt hollow. She realized she didn't even know exactly how long she had been down here alone, without food or water. All she had was the dark silence of her own company.

Axton's feet stopped in front of her listless form. She couldn't muster the strength to get up—to move.

He placed a plate of solid food on the ground. Bread and hard cheese were sitting in front of her, as well as a cup of water. It drew her gaze away from the faefire. Axton still hadn't said anything. She held her breath—

waiting for an explanation—waiting for him to admit he had made a mistake. That confession never came.

"You left me." His voice was detached—cold. "I remember coming to in the driver's seat of my car, frantically looking for you. The next moment, I was back in my apartment. I didn't know what was going on." Axton squatted in front of her, resting his elbows on the knee of his black pants. He picked up a small stone from the ground, tossing it at the wall. Morana flinched at the sound and finally looked at him. "Inara found me in the apartment." His face twisted, disgust shadowing his features. "You *left*," he spat.

Morana tensed. Her skin was clammy, her hair damp from the humid air of the prison cell. She hardly felt anything looking at the man who had betrayed her. She may have left him, but she had left him with the assumption that he would be taken care of, and that she would return. Axton, on the other hand, had thrown her into a cell after making a bargain with a goddess.

The slap still lingered on her skin, a scar and reminder of all the times someone had forcefully taken from her. Axton had willingly kissed Inara, his unmarred flesh painting a picture of their relationship—something she still couldn't make sense of. He could have fought the bargain, but he was all too willing to participate and starve her. Her chest tightened, but the sadness was soon replaced with a bitter rage.

"I'm capable of all manner of things," she warned. Her eyes were steel, unwavering in the presence of the man she now despised. Every ounce of emotion had drained the moment she realized what he was doing. Maybe it was selfish of her, but she had been told once that people weren't selfish enough.

Axton scoffed, standing up to his full height. He was wearing another white button-up; the sleeves rolled. For a moment, it reminded her of Matthias. There was no guarantee that Death would come after her, but based on his track record, the way he relentlessly sought her, she hoped he would.

Inara entered the room behind Axton, her strange eyes glittering in the faelight.

"Did you learn anything?" Inara asked.

"No." He strode toward her until he was standing in front of the goddess. She patted his chest. "Quite alright." Her eyes shot to Morana, vicious intent lurking in her gaze. "Strip her down."

Morana's back straightened, her shoulders squaring. Axton wouldn't—he *couldn't.* She could hardly bring herself to believe that the hands that had touched her so gently, coaxing her to begin to trust, would be capable of such cruelty. Yet, he obeyed. He turned to her, grabbing the neckline of her dress and shredding it in three rough pulls. Morana tried to fight his grip, thrashing and pushing herself away from him, but it was no use. She was stripped completely bare, with nothing but the grim of the cell coating her skin.

"Turn her around," Inara commanded.

Axton grabbed her arms, pulling her to stand. The warm touch that had once caressed her gently and caused shivers to rake over her flesh now bruised. Morana clenched her teeth, glaring directly into the hazel eyes that she would never forgive.

Axton roughly turned her, forcing her into a kneeling position, and then slamming her head to the floor. The ground sent a shock wave of pain through her skull. She was in the fetal position, back bared for the relentless torture she would likely endure.

"Ana," Inara mocked, voice laced with amusement. Morana's throat tightened at the use of that name. "What does Matthias want with you?" she asked.

"I don't know." Morana's voice was hardly a whisper.

"Speak up, child."

The first lash blindsided her. A burning fire was scorching her skin. She couldn't see what Inara was using, but it felt like pure, unadulterated power. It was nothing like the shadows. It seared her skin, making her cry out in pain. Axton's hands still fought to hold her in place, shoving her scarred cheek to the ground.

"I don't know," she said louder.

"Hmm," the goddess mused. "I don't believe you." The words had a bite to them. Her power whipped out, crashing against Morana's already sensitive flesh. She screamed again. A stray tear fell down her face, stinging almost as much as the lashing she received.

Inara did not cease. She asked the same question. Morana gave the same answer, then paid the price for her incorrect responses. When the blood dripped down her back, staining the floor a deep red, Morana gave in. The pain was too much. She let the darkness take her.

She was dreaming.

Axton and Matthias stood in the cell with her when her eyes opened. She was lying in the fetal position on the floor, unaware of how long she had been passed out after the lashing.

Morana sat up, but they didn't look at her. She couldn't make out their whispering filling the cell.

After a moment, she stood. Axton immediately looked and walked to her in two strides before forcing a bitter kiss on her lips. His grip was bruising on the back of her neck as he crushed his mouth to hers. Bile rose in her throat and before she realized what was happening. Before she could push him off, he sank his teeth into her bottom lip. The copper flavor coated her tongue, tasting like honeyed poison and broken promises.

Morana reeled back, pulling her hand to her mouth. Blood stained her fingers as the room swayed. Axton's features changed, shifting into an immense serpent that dwarfed her where she stood, and back to a man.

When his form stopped shifting, he finally remained like a snake coiled on the ground.

She stomped on the beast, grunting with the full force of her strength. The snack twisted and slithered away, disappearing into the darkness.

Matthias was next to her in an instant. "I'm so sorry," he whispered. "I wanted to protect you." He leaned down. She didn't have the strength to pull away. Her mind was foggy from the venom of the snake's kiss. Matthias wrapped his lips around the bite, sucking deeply. The haze over her mind slowly lifted the longer he worked. It sent pleasure into her body, a heady need taking over as he sucked the venom from her blood. Morana moaned at the familiar push of shadows under her skin, the power she so dearly missed. She wrapped her arms around him to drink in more of it, and he allowed her, caressing her and promising reprieve from the monsters that lurked in the light.

She could hear a song playing in the background. The language and tune were unrecognizable, ancient, but the noise brought comfort to her quickly fading mind. She was lost in what he was doing, begging for it to continue, never wanting him to stop healing the sting of betrayal that coated her lips.

Her eyes weighed heavily when Matthias finally pulled away from her. He ran a finger gently over her forehead, soothing the tension there. There was a kindness to his eyes, one that brought peace.

"Sleep," he said. His voice was a deep rumble.

Morana allowed sleep to come, wishing Death would embrace her completely.

There were new footsteps in the cell when she came to. Morana's eyesight was blurry as a woman strode toward her. She couldn't make out who it was and dreaded the thought of being whipped again. There was no strength left in her as she lay prone on the cold, hard ground.

When the woman tried to grab her, Morana lashed out, pushing against the toned body with brown skin. She was so weak. It did nothing but exhaust her further, and she eventually gave up.

"It's alright." Sarnai's voice was easily recognized, though it was gentler than she would have expected. Morana's nerves settled, an overwhelming peace washing over her. "I'm going to get you out of here."

The last thing Morana remembered was being lifted before the sweet surrender of sleep took her once more.

Twenty-Four

The crackling of a wood stove and the scent of spices and herbs woke Morana up from her deep slumber. It was so different from the vomit and piss that assaulted her senses in the cell that it took her a minute to adjust.

Sarnai was standing in the small kitchen of the one-room cottage decorated with deep browns, rich emerald greens, and dried herbs hanging from the ceiling above. Sarnai was crushing some brightly colored herb with a mortar and pestle. She took a pinch of what looked to be crushed flowers and added it to a steaming cup. The silver webbing glowed brighter across her forehead as she worked. Her delicate fingers wound around a small golden spoon, working to stir the tea.

Morana sat up, realizing she was in a small bed in the corner of the room. She was greeted with a pounding headache. There were plants all around them, growing along the wooden walls, and the one stone wall over by a small seating area. The forest-colored comforter twisted around her aching legs. She was wearing clothes now—a large white shirt that came down to her mid-thighs. Her skin was clean, and she reached up to feel her hair. The tangles were gone.

Morana's chest tightened at the memories, her stomach hollow and aching. Sarnai had come for her, pulling her out of that cell. Her mind struggled to settle—to believe what she was witnessing.

Sarnai turned, carrying the cup toward the bed.

"Perfect," the goddess spoke. "You're awake." She shoved the cup into Morana's hand. "Drink this."

"What is it?"

"Just drink it." Annoyance only colored Sarnai's tone for a moment before she softened. She took a seat in the golden cushioned chair next to the bed with an expectant look. Morana blew on the liquid, feeling a sense of calm wash over her as the aromatic steam hit her in the face, washing away the memory of damp air and the harsh slap of Inara's hand. "It'll bring the shadows back. That place suppressed your magic. I'm not even sure how she did it."

"Are you a witch?" Morana asked, her voice raspy.

Sarnai chuckled, a soothing amusement in the sound. "A *bitch*?" she began. "Yes, absolutely. A *witch*, however, no. I'm a goddess." She smiled then, running her tongue across straight white teeth before she spoke. "A bitchy goddess."

Morana huffed a laugh. She brought the cup to her lips and drank the tea. It was bitter on her tongue, tasting of licorice and rust. Her eyes squeezed shut as she forced herself to swallow. The memories of Mabon lived there behind her heavy lids. She could see Matthias standing and watching her dance with Ronan, feel the heady pleasure of the wine. Her chest tightened as she saw Axton, felt his lips brush over hers, a snake biting her flesh and making her bleed. She inhaled deeply, but her fingers were trembling now, her back stinging with the memory of Inara's harsh power.

"Where is Matthias?" she asked. She opened her eyes before setting the cup down on a copper side table.

"Busy running a kingdom." Sarnai got up, moving to the stove where something was boiling. "That and starting a war over your abduction."

The air was sucked from the room, briefly freezing time while Morana took in the word spoken.

War.

"You're not serious." Morana's face had fallen. She hardly believed that Matthias had gone to *war* over something like this. He knew the risks, knew that the court was chasing her. But who was she to make him willing to throw his entire court into a war for her?

"I didn't say I agreed with the theatrics," Sarnai huffed out a breath. "But he's pissed. He nearly went crazy trying to find you."

Morana chewed on that as a comforting warmth bloomed in her chest. She desperately wanted to see him, desperately wanted to throw herself at the god of death and beg for him to never leave. It was strange, considering all that happened, but she felt it almost viscerally.

"Everyone is calling me the *Queen of Darkness.*" Her eyes were pinned on the goddess as if her stare alone could retrieve the answers she sought. "What does that mean?"

Sarnai looked uncomfortable, shifting between her feet while stirring whatever was in the pot.

"There's an old story about a goddess called Lady Death," she began. "It's an ancient story." She used a ladle to pour the soup into a stone bowl, adding a spoon before bringing it to the side table and gesturing for Morana to eat. Morana took it reluctantly, but after a few bites, she began devouring the lentil stew. Axton never brought her anything to eat in that hellhole.

"I've never heard anything about a queen of darkness, though," Sarnai continued. "Lady Death, however, was a common enough tale." Sarnai sat on the golden chair again, leaning back with her hand under her chin, her umber eyes serious. "Lady Death was a major god." She examined the webbing on her arm as if it were a script to the distant tale. "There were major gods, gods before Matthias and me, gods that were infinitely more powerful. Lady Death was one of them."

"What happened to them? The major gods, I mean." Morana leaned in, hungry for the details now that she devoured her soup.

"Said to be sleeping in the Wastelands to the north. Lady Death was never actually seen. Raidan was another major god, real enough. He became power-hungry, looking to conquer the realms and join them as one under his rule. He was a brutal god, vicious and evil, playing games with the people who served him."

"What games?" Morana interrupted.

"He had his people, his followers. He would send them to destroy cities, slaughtering men, women, and children in his name. Raidan would purposefully cause pain and strife in order to flaunt his power, get people to worship him."

"And people chose that? They didn't see through to the god's cruelty?"

"Desperate people don't see corruption, Morana. They long to see the good in everyone, hoping that someone will save them." She stood up, walking to grab her own cup of tea from the small counter. Moving to sit back in her chair, she continued. "Lady Death was meant to put an end to his cruelty, but she never showed."

"Is this a true story?" Morana interrupted.

Sarnai eyed her suspiciously. "It's just legend, older than Matthias. The sleeping gods are true enough, but we have never seen such power, such cruelty. There are relics, though, those remaining and passed down by the gods to their children, ones designed to kill gods and not fae."

"Matthias has parents?" It never occurred to her. She thought he just spawned from the inky darkness that he wields.

Sarnai laughed at her incredulous expression, leaning back in the chair. "Matthias isn't the first Death god to exist. There have been many."

"How old is he?"

A wicked smile graced her full lips. "Younger than me." She folded her arms, gazing at Morana with intention, daring her to ask the question burning her throat.

"And how old are you?" Morana took another sip of tea. "Thousands of years old?"

Her eyes glittered as Sarnai stared at the woman on the bed in her cottage. She stood up again, pushing up from the chair. "You need to rest," she advised.

"When can I see him?" Morana called after the goddess. It sounded desperate, and Morana cringed at the strange way she had expressed her desire. She wanted to see him, to figure out what had happened. Inara had whipped her, broken something in her while she was held in that cell. Axton couldn't be trusted. Her throat clogged with the tears she longed to cry. He had shoved her to the ground, forcefully stripping her bare. She could still feel the cold concrete crush against her face. Morana closed her eyes again.

"After you rest." Sarnai patted Morana's arm before moving across the small cottage. She was graceful, kinder than Morana had realized.

The soup satisfied as Morana continued to eat, watching the goddess stride to the door. "You're not as bad as I thought, Sarnai." Humor danced in her smokey gray eyes as Morana beheld the creature. She had always liked her, but she would never admit that.

The goddess turned around, another smile on her face as she looked over Morana lying in the bed of her cottage. Morana assumed they were in the flora kingdom, not the land of the gods. The vibrant colors of plants lining the walls, and the misty air clued her into their location. That and Sarnai's presence, her clear ownership of the cottage.

Sarnai looked her up and down, observing her with predatory focus. "You're right," she finally answered. "I'm much worse."

A soft smile overtook Morana's features as she sipped the broth. Sarnai reached the door, opening it and closing it with a gentle click.

Morana leaned back, her head resting on the pillow behind her.

It was then that she felt it, the slow pulse of shadows under her skin. They were faint, not nearly enough to switch realms, but it brought comfort— reassurance. As it was, the tea she was given worked.

Morana called on the shadows, relishing in the solace they provided. She let the inky blackness skate across her arms in the misty light of Sarnai's cottage. As she worked, manipulating them became easier, but there still wasn't enough to go anywhere. Maybe if she waited, her full abilities would come back, and she could escape this cottage to go back to the land of the gods—to Matthias.

She didn't know why she wanted to see him so badly. Maybe it was the dream she had had in the dungeon after Inara had whipped her. Maybe she was desperate and alone.

There was only one thing she was sure of; after it all, Axton would pay for what he had done.

Twenty-Five

The scent of cardamom woke Morana from her slumber. A steaming cup of tea sat ready for her on the copper side table. She could feel the shadows strengthening just beneath her skin. Reaching her hand forward, she allowed the darkness to coat her skin, bringing the comfort of her power's return. It was almost fully back.

She hadn't expected how vulnerable she would feel without these abilities that she had been harnessing. When she was in the chamber, alone and cold, she felt powerless to defend herself. The reminder of Inara's presence sent a cold chill down her spine. That was when the stinging began.

She reached under the large shirt she still wore, feeling the places that had burned with what felt like fire when Inara unleashed her power over her flesh. She couldn't feel scars there, as if the abuse never happened. Nothing marked her body, indicating the betrayal that still etched and carved marks on her heart.

Closing her eyes, Morana took a deep centering breath, willing her mind away from the memories of being stripped bare by the man who had claimed to care for her. She could almost feel his grip on her as he shoved her face to the stone floor. A tear slid down her cheek, and she swiped at it. The liquid coated her fingers, and she glared at the proof of lingering sorrow. She had followed him to prove her loyalty—to fix her mistake in abandoning him. There was a time when she would have never allowed herself to cry this much—feel this much. That felt like a lifetime ago.

Flipping the comforter off her bare legs, Morana stood up in the cabin and took a sip of the cardamom tea Sarnai had left for her. It was rich and inviting, with a hint of sweetness. Morana took a second sip before looking around the cottage. She hadn't been able to take in Sarnai's space earlier, and now that she was alone, she was becoming curious. It was cooler now than whenever they had first come to the flora realm. Morana chuckled at the memory. So much had changed.

Sarnai's cottage contained the bed with the side table against a wood-paneled wall. It was one room, with a few cabinets and a small countertop for a kitchen next to the wood-burning stove. A wall of gray, natural-looking rock sat on the other side of the room with the emerald couch and a wooden chest littered with books and old parchment.

The small windows allowed misty light to float in, coating the cottage with a warmth and comfort. It still wasn't enough to heal the wounds—not entirely.

Morana walked on creaking wooden floors to examine the books Sarnai kept on the table. Maybe she could learn about the strange woman that appeared every so often in the land of the gods.

She trailed her fingers over a leather-bound book before picking it up to examine its contents. The pages smelled of ink and felt stiff with age. Morana turned to a random page, gently running her fingers over the lettering. This book must have been important if Sarnai kept it in her private cottage.

As she read, Morana laughed, the sound raspy on account of her not talking for such a long period. As soon as she read the word *cock*, amusement shadowed every other emotion stirring within her. It seemed that Sarnai enjoyed a good historical romance just as much as the next person, but this one was particularly graphic. Continuing to read, Morana smiled at the idea that Sarnai had kept something like this on her table while a guest resided in her home. It was very detailed. She laughed again, reading the words *massive length.*

"What's so funny?" A gravelly voice sounded in the room and sent her heart plummeting to the wooden floors below. Morana snapped the book shut and turned to see a disheveled Matthias standing by the door near the kitchen. His dark hair was mussed, and his black button-up wrinkled, as if he had been wearing it for days, or, at the very least, picked it up off his own floor. Dark circles were etched beneath his wild eyes. When they met her own, some of the frantic energy dissipated. His shoulders sagged.

Emotion flooded her as she thought of Axton, and the doubt she had placed upon Matthias before they went to Mabon tightened her chest. In that moment, she had believed the things Axton said, blindly following him to what would have been her end. The last person she had expected to betray her did, and the god of Death stood before her, ready to wage war on her behalf. At least, according to Sarnai.

His deep eyes glittered in the misty light of the cottage. She could have sworn he looked happy to see her as he was standing there, alive and breathing. His sleeves were rolled up, and a flash of Axton's hand entered her mind. She remembered the callous way he had shoved her. Morana winced, her fingers trembling until she registered the crows inked across Matthias's forearms. This was Death. She saw the familiar moth tattoo on his hand, and for a moment, pictured the other tattoos etched into his flesh beneath that shirt.

She couldn't explain her emotions—the way it felt as if she were finally safe in the presence of Death. Her shadows called to him in a way she hadn't noticed before. Always reaching out to mingle with his power. She watched as they snaked down her skin, stretching toward the ominous god. After all she had endured, after all she had doubted and believed, Matthias was here, looking like he had ripped apart the world to find her.

Without thinking, she moved forward, wrapping her arms around his waist and burying her face in his chest. Matthias tensed but welcomed her just the same by crushing her against him. His hand was gentle as it brushed a strand of hair back. He inhaled, taking in the scent of whatever soap Sarnai had used. He needed this, too. She felt like a ridiculous child—vulnerable and needy, but she had so very little left.

Axton had shown the truth. Now that Morton was dead, and there were no ties to her old life because of her own senseless running, this was all she had. She wished she could be stronger, wished that she could keep a careful distance from the god because that's what she would have done before, but there was nothing left for her in the human realm. After everything, she needed someone, even if that someone was filled with the same darkness that now resided within herself.

His hand gripped the back of her head gently as he held her there. There was no fire in his touch, just the comfort of a warm embrace.

"Sarnai reads romance," she finally answered, another light chuckle leaving her lips.

"I could have guessed that." She could feel his voice rumble in his chest as he held her close. "Plants make terrible company."

There was a pause. Morana released him. A flush crept to her cheeks as embarrassment washed over her as she realized how helpless she seemed—clinging to Death like he was the very essence of her being. She fought to bury the emotion, carefully masking what she was feeling in his presence. Tears threatened to escape, but she kept them at bay, not wanting to think about the scars that should have been engraved into her flesh but weren't. The kiss she shared with Axton flashed through her mind, and she cleared her throat. Closing herself off once more—the old habit she couldn't shake.

"Have your abilities returned?" Matthias asked, hands in the pockets of his black pants.

She let it spill over her skin again, consuming her in the shadows. Allowing her to disappear briefly, hidden from the world. Matthias could still see her. He could see through that magic easily. "I would like to go back," she said. Her eyes were pinned on the only comfort she had found since before Mabon. This small cottage brought peace, but she couldn't stay here forever. "To the land of the gods," she finished.

Matthias looked at her as if he wanted to tell her something, a crease entering his brow. "Go into my mind," he commanded.

Her mouth dropped open. "What? I don't know if I—"

"Try." He insisted, taking a step toward her.

The world fell away instantly, doubt disappearing as she lost herself to the shadows, entering the mind of the god standing before her.

They were standing weightless in the cavern of his deepest thoughts. She had been here before, during her training. Matthias was smiling, striding forward before stopping a foot away from her.

"I want you to see," he spoke. "I want you to know the truth."

The words struck her, a confirmation of the one thing he had always offered her, the truth, even admitting to sending someone to kill her. Sometimes the truth hurt, but sometimes it was a comfort, even in the face of darkness.

He reached out, touching her cheek and pulling her into a memory, viewing the world from Death's eyes.

She was in the human realm, kneeling in a familiar dark warehouse with a green-eyed fae trembling beneath her, or Matthias rather. The shadows wrapped around the fae, pinning him in place. The fear on the assassin's face was palpable.

"Tell me where she is," her voice rumbled. It was as if she were Matthias, feeling his emotions and reliving the memory the way he experienced it. Fierce anger burned in her chest as she kneeled on the man's chest, holding him in place. The raging storm of malice was accented with a hint of panic. Panic for her?

"It's warded," the assassin croaked out. "Deep in the mountains of the Court of Light. You can't go in. Your shadows won't work there." The man coughed as the shadows wrapped around his neck, making him believe *the worst. He couldn't breathe—not well. Sweat was dripping down his temple.*

"How did Inara get her out during Mabon?" Matthias asked. "I had to trick you into the human realm. How did she get her out of there? She would have had to lure her. What was the trick?" Deep rage settled into her bones as her hand reached out, replacing the shadows. She was really choking him now, seeing red. She loosened her grip slightly.

"The boy," the fae confessed. A deep snarl ripped from her chest. Dark thoughts swirled in her mind as she glanced down at the man. She could smell the blood she longed to drain from his veins, taste the bitter wrath on her tongue. She pulled a dagger out of her boot—Matthias's boot—then the wall slammed in place, blocking her off from his mind once more.

"What did you do to him?" she asked, staring at Matthias in the cottage. She had been aggressively thrown from his mind; his fortress unbreakable.

"Handled it," he answered, his eyes boring into her own. "Now maybe you can explain what happened." He swallowed. "Did she hurt you?"

Morana stared at him, the pain searing her back once more, a faint memory of what she endured. She felt the hollowness of hunger, the thirst that had consumed her, and the fog that had taken over her mind in her time as a prisoner. She couldn't tell him, couldn't bring the words to her lips, but maybe she could show him. If he trusted her enough to allow her into his memories, she could do the same for him.

"Why don't you look for yourself," she whispered.

He was there in an instant, living through the torture with her. She let the memory play, trying to detach herself from her body when Axton ripped her dress and shoved her to the floor. Every emotion replayed as she felt her face hit that stone again, the pain of Inara's lashing. Agony slithered its way into her soul.

When it was over, when she pushed the god of death out, Matthias just stared at her. Anger radiated off him in waves like she had never seen before, making his presence more intimidating. In that moment, she was reminded of who he was, the power he held.

"They whipped you," he growled as his lip peeled back in a snarl. "With her magic." His jaw clenched, hands flexing at his sides to restrain the rage. She had tasted his wrath while in his mind and knew how forceful it could be. "It's been two weeks. They whipped you and starved you."

"I just want to go home." Morana was desperate, fighting the tears that threatened to break through. It had been almost too much to relive everything that occurred, and she could see the way Matthias was wrestling with it.

"Home?" Matthias asked, a softer expression overtaking his face as he observed her distress.

"With you." The words were pitiful, and she knew it, but he was all she had left.

His eyes widened before his features softened again. The pad of his thumb trailed over her lip as he inhaled. Her stomach twisted at the tenderness of it.

When his hand dropped away, Matthias looked pensive. He ran a hand down his face and stepped forward. "I have a lot to do in the Court of Shadows," he admitted. "The palace is filled right now. Nobody is in the land of the gods." He ran a hand through his hair, twisting his fingers through the mussed dark strands, a motion he must have been doing a lot of recently. "You can come with me to the fae realm, but I can't promise it will be safe. We've been fooled once already" She could see the worry in his eyes.

Morana momentarily remembered the way Inara had kissed Axton. The cold and calculated way he had walked to her cell, pretending to demand information he had no desire to retrieve. As if he knew what the cost for her lack of knowledge would lead to. The tears lost their grip on her emotions. Instead of emptiness or the sting of betrayal, a dark storm of anger swarmed in her chest, thrashing for its release. It hailed and churned, working her into a demon to be feared. She would not relent until the son of a bitch got what he deserved.

"And I can't promise I won't kill them for what they did," she whispered, barely containing the hurricane of wrath.

A smirk appeared on his face; one eyebrow cocked in response to the promise she just spoke. He reached forward, wrapping his hand around the back of her neck.

He leaned down, eyes looking into her own with the depths of all they had just shared, the way they had accessed each other's minds with undeniable trust. She could have been lost in the dark gaze that had become so familiar to her. The one that had helped her claim this power for herself. He was continuing to do that, pushing her toward mastering who she was meant to be.

"Good girl," he almost growled.

And then they were gone.

Twenty-Six

Obsidian floors greeted her as she arrived in the palace of Ascella, still dressed in nothing but a large white t-shirt. Morana pulled at the garment, frantically trying to cover more of herself while Matthias moved swiftly past numerous servants.

The castle was full, much more crowded than what it had been the first time she had come here. She supposed everyone from the land of the gods had been moved, considering all that was happening.

A blonde woman wearing a simple linen dress stopped before Matthias. He was talking quietly, and Morana couldn't make out what he had asked. She hurried to catch up, noticing the way the woman glanced at her bare legs, her eyes widening before she averted her gaze. Morana tugged the shirt down more, wondering what the staff must be thinking. Did they know about her kidnapping?

"The tower is open, yes," the servant informed. She glanced back down the hall. The black floors contrasted against gilded walls. It seemed that everything in this palace was black and gold, something starkly different from Matthias's home in the land of the gods.

Matthias rushed down the hall, grabbing Morana's hand and leading her to a spiral staircase at the end of the corridor.

The stairs wound around the tower, leading up to someplace unknown. Morana ran her hand along the banister, ebony wood carved in designs, speaking of the other palace. They walked the stairs until they reached the top. The door was open, leading into a large bedroom.

It was lavish compared to the room she had stayed in before. This one accented in silver and gold with dark gray walls and dark wooden floors. The gray comforter was sprawled across the bed that sat in the center of the room against the back wall with a gold and crystal chandelier suspended above.

A fireplace sat at the center of the room, contained in a square column that stretched from floor to ceiling. The fire was already going, casting orange and yellow light over the dark walls.

Morana halted just inside the room.

"You can stay here," Matthias began, black boots clicking on the wooden floors. "Willow will be up soon." He turned to face her, dark eyes glittering in the light.

"Where will you be?" she asked. She didn't want to admit it, but as she stood in the palace, memories flashed of the assassin that Inara had sent. She could feel the sharp sting of a dagger run across her face, the way her knife felt cutting into the women, twisting and hitting flesh and bone. Morana shivered.

Matthias's expression distorted, speaking of what he could now see her struggling with. The anger she had felt in the cottage slowly disappeared. She had to admit that she was afraid, afraid to sit with her own thoughts, afraid to touch that hidden part of herself, the one that would surely come up while she was alone.

"The lords are being called the palace," Matthias finally answered. "All four of them." He stepped forward, standing a foot away from her. His eyes were soft. "We will pay her back for what she did." His expression darkened as he brought a hand up to the side of her face, fingertips twisting in her blonde hair. "We just need to figure out how it is we plan to do that."

Morana nodded. She couldn't look away from the marbled shades of dark brown and black in his eyes. The shades twisted like the smoke of the shadows. "And what will I do?" She swallowed the fear, reminded herself of the promise she had made less than an hour ago. "Will I be allowed in the room? To sit at the table? I am the one that was beaten, Matthias."

He looked at her then, seeing through all that she fought to portray. She felt as if he could see the fear, see the trembling girl lying within. The small child that had never had someone care for her, not fully. The one that she had ignored while she picked up the pieces of her life and kept moving forward, never staying in one place or moment too long. He could see her.

"You are welcome anywhere here." He spoke with a ferocity that sent shivers down her spine. "I would never deny you the chance to do something about the things that torture you, the scars that now exist." His hand was still on her cheek, stroking gently. "But for now, I want you to take care of yourself."

The statement struck her, reminding her of a conversation they had had the first time she had entered this realm. It reminded her of a sunroom atop a small restaurant in Ascella, the one where he had spoken truth to her, the truth about being selfish. Could she handle the darkness within her? The desperate and vulnerable emotions that tried to break free, and the untamed rage that simmered just below them.

Morana placed her hand over his, running her thumb across the moth tattooed there. She closed her eyes, preparing herself to do the work she had avoided for this long, knowing that he knew she needed to do that work too.

"Okay," she breathed.

For a moment, she thought Matthias might kiss her. He looked like he was battling with the thought. Instead, his hand dropped away, and he nodded once, turning to exit the room.

As he opened the door, a familiar woman strode through the entrance, dressed in a simple sage-colored tea-length linen dress, buttons trailing down from the scooped neckline. She looked beautiful in a way that Morana hadn't noticed before. Her black hair hung loosely over her shoulders, a friendly smile on her face.

"Miss Morana," she spoke.

Morana ran forward, hugging the woman, clinging to her tightly.

Willow's eyes were wide as she wrapped her arms around the broken girl before her, gently embracing her as tears threatened to break free.

"Shall I run you a bath?" she asked.

"That would be nice." Morana squeezed her tighter, her chin resting on the servant's shoulder.

"I will admit, this is strange." Willow loosened her grip and stepped away, looking at Morana and eyeing her. "But Matthias informed me of where you were." A darkness crossed her expression. "Are you alright?"

"I'm fine." Morana wiped the tears away, looking at the wardrobe that sat against the wall. "Are there clothes in there?"

Willow winced. "Yes, but we haven't moved everything yet. There are mostly dresses, and a few items you can use to sleep in."

"Right." Morana moved to open the wardrobe, taking in the elaborate dresses and a pair of black sweatpants, and simple shirts folded neatly at the bottom.

Willow moved, entering the bathing room where Morana heard the water run. She stood there, breathing deeply and choosing the sweatpants and shirt. She didn't know how long she stood holding those clothes, taking in the feeling of safety in her new surroundings.

Willow appeared around the corner, wiping her hands on her dress. "The bath is ready." Her voice was gentle. "I will leave you to it."

Exhaustion consumed her mind before she turns slowly. "Thank you," she whispered, a faint smile on her face.

The water was slowly cooling as Morana watched the shadows dance across her skin, the promise of protection her power provided comforting her. She had been sitting with her thoughts for hours, skin wrinkled and pruning.

She had sorted through the mess of emotions regarding her father. Something she hadn't thought about in years. Her heart hardened by neglect and abandonment. The tears came fast, leading her to a frenzy of heartbreak over the last month since her world had been turned upside down, the one person she had trusted for the longest betraying her in an instant.

A mirror sat facing the bath where she had stared at the lightly tanned skin on her back, unmarred, untouched. Was it even real? Matthias had believed it to be, and he had been moving through the painful memory with her. She couldn't help but picture the anger he felt because of all she had endured. Did he regret sending that man to Ashford? Taking part in some of the trauma that wound its way around her heart?

It didn't matter. Those moments in the alley, that man she had avoided, they were nothing compared to the days she had spent slowly losing her mind in the Court of Light. They would never compare to the stinging slaps Inara had placed over the scar of her assassination attempt. And absolutely none of those things would add up to the poison kiss of Axton's betrayal.

The anger had settled, leaving her with a burning desire to do something, be something, change something. She longed to accept the darkest parts of those feelings.

Vengeance, when done right, wasn't a reckless rage fighting to harm those who had hurt you. Vengeance was a dark companion living at the very core of your being. A creature that demanded justice, no matter the cause.

Morana got out of the tub, drying her body with the cream-colored towel Willow had left for her.

She threw on the lounge clothes she had pulled from the wardrobe; her damp hair seeping through the shirt. She sat on a bench, gazing out the balcony windows. As the sun settled on the horizon, she feared the moments she was about to spend alone. Would the shadows provide enough comfort for the night ahead?

"Willow said you've been in your room alone all day." She could feel his presence in the room without turning to look at him, the shadows that still comforted her flesh calling out to whatever magic he held within himself.

"How were your meetings?" she asked, glancing sideways at the death god now standing by the fireplace.

"Tense." Matthias moved forward, closing the distance between them.

The click of his shoes on the floor sent unsuspected fear through her blood. She could feel the stinging pain lancing across her back, causing her to shut her eyes. The image of Matthias sucking the venom from her lips, the strange dream she had had in that place, flashed across her mind. She came out of it.

Her emotions were more vibrant, harder to bury now that she had dug them up and explored what they were.

"Matthias," she said. Her voice was soft as she looked at him, standing with his hands in his pockets, his dark hair falling gently across his forehead. "Would you stay with me?" she asked—unashamed.

"Just until you fall asleep?" he questioned. There was a gentleness to his voice now, something that rounded the rough edges, the deep gravel usually in his tone.

"However long." She looked at him then, her eyes communicating the depth of her emotion. She was laying herself bare before him.

"I can do that." The shadows embraced him, and he was gone.

Confused, Morana made her way to the king-sized bed, nestling herself under the layers of blankets and sheets—waiting.

Matthias reappeared, shirtless and in a pair of black sweatpants. She glanced at the crows inked across his chest, the way they moved through the light of the moon, symbols of death, and symbols of the light that you could find in the dark abyss. The way the moon and the stars were gentle, shining in the pitch black when all seemed lost, when fears twisted and spooked, the place where many gave up. The stars and the moon were gentle and seeking, easing the searing pain of loss.

Matthias lifted the blankets on the other side of the bed, climbing in and keeping careful a distance between them.

Morana was lying on her back, staring at the ceiling above them and listening to his gentle breathing—a reminder that Death was a person, and he was very much alive.

"I had a dream while I was in there." She swallowed. "When I wasn't quite—" she struggled for the word, brows furrowing. "Right," she finished.

She could feel the shifting of the mattress as Matthias moved closer. The sun was fully set over Ascella. She could see it outside of the balcony, behind where he was now turned, facing her.

"Axton turned into this serpent," she disclosed. "He—he bit me—poisoned me." She turned to face him, gauging his reaction.

"That doesn't sound so far from the truth." They were facing one another now, his breath coasting over the tear-stained skin on her face.

Matthias reached up, easing a strand of her hair behind her ear. She inhaled sharply, surprised by the touch. For a moment she saw it then, this man, the one that had sent a goddess to find her, the one that was working to tear down all that had scared her. He was the stars, the gentle and seeking presence that asked her to look at the shadows within herself, to deal with her emotions, unearth them and be unashamed.

"You were there," she confessed. It looked as if he were holding his breath while she glanced at his lips. "It was strange, but you sucked the poison out—in my dream, I mean."

He chuckled then, a sound that made her smile. "You had a dream where I was sucking poison from a wound on your heel?" Matthias reached forward, resting a finger beneath her chin.

The surrounding air changed, crackling with a familiar tension. One that she had once fought against. Morana's lips parted, and Matthias trailed his thumb across the sensitive skin. She shuddered, heat pooling between her legs.

"Not my heel," she breathed. Her eyes heated with desire. He met her there, his expression darkening in the fading light of the fire.

His hand moved over her cheek, down her neck, a gentle caress that sent her heart racing. He rested his hand on her shoulder.

"No," she whispered, wrapping her fingers around his wrist and pulling his hand to her lips, tracing them with the tips of her finger. "Here," she answered. His bare chest was rising and falling rapidly, the dark stubble coating his jaw making her ache with desire.

"Is that all?" he asked. His voice sounded like he was fighting back a groan, throaty and enticing.

"That's all."

Matthias shifted forward, pressing a kiss to her lips. His mouth was warm, and she whimpered at the contact. He moved, adding pressure and threading his fingers in her hair. She could feel the rumble in his chest, a noise that had her stomach curling.

He pulled away, breaking the kiss and gazing at her with lust-filled eyes.

"Let me know where my lips end up in your dreams tonight," he spoke low. "I may oblige you tomorrow."

A small smile formed on his lips; the ones that had just been pressed to hers before he turned.

She shifted onto her back, breathless and light. Something was freeing about allowing herself to feel, about allowing him to see the depths of who she was.

Morana took a deep breath, closing her eyes and allowing herself to forget—if only for tonight.

Twenty-Seven

The morning light filtered across the luxurious room. Morana sat by the fire, watching the flames flicker and dance with the rays streaming in from the window. She had slept peacefully last night, embraced by Death. His presence had kept the nightmares away.

She could hear water running from within the bathing chamber. She got up, striding to the entryway and leaning against the doorframe. Her gaze roved over the god, brushing his teeth while standing over her sink. Her cheeks heated as she watched the flex of his arms beneath his rolled-up shirt. The moth on his hand stretched over veins and tendons.

Matthias had shaved, dressed for his life as a king. The disheveled man that retrieved her from the flora kingdom now looked as confident and powerful as ever. He leaned down, holding her gaze and spitting in the sink. A sharp inhale left her now parted lips as tension crackled in the air. Matthias took the pad of his thumb and wiped at his full lips. The ring on his finger catching in the light. He looked away, breaking her trance and placing the toothbrush in a cup by the sink.

Let me know where my lips end up in your dreams tonight.

She cleared the desire clogging her throat. "More meetings?" she asked, folding her arms across her chest.

"The lords are here." He wiped his hands on a towel before running one through his dark hair. When he met her gaze in the mirror once more, her pulse quickened to a wild pace. He leaned over the sink, the crows flexing on his tattooed flesh as he met her eyes again. "All four of them."

Morana tucked a strand of stray hair behind her ear, a crease appearing on her brow. "What exactly are you discussing, Matthias?" She was nervous, anxiously wanting to know what he was planning on doing and the reasons behind his actions. "Sarnai mentioned war," she confessed.

Matthias raised a brow, turning and leaning against the sink, hands still resting on the surface. "We are planning on taking their court to war," he answered.

Morana stuttered before speaking. "Over kidnapping? Over—" she fought for words. "A war over some strange mortal from the human realm? I want vengeance as much as the next person." She had planned to use this bitter rage lying dormant in her chest. She just hadn't figured out how. "But honestly, an entire war can hardly be justified."

His eyes were penetrating. "I escorted you to Mabon, and Inara found a way around the deep magic that binds us. That time of peace is important." His gaze darkened, something sinister crossing over his face. "She took you to a dungeon, laced with magic, to drain your own. She whipped you, used that time of peace, that *boy*," he spat the word as if it tasted vile on his tongue, "to lure you away." Matthias took a deep breath, running a hand down his face. "The implications of something like that—of harming one of our own."

Her head snapped up. "I'm one of your own?" she asked, allowing her vulnerability to show, the deep longing to be accepted in this place.

"That's what the shadows say." He cracked a subtle smile, watching her as black mist swirled in his presence, reminding her of the power they shared, the power found in his court.

Morana raised a brow, a wicked smirk forming on her lips. "Then I suppose I should get dressed."

Matthias ran his tongue across his white teeth, amusement dancing in his eyes.

Morana adjusted the red satin clinging to her body as her heels clicked on the marbled floors of the palace in

Ascella. She hadn't liked the dresses before, but something about wearing this felt empowering. Axton had torn a dress from her body, forcing her to bend to the will of a monster. Morana raised her chin. She would reclaim everything he had stolen from her.

Matthias was walking next to her, leading her to where the lords were now waiting. She pulled her hair to one side, draping it gently over her shoulders. It had gotten longer in the last month.

Two massive, golden double doors were before them. Matthias turned to her, a serious expression. "You're sure you want to be involved?" he asked.

Morana allowed the simmering anger to boil in her chest, remembering the way Axton had held her down, the way he had insulted her with his actions.

Morana nodded, and Matthias opened the doors.

Inside the room was a large, rounded wooden table. Five bodies sat around, standing as they walked in. Morana caught the confused gazes of the two strangers before her. Her nerves slowed when she caught sight of Sarnai, Ronan, and Garian. She kept her sights on the familiar fae and the goddess in the room, drawing strength from their presence.

Sarnai strode forward, wrapping her arms around Morana.

"Is the dress too much?" she whispered. Sarnai smelled of soil and mist. She kept her hands on Morana's shoulders as she leaned back to look at her.

"Actually," she began, a devious smirk on her face. "I believe you are severely underdressed."

Morana took in the goddess's silver gown, the light in her eyes, and allowed a smile to break across her face.

"I didn't know you read romance," she remarked. And Sarnai's eyes glittered in the dim light. Morana recognized the lighting here, the fires that seemed to burn with a preternatural glow.

Faefire.

"Of course I do," she chuckled, patting Morana on the cheek. "You might benefit from a little romance too, don't you think?"

"Couldn't agree more," Ronan was standing behind Sarnai, his bright eyes meeting hers before Sarnai moved to go to her seat.

"Lady Morana," Ronan continued, gently picking up her hand and pulling it to his lips. "It's great to have you back."

"I told you, Ronan." Morana pulled her hand away. She knew Ronan was harmless—had felt relief at his presence, but something about another man touching her burned her skin. The memory of Axton's assault still clung to her like a wet garment she was desperate to peel off. "I'm no lady."

He chuckled, leading her to a seat next to where Matthias had made himself comfortable. "You can't blame me for trying."

Garian was seated, staring at her with an unfamiliar intensity. When her eyes met his, she saw something like relief.

An unfamiliar woman with deeply tanned skin and dark curly hair piled atop her head sat back in her chair, tapping a manicured nail on the wooden table. Her full lips were set in a frown. "What's with the girl?" she asked, her tone tight.

"This is *the* girl," Garian chimed in, looking at the firm woman at the table.

"The one who was taken?" The woman's voice was louder now, cracking beneath the shock of her revelation. She quickly composed herself, one hand running down her face. "A liability." Her brown eyes sent ice toward Morana.

"She is to be welcomed." Matthias's deep voice was low—commanding. "This is Elivira," Matthias informed. "Lady of Namid. The forested city just before the border to the Court of Light."

Morana glanced at her lush features. Her nose was tilted up, lips full and dripping with malice. Morana fought to keep her face under a careful mask. "You believe me a liability?" she asked, allowing bitterness to slip into her tone.

"You are the reason we are having this conversation," she spat. "You are a liability."

"Bullshit." Morana raised her chin, challenging the woman. She wouldn't be labeled a liability. "I wanted to attend this meeting."

"And what makes you think you can assist this court with a looming war?" Elivira asked. Morana noticed the way her eyes glinted in the light. She was presenting a challenge, sizing up the strange woman Matthias had just brought into the room with the lords of his court.

"What makes *you* think I can't?" She allowed the shadows to coat her skin, the heady power put on display. Matthias didn't say anything. He sat quietly, arms folded across his chest, waiting to see what she would say. "This involves me, does it not? I'm not some damsel in need of saving."

Elivira laughed—a bitter sound. "Your previous situation seems to say otherwise."

Morana's eyes blazed with the raging fire that formed in her chest. She stared at the woman, pushing shadows in to access Elivira's mind. It was intrusive, and she didn't care. She needed to know.

Elivira flinched as she tried to block Morana out. The woman's eyes widened before steeling to tell Morana that she hadn't expected that power or the way Morana refused to hesitate.

"I was kidnapped, imprisoned, and whipped naked on the floor of a dungeon that sucked the shadows from beneath my skin." Morana leaned forward, resting her elbow on the table. "I have no qualms about cashing in on revenge." Elivira's jaw ticked. "The revenge I am owed."

Matthias was smiling, his arm resting on the back of Morana's chair while his other hand tapped the surface of the table.

"I guess that answers that question," he said. "You have information about the book." Matthias began, and Elivira shifted in her seat.

Morana's eyes moved around the room, taking in the two older men in the room. They hadn't spoken yet. She didn't bother interrupting.

"The blood book is in a temple just outside of Zora."

One of the older men chimed in, his thick white beard moving as he talked. He was broad, his white hair pulled back into a bun. "The blood book," he began, "Where did you get this information?"

Elivira glanced in at him, a serious expression on her face.

That's Hames.

Matthias's voice rang clearly in her mind. She glanced in his direction. His dark eyes met hers briefly, a small smile on his face before he looked back at the broad man across the table.

You should keep your mind more guarded.

Morana stretched the shadows toward him, entering his mind freely. He had left it open. She smiled.

As should you. She saw him react, knowing he had heard it.

Elivira leaned forward. "My city borders the courts. Fae pass through all the time. A woman from Zora was heard speaking of the blood book in one of the taverns. I think it would be worth collecting before we move forward with an entire war."

"What is a blood book?" Morana asked.

Elivira scoffed, clearly irritated at her ignorance.

Morana didn't let the expression through, wouldn't allow herself to be belittled.

"It's tied to Inara using blood magic," Garian informed. "The book will house her memories. There is one for all the gods. It helps to document their histories."

"It's a journal," Morana remarked.

"More or less," Garian's expression never changed, but she saw the subtle glittering in his warm gaze.

"Elivira is right," Matthias finally said. "We should retrieve the blood book before doing anything else. It could tell us more about what Inara wants with the boy."

"The girl's lover?" Hames asked, glancing at Morana.

Morana tensed, her fists balled under the table. The rage was consuming as she fought to hold herself together. Memories flashed in her mind, the same ones that brought that burning fire to beg for payment for what he had done. Now that her shadows returned, they begged for vengeance as much as she did, undulating in anticipation just beneath her skin.

Easy. Matthias whispered into her mind.

"He's how she lured me away from the palace." Morana's tone turned dark, laced with the poison of betrayal. "But no," she started, "He is not a lover."

"So, who plans on retrieving the book?" Sarnai asked, feet propped up on the table's surface. She was staring at her nails, hardly bothered by the tense conversation. "I already retrieved the girl." She smiled at Morana.

"We will go," Matthias answered, a dangerous glint in his eyes. "I have a blood book of my own. I'll know how to retrieve it."

And where is yours? Morana asked.

Matthias smirked, the only sign she had spoken to him. *Wouldn't you like to know?* He answered.

"We shouldn't go alone. We will need at least two more," Matthias finished, looking around the room.

"I'll go," Ronan chimed in, looking to Morana and winking. "I would never turn down an opportunity to travel with a beautiful woman."

"Elivira, we will need you as well. You're the one with the information," Matthias said, ignoring Ronan's flirtations.

The woman huffed in frustration.

"We won't be able to shadow into Zora." Matthias was looking at Morana. "We can go to the border, then make the day's journey, but we don't want them to track our magic."

Morana nodded, fear creeping up her spine. "So, no shadows?" she asked, doing her best to hide the emotion from the lords seated in the room. She just got them back and had been keeping them close. Their nearness gave her strength, allowed her to push past all that happened. The idea of suppressing them made her pulse quicken as trepidation closed around her throat.

"No shadows," Matthias confirmed.

She looked next to him where Garian was seated. The man was smiling, and it almost wiped away the fear she felt—almost. "I hope you've been practicing what I showed you, strange mortal."

Twenty-Eight

Morana awoke to a familiar presence seated at the end of her bed. She had spent the previous afternoon talking with Sarnai as she showed her the library here in the palace of Ascella. Touring her through the gardens and introducing her to the staff.

The fire was fading, the room cooler than she expected. Morana glanced at Matthias sitting at the end of the bed. She didn't know when he had shown up, when he had decided to sleep with her, but she was thankful he had.

She looked at the skull tattooed on Matthias's back. Shadows made up the intricate details of the tattoo. They seemed to pulsate and swirl, much like the powers that rippled underneath his skin. She admired the way his muscles shifted as he leaned forward, setting a coffee cup on the tray in front of him.

"Did you have any pleasant dreams?" he asked without turning around.

Morana flushed. "No dreams." She didn't bother hiding her relief at that, sitting up on the bed and leaning against the mountain of pillows behind her.

Matthias chuckled, standing and moving toward the bathing chamber. He paused before entering, looking back over a shoulder. "This room was my mother's," his voice was low.

"You had a mother?" Morana figured he did after her conversation with Sarnai, but it still was a shock. To think that the powerful god cloaked in dark mist hadn't just appeared was difficult to wrap her mind around.

Matthias laughed, turning around to face her and leaning against the door frame. "Of course," he said.

"But you're a god."

Morana realized then how much of who he was she didn't know, didn't understand. And still, she trusted him implicitly.

"And so was she," he offered. His dark eyes lingered for a moment as he thought. "The temple in Zora," he began. "It's more of a tomb. That tomb belongs to a god named Lux."

Morana's heart lurched at the sound of that name. She had read about him before, in the land of the gods. She remembered the story.

"I know about him," she said, pulling the blankets off of her legs and standing. "Inara seduced him, right? He was the god ruling over her court before." She tucked her hair behind her ear. "There was a book in the land of the gods. I got it to open. I was trying to learn more about Inara after that dream."

"He ruled her court." Something dark shadowed his expression, sending chills over her skin. "She keeps the blood book in that tomb. The book that details her memories." He rubbed the back of his neck with his hand, eyes breaking away from hers. "It'll be warded and difficult to get into."

Morana saw it then, the insecurity cracking his façade. He was nervous about this, nervous about stealing whatever this book was. In the meeting, they had explained that all the gods had them.

"Like your blood book?" she asked, a small smirk on her lips.

Matthias's eyes met hers once more. He smiled then, a knowing expression. "Like mine."

Morana thought about the mission they were about to complete, stealing a personal relic from a god, using it to begin a war. She didn't know exactly what she felt, but she was realizing how dangerous Inara was. She briefly felt the familiar scalding scars on her back, the ones that weren't really there.

"She killed that man, didn't she?" Morana asked.

"She did." It was a simple answer.

Morana remembered the sword, the one the text spoke of, wondering if that was the answer to the question she had asked outside of Reese's shop.

She smiled again, gauging his reaction at her words. "So, I suppose it takes a little more than a nice dress to kill a god."

Matthias lingered in the doorway, looking up at her through the stray strand of dark hair that had fallen across his eyes. A small smile pulled at the corner of his mouth. "It takes a weapon designed by one of the major gods to achieve that, but don't worry. Those gods are dead, and that sword you talk about went missing long ago."

The thought gave her little peace. That familiar simmering stirred in her chest, fueling the desire to repay the goddess for what she had done. A sword like that would be a valuable asset.

She didn't like the way she didn't want to be alone, felt strange having such an urgent need to remain in Matthias's presence. It made her feel weak, and weakness wasn't something she needed—not with the task at hand. After the day spent contained in her rooms, draining everything she hadn't allowed herself to feel, she was exhausted.

"Matthias?" she whispered as he grabbed a shirt from the bathroom floor, shrugging it over his shoulders.

Matthias paused.

"Yes?" His voice was soft, coaxing the confession out of her. The thing she longed to tell him.

"Thank you."

"For what?"

She didn't know. She hardly knew what she was thanking him for. It could have been his presence, his willingness to keep the loneliness at bay. Or it could have been the way he saw through everything that she was. It could have been the way he had seen her emotions as he lived through the memories that made her. That was invaluable, something that she couldn't stop herself from appreciating.

"I—" she stuttered. Deciding how she would answer. "Thank you for seeing me."

Matthias nodded before turning toward the exit of the tower bedroom.

He paused for a moment, glancing back at her. "There are clothes on the table. You'll need to get dressed as we will leave for Zora soon."

Right.

Morana kept her eyes on his back, thinking about what he had asked her when she had woken up. He had asked her about her dreams, and she had lied, knowing what he was actually asking, but she trusted this man, and if she were being honest, she liked the effect he had on her.

"My lips again," she whispered. It caused him to pause. He didn't say anything, just held his hand on the doorknob, still turned away.

"You asked me if I had any good dreams." She couldn't hold back the smile when his eyes glanced back.

Matthias chuckled; a sound sweeter than anything she had heard before. "Right," he responded. She saw the way his full lips curved into a smile, the way the image brightened the room.

For a moment she thought that maybe she had gone crazy, sleeping in the same bed as Death, flirting with him. She wanted everything he had to offer. Death was the comfort she craved, the consistency and realistic expression of who he was. He wasn't afraid to tell the truth, and he wasn't afraid of the things she had shown him—the things about herself.

Matthias exited the room, leaving her to prepare for the journey ahead.

The temperature was cool around the palace grounds, the leaves on the trees turning shades of yellow, orange, and red. Morana glanced down at the leathers she wore beneath her cloak and the belt clasped firmly around her waist, giving a place for her sword to be sheathed. The dagger was strapped to her thigh.

Ronan and Elivira had brought the horses out from the stable, packed with everything they would need for their overnight journey to Zora. Nerves skated over her limbs, her stomach fluttering in anticipation. They would shadow to the border, and once they crossed, she wouldn't be allowed to feel the familiar comfort of her power.

She was fidgeting, anxiously awaiting the arrival of the horses. There was fear burning in her chest, reminding her of the last time she had gone without the shadows, how they had failed to protect her.

Matthias had assured her they could use them to shift out of Zora, just not while they were there. It was too much of a risk to be traced or seen with the powers of his court.

Another body appeared behind her, and Morana turned. Garian was standing there, dressed for travel, with a stoic expression etched onto his face. It was so rare to see emotion from the lord, but it was there. She had known it during that meeting, and deep down, she felt that the ill-humored and crotchety man actually liked her.

"Here to see us off?" she asked, patting the hilt of the sword at her side. "I'm eager to prove my lessons were successful." Morana gave him a bright smile, an attempt to continue to win him over.

"I'm coming with you," his voice was gruff, his face expressionless.

Morana looked at Matthias. The death god didn't look surprised, as if he had known this would happen.

"I'm not sure you've had enough lessons to actually defend yourself. I'm here to provide extra assistance."

Morana feigned a frustrated sigh. "That's actually a bit of an insult, Garian." She could have sworn he smiled, just barely.

Elivira came out with two horses, followed by Ronan leading another two.

"If Garian's coming, don't we need a fifth?" she asked.

Matthias wrapped an arm around her shoulder, pulling her closer. He smiled, and she followed his gaze. "I didn't know if you could ride." He pointed to the largest horse, a dappled Percheron gelding carrying a large saddle. "We are both riding that one together."

She looked back to Matthias, reading the amusement flickering in his eyes. Her blood heated at the knowing smirk pulling at his lips.

"Do you think that's a good idea?" she asked.

"Do you?" Matthias smiled then, allowing his arm to drop away from her.

He grabbed the reins and led the horse to a mounting block in the grass. "Do you need help?" he asked, still smiling from their previous exchange.

The others had already mounted from the ground.

"I know how to ride a horse," she grumbled, stepping up the three steps and taking the reins in her hand. Her right hand was atop the back of the saddle.

She had to admit, this horse was huge, probably on account of carrying two people. She struggled to reach the stirrup.

"Everything alright?" Matthias asked. His tone was taunting, and it sent frustration skittering across her chest.

"I'm fine," she huffed, shoving her foot into the stirrup, and whipping her leg around, careful of the sword dangling from her side.

Matthias mounted behind her, sending a wave of heat through her blood as he pressed in close. She tried not to think of all the places their bodies were touching, tried to focus on where they were going.

He had one arm wrapped around her waist, holding her close, and the other wrapped around to hold the reins. The horse stepped forward and back, anxiously standing and ready to move. Morana swallowed.

She felt his thumb brush over the fabric on her stomach, eliciting a sharp breath from her lips. Matthias chuckled and leaned down, his mouth just next to her ear. He repeated a phrase she had heard him say before, one that had her picturing a warehouse.

"Don't blink."

And then they were gone.

Shades of gold and deep auburn colored the forest, telling Morana of the season in this part of the realm. She wondered what it was like back home. She swallowed. Home. She wasn't sure she had one of those anymore.

Morana sat with Matthias behind her. They had been walking on horseback for hours, moving over the muddy ground in the Court of Light. There were no people here, just the peaceful wilderness surrounding them. It eased some of her fears, gave her a sense of comfort she didn't know she had needed.

Ronan hadn't stopped talking, filling the forest with conversation as he attempted to charm Garian into actually befriending him. Garian hardly reacted, grunting in frustration every few minutes.

"Not to bring up a poor memory," Ronan began, his horse coming alongside the gelding her and Matthias were riding. "But I enjoyed dancing at Mabon. You certainly impressed me with your moves."

"Yours left something to be desired," she taunted, rolling her tongue along her cheek.

Ronan laughed then, blue eyes sparkling in the fall light that flickered through the trees.

"I assure you my physical performances leave nothing to be desired." Ronan winked at her, still attempting to flirt despite her disinterest. She had to admit she found it funny. A chuckle broke loose from her lips.

"Is that why you cycle through so many women, Ronan?" Garian asked, his low voice carried through the trees. "I would assume if a woman was truly satisfied, she would continue to come back. You would have had a wife by now." A flicker of emotion crossed his face, breaking the severity that she was used to. "Your city will catch on. It could ruin your reputation."

Ronan laughed then, a jovial sound. "My reputation is already ruined."

"Ah," Morana chimed in. "I would hate to make it worse."

The conversation grew quiet. Elivira was leading, her horse moving with quick strides. She hardly participated in the conversation, her sole focus on business. Matthias allowed their horse to fall back, just behind Ronan and Garian.

"You said I kissed your lips in your dreams last night," Matthias stated, his voice low as his breath caressed the shell of her ear. Morana shifted uncomfortably, her body feeling extremely hot. She wanted him, but the view of the other lords caused her to pause. This wasn't the time to reflect on her burning desires.

"A lie," she spoke, allowing the small smirk to remain on her face. "I just wanted to see how you'd react."

"And how did you want me to react?" he asked, pulling her closer to his chest. "Did you want me to kiss you again?" There was a pause before he gently brushed his lips over her skin, just below her ear. Her breath caught in her throat. "Shall I allow you to sit on my throne while I do it?"

The memory flashed in her mind. She recalled his lips pressed to hers, the way his touch had burned her skin with delicious heat. He had pushed her down on the throne, demanding her to remain in that position. She liked the freedom with him, the way he *wanted* her to defend herself and make her own decisions. Morana could feel the flush over her skin as his warm chest pressed into her back.

"I did like the power," she rasped, leaning her head back against his shoulder and tilting it, giving him more access.

Matthias's thumb made gentle circles on her stomach before moving slowly to her thigh beneath her cloak. She didn't want him to stop, almost begged him to continue. Her body was begging for release after all she had been through—pleading for closeness and pleasure.

"And where else would you have me kiss you, Morana?" His voice was husky, laced with seductive promises. "Where would it feel most powerful?"

She couldn't think beyond his hands, the way he moved his fingers to trail up to her waistband, over her pants, and lower.

"What are you doing?" she asked, holding back a moan.

"Something I've wanted to do for a while." His hand stilled. Her head still resting on his shoulder, his body pressed up against hers. "Would you like me to stop?"

"What if they see?" Morana's spine straightened, her eyes flicking wildly around the forest.

"Don't make too many noises, and they won't know a thing." The words had her panting, fighting any noises that built in her throat.

He shifted forward, pressing his body against hers, one hand still tucked under her cloak, resting on her upper thigh. She could feel his hard length pressed behind her, driving her to the brink of madness.

"If they won't see," she breathed, leaning into his touch, begging him to take. Her braveness surprised her. She didn't think of herself as someone to do something so intimate in an open place where she could be caught. But then again, she didn't think she even knew who she truly was. The mask she created all those years ago became her identity, and Matthias took it and shattered it. It left her as exposed as she was now. Usually, she would run, but instead, she ground into him.

She felt his chest rumble behind her, his hands slowly moving to her waistline, that moth tattoo inked over the veins in the hand that no one could see. She could feel it though, feel when he skimmed his fingers along her flesh, feel when his hand glided between her skin and the fabric of her pants, feel when a finger pressed directly where she needed him most, damp heat flooding her very being.

"Tell me, Morana," His voice was still a whisper, the horse still hanging back from the others. She hardly thought about where she sat, hardly recognized her surroundings, or what they were doing beyond that one finger stilled at her core. "How shall I make you feel powerful today?"

She moaned softly as his finger moved, sending pleasure through her entire body.

"Shh," he whispered, his finger stilling for a moment. "Tilt your hips forward."

She obeyed, settling back further as his finger moved down, dipping into her and curling inside. Morana bit her lip, her chest rising rapidly at his touch.

Her back arched when he pulled that finger out, gently pressing the tip against her inner walls as he moved to that spot again, softly circling—circling and then dipping back in.

He repeated his motions, over and over, his pace steady as he brought her over the edge. She fought to keep quiet as she came crashing down, a heady wave of pleasure washing over her body as he stroked her until she settled.

Matthias groaned, gently kissing her neck as he gasped for breath. "*Fuck*," he whispered. She could feel his solid length press into her from behind. She shifted and Matthias pulled his hand from her pants, unwinding his arm from her waist. Glancing over her shoulder, Morana turned and watched as that glistening finger dipped between his lips. His brows pinched together, and another groan rumbled in his chest. Her cheeks heated at the sight of him.

"Oh my god," she whispered, leaning forward and gripping the pommel of the saddle. Her breath was still coming out in shallow pants.

"You are referring to me, aren't you?" He laughed, and she joined him, the sound drawing Garian's attention from up ahead. The lord raised his eyebrows, eyes widening before he looked forward again. Was that a blush creeping up the stoic warrior's face?

"Oh no," panic wound its way around her throat, gripping her tightly. "Did he—"

Matthias just laughed again. "He's a married man, Morana. Don't worry about it."

Embarrassment flooded her cheeks, causing her to place some distance between herself and the solid body behind her.

"I didn't know he was married," Morana stated, distracting herself.

"She lives in Nashira with their toddler."

Morana turned to look at him, her brows furrowed. She twisted to face forward, glancing at Garian on the horse up ahead. "I find it difficult to imagine him with a young child. He's not exactly warm."

"He has his moments."

Elivira halted up ahead, her gaze cast out through the trees. A tension moved through the air, allowing panic to grip Morana's heart, heightening her senses to what was happening.

Ronan and Garian halted as well, looking out to see whatever Elivira had seen.

A soft music filled the air, lulling and intoxicating. Morana could hear it increasing in volume, drifting through the trees wrapped in golden autumn light, settling the adrenaline that had raced through her veins, muddying her thoughts. She could only think about that sound, the peaceful singing coming from the mist that now rose in the forest.

Matthias tensed behind her, but she hardly acknowledged his reaction, still gazing out at the mist, listening to the sound that longed to pull her in.

Morana's mind wrapped around peaceful memories, resting somewhere between sleep and wakefulness. Matthias dismounted, unsheathing his sword, preparing to fight.

"What is it?" Morana asked, watching the others dismount.

"Veeden," Ronan answered. His usual temperament replaced with a tense seriousness that now overshadowed his expression.

"A siren of the wood," Matthias finished. "How comfortable are you with your sword?"

Morana fought the raging desire to move forward, to meet the mist, and all it offered. She dismounted, listening to the sound float in the air around them. It was as if she could touch that sound, hold it close, and keep it, something to chase away the darkness.

"Don't call the shadows," Matthias warned, but now that she looked at him, she saw him straining to fight the effects of the Veeden—the siren.

"Aren't they creatures of the Wastelands?" Garian asked.

"They're supposed to be," Matthias answered, his tone tight.

The fog thickened, making it increasingly difficult to see the other lords. Matthias's figure slowly disappeared, swallowed by the gray haze that was growing with the volume of the siren's song.

Morana looked around. "Matthias?" she called softly. There was no response, only the silhouette of a woman moving through the trees.

The trees were swaying. Or maybe it was her? Regardless, Morana fought to keep herself lucid, but the song kept begging to drag her under—pull her out to sea in the way it was told in stories.

The woman appeared, her naked form taking shape as the mist parted around her. Her skin was like bark, textured and gray, and she was singing with her long silver hair set in waves that hung below her waist. The song consumed her—the words leaving the woman's lips as the creature stepped forward, prowling like a woman tracking down prey.

"Queen of Darkness," the Veeden's voice had a musical quality to it, coasting along the song she had been singing to draw Morana in. "Can you hear him calling you?" The woman was close now, circling Morana through the fog. "Can you hear him begging to give you your heart's desire?"

"Who?" Morana whispered. The fog still clouded her mind and senses.

"Raidan's calling, child." The siren reached a long black fingernail out, tracing it over Morana's features with a gentle touch. "Give in," the woman breathed.

Morana closed her eyes, a heavy presence settling over her, weighing on her shoulders. The Veeden's lips were hovering just in front of hers. She could smell the moss and dirt scent of the siren's breath.

"Give in," she hissed. Morana wanted to. She had wanted nothing more. A sharp nail dug in just below the scar on Morana's cheek. The agonizing sensation of flesh ripping sobered her mind, dragging her from the sea that threatened to consume her.

Morana didn't react, thinking through her next move. She felt blood run down her jaw, dripping on the hand that now rested on the hilt of her sword.

Her hand tightened around the hilt as she opened her eyes, met with the contorted face of a siren ready to consume. Morana tried to pull back as the woman struggled to drag Morana's mouth to hers. Bile rose in her throat as Morana fought against her tightening grip, the biting sting of that long black nail still digging into her flesh.

"Give in," the Veeden shrieked.

Morana wouldn't. She unsheathed her sword, ripping herself away from the grip of the creature of the wood. The sword gleamed in the fading light, cutting through the mist.

"I will not," Morana declared.

The monster's features twisted, its lip peeling back as she morphed into something ugly and evil. A sinister smile crossed its face, its skin dull and leathery. "You will give in to Raidan's call, Queen of Darkness. You will."

The Veeden didn't move as Morana brought the sword down, cutting its head from its body in one swipe.

The blade met the resistance of flesh, pushing through whatever bone and black blood lay within the creature.

The head rolled, smile still stretching across the Veeden's face as the body crumpled to the ground next to the detached skull.

Shock shot through her heart as she fought to catch her breath. Her stomach was churning, threatening to expel its contents on the forest floor before the mist faded. Autumn leaves broke through the fog as a quietness settled. Matthias, Garian, Elivira, and Ronan appeared with their swords drawn and eyes frantic. Morana wrestled with her uneasy stomach and stood straight. She had done it—had protected herself.

She wiped the crimson staining her face, the black blood dripped from her blade. Matthias glanced at the head shoved into the mud, his eyes wide.

"Taken care of," Morana asserted, kicking at the head and fighting the bile in her throat before turning.

Matthias walked forward, running a hand along the small puncture wound below her scar. She could see the debate, the desire to heal. He couldn't call on his power, not out here, not while they still had to retrieve the blood book.

"Don't," Morana grabbed his wrist, gently pulling his hand away from her face. "Leave it."

"I told you she was an exceptional student," Garian chimed in.

"Please," Morana scoffed. "You hardly trained me."

Garian cracked a smile.

"Natural talent, then." Ronan's usually light temperament disappeared. There was only raw shock remaining on his face as his blue eyes widened. He sheathed his sword, never letting go of the hilt—as if the weapon were a lifeline that held him steady.

"You wouldn't know natural talent if it bit you in the ass," Matthias joked, keeping his eyes pinned on Morana's. There was concern in the hard set of his jaw, the crease forming on his forehead.

The nausea settled, replaced by a numbness she couldn't touch yet., something. She figured the feelings would come later, and she would welcome it instead of burying it six feet under.

Elivira appeared before her. "We need to get out of these woods before more creatures show up." Elivira used her sleeve to wipe dirt from her full lips. "The caves aren't that far, and the horses waited."

Morana didn't say a word. She merely moved to their gelding, mounted from the ground without thinking, and waited to finish the last few miles to the caves.

Twenty-Nine

Morana kept replaying image of slicing the creature's head from its neck. She could feel the metal cut through gruesome flesh. Hearing the slick slide of the weapon and crack of bone, she trembled. The reality of what she had done, the head rolling on the forest floor as the ominous whispers hit her in the dead of night. The crimson stain of death settling on her bones.

Morana wandered from the cave where the others were sleeping. Matthias was missing, but it was almost as if she could feel him. She wandered the rocky hill, guided by the full moon that hung overhead. The stars were out, gently glittering above.

She could hear the rushing of water, the river they had crossed on their way to the caves where they set up camp. About a mile downriver was the wooden bridge where their horse had nearly shied, refusing to cross.

As she came to the foot of the hill, met with the sight of soft blue light glistening over the water, she saw Matthias seated at the river's edge. His knees were up, elbows resting there.

Morana didn't say anything. She just merely walked forward, sitting next to him in the silent darkness. They didn't speak, only stared out at the rushing waves, the trees beyond the river stretching overhead, hiding the creatures that lurked beyond.

She looked down at her hands in her folded lap—still shaking. All she could see was the sinister smile of the Veeden. The words hissed before she hacked off its head.

You will give in to Raidan's call, Queen of Darkness. You will.

The words unsettled her almost as much as the feeling of flesh meeting steel.

A warm hand covered her quaking fingers, the moth tattoo muted in the light of the moon. Morana turned to look at Matthias, met with the understanding in his gaze.

"I'm sorry," he breathed. "For the scars that are now placed on your heart." He reached his other hand up, trailing it over the two marks etched into her face. "And for these," he continued, "Though they serve as a reminder of the strength you have."

Morana looked away, allowing his hand to fall away. She chewed on the words before she spoke. "I now hold a scar for each life I've taken," she whispered.

Matthias was pensive, but he didn't speak, just kept his gaze pinned to her, mulling over what she had confessed—the real reason behind why she wanted to keep them—why she wouldn't allow him to heal the marks marring her face.

"Is that why you wanted to keep them?" he asked. "To remember?"

"Sometimes I don't feel things right away." Morana looked down at her hands, still trembling. "I know it's a reaction, something I started doing because of how I was raised." She ran her hands down her legs, trying to wipe the terror away. "I got so used to burying everything, it became a habit. Why not wait to feel until I felt safe?" A small smile formed on her lips. "I've dealt with a lot since being around you."

"Does that mean you believe me to be safe?" Matthias questioned, a smile of his own decorating his lips.

"You are not safe, Matthias." She chuckled, leaning back on her hands. "But something about knowing that to begin with is comforting."

He hung his head between his legs, a small laugh escaping and disappearing into the soil below.

Her face turned serious once more. "I kept the scars for them," she admitted. "Even if they both were trying to kill me, even if one was a creature, it doesn't mean I didn't care. I killed them. I took two lives."

Matthias's gaze was dark. "It gets easier." He ran a hand down his face. "It shouldn't, but it does."

"For a god of death, I haven't seen you do a lot of killing."

"I haven't killed a human if that's what you're asking. Plenty of fae have been executed by my hand, though." He shifted to stand, pulling his shirt up over his head. His weapons were gone, abandoned in the cave where the lords were sleeping.

Morana watched as he stripped out of his pants, left in only underwear. Her pulse quickened as she took in the lean muscle and twisting darkness that seemed to follow him.

"What are you doing?" she asked.

"Going for a swim," Matthias smiled as he moved to the water, turning his back on her as he tugged his underwear off. Morana flushed as she got a full view of his toned backside.

Heat washed over her as she watched him jump into the river, turning and swiping the damp, dark hair away from his forehead.

"Are you coming?" he questioned.

Morana hesitated a moment before deciding to follow. He had already seen her naked once, and after what they had done on the horse—

Her heart picked up in pace as she stripped off her clothes. She unclasped the bra at her back and allowed it to fall onto the muddied grass of the riverbank.

The air was cool, and she prepared herself for the biting sting of water as she jumped. The river and moonlight consumed her, the silence bringing a peace to the anxieties she held.

When she broke through the surface, Matthias was there, grinning with teeth white. He splashed water at her, and she closed her eyes tightly, a small shriek leaving her lips.

Morana skidded her hand across the quiet waves, sending droplets directly for the god. She laughed then, caught in a moment of despair, fear, and joy—the life she had found in the darkness—the life she had found in death.

Matthias moved closer as the water settled. She could feel the floor of the river beneath her feet, the dirt shifting as he walked even closer, his naked body in front of her. Morana halted, looking up into onyx eyes, her breathing shallow.

Her mind flashed to the way he had touched her on the way here, the way he had her riding his hand, fighting the moans she so desperately wanted to release. She brought a hand to his chest, feeling the slick skin and light dusting of hair.

"Do you feel powerful, Morana?" His tone was dark, laced with desire.

"No," she said, lowering her own tone. "But I think you can help me with that."

Matthias's lips parted as he closed the space between them. She could feel him everywhere, his body pressing flush against hers, his thickness pressing into her leg. She let out a shuddering breath as he wrapped his hands around her waist; the water shifting in gentle waves over her skin.

Matthias leaned down, pausing before his lips met hers, a question there in the movement.

She didn't bother answering, just closed the space between, crashing her mouth against his in one reckless motion. The heat of his lips encased her, sending jolts of pleasure through her blood.

He tasted of secrets and solace, moving with a desperate hunger to consume. She would let him and bared herself to him fully in the moonlight.

Morana wrapped her legs around his waist, his hands running along the backs of her thighs, lifting her with her waist just beneath the surface of the water. Matthias groaned as his hard length brushed over her entrance, sending fire into her veins.

"I don't know how this works," she breathed, breaking the kiss. "You're a god, I don't know—" she didn't know how to formulate words as he pressed his lips to hers again.

He broke for a moment. "If you're wondering about protection, there are herbs you can take. Sarnai has them. We will be home tomorrow, or today. I don't know what time it is." His chest was rising and falling rapidly, barely containing the beast beneath inked crows flying across a night sky. He was panting as she ran her hands through his dark hair.

"Herbs, right," she moaned as his length brushed over the heat that was quickly pooling at her core. "Go on then."

Matthias chuckled before meeting her lips again. One hand moved up to caress her breast, gently squeezing.

Her head fell back as he kissed and licked up the column of her neck, his movements becoming more fevered.

He kissed her collarbone, nipping at the skin there and sending pleasure racing up her spine. The sting pushed her, desire quickly taking over. She moved her body, trying to get him to hurry.

"Impatient," he mused, still ghosting those full lips over her sensitized flesh.

"I'd like to meet death now," she breathed, her eyes fluttering closed. "I'm not afraid anymore."

Matthias paused, and she could have sworn his breath halted for a moment. Once he snapped out of it, he pushed his thick length into her, completely stretching her at the size of him. He pulled out slowly before thrusting into her in a way that sent her head spinning, filling a hollow part of her she hadn't realized she held.

Matthias moved, marking her with every bite, every lick of his tongue. His movements were frantic as he buried himself in her, groaning with every motion. He couldn't get enough of her skin, hungrily threading his hands into her hair. His grip tightened as he pulled her head back, his tongue trailing over her jaw.

She moved her hips in time with the pace he set, grinding against him until she was climbing, working toward a release she knew would be her undoing.

Her nails dug into his back, scratching that shadowed skull tattoo in desperation. Matthias didn't stop, biting her lip and sucking the wound.

His breathing grew harsh in the night as he slammed into her. She let out a throaty noise; her release just within reach.

"Fuck," she breathed.

Matthias slammed into her again, gripping her firmly as a dark rumble sounded in his chest. The sound sent her over the edge, rising and falling with the crashing waves of the river around them. She hung there, suspended with the stars, while he quickened his pace, finding his own release and shuddering.

They fell into one another, arms wrapped tightly as they shared breath. She exhaled, her mind deliciously empty of the worries that haunted her. His firm grip held her. Morana could feel the echoes of shadows rippling beneath her skin. The comfort she took in the safety of their presence returned. She couldn't use them here, but they were there, lurking beneath the surface. Matthias was there, too. He had been there, and for the first time in three years, she didn't feel so desperately alone.

When she finally came down, her forehead resting on his firm shoulder, Morana laughed, realization appearing as Matthias continued to hold her beneath the stars.

"I just fucked a god," she said.

Matthias chuckled, squeezing her thighs. "And how do you feel?" he asked, knowing full well what her answer would be.

"Powerful," she whispered.

"Did you dream about me, darling?"

Morana opened her eyes, faint sunlight streaming in from the mouth of the cave. Ronan was hovering over her, blue eyes glittering and a smile on his dirt-streaked face. Even with the smudge marring his features, he was attractive. Yet, she found herself more amused than taken by his devilishly handsome looks.

"She certainly wasn't dreaming about *you*," Garian remarked. He sat by the fading fire, carving a piece of wood with his knife.

Morana flushed, sitting up on the bedroll of the cave. She hadn't gotten enough sleep, the exhaustion from the Veeden settling into her bones. She thought of last night, heat working its way to her cheeks.

Looking around, she spotted Matthias leaning against the wall at the cave entrance with a cigarette between his lips, the lips she had become familiar with by now.

"Right," Ronan said, extending a hand to help her up. "It was worth another shot." He winked as she placed her palm in his, standing and brushing dust and dirt from her pants. A tight braid dangled at her back, and her cloak draped over a large boulder in the corner.

"I haven't seen you do that in a while." She nodded toward Matthias, gesturing to the cigarette he had between his finger and thumb. Smoke blew from his mouth.

"You didn't seem to like it." He tossed the butt out of the cave and into the crisp air, pushing off the wall and striding toward her.

He was standing in front of her, a smug expression on his face. She couldn't help but remember the way those hands felt gripping her legs, the way he thrust into her.

Morana looked away, voice a whisper. "Oh, I like it." The sight had her biting her lip. Something about the way his lips wrapped around the cigarette sent her thoughts spiraling and a familiar curling sensation wound its way around her stomach.

"Then good thing I'm a god and don't have to worry about something like a cigarette killing me." The smirk broke on his face, dark eyes glistening.

Morana cleared her throat, striding over to where Garian sat.

"What are you carving?" she asked, observing the piece of wood in his hand. The winged creature was taking form beneath the blade of his knife.

"A dragon," he answered, "for my son." He grunted, fighting off some emotion. Garian was usually good at casual indifference, but how long had he been away from his family?

"Matthias told me you were married." Morana looked over to Ronan and Matthias gathering bedrolls. Elivira had disappeared, and Morana figured she was out caring for the horses.

"I am." Garian tossed the dragon carving in his hand. It was remarkably well made. He smiled as he looked at his work. "Theo's a smart kid." He held the carving in his grip tightly. "Loves dragons and monsters."

"You miss them?" Morana asked, glancing at Garian's jaw, his dark skin glowing in the morning mist.

"More than I care to admit." He grunted, weapons hanging from his belt as he stood up. He said nothing else, just walked to gather what he had already packed.

Elvira appeared then at the cave entrance, tossing a bag to Morana. She caught it; eyes held on the strange woman. She wasn't friendly, but Morana didn't dislike her. In fact, she admired her, the way she had challenged the stranger in that meeting room.

"You should eat," Elivira spoke. "The horses are ready. Ronan, go make yourself useful and get that stuff out of here." Elivira sat next to Morana, stretching her legs out ahead of her. Her dark hair tied in a bun atop her head. She pulled out a piece of dried meat, ripping it with her teeth.

"How long until we get to the blood book?" Morana asked, pulling the mix of nuts and dried berries from the pack. She was starving, the dried meat, hard cheese, and trail mix hardly satisfying. Last night, Garian had trapped a few rabbits, cooking them before they retired.

"It'll be about an hour."

Morana was pensive, watching as Garian threw his pack over his shoulder, striding out of the cave. Elivira didn't talk. She had come on this journey, even though she believed Morana to be a liability. She hadn't complained, accepted what Matthias was asking her to do.

"I know you don't like me," Morana began.

Elivira scoffed. "What makes you think that?" she asked, glancing at Morana. There was no taunting to her voice.

"I—" Morana didn't know how to answer.

"I do like you." Elivira took another bite, speaking after swallowing. "You held your own in that meeting room. You decapitated a Veeden." She smiled. "A pretty badass move, if you ask me." Elivira stood up, finishing the piece of dried meat she had been eating. "You endured torture and came out with a heart of vengeance. You're exactly the kind of woman I would like for Matthias to keep around."

A knowing smirk formed on her lips, her tongue trailing over the inside of her cheek before she walked away.

Morana flushed, touching her lips before packing the food away. She wanted him to keep her around too, and the thought terrified her.

She grabbed her weapons, strapping them to her sides. She donned the cloak and walked out of the cave where the horses were waiting, packed with each of the lords and Matthias waiting.

She moved forward to her horse, Matthias holding the reins, a wicked glint in his eye.

"After you." He gestured to the stirrup, and Morana swallowed, placing her hands on either side of the saddle while Matthias helped her up.

He mounted, pressing his body against her back. His firmness reminded her of the river, and the fire that burned there.

"Not long now," He spoke softly, wrapping one arm around her to hold the reins.

She breathed deeply.

One more hour.

Thirty

Morana shifted, fighting the pull of sleep as the horse moved through the forest. They had left the caves, only to find themselves out of the forest for a brief time before the trees rose from the ground once more. This time, steep ravines and the comfort of large hills to one side accompanied them. They followed the line of hills, keeping close to the rocky walls stretching to the blue sky.

Morana fought the hallucinations of rising mist as she felt the cut of her blade on flesh, a ghost of a memory from her run-in with the Veeden. The eerie whispers filled her head, making sinister promises that unsettled her. The only comfort she found was in the god pressed against her back, guiding the horse as she leaned back against his chest, focusing on breathing.

"You've never actually shown me what you do in the human realm," Morana mused, as she shifted in the saddle. The long hour wore on her backside.

"I didn't realize you wanted to know." Matthias clucked, urging the horse to keep up with Elivira.

"Sometimes I feel like the human realm doesn't exist anymore, or like it was always just a figment of my imagination—like this is all there has ever been."

Matthias chuckled. It was a sound that brought a smile to her lips. "I can assure you there is far more beyond the human realm. I don't go nearly as often as I'd like, but I would be happy to bring you with me." He squeezed the arm that was wrapped around her just slightly. "Though I will warn you, it's difficult to watch."

"Do you kill people?" Morana brought her fingertips to the puncture wound on her cheek, the dried blood there that the Veeden had left. She felt for the scar just above it as well, remembering the assassin's blade sliding across her skin. She hadn't bothered to ask before, assuming killing was his job, but brutal killing didn't fit with the image he now presented. Matthias wasn't who she thought he was.

"I don't actually kill people in the human realm." She could hear the seriousness in his tone. "My duties as king sometimes call for it, but humans aren't fae."

Morana looked ahead, watching Elivira stop at a large door carved into the side of a rocky foothill. The columns rose on either side, a testament to the skilled masonry that made up the entrance.

The shadows threatened to break free as Morana felt the magic of the place. She fought to keep them at bay.

Garian and Ronan dismounted first, followed by Elivira and then Matthias, who was waiting to help Morana dismount.

She stared at the stone doors as she stood there, taking in the elaborate designs etched into the surface. There were strange markings running up the two columns to either side.

Elivira strode confidently for the door, grabbing the large handle and pulling, but nothing moved.

"You won't get in like that," Matthias informed. He wasn't mocking her, just giving information before he turned to Ronan.

Ronan nodded and unsheathed the dagger at his waist. He gripped it, knuckles whitening, before cutting a line across his flesh, just below the crook of his elbow, horizontal across his forearm.

Morana flinched, drawing back at the sight of blood welling. Ronan noticed the reaction, his blue eyes taking on their usually amused light.

Curiosity covered her shock as Morana watched the lord step to the entryway, tracing the carvings on the stairs with deep crimson blood.

As Ronan stepped back, eyes still pinned to the stone, the symbols changed, a golden glow emanating from the etched carvings.

Wind whipped around them, magic rumbling through the earth as the glow faded. The light slowly disappeared—the blood gone. They stood in silence as the air became stagnant.

"Runes," Ronan whispered. "It will work."

A soft click sounded, and the doors swung open, greeting them and encouraging them to venture into the temple.

They walked forward, the deep magic changing the surrounding air. Inside the temple were two colossal statues on either side of the long hall. They looked like gigantic wolves carved in stone, teeth barred as they guarded whatever lay beyond.

The yellow light floated in the temple, giving the stone floors a golden hue. At the end of the long hall sat a glass case with a man, perfectly preserved, clutching a sword to his chest. He was lying flat, and as they moved closer, entering the bowels of the temple, Morana realized why Matthias had called this a tomb instead.

She shivered at the eeriness of the man. Long blond hair like a warrior, tanned skin. He almost looked as if he were still alive, and the closer she got, the more it seemed so.

Standing directly in front of the glass coffin, Morana traced a finger on the lettering of a plaque. The script had one name and a phrase in a language she couldn't read. The name drew on something familiar, something she had heard or read before.

Lux

Morana inhaled sharply, turning to Matthias, who was now standing by her. "Lux, as in the god? The one Inara killed."

Matthias's brows raised, and his shoulders turned rigid.

"It seems so," Elivira said as she walked around the room, poking and prodding the walls for any hint of where the book was.

Morana could see nothing else beyond the coffin that sat in front of them.

She traced the letters of his name. It felt familiar.

"Here," Ronan said. There was another rune etched into the wall just beyond where the dead god was resting. "This is it."

Ronan dipped his finger into the blood pooling on the cut he had made, tracing the rune with careful concentration.

That same yellow glow took over the entire tomb, lighting it from within just as something clicked on the stone slab that held up Lux's casket. A small door opened, and Matthias moved forward to retrieve a book, golden in color, with a delicately designed piece of metal holding it closed.

"Inara's blood book," Elivira breathed.

"Right." Matthias gazed at the book before looking around the tomb frantically. "Okay, we need to go." He put the book inside his pack. "The shadows won't work until we are out of the temple, and those stone carvings—"

He never finished the sentence.

A deep growl sounded from the entrance to the tomb. Morana turned to see a large dog, almost like a wolf, with a humanoid body and eyes of glowing ember.

Panic rose as she reached for her sword, watching the dog prowl toward them. It was massive, its lips peeled back in a vicious snarl.

Morana unsheathed her sword, readying herself for battle. She watched as the three lords and Matthias had already grabbed their weapons, ready for an attack. She longed for the comfort of the shadows, but she couldn't feel them in this place, bringing back memories and the desperate fear she had felt as Inara's prisoner.

Garian stepped forward first, sword in hand. The movement had the dog snapping its neck, shooting its ember eyes in Garian's direction. Then the creature lunged.

Garian struck true, plunging his sword into the belly of the beast, but the monster was unrelenting. Sweat beaded on his brow as he fought with the creature before Ronan appeared behind the animal, slashing his sword across its back. The dog wailed, a piercing sound sent up across the stone as black blood dripped into its fur, floating down to the floors below.

Bile rose in Morana's throat as she watched them fighting. Matthias stepped in as she stood panicked, her sword held tightly in her grip.

The monster turned, pulling itself off of Garian's sword, the wound stitching instantly. The damn thing could heal itself.

Matthias thrust his sword upward, penetrating the wolf's jaw. His sword cut straight through to the other side, coming out between the creature's eyes. The wolf howled, using its humanoid hand to grab the sword from Matthias's grip.

"No!" Morana screamed as the wolf snapped its jaws, gripping Matthias's leg. Ronan stabbed it again from behind, his jaw clenched as he fought for the king of his court. Matthias's leg bled, unable to be healed because of the magic of the tomb. Nobody could call their power.

"The sword," Elivira shouted. She was standing by the glass tomb, desperately trying to move the lid from the top. Morana glanced at the sword in the hands of the dead god.

She ran over, helping Elivira to move the lid. It was heavy, and she grunted as she pushed, sweat dripping down her back. They got the coffin open enough for Morana to reach in and grab the sword. The hilt of it sent pain racing up her arm, igniting her blood and making it boil. She screamed again, barely able to focus on the battle surrounding.

"That can only be one fucking sword," Elivira yelled, jumping in to fight the wolf off Garian. "A sword like that can kill a god. It can certainly kill this creature."

Morana realized what she was saying. This was the sword from the story she read about Inara. Inara had stored her blood book in a tomb where the god she had killed was laid to rest, forced to reside with the weapon that killed him. The irony was not lost.

Morana ran forward, her blood still burning from the magic of the weapon. Ronan was pinned under the wolf, his shoulder bloody, when Morana moved to strike the creature. It turned, lunging at her with snapping teeth.

"Fucking hell," she breathed as the monster swiped a claw at her, marring her shoulder, making it bleed. She shrieked, the pain biting and distracting. As the dog moved to jump on top of her, she fought to lift the sword, successful as she drove it through the creature's gut, blood spurting and falling to wash over Morana's clothes.

She was panting as the creature stilled, the sword still embedded in its belly. The full weight of the dog fell on top of her, and she struggled for breath before Garian and a limping Matthias pulled it off.

"Not bad with the sword," Garian remarked. "One designed by a god, no less."

Morana scowled, willing herself to stand, smelling the coppery scent of blood. "I'm really tired of the compliments you make after I kill." She touched her shoulder, blood coating her fingertips.

"And I'm really tired of you being the one doing all the killing." Garian smiled—barely, and Morana let out a sigh.

Her hands were trembling again in light of what she had just done.

Matthias was beside her, leg still dripping blood on the stone. He touched the wound on her shoulder.

"I suppose you want to keep this." She flinched as the pressure of his finger stung.

"Another scar, another death." Morana dropped the sword, allowing Ronan to pick it up before working her way out of the temple.

As soon as they walked through the doors, she felt the familiar sensations of her powers. It curbed some of the anxiety coursing through her.

"Can we go now?" she asked, still in shock over what had happened.

Matthias grabbed the horse by the reins, looking around at the company around them. "I suppose that's a good idea."

Morana let the shadows take hold, watching them wrap around each and every one of the lords. She pictured the open paddock of the stables at the Palace of Ascella, just near where they had left.

In an instant, they were falling into the abyss. Only to end up standing exactly where they desired.

Morana stood over the book, the gray walls of the room where she had first met the lords around her, closing her slowly into a box of hopelessness. They couldn't get the golden book to open. The strap that latched it shut held firm.

Sarnai walked in, handing her a steaming cup of something. It wasn't the first time the flora goddess had pressured her to drink some strange herbal concoction.

"This one's a little different." Sarnai put her arm around Morana's shoulders with a smile on her face. She leaned to whisper in Morana's ear. "Matthias, let me know you might need this."

"It's warded," Garian spoke from where he was seated against the wall. His head had fallen back against the wall. Morana saw the blood and dirt streaked on his face, the exhaustion that was setting it. It was setting in for all of them. "There's no telling how we will open it. No telling what kind of crazy magic Inara used."

Matthias strode into the room with a steaming cup gripped in his tattooed hand. Morana glanced from the cup to his uneasy eyes. He didn't know how to open this book either.

"Look," Elivira began. She was sitting on the table and leaning over with her elbows on her thighs. She ran a frustrated hand down her face. "I merely figured out the location. Knew it would be in the foothills around Zora. I can't be asked to figure out how to open it."

"I did the runes," Ronan said, leaning against the far wall and pointing to the scar on his arm. He touched it gently, the skin slowly stitching back together with the power he held. He smiled. "So, it's not on me. Though I did bring back that damn sword." Ronan gestured to the sword on the other side of the table, the one they had stolen from the tomb.

"I trained the wild woman," Garian added. "Trained her well if her body count means anything."

Morana grimaced. "You lazy asses." Her brows furrowed as she stared more intently at the book.

Elivira laughed and hopped off of the wooden table. She patted Morana on the back, a small smile on her full lips. "Of course we are. We work for Matthias."

Morana tried again, prying at the cover of the book. It was no use—a familiar place to be.

"I suppose we can't read it," Ronan said.

"No shit," Morana stepped back, allowing Matthias to observe the book.

"What does it take to confuse a god?" she asked, a smirk playing on her lips.

"This fucking book." Matthias set the cup down, reaching in his back pocket and pulling out a cigarette and lighter. He lit the end, inhaling deeply. Something about the way his lips wrapped around it had her heart racing.

Matthias looked at her, a wicked and knowing glint in his eyes.

They would never open it. They needed someone who could—someone who knew more about opening books.

Cain.

Morana grabbed the book, exiting the room swiftly. She found herself in the hallway, looking around.

"Where are you going?" Matthias asked, following behind her.

"Where are the libraries here?" she questioned, moving down the hall. She didn't know if she was going in the right direction.

"Down the stairs, off the first floor." Matthias was right on her heels. "Why?"

"Cain," she said.

"The scribe?"

"You said everyone from the land of the gods was moved to this palace." Morana turned to look at him, clasping the book tightly to her chest. "Cain can open this book. He helped me once. The boy knows books."

Matthias chuckled.

"I'm being serious. That boy could probably do this. He was there. He helped me open a book about Inara, and he knows abnormally much about everything. We need to find him."

Matthias stared at her, taking in the words.

"How old is he, by the way?" Morana looked at Matthias for an answer.

He smiled. "He's sixteen."

"So, the fae—"

"Garian is two hundred thirty-eight."

Her eyes widened. "The library," she began.

"Right." Matthias grabbed her arm, shadows pulling at her. And then they were gone again.

The library in the palace of Ascella was larger. From the center, Morana could look up at the glass dome above them and see the railings lining the three floors above them. The shelves were dark—as was the entire palace.

Morana looked at Matthias. "Where do the scribes usually work?"

"The fourth floor," Matthias answered, grabbing her hand in his and pulling her along behind him. They moved to the stairs, quickly ascending until they reached the fourth floor.

Morana moved through stacks of neatly placed books, looking for red hair and a smattering of freckles in the dim lights of the library.

They came to a table on the fourth floor of the library where Cain was sitting, writing and copying from a book in his lap. It reminded her of the last time she had confronted him.

Morana rushed forward, slamming the blood book on the table in front of the boy.

Cain jolted in his seat as his eyes went wide as he stared at the book. He slowly lowered his pen to the table, swallowing hard. His head was flicking between the god and the girl who had interrupted his thoughts.

"We need you to open this," Morana insisted, gesturing to the book that now rest on the table.

"And what makes you think I can help you with that?"

"You've helped me before."

Cain pointed to the golden book on the table. "That is a blood book from one of the gods, not the book the *Histories of the Seelie*. Who does that book even belong to?"

Cain was staring at Matthias, a question in his eyes.

"Does it matter?" Morana asked, frustration quickly rising.

"It's Inara's." Matthias offered, pulling his cigarette back to his lips.

Cain's eyes went wider, and Morana thought the boy might pass out right there at the table.

He reached forward, inspecting the book and running his fingers over its surface. He picked it up, holding it to the light and turning it over before setting the book gently back down on the table.

"This could take days." The boy scowled at the tome as if it were a puzzle he was now trying to figure out.

"That's fine," Morana stated. "We just need it opened."

Her memory flashed to Axton's hands on her, pulling at the fabric of her dress, yanking her to her feet, and slamming her head against the hard stone. She could feel the weight of burning fire crashing over the skin on her back. She could see the kiss that Axton shared with Inara, the way she treated him like a dog.

They needed to learn what she was doing with Axton.

Cain grabbed the book again, working to study the designs etched into gold.

Morana stared at him, waiting for answers before she felt Matthias's hand at her back.

"We better pass the time elsewhere," he said.

Morana nodded, allowing the burning desire to consume her, only to be tamed by the hope of answers.

Thirty-One

With Cain working on the book, Morana had time to sit in the still quiet of her room. Moonlight was streaming in through the balcony, lighting the dark walls and sparkling on the golden accents.

She sat on the balcony, freshly bathed, with her knees drawn to her chest. The lights of Ascella glistened, the vast city stretching out with cobbled streets and creeping vines. Autumn colors had settled in, leaving crisp leaves floating in the wind just outside the balcony.

Morana rested her arms on her knees, placing her head there, her blond hair ghosting over her legs. She wore black leggings and a white, long-sleeved top that she had covered in shadow. She had missed using her powers on the way to Zora, missed the security they provided, the peace found in the dark mist.

She felt his presence then, and she didn't need to look to know that Matthias was in her room, stalking towards her. She figured he was here to keep her company tonight. The weight of his presence was heavy, meaning more than she cared to admit—even to herself.

"Put some shoes on." His low voice rumbled across the floors. Morana turned. He was dressed differently, a white t-shirt clinging to his muscled form, a familiar leather jacket, and black ripped jeans. She liked him like this.

"Where are we going?" Confusion coated her features, furrowing her brow as she took in what he was wearing. She could have guessed where before he said it.

"The human realm." Matthias ran a hand through his hair. "I want to show you something."

Morana stood, slipping on a pair of canvas shoes, something that reminded her of the life she had left behind.

"Is this part of your death god duties?" she asked.

"More or less."

Matthias walked over to her, gently brushing a strand of hair behind her ear, allowing the darkness to consume them. "Keep yourself hidden. You won't want to be seen."

Morana descended into the abyss while allowing her power to hide her form. Nerves moved through her at the thought of returning to the human realm—brutal memories threatening to break the peace she had found in the Court of Shadows.

They were suddenly standing in the dusty bedroom of an old house. A blue floral comforter drawn over the frame of a sleeping man, face wrinkled and ashen with age. He was breathing peacefully.

Morana saw the medication littering the side table, the half-finished plastic cup of pudding. Everything in this place smelled old, the lingering aroma of death fast approaching.

"Is he dying?" She asked as silver lined her eyes, the tears threatening to spill over. There was no hiding what she felt, not looking at an image like this. She didn't know this man, but the image struck her, a reminder of mortality, the fragility of life.

"He is." Matthias's features hardened, a tense expression on his face. It was as if he had seen this many times before. "You once asked me about what I did in the human realm. I wanted to show you." The shadows were twisting around them, keeping them hidden from view. "This is what it is to be a god, Morana—the truth of it."

She heard the creaking of a wooden door to their left. A small girl, close in age to Morana, walked in, brown hair tucked behind her hears. A hard edge that formed long before this night, encased her blue eyes, and Morana saw a familiar wall around her that was built for safety—for keeping people out.

As soon as the door clicked shut, the girl's features softened, her eyes turning glassy with tears. There was a likeness in her face. It reminded Morana of the man, even while he lay just moments from death. This had to have been her grandfather.

The blue-eyed girl crawled beside the man, careful not to rest any weight on him as she held the hand he had on his chest. She was clinging to him for dear life.

Her tears were silent, hidden away for just this moment. Morana joined her, a steady stream washing over the two scars she wore on her cheek, the ones reminding her of the lives she had taken, the things that had made her tremble and made her anxieties come to life.

"This one's lived a good life," Matthias spoke. His voice was low, coated in magic designed for Morana's ears only.

Morana gave him a questioning look.

"I can just tell," he offered, jaw tight.

The girl began speaking, talking of many memories lived. She detailed mornings of crisp newspapers and steaming cups with the scent of coffee. She spoke of blue numbers written on lined parchment and companionable silences with depth far greater than any passionate discussion or vulnerable conversation.

"This moment feels private," Morana whispered.

"Aren't all moments, really?" Matthias asked, keeping his eyes on the dying man. "It just depends on what you choose to share that takes a moment from private to public. What is secret for one, is freely given for others. The shadows don't ask for permission. They see it all."

"What are we here to do?" Morana wiped the tears from her cheeks, deep sorrow setting in her bones at the image before her.

"Ease his mind."

The room turned quiet, carrying the solace of Death.

The silence ended at the sound of a broken voice, shattered and small. Morana saw pieces of herself in the desperate girl. When she had walked in, there was that familiar hardness to her, a protective wall wrapped around her, blocking out the world and all that she felt, but in the safety of this room, in the safety of his presence, the girl allowed herself to fall.

"You always said you were proud of me," the girl croaked, her hand still wrapped around the fingers of the listless man. It made her look like a child. "You always made sure I knew. You never let me doubt it."

The tears burned, coming faster and harder as Morana watched the scene unfold. She couldn't stop the stabbing pain of loss that struck her. To watch something so emotionally hurt. She couldn't believe this was something Matthias had done before. Why he continued to do whatever it was they were trying to accomplish by standing cloaked in wisps of darkness.

"What am I going to do now that you're going to be gone?" the girl whispered, closing her eyes and leaning into the man's shoulder. "I miss when you could hear me and tell me what to do. You always knew better than anyone else." Her eyes were still shut as the girl let the well of despair rise.

"Will she be alright?" Morana looked at Matthias. There was a new expression on his face. It was layered, and Morana desperately wanted to peel those layers back and uncover what rested beneath.

"She will." He stretched out his hand, shadows wrapping around the entire room as it became dark, pitch-black as the longest night.

There was peace in the night that wrapped around them and caressed them gently. Morana knew it was Matthias's power because she felt it too, slowly easing the sorrow.

Morana reached out to melt her power with his own. She wasn't sure exactly what she was doing, but she had practiced enough to know she could form the darkness, shape it to what she needed, and the idea had already taken root.

She split the mist, creating the illusion of sparkling stars above them. The lights covered the sobbing girl as if she were under a vast night sky, letting her see all the beauty she could find in their pain.

"It's peaceful," Morana breathed, tears still lining her eyes at the depth of emotion.

"Death can be."

It was a truth she knew too well.

"I've seen that," she expressed. "Do you do this often? Do you come to the human realm to give peace to those fading from this world?"

"Not often enough." He cleared his throat, working through what he was feeling. "What kind of god would I be though, if I could bring comfort, to meet people in their darkest hours and wrap them in something that could heal—if only briefly—and I never used that ability?"

Morana looked at him, the full lips and tanned skin. She saw Death then—really saw him in the same way he had seen her. He was the image of a god, desperate to lead and desperate to care. She was descending into a depth of something she hadn't allowed herself to feel before, her heart warming in her chest.

"You are good, Matthias." She wrapped her hand around his to stroke his inked skin. She laced her fingers through his own. "A good king, a good god, and a beautiful mystery."

Matthias looked at Morana briefly before turning his gaze to the reason they were here. "We should go back," he said, gently squeezing her hand. "He's about to go."

"We could take a walk first. I've missed being in the human realm, and I don't want to leave just yet."

Matthias nodded and Morana looked back at the man, his breathing slowing to still under the sky they had created. One last tear trailed down her cheek as the elder gentleman was swept away. His soul was now floating to wherever people truly go after they die.

Matthias turned to face her and reached up, brushing the tear away and placing a gentle kiss on her forehead. The shadows engulfed them, and they were gone, standing on the trail of a forested park.

"How old are you, Matthias? How old are you, really?"

The moonlight filtered through the trees and dappled the forest floor. Morana stepped on crisp leaves, the sign that fall had appeared in the human realm. When she left, it had still been late August. So much time had gone by, and also so little. She hardly remembered what it was like to live without the power that lie in her, the power she just used to heal.

Morana looked up, a clear night sky above them. Showing the same stars and symbols she had created just moments ago. It was still peaceful. Amid of all the pain she had just witnessed, she could find peace walking beneath the stars with Death.

"Too old," Matthias answered, the side of his mouth quirking up into a smile. Morana saw the tattoo peeking above the collar of his t-shirt, knowing now that it was the tip of a crow's wing. She thought about the way the planes of his chest felt under her palm, her face heating.

"That's not an answer." She bit her lip and bumped her shoulder into his, not knowing if he would actually tell her. Death had to be old, but Sarnai had once said he wasn't as old as her. Garian was old, but he was fae and not a god. "What is it? Like thousands of years?"

"Not yet." His hand grabbed hers, his fingers brushing gently against her skin. She ran a finger over the inked hand. "Though you are about to find out that you slept with an old man." Matthias laughed, and she couldn't get enough of the light in his eyes when he did.

"Are you older than Garian?" she asked. "You are a god, though he certainly looks older."

"I'll be seven-hundred twenty-four soon."

Morana's head snapped to look at him. She stopped walking. It wasn't surprising. He certainly didn't look that old. "Oh my god." She stared at him; a taunting look in her eyes. "You're a predator."

"It doesn't necessarily work like that. I'm relatively young in terms of the age of a god." He studied her, trying to find any sign of discomfort.

"So, you're like twenty-four, but seven-hundred twenty-four in dog years?"

"Sure." Matthias smiled, looking out to the trees as they started walking again.

The forest was quiet, save for their footsteps. Morana watched the light move over leaves and gravel, her mind wandering. She felt a pang in her chest at the realization of the life she had given up. Even so, there really wasn't anything here for her. Certainly not her father—wherever he was.

"Tell me about your parents," she asked, voice quiet. She didn't know what he would say—if he would answer at all.

Matthias unlaced his fingers from hers to put an arm around her shoulders, kissing her temple firmly.

"How is a god created?" She traced her gaze over his full lips.

"You're interested in creating one?" There was a wicked glint in his eye.

"I'm being serious."

Matthias's face fell. He thought for a moment. "My father ruled the Court of Shadows before me. He ruled when the Court of Shadows went by another name." He leaned in a bit. "The Unseelie. He was around when Inara killed Lux." Matthias's voice changed, dropping lower and filling with sorrow. "My mother's crown is in the hall of relics. It's beautiful really, with black and red stones. She wasn't a god, but one of the major gods gifted her with the same life span as my father. They died when I was twenty. I was an adult by then. Even though I had been preparing to take over the Court of Shadows, even as my father had taught me all it was to be a god of death, I wasn't prepared for them to go."

"One more question." Morana leaned into his arm around her shoulders. "What about your blood book? Are you afraid someone will take it?" She was starting to understand the importance and power the books held.

"Are you wanting to read my memories, Morana? Is telling you about my family not good enough?" He was smiling now, looking down at her as the light of the moon highlighted his features, the dark stubble that now coated his jaw.

"I'm sure you'd let me into your mind again." Morana held his gaze. "You'd show them to me if I asked." She believed it, believed what she had said with everything.

Matthias stopped, placing a hand on her cheek and running his thumb along the two scars there, the ones reminding her of the lives she had taken. He ran his other hand over the scar that was now carved into her shoulder.

"Tell me this, Morana," he began. "Why do you want to keep these scars? Aren't the ones on your soul enough?"

She stared at him, feeling the way her skin heated at the gentlest touch. He spoke as someone who had seen death time and time again, someone who didn't understand why you would want all those reminders. His gaze was searching. She had thought about it that day she had spent alone in the castle. It was the day when she had finally touched all the emotions she had kept buried for years.

"I was just thinking. If my soul becomes so scarred that I can no longer feel the sting of death, if I have my skin marked too, it will be a reminder that I can choose to never be too far gone." Her brows furrowed. "That sounded stupid and made little sense." Morana shook her head and looked away. "I guess I'm saying that my hands have trembled after every kill. If ever there comes a day when they stop, at least I have the scars to remind me of how it felt at first. The scars will draw me back to compassion—keep me from becoming a bloodthirsty animal."

"You certainly are bloodthirsty." Matthias leaned forward slowly as the air crackled between them. The shadows wrapped around them. He used his power to caress her skin. It ran like a touch down her arms, over her chest, between her legs. She inhaled sharply at the sensation before drawing on her own power.

As the inky mist pulled from her chest, it stuttered briefly as Matthias's power lessened. That's when a crack sounded in the forest.

Morana's stomach dropped, the panic rising like a flood. Her eyes were frantic, desperately trying to see who was out there. She had been hunted before, and a familiar race of adrenaline shot through her veins. Her mind couldn't focus as she drew her power closer, allowing the shadows to twist over her skin. Inara was still searching for her, hunting her. Now that they had the blood book, did she find them?

"We need to go," Matthias said, his tone tight. The shadows increased as he drew on more of his power. Morana didn't miss the way Matthias winced just before they disappeared.

Thirty-Two

Morning light broke through the balcony doors, meeting the lingering light of the fire. Morana turned to see Matthias standing with his back against the wall. He had stayed here again. He hadn't missed a night since the day she had asked him to stay.

"You slept in." He was smiling now, face cleanly shaven and clothes neat. He looked every bit the king of darkness, the god of shadows and death.

Morana's stomach growled in response as she kicked off the blankets. Matthias's chuckle sounding in the room.

"Breakfast was already served. I know you haven't eaten in the hall here. Willow is in the kitchens this morning. I'm sure she wouldn't mind you showing up and begging for scraps." The black mist rose, and Death was gone, fading away before she could say anymore.

Morana chose a forest green gown, not bothering to address her hair. She added enough makeup to look presentable and made her way down to the kitchens.

The room was warm and smelled of baking bread. Servants were moving around, chopping vegetables, and preparing for lunch. She spotted Willow standing by a hearth, poking the fire with an iron.

Morana almost laughed.

"Those make a great weapon," she said.

Willow turned around with her wide blue eyes widening in surprise. "You missed breakfast, Miss Morana."

"I was out late."

Sarnai appeared through another door, carrying a steaming cup, her elaborate dress billowing behind her.

"There you are!" She walked around to shove the cup into Morana's hands. A familiar scent coming from the herbal concoction. "I walked this all the way to your room to find it empty," she scolded.

Elivira appeared then. She wasn't in a dress, still wearing leathers similar to those they wore on their trip to Zora. Morana hadn't talked to her since inside the cave.

She came in and grabbed a pastry off the counter, turning to eat it casually.

Willow glared at her. "You can't do that."

"I'm one of the lords. I think I can. Especially since I'm not opposed to pulling the power card for this delicious work of art the kitchen staff has come up with." Elivira leaned over the counter, taking another bite of the baked good and looking at Morana's cup. The smirk faded, and she wrinkled her nose. "Is that what I think it is?"

Sarnai smiled, winking at Morana before answering. "Why? Do you need some?"

"I don't need that." Elivira looked at Morana. "When did you even have time?" Her face drained of color. "I sincerely hope this was after the trip."

Morana blushed, turning to Willow. "Something to eat?" she asked.

Willow set some plain pudding in a jar with seeds in it in front of her. There was a layer of jam and fruit stacked on top.

"What is this?"

"If you don't want it, then you're welcome to starve." Willow tossed over her shoulder, grabbing the fire iron to continue her prodding.

Morana ate the food in silence, drinking the tea as well. The pudding was good, better than she expected. A reminder of where they had been last night flashed in her mind as she remembered the dying man. The sorrow still sat heavy in her bones.

Matthias appeared with Cain. His face was serious in the busy kitchen. He said nothing before gesturing to Sarnai and Elivira to follow. Morana dropped the spoon and walked out of the kitchens, feeling the urgency of what was coming.

"I got the book open," Cain began as soon as they entered the hallway. Morana let out a startled breath, her heart picking up in pace at the thought of what they would uncover. "I've read some of it. There's something important that we need to look at, especially if you're considering using this to launch a war."

Matthias walked next to her; tension woven in his shoulders. She could see it in the way he walked.

"Have you read it?" she whispered.

"Some of it."

They made it to the library, quickly returning to the table on the fourth floor.

Sarnai sat on the table's surface next to Elivira. Matthias was standing on the opposite end of the table, staring at Cain. Morana was looking at the opened book. She couldn't believe how fast Cain had pried the damn thing open. Staring at the leather, she chewed her lip, nervous about what they would find.

"The pages before this are *missing*. That is unheard of for a blood book. All the gods are bound to these. How the magic of the book can be disrupted, I'm not sure." Cain ran a hand through his curly hair, fingers tangling in the strands. He let out a harsh breath. "I can't see anything regarding how that could have happened, but this entry, just after the missing pages. This caught my attention."

Cain read aloud.

The Wastelands were always bitter and cold. I hate the snow and the mountains where the gods sleep. I am certain now, more than ever, that the girl who appeared in my palace for mere moments is, in fact, the Queen of

Darkness. The whisperings must be true. She will have two options: accept the call or end her own life.

I refuse to end my reign. I have worked too hard to be conquered.

"Queen of Darkness," Morana whispered. "Sarnai, you told me you didn't know what that meant, but you told me the story of Lady Death?"

"This is impossible," Matthias breathed. He swallowed hard.

"You'd have to have more than the shadows in your blood for that to mean anything," Elivira added. Her scrutinization made Morana uncomfortable. She shifted on her feet.

"She's gone insane." The webbing on Sarnai's forehead flickered, glowing brighter for a moment.

"There's more about the boy's bargain. The bargain is true. He is bound, and it was unbreakable, but there has been more since then." Cain flipped to the page and Morana grabbed the book, reading silently.

His hands ghosted over my skin, and I swore it was better than anything I had ever felt. This wasn't part of the bargain, but I had to admit, I would be a fool not to accept this level of attention.

Axton wrapped his lips around my—

Morana slammed the book shut. The simmering rage now boiling, threatening to break free. Her face was hot, and the kiss they shared in the dungeon seared her memory. The burn of betrayal scalded her all over again. His loyalty to Inara ran deep—deep enough for him to shove his tongue down her throat—to betray and bruise and tear the dress from Morana's body. Bile rose in her throat as Morana stared at the damned blood book.

"I read something else before I called you up here," Matthias added.

"Something about her sexual escapades?" Morana spat.

Sarnai just looked confused, but the emotion was too much. The level of betrayal was far beyond what she had originally anticipated.

"That sword Ronan brought back with us, the one you used to kill that dog." Matthias leaned his hands on the table, face serious. "It was the one she used to kill Lux, and it is one that could kill a god. She isn't the one that has it."

"So," Elivira began. "You still want to take our court to war, and you want to kill the bitch."

Morana's jaw ticked. "I agree with killing the bitch." She let the burning wrath ignite, burning higher and higher. "And Garian said once before, I've become good at killing." She lifted her chin. "I wouldn't mind a war."

Thirty-Three

Shadows twisted in her dream world. She was standing in the nothingness of her mind. The power was her only company. Morana ran a hand through her hair, breathing deeply. This space was one she had grown to love. Her power resided here, and she was finally feeling comfortable with herself—the version she had kept hidden for so long.

Morana was sitting, her legs curled to her chest as her cheek rested on her knee. Running a finger over her lips, she thought of Matthias, the heat of his body, the slick sensation of his tongue requesting access as they kissed.

She thought she could hear his voice whispering in the darkness. The sound became louder—pleading as the shadows begged her to listen. Her limbs were coated in dark mist, hairs standing on end as the peace she had felt disappeared—replaced with an urgency she couldn't understand.

Matthias's voice echoed once, clear as it boomed through the darkness.

"They found me."

Morana stood up, spinning as she tried to see anything but the dark chamber of her mind.

"They found you?" she called. Panic took root in her chest, vines wrapping tightly around her heart and squeezing to the point of pain. "Matthias?" Her voice echoed in the void. "Where are you?"

"The land of the gods."

Something was wrong. Morana could feel it in her bones, feel it in the shadows that refused to stop drifting over her skin, whispering dark secrets in her ear. Matthias wasn't there when she awoke. The castle was quiet, but she *knew.* It had been real.

She descended the tower, finding her way to the hall. Nothing seemed to be amiss, and she thought for a moment she had been going crazy, panicking as a result of the trauma she had experienced. Still, there was the incessant nagging of the shadows in her head, the one that reminded her how she could feel his power, sense when he was close—like calling to like.

Morana walked the halls, canvas shoes padding silently across the black floors as she tried to ease her mind. Sarnai showed up, pulling her into an alcove in the corridor, a desperate look in her eyes.

There was an urgency to the set of Sarnai's jaw, a tension in her shoulders. The usually graceful and unbothered goddess glanced down, umber eyes burning with fire. Morana knew what she would say before she opened her mouth.

"Matthias isn't here," she whispered. Her voice was harsh—urgent. "I went to the land of the gods," she admitted. "Morana—"

Morana's heart quickened, the familiar rush of adrenaline running to her head as she fought to listen to what Sarnai had to say. The flora goddess was usually composed. Morana had never seen her this worried—frightened.

"The palace is destroyed." Sarnai's eyes were wild, her hands trembling where she held Morana in place, her grip punishing as Sarnai fought for something to steady her. "Everything's tipped over. It's like someone was looking for something, looking for him."

Morana tensed, sheer dread weighing her to the floor. The blood was roaring in her ears as time slowed. Matthias was gone. The palace was destroyed. Where did he go?

"I need to see for myself."

"You shouldn't—" Sarnai gripped her hands tighter, but Morana pulled from that grip, calling the shadows and picturing the foyer in her mind. She could see the red carpeting and woodwork lining the walls.

She didn't hesitate. Part of her knew what she would find, but the fear was still palpable.

Sarnai disappeared from sight as the shadows consumed, twisting before throwing her into the land of the gods.

Everything was overturned, and her world was burning.

Morana looked around the palace, taking in the destruction. She couldn't lose it, not now. She did something she hadn't done in a while. Morana took the fear and chaos swarming inside her chest and shoved it deep in the grave, running through the halls of the palace she had nearly called home.

She couldn't sense him here either, couldn't understand what had happened. There was dread here in the emptiness of the house. She had grown close to the god—trusted him. His presence was a constant protecting force. Morana dug her nails into her palms as she began running, finding her way to the hall of relics. Time was moving slowly as she observed the objects lining the tall shelves.

A crown caught her eye, delicate and intriguing with ruby stones and crystals black as night. It was beautiful. It took her a moment, but Morana realized who that crown belonged to. The recognition made the anger burn brighter.

The blue glow from the fountain distracted her, and she found herself moving to the Basar in the same way the Veeden had drawn her in. Power swirled in the water, begging to be used. She wasn't thinking now, her mind void of thought and filled with the whispering voices of the shadows.

Matthias had told her that the Basar could show her the past. Maybe they could show her what had happened.

There was the chance the Basar would consume her, that she wouldn't have the strength to pull herself away from the fish.

She didn't care.

Looking down at the translucent fish emanating blue light, Morana stripped off her shoes and touched the surface. She felt a gentle pull at first, a fish suckling the tip of her finger before it dragged her under. The sting of a thousand bites on her body made her lungs burn as she breathed in water. She lost consciousness, descending into the vision.

Matthias was here. He was alone in the land of the gods, the sword in hand. Morana watched as he descended a set of stairs, moving lower and lower underground. His eyes were panicked, as if he sensed someone here.

He entered what appeared to be a dungeon and drew a rune on a wooden door to the left. The blue glow lighted the dungeon. Morana tensed, the dripping sound and solid floor reminding her of the dungeon she had been trapped in with Inara. This one was different, though. The door opened, and Matthias placed the sword atop a stone slab before exiting and snapping the door shut.

He was running then, the sound of crashing objects sounding upstairs. There were no shadows. He wasn't using them, and Morana couldn't understand why.

He entered the demolished foyer, the same way it was when Morana had entered the land of the gods.

Matthias paused, slowly turning to be met with hazel eyes. Axton was standing there, eyes hard. He was holding a black object in his hand. Inside, the ball looked like dark smoke, twisting and twirling.

"Where did you get that?" Matthias asked. He was panting now, barely able to breathe.

"A gift," Axton informed. "From Raidan."

"Raidan," Matthias breathed. His eyes turned sinister, twisting with the bitter rage he felt. "Inara has you doing her dirty work now. Draining my power for what, exactly?"

"You're going to the Wastelands."

Morana fought. She thrashed beneath the water as the vision ended, desperately trying to climb her way to the surface. The fish were consuming her, biting away at her raw flesh. She frantically moved her arms, trying to break through the surface.

A Basar tugged on her hair, driving deeper and deeper into the fountain, sending her to the bottom. She couldn't breathe and she could feel the water invading her lungs.

Her mind turned hazy, barely clinging to reality as she touched the floor, fish surrounding her.

The Basar were relentless, and she suddenly understood why Matthias had grabbed her wrist, warned her about these creatures so long ago. Inara had wanted her to jump in this fountain, to use the strange fish to pry into Matthias's mind.

She didn't need to. He would let her in if only she'd ask. Pain deeper than the stinging of flesh marred her bones, striking her heart until she couldn't think. If this had resulted from stealing the blood book, she knew she would blame herself. The guilt had eased these past weeks, but a new guilt had surfaced. This one was sharper and more painful than the last.

She thought of Matthias in the river and the glow of the water on his skin. She thought of how it had felt to have his hands on her, his lips on her, and the way she had clawed at his back.

Images flashed through her mind—memories—one after the other. She saw every moment spent with the god and couldn't help but wonder if the Basar were showing her another vision, or if she was merely reliving her entire life.

Death happened on its own. Matthias didn't have to be there. He may have been the god of death, but he didn't cause it. Matthias came in the night, sticking to the shadows and easing the pain of loss. He was the one that ruled the fae, the king of shadows, and the god of darkness.

Matthias wasn't here to ease her mind as her consciousness faded. She descended as a scream left her lips, muffled by the water twisting around her.

Thirty-Four

Morana moved through the halls of the palace in Ascella, black strapped heels clicking on the obsidian floors, keeping time with the beating of her heart. The rage that had burned and boiled was now cold, like the glassy ice over a frozen landscape. She could picture the overturned books and glass shattered on the red carpets of Matthias's palace in the land of the gods. It only hardened the ice in her soul. Morana knew who was to blame, and she was out for vengeance, just like she promised.

Her hair was delicately pulled up into a low bun, wisps of hair loose around her face. Her dress was flowing and black, the neckline plunging low. A layer of red fabric rested under the black overlay, peaking through as she walked. She hated dresses before, but now they made her feel powerful—beautiful. The black fabric marking who she willingly belonged to, telling the world what court she stood behind.

The dress was perfectly accented by the silver crown on her head. Deep black stones set and surrounded by rubies. The crown was delicate, but also powerful. She looked like a queen, and in some ways, she was. She had fought her way out of that fountain, called the lords to Ascella, and explained what she planned.

Darkness surrounded her as the shadows twisted and swirled. That same darkness bore into her soul—cold and calculating—as she strode to the entrance of the throne room, where she would finally take hold of what was hers.

She could see the events as they played. The visions from the Basar that clued her into what had actually happened, how Matthias had been taken. The human who had kidnapped a god.

She scoffed, thinking about how Axton must have felt pulling off something like that. He had taken ahold of Death, conquering and rising above. If Axton wanted to play as if he were powerful, if he wanted to use his bargain as a fucking excuse, Morana would play along then too. She wouldn't let the asshole get away with it. This frozen landscape would consume him, lay him to rest beneath the ice of this lake. He would drown in the same way she had almost drowned in the fountain just to learn the truth. She fought her way out, but he wouldn't.

Morana walked through the doors to the throne room lined with symbols of death. The lords of the Court of Shadows stood there waiting for her, accepting what she had decided with open arms, committing to it fully. Hames and Elivira stood in the room, awaiting her show of vengeance and wrath. Garian and Ronan were otherwise preoccupied, but they would enter momentarily.

Morana took her seat on Death's throne, power emanating from her figure. Her gray eyes were bright, shining through the inky mist that coated the room, drifting across the floor as she willed it. It was a show of power, the power that Matthias had awakened in her, taught her to use and control.

She could have lost herself to the sorrow of his disappearance, but she was more than that. She had willed herself to deny sorrow before. And in this room, the only emotion she would allow herself to feel was the increasing wrath she longed to wield.

She ran a finger over the sensitive skin behind her ear before lifting the hand, gesturing to the doors.

The black metal opened, and the slamming sound mixed with yelling sent pleasure down her spine. She inhaled, closing her eyes, thinking of how she would enjoy what was about to take place.

Garian and Ronan had a firm grip on the screaming man in chains. They dragged him forward. Sweat was dripping down his temples, dirt and blood streaked his face and coated his brown hair. He was thrashing and clawing like an animal to get away from them, begging to be released.

Morana lifted her chin, staring down her nose at the sad excuse of a human before her. She could play this part well, the power of the shadows flicking between her fingertips, growing and whispering until they consumed her every thought. Her hands tightened around the throne, bracing her as he looked up.

That was when he saw her, seated on the throne atop the dais, a crown of ruby and tourmaline atop her head. She looked every bit the queen of darkness, every bit the role she was playing.

She stared at the man, broken and bleeding before her. He had stopped screaming, his features turning hard as he glared.

Morana felt nothing.

They stopped before the throne, throwing the man to the ground. Garian and Ronan used their shadows to hold him there, keep him from running.

Her prey was right where she wanted it, and she would become the hunter this time.

"Axton," she spoke, voice smooth and laced with sinister promises.

He spat at her; his face contorted in rage. "Fuck you, Ana."

She didn't even flinch.

"Never again." Her lips peeled back as she glared at him, sending shards of ice in his direction. She hoped the shards would stab through his heart, hurt where she wanted him to hurt most—make him bleed. "Where is he?" she asked, holding onto her cold composure.

"I don't know," Axton snapped. The chains were rattling between his wrists. Garian and Ronan focused on holding him there, their shadows running over his skin, convincing him he couldn't move.

"You lie." Morana lifted her chin. "Maybe I'll send you in to be eaten by the Basar while they show you exactly how deep this lie runs. I made it out of that ridiculous fishbowl. My hope is that you wouldn't be able to do the same."

Axton blanched. His body stilling on the ground. It sent intense pleasure through her to see him there. He tried to keep his grip on his dominance, but he would eventually roll over.

Morana stood up, sauntering down the steps of the dais to Axton. The darkness keeping her company—a menacing and beautiful sight. The shadows twisted over her skin, trailing along her legs, kissing her cheeks. The power was heady.

"I've kept a mark for every life that I've taken," she began, voice low. The pink flesh on her face and shoulder clear to see. "I kept the scars they gave me." Morana leaned down; her face dangerously close to his. Garian and Ronan held firm so he couldn't touch her. "Did you know that there were no scars on my back where Inara whipped me? No scars from when you stripped my dress off my body and held me down?"

Axton didn't speak. His hardened hazel eyes spoke of the deep hate he now felt. There was no love there—no caring. She could see nothing remaining of the dimpled boy that had almost stolen her heart—almost.

"I will not let you hurt me," she snarled. "Elivira helped me solve the problem."

Morana pulled strands of hair to the side, revealing the small serpent tattoo Elivira had inked into her skin. It was black and white, twisting with detailed scales.

The lord chuckled. Elivira was smirking from across the room as she watched the scene unfold.

"Do you know what this mark means?" Morana asked. "What it means for you?"

Morana stood straight, stepping back to the throne, standing at the top of the dais.

"How does it feel to be just like him?" Axton seethed. The words had no effect, no fire to melt what had already solidified in her soul. "To cause death and destruction wherever you go?"

She could now see the fear just beneath the surface. Axton knew that this wouldn't end well for him as he tracked her movements when she touched the serpent tattoo. She knew the truth behind why she had wanted to mar her skin, the truth of what she was about to accomplish, the vengeance she would take for herself—for Matthias.

She couldn't let Matthias stay in the Wastelands. She had mentioned the comment about Raidan to the lords. The confession led to a serious discussion about what they would do next. War was inevitable, but without a king, they couldn't start it. They needed to retrieve Matthias first.

He had once liked the way she looked sitting on his throne, told her as he pressed his lips to hers, the heat of everything they were together permeating her body. She would rule now, sit on the throne and break apart the world to find Death, greet it with open arms.

Axton would do the same.

Morana grabbed something that lay beside the throne, black and sleek. A familiar rush ran through her veins. This was what she was used to, her only choice for the man she hated—the mortal.

She didn't respond as she walked down the dais and stood before her tormenter again—the liar in chains.

Morana lifted the gun, finger firm on the trigger. It brought back familiar memories at the gun range, all the time she had spent getting to know Axton. It was all wasted, just like his ridiculous life.

She smiled then, letting him see exactly why she had marked her skin, exactly what she was planning.

"You wouldn't," Axton whispered.

He didn't know her. She had said once that she was capable of many things, and Morana was starting to believe it.

"You are just like the god of death, just like that fucking fool. How does it feel, Ana?"

Morana didn't hesitate before she pulled the trigger, gruesome matter splattering across the floor and walls, decorating the dark throne room in crimson blood.

Axton's body slumped to the ground, void of any life. Morana scoffed. The goddess of life couldn't keep him here, couldn't keep him away from the all-consuming bloodlust that now invaded her skull.

She lowered the gun slowly, one word on her lips. She spoke that word as a whisper. One last statement to the dead man in the Court of Shadows.

"Powerful."

ACKNOWLEDGMENTS

There are so many people I have to thank when it comes to this book, and I'm never very good at wording this stuff. So, here we go.

First, I want to thank my editor, number one hype woman, and friend, Kenna. I literally could not do this without you. Thank you for pushing me, believing in me, and never balking at my craziness. I can't wait until your books are sitting on the shelves next to mine. Don't forget me when you make it big.

I would like to thank my dear bookish friend, Wednesday. Your encouragement and kindness mean so much to me. Thank you for sharing stories with me and laughing through it all.

I could not write this without thanking Kate. Friend, you were the first person to actually read my writing when I decided to write a book. I can't wait for the release of your novel, and I'm also thankful for the one time you dyed my hair blonde.

I want to thank my family for their support, my mom for sharing my passion for books, my grandmother for her fierce loyalty and constant phone conversations, and my cousin Olivia. Olivia, you will never read this because it has way too many words. So, your acknowledgment will be lost to you. It's actually kind of funny. This is really one big inside joke with myself.

Thank you to my husband for all of the inspiration. Hopefully, nobody reads this sentence.

I'd like to thank Erin for making such beautiful graphics for the interior of this novel. You're literally amazing for doing that for me.

I would also like to thank Ali for being an amazing narrator for ACOW, and for being herself in general. I fully believe in you and your ability to make it big, friend. Keep going!

A special shoutout to the fifth lord, Gael. You served no purpose whatsoever, and I'm sorry I had to cut you from this book. Five was a nice number, but I didn't even know who you were so . . . bye.

A special thanks to the horse that sacrificed his dignity so Matthias could get some on-the-road action.

Finally, I would like to thank my grandfather who passed away during the course of writing this book. Thank you for showing me that a person's value is based on their existence and not their merit. Thank you for the way you saw the shadows in others and chose to call them beautiful. Everything I am is because of you, and I miss you eternally.

CPSIA information can be obtained
at www.ICGtesting.com
Printed in the USA
LVHW041927260422
717290LV00006B/165

9 780578 367330